M. A. Hunter has been a huge fan
young age and always fancied th
That dream became a reality whe
The Missing Children Case Files.

Born in Darlington in the north-east of England, Hunter grew up in West London, and moved to Southampton to study law at university. It's here that Hunter fell in love and has been married for fifteen years. They are now raising their two children on the border of The New Forest where they enjoy going for walks amongst the wildlife. They regularly holiday across England, but have a particular affinity for the south coast, which formed the setting for the series, spanning from Devon to Brighton, and with a particular focus on Weymouth, one of their favourite towns.

When not writing, Hunter can be found binge-watching favourite shows or buried in the latest story from Angela Marsons, Simon Kernick, or Ann Cleeves.

Also by M. A. Hunter

The Missing Children Case Files

Ransomed

Isolated

Trafficked

Discarded

Repressed

EXPOSED

The Missing Children Case Files

M. A. HUNTER

One More Chapter
a division of HarperCollins*Publishers*
1 London Bridge Street
London SE1 9GF
www.harpercollins.co.uk

HarperCollins*Publishers*
1st Floor, Watermarque Building, Ringsend Road
Dublin 4, Ireland

This paperback edition 2021
First published in Great Britain in ebook format
by HarperCollins*Publishers* 2021

A catalogue record of this book is available from the British Library

ISBN: 978-0-00-844341-2

Printed and bound in the UK using 100% Renewable Electricity
by CPI Group (UK) Ltd

Content notices: paedophilia, sexual assault, drug abuse, child abuse.

Dedicated to all the victims
of abuse who have suffered,
and those who continue to suffer.

The old moon is tarnished
With smoke of the flood,
The dead leaves are varnished
With colour like blood,

A treacherous smiler
With teeth white as milk,
A savage beguiler
In sheathings of silk.

— *Sea Lullaby*, Elinor Wylie

Chapter One

THEN

Portland, Dorset

It had been several minutes since she'd watched her sister stomp away from the yard, and whilst she still didn't really have much concept of time, the fact that the shadow of the house was now totally covering the driveway indicated it was getting late. The shade brought with it cooler air, and the little girl on the skateboard rubbed at her upper arms with her hands, as if enough friction would cause the goosebumps to simply shed from her skin.

Despite her previous protestations to the contrary, riding the skateboard up and down with nobody to watch and cheer her progress really wasn't as much fun as she'd thought. She was now able to just about hold herself on her standing foot, while propelling the board with the other, although the uneven surface of the paving slabs made for a bumpy ride.

Stepping down from the toy, she moved to the edge of the yard, leaning over the low brick wall, the wrought-iron railing pressing into the top of her jeans, and strained to see whether her sister was on her way back yet. Grandma's house was only a four-minute walk away according to her mum and dad, and her sister must have been gone for at least two or three times that long. She pictured her sitting in Grandpa's old reclining chair – the one with the plastic handle that made the bottom of the chair shoot out and scoop up their feet. Grandma didn't like to sit in it herself, not since he'd died, so it meant it was always free for the grandchildren to fight over whenever they'd pop round.

She pictured her sister on the fully reclined chair, watching cartoons and tucking into a large bowl of Grandma's apple crumble and thick yellow custard. She could practically taste the cinnamon and brown sugar as she imagined her sister tucking into the pudding. Envy gripped her mind, as Grandma offered a second helping because Anna had managed to walk the route unaided, and she was the only one there to eat the crumble.

Pushing her head further over the railing, she looked to the left and the right, in case her sister was playing some kind of game, and was secretly hiding just out of sight, so that Emma would only think she'd gone to Grandma's house. But the road was empty, save for the snake-long line of cars that clung to the pavement edge as if they might all fall if one moved away. The street was deathly quiet. No neighbours; no children playing; no dogs barking; no sign of Anna.

Emma's eyes narrowed, and her lips pulled themselves into a huff. It wasn't fair! Just because Anna was two years older, and was able to better remember landmarks and road names, didn't mean she should be allowed extra helpings of Grandma's apple crumble. Abandoning the skateboard, she stomped to the front door and pulled the handle down, letting herself inside. She was taken aback by the blast of warm air that wrapped itself around her shoulders and carried her inside. She hadn't realised just how cold it was outside, and couldn't help smiling at the toasty brush against her cheeks. Closing the door to the draught, she hurried inside, throwing herself at her dad's armchair in front of the television; the one closest to the radiator.

She could hear the low rumble of voices somewhere nearby – possibly the kitchen – but her dad didn't appear to be watching the racing cars on the television, so she flipped through the channels, searching for the cartoons she'd imagined Anna watching. All she could find was horse racing, a black and white war movie, and some programme with an old man talking about the history of the church he was standing beside. Switching off the box, she looked around the room for something to do, before spotting her dad's bag of wine gums. They'd given them to him for Father's Day, and he must have opened them to enjoy with the racing. He always offered them one when he opened a new bag, and she was sure he would have offered her one if he realised she was in here now.

Shifting her weight to her knees, she craned her neck over the back of the armchair, trying to see whether either of her parents were likely to emerge from the kitchen anytime soon, but it was impossible to tell with the door closed.

He wouldn't be upset if she had just one. She'd choose an orange one because he always said they were his least favourite. If anything, she'd be doing him a favour in eating an orange one, so then he wouldn't have to. And if he was in here now, she was sure he'd offer her one anyway, so where was the harm?

Her hand was clammy as she stretched her arm out towards the bag, keeping one eye on the kitchen door in case it was suddenly thrust open. She felt the sharp edge of the plastic bag brush against her fingertips, rustling as it did. A sudden bump behind her had her arm freeze in mid-air, and the gasp catch in her throat. Rolling her head back towards her shoulder, she half expected to see her dad there, staring her down for stealing one of his wine gums, but the kitchen door was still closed.

It was now or never. Mum or Dad could be out at any second, and her mum would probably disapprove of her eating a sweet so close to dinner time. Taking a deep breath to settle her nerves, Emma dug her hand into the bag, and fished around until she found the orange prism of sweet and quickly popped it into her mouth, savouring the citrus bite. A moment later, the kitchen door opened and her parents emerged, continuing their conversation, oblivious to her presence just behind the armchair.

'So, we're agreed,' her dad's voice carried. 'We go tonight and we don't look back?'

Her mum's voice when she replied sounded pained and hollow. 'If you think that's for the best.'

'I don't see any other way,' he replied. 'You get the girls in, and I'll make the call.'

Emma chewed the sweet as quickly and quietly as she could, eager to hide the evidence of her crime. She heard the front door open and her mum's voice calling for them both, but remained where she was until the last of the gummy was safely swallowed.

'Girls?' her mum's voice called out as she stepped back indoors.

Emma swivelled back onto her knees and peered over the back of the armchair. 'Boo!'

Her mum caught her breath, and pressed a frail hand over her chest, her face a deathly pallor. 'Oh, there you are, Emma. You made me jump. Where's your sister?'

The warmth of the room and the lure of the wine gums had totally distracted Emma from the real reason she had come inside, but now the image of the reclined chair and big bowl of crumble and custard came flooding back into her mind.

'She went to Grandma's house,' Emma said bitterly. 'Can we go before she eats all of the custard?'

Her mother's brow furrowed. 'Very funny. Where is Anna really?'

Emma adopted a stern face, put out by the doubt cast upon her response. 'I told you: she went to Grandma's house.'

The frown deepened. 'You're being serious? How did she get to your grandma's house?'

'Duh, she walked, obviously.'

'When was this?'

Emma shrugged.

Her mum continued to watch her, as if waiting for some punchline that wasn't coming, before lifting the phone from the wall and pressing the speed dial button. 'Hi, Mum, it's Bronwyn… Yes, we're all well here… I was just wondering whether I could speak to my daughter please? I need her home because we need to go out soon… Anna of course…' She turned to face Emma, but kept the phone to her ear. 'What do you mean she's not there?'

Emma peeled herself from the armchair, sneaking a glance

at the packet of wine gums, certain her dad wouldn't mind if she had a second but not daring to risk snatching one with her mum in the room. 'When's dinner?' Emma said, no longer interested in observing the telephone call. 'I'm starving.'

'Hold on, Mum,' Bronwyn said, lowering the phone to her shoulder. 'Emma, where is your sister?'

Emma stopped her journey to the kitchen. 'I told you: she went to Grandma's house.'

'When was this?'

Emma shrugged again. 'I don't know. A while ago.'

'What happened? Why did she say she was going to Grandma's?'

Emma hadn't wanted to mention her part in the argument that had ensued over the skateboard, but the way her mum was glaring at her now made her think twice about lying. 'She was being bossy about my new skateboard, and I told her it was mine and I wanted to play with it. She shouted and then said she was going to Grandma's house.'

'But when did all this happen? You two couldn't have been in the yard for more than…' her words trailed off as her eyes fell on her wristwatch, swiftly widening as her mind calculated the difference. 'Oh God, I didn't realise it was so late.' She returned the phone to her ear. 'Hi, Mum, listen, if Anna does show up at your house, can you call me straightaway, and I'll come and collect her? No, no, nothing to worry about, I'm sure… Yes, thank you. Love you too.'

She returned the phone to its spot on the wall, taking a deep breath and then dropping to her knees in front of Emma. 'Now listen, Mummy won't be cross, but I need to know where your sister really is.'

'I told you—'

'I don't care about any of that,' she interrupted, puffing the fringe from her eyes. 'I don't know what prompted the two of you to construct this prank, but it isn't funny anymore. Okay? I just need to know the truth. Where is Anna?'

Emma opened her mouth to speak, but Bronwyn cut her off again.

'No lies this time, Emma. I won't be mad if you just come clean. Is she hiding in her bedroom? Or somewhere in the back garden?'

Emma shook her head, not happy with her mum's tight grip on her upper arms. 'I'm telling you the truth. I don't know where she is. She said she was going to Grandma's house. She climbed over the wall, and walked as if she was going there.'

The blood had yet to return to Bronwyn's face, and she was clearly struggling to keep her voice calm and even. 'If you're lying to me, Emma, you will be in big trouble. Do you understand? I will confiscate your skateboard if I find out that you're covering for your sister.'

Emma resented the threat to the skateboard, and pulled herself free of her mum's grasp. 'I'm not lying! She went to Grandma's house. That's what she told me.'

Bronwyn straightened and moved through to the kitchen, fumbling with the key in the patio door. She pulled it open and stalked into the small square garden, eyes darting left and right, but there really wasn't anywhere to hide within the frame of the six-foot fence panels.

'Anna? Anna? Are you out here?'

Gulls squawked in response, but there was no sign of the little girl with a mess of dark hair and glasses.

Returning to the kitchen, Bronwyn gave Emma another pained stare, hoping for a different response, but Emma didn't have one to offer. Hurrying upstairs, Bronwyn opened the door to Anna's bedroom, checking in the flat-pack wardrobe, under both duvets, and the windowsill beyond the closed curtains, but there was no sign of her.

'I've spoken to Dev,' Emma's dad said absently, studying the screen of his mobile phone as he appeared in the doorway, 'and everything's sorted for tonight. I'll throw some things into a case while you get the girls into the—'

'Anna's missing,' Bronwyn said, clutching her throat with her hand.

Chapter Two

NOW

Market Harborough, Leicestershire

It's nearing six when we leave the motorway, passing farmland on all sides as we head through Leicestershire. It's the first time during our journey up here that conversation has finally stopped. Poor Jack looks exhausted as he stifles a yawn and puts the takeaway cup of coffee to his lips as we idle at traffic lights, but he quickly winces.

'Are you okay?' I ask, assuming it's one of his injuries causing the pain.

He nestles the cup back into the plastic holder behind the automatic gear stick. 'Cold coffee,' he says, swallowing painfully. 'Might be an idea to get a fresh burst of caffeine before we head into the police station. I don't know about you, but I'm shattered.'

I'm sure my body is equally tired, but any signs of fatigue are being squirrelled away, as I feel more alert than I have in a long time. I was all set to send Maddie the outlines of two books detailing everything we've faced in the aftermath of Aurélie Lebrun exposing the presence of a secret ring of paedophiles and traffickers operating along the south coast of England, when a call from DS Sarah Yates from Leicestershire Constabulary interrupted me. After what she told me, I saved the draft email, packed up my laptop and an overnight bag, and bailed out of my flat. I still can't believe that the suspect in the fatal shooting of Sir Anthony Tomlinson is demanding to speak to me and that the police are prepared to grant her wish in the hope of extracting a full confession of murder.

How could I feel tired with that hanging over me?

'We can stop for coffee if you need it,' I say, smiling at Jack, uncertain how else to show my appreciation for him driving me up here despite his extensive injuries.

He was attacked by an amateur boxer while chasing leads linking Tomlinson to the ring, so I can't help feeling responsible for his current condition. He assures me he bears no grudge, but he should be resting rather than driving me four and a bit hours from Weymouth.

'It might be an idea to get a snack before we drive over there too,' Jack adds. 'We've no idea how long this is going to take.'

I know he's talking sense, and sustenance is a good idea, but I'm desperate to get in there and hear what the suspected shooter – Kylie Shakespeare – has to say for herself.

'Okay,' I say reluctantly, not wishing to annoy him, 'but I did tell DS Yates we'd be there between five and six, and I don't want her to think we're not coming.'

Jack moves the car forward as the light switches to green. 'Of course. I wasn't thinking. That's fine.'

My head snaps round. 'If you're hungry, Jack, then you

should get something to eat. All I was saying was, could we make it a burger at a drive-thru, or similar? Or maybe you could drop me at the station first, and then grab some food after?'

He meets my stare, but there is no animosity in his eyes, which is a relief. 'You're right; I'd forgotten what you'd said to DS Yates. We'll head straight to the station, and then I'll grab us something afterwards. Are you sure you're okay about all of this?'

I frown, confused by the question; why wouldn't I be okay?

'It must have crossed your mind,' Jack continues, splitting his gaze between the road and my continued confusion, 'that this could be another of their traps?'

'The "their" he's referring to are those connected to the trafficking ring who have been producing and distributing underage pornographic material, and we suspect killing the children they've been abducting and abusing. The same people who hacked our phones and tablets with software to track our GPS and keystrokes. Thankfully, Jack is more tech savvy than I am, and has removed the incriminating software, so I finally feel like we can talk without being overheard.

'Of course it's crossed my mind,' I admit.

The reason Jack is having to hide how much pain he's actually in is that he followed an anonymous tip about someone guaranteeing information to tie Tomlinson to the ring, but after Jack arrived at the pub to meet the contact, he was driven off the road, and was lucky to survive. His car is still at the garage being repaired, which is why we're in this courtesy car. I've thought about little else since DS Sarah Yates's phone call. Whilst I've been busy putting together the pieces of the jigsaw, Tomlinson is killed in suspicious circumstances and the suspect demands to speak to me. I'd have to suffer with anosmia, not to sense that something smells very fishy here.

'But what choice do I have?' I say to Jack now. 'Whoever this Kylie Shakespeare is, she might have valuable information that will help us tie Tomlinson to our investigation. We've talked at length about how such a ring could go undetected for all this time. We're talking more than thirty years of children going missing and those sick films being made. Just think, if it weren't for my crusade against Arthur Turgood and his conspirators at the St Francis Home, we never would have found the video files on his hard drive. I'm an investigative journalist first and foremost, so how can I turn down the chance to tie it all together?'

'That's exactly what worries me most,' Jack says, sighing and turning down the heating. 'We've had to fight to get as far as we are now, and just when we thought they were shutting us down by applying pressure to have the official NCA investigation closed, up pops the key to all our problems. You can see why I'm more than a little suspicious about all of this, can't you?'

I know his question is because he's concerned about me, rather than that he doubts my integrity as a journalist.

'Absolutely, but it's not like I'm having to follow the lead down some darkened alley where I could be in danger. I'm meeting her in a busy, bustling police station, surrounded by those who've made it their vocation to protect the public and serve justice. If anything, I couldn't be safer.'

'Mmm,' he mutters, but doesn't offer any further thoughts on the subject. 'And you definitely don't recognise the suspect's name?'

I've been racking my brain since we left Dorset for any kind of connection to a Kylie or the family name Shakespeare. Aside from the bard himself, I don't know anyone with that surname, and there are no contacts in my phone with the name Kylie. It could of course be a false name, but surely the police would have to verify her identity before proceeding with booking her in and interviewing her? I've even messaged my best friend Rachel to see what she can find about the name, but her internet searches have been as unproductive as mine.

My phone vibrates as she messages me again, confirming there is no Kylie Shakespeare listed on the Anna Hunter Foundation database. The charity, of which we are trustees, allows those who've suffered as a result of a missing person to seek either emotional or financial support.

Jack turns on the car stereo. 'It's nearly six,' he adds. 'We should probably check whether there's any further news being reported about the shooting. The last thing you want is to be blindsided.'

He tunes the radio into a local station, and we wait for the news to start.

'More now on the fatal shooting at the home of local resident and former Metropolitan Police Commissioner Sir Anthony Tomlinson. Leicestershire police have yet to make a further statement in respect to their investigation following what was relayed shortly before lunchtime. We know that the victim's neighbours called police at around about six o'clock this morning to report the sound of several gunshots in the vicinity, and a passing patrol car was on the scene minutes later. The small cul-de-sac was quickly cordoned off, trapping the suspect inside the Tomlinson family home, a modest four-bedroom property with no method of escape save for via the road. A line of communication was opened with the suspect, and after several hours of negotiation, she allowed the police to enter the property and bring her out in cuffs. We believe Sir Anthony was the only person at the property at the time of the incident. The suspect was taken to the police station in Market Harborough at around ten o'clock, and is yet to be released. We are expecting a further statement from the Detective Inspector leading the investigation before eight o'clock tonight. Our thoughts and prayers are with the Tomlinson family this evening.'

Jack and I exchange glances. I suppose no news is good news; I'm relieved there was no mention of the demand that I come to the police station, but as we enter the town centre, I'm suddenly worried that I'll have to fight my way through a throng of reporters all eager to get an exclusive scoop. Given my history, I'm not entirely sure what they would make of my presence here.

Thankfully, there is nobody waiting outside the station as we arrive on Fairfield Road. I'm not sure what I was expecting, but the building looks more like a social hall than a police station, save for the navy-blue stripe running through the middle of the brickwork. A rundown wooden bus shelter and public bench block our view of the front of the building, but although there are lights on inside, the place looks closed up for the night.

'Your guess is as good as mine,' Jack says as he spots my furrowed brow. 'This is definitely the right place, isn't it?'

I double-check the satnav, before searching online, but this is the address of the only police station within a couple of miles of the town centre. Surely if they'd moved her to a different station, DS Yates would have phoned and advised.

Unfortunately, she called from a withheld number so I've no way of phoning her back to check.

Jack indicates at the next junction and pulls up at the side of the road. We've parked on a thick yellow line, but there don't appear to be any traffic wardens around, so hopefully we'll be safe. Unfastening my seat belt, I exit and hurry to the front door, but my worst fears are confirmed by a laminated page in the window.

'They closed at four,' I tell Jack when he's hobbled over. 'I don't get it. DS Yates definitely told me to come here, and she knew I wouldn't be arriving until after four.'

Jack presses his face against the window, his breath misting the glass. 'There is a light on inside,' he mumbles, 'so there must be someone here.' He bangs his fist against the glass several times.

A moment later, a pair of eyes appear on the other side of the glass, and a bony finger points at the laminate.

'DS Yates phoned me and told me to come down here,' I shout through the glass. 'My name's Emma Hunter.'

The eyes narrow, so I hold out my open passport to confirm my identity. Jack too holds up his warrant card. A moment later the eyes return and the officer in black unlocks the door, allowing us to enter.

'Who did you say called you?' he asks.

He can't be much older than Jack, though has more of a wiry frame, and his thick brown hair is pulled into a messy bun at the back of his head.

'DS Sarah Yates,' I explain. 'My name is Emma Hunter and I'm a writer-cum-journalist. She phoned me around one, and asked that I drive from Weymouth to see her.' I pause, choosing my words carefully, before whispering, 'It's in relation to the shooting this morning.'

He considers the two of us for a moment, before turning to Jack. 'And you are?'

'I'm PC Jack Serrovitz from the Met. I work with Emma occasionally and I drove her up here.'

Satisfied, he takes a long gulp from his mug of hot chocolate before allowing us entrance to the station proper, and asking us to wait in the reception area while he calls it through. It's cold inside the reception area, and I cup my hands to blow warm air into them, having left my anorak in the car.

'You want my jacket?' Jack offers, but I shake my head with a smile. Now is not the time for chivalry. I still haven't forgotten the disappointed look on Rick's face when he saw Jack and me together when we left my flat. But I need to push all thoughts of my complicated love life out of my head.

The hipster police officer returns with a grim expression on his face. 'DS Yates is currently in a team brief, but will come down as soon as it ends. You've been asked to wait here.'

I nod my understanding, though would much prefer to be somewhere warmer. 'I think she wanted me to speak with the suspect, Kylie Shakespeare, so would it be possible for us to wait somewhere for that?'

He shakes his head. 'I was told that's not happening anymore, and you're to wait here until DS Yates arrives.'

My chest tightens. 'What do you mean that's not happening anymore? We've just spent five hours in a car driving up here.'

He holds his palms out apologetically. 'I'm sorry but I really don't know. That was what I was told. I'm sure DS Yates can explain matters when she comes down.'

He takes his leave and returns to the small office behind the reception desk.

'You should go and get something to eat,' I say to Jack. 'It doesn't need both of us to freeze.'

'That's all right, I don't mind waiting with you. It's nice to be out of the car to have a stretch, to be honest.'

I'm grateful he's said that, as I have a horrible feeling sinking through my body right now. The reception area isn't very big, and is lined with chairs, but I manage to find a little circuit I can pace just to try and warm up. I'm about to ask Jack whether I can go and collect my anorak from the car when a youngish woman with dark-brown hair and perfectly shaped eyebrows comes through the security door beside the reception counter. She looks tired, her shoulders hunched slightly, and the blouse which was probably neatly pressed bears the strain of a suit jacket being slipped on and off repeatedly over the course of the day.

'Emma?' she asks softly as she approaches.

'Yes,' I say warmly, 'and you must be DS Yates?'

She doesn't reflect the positivity I'm projecting, and the sinking feeling in my gut worsens. 'Thank you for coming up; hopefully traffic wasn't too bad?'

I shrug. 'It was fine.' I point to Jack. 'This is PC Jack Serrovitz, who was with me when you phoned.'

She nods a greeting to Jack, before returning her attention to me. 'Do you think we could go for a quiet chat?'

I nod eagerly, hoping the next room has some kind of central heating. We move off before she turns and puts an arm out in front of Jack. 'Sorry, I just need to speak to Emma alone.'

Jack's anxiety is apparent as his eyes search mine for reassurance.

'You wait in the car,' I suggest, 'or go and grab some food. I'll phone when I know more.'

He sighs, but returns to the main door where the hipster officer unlocks it and allows him to leave.

DS Yates types in a security code and the door buzzes as we head through to a corridor which has doors leading to rooms on the left and right. I've spent enough time in police stations in recent years to know they probably lead to interview suites. We stop at one and she opens the door and shows me in. I'm surprised to find another woman already seated inside.

'Emma Hunter, this is my DI, Marina Oakley,' Yates says.

I nod in the woman's direction, but she makes no effort to stand or offer her hand to shake. When I sit across from her, I can see now her large frame is in stark contrast to the stick-thin Yates.

'Can I get you anything to drink?' Yates asks, but I decline, despite my mouth growing drier by the second.

Something is very wrong here, and I now wish I'd insisted Jack accompany me. Each of them has a pad of paper in front of them, and as I see Oakley open hers, the first page is full of questions scrawled in indecipherable handwriting.

'Before we begin,' Yates begins, making herself comfortable behind her colleague, 'I do need to advise you that the following interview will be conducted under caution, and—'

'Wait, what?' I stammer. 'Under caution? What for? I don't understand what's going on. You said we were coming in here for a quiet chat.'

Yates and Oakley exchange glances before Yates continues, 'I will explain what is going on, but we just need to ask you a few questions first, Emma.'

My heart is racing, and my eyes dart to the closed door behind the two of them. 'Questions? Questions about what?'

'We'll come to that,' she replies firmly.

Jack's words from the car echo through my mind: *this could be another of their traps.*

My neck is flushing, and my breaths are short and shallow. 'Am I under arrest? If so, I deserve to know why.'

'You're not under arrest, Emma, but by conducting the interview under caution, it allows us to rely on the content in future. If you want to call a solicitor, you're more than welcome to.'

I feel physically sick, and wish Jack could hear my silent pleas for help.

Chapter Three

NOW

Market Harborough, Leicestershire

I've listened to the police caution suspects on interview tapes more times than I can remember, but hearing the words delivered to me in person sends a shiver the length of my spine. I know I've done nothing wrong, but when I think of how the ring have battered and bullied to close down our investigation, I'm terrified by the prospect of what's around the corner that I can't yet see. It also troubles me that the interview is being recorded, which suggests there *will* be further use of it in the future.

'Let's begin with your relationship with Kylie Shakespeare,' Yates says, Oakley's ballpoint poised on the page. 'How do you know her?'

There is a fog over my mind making it impossible for my sixth sense to predict what's coming *and* process what's just been asked. 'Um, what? I-I don't have a relationship with her.'

It isn't the best start: stuttering my words and failing to

sound authoritative is not going to help. I've listened to suspects who've later been convicted of crimes nonchalantly refuse to speak, almost singing, 'No comment' as they gleefully refuse to cooperate. I need to channel that kind of certainty when I speak, but I feel anything but convinced of my innocence. What if I've been set up to take the fall for something, like when Jack was lured to that pub to be set upon by that amateur boxer?

'She seems to know who you are,' Yates counters, deliberately adopting a confused expression as if I've just told her the world isn't round.

'What can I say? There are lots of people who know who I am,' I respond aiming for coquettish and failing miserably.

'And why's that then?'

This is unbearable. Even though I've done nothing wrong, I feel as though I've been caught with my hand in the cookie jar, and I hate the feeling. Does she really want me to say that as a bestselling writer, my name and backstory are known by the hundreds of thousands who've bought and read my work?

'On account of my books,' I plump for, hoping it will be enough, but her expression remains haunted.

'Ah, so Miss Shakespeare is one of your readers then? A fan.'

'I-I don't know. I've not met her – at least I don't think I have.'

'Which is it? You've either met her or you haven't.'

I gently massage my temple as a headache lurks nearby. 'What I mean is, I'm not aware that I've met anyone by that name, but I do meet a lot of people at various book signing events. I'm not saying that this woman has read any of my books, but for all I know it's possible.'

'So, to clarify, you do not *believe* you've ever met Kylie Shakespeare before?'

I don't like her emphasis of believe, as I sense it's part of the trap she's planning to spring later, but I can't see what that looks like.

'As far as I'm aware,' I confirm.

'Have you ever had cause to interact with her in any other way? Email? Phone? Text message?'

'Again, as far as I know, no, I haven't.'

I gulp audibly as I think of the spyware that Jack located on my mobile. What if it's possible that the hackers who downloaded the software have been secretly holding conversations with this woman behind my back? It seems ludicrous, but I'm not tech savvy enough to know if that's possible.

Yates whispers something to Oakley behind her hand, before the Detective Inspector nods. I know in the deepest recesses of my mind this is a common ploy used to throw off the interviewee, but it doesn't stop my pulse quickening another notch.

'Are you sure I can't get you something to drink before we continue?' Yates asks, suddenly all smiles.

She's trying to worm her way into my subconscious. If I tell her my mouth is as arid as the Sahara, will she take that as a sign of my guilt, even though I've nothing to feel guilty about? Or if I refuse, will she take that as a sign that I am compliant in whatever I'm suspected of? Or is she just taking pity on me because the questions so far have merely been to break the ice, and we're yet to get to the crux of why they've dragged me in here? I don't know what to do for the best, and quickly shake my head.

'Okay, we'll move on then,' she says, ticking something on her pad.

'On second thought, I would like a drink,' I say, my tongue unnaturally swollen; at least, that's how it feels.

Yates raises her eyebrows in surprise. 'Not a problem; I'll get us some water.'

She leaves the recorder running, explaining that she is stepping out to get me a drink. The sound of the door closing seems to echo around the room, and I don't know where to settle my gaze. DI Oakley is studying her notebook, the ballpoint pen scratching against the page. Should I make small talk, to throw them off the scent of my panic? If only making small talk were one of my strengths! I'm about to attempt something when the door bursts open again, and DS Yates places three stacked paper cups on the desk, along with a translucent jug of water. She doesn't pour me a drink, just leaves the jug standing there enticingly. She announces her return for the recording, and I buckle.

'Can I just help myself?' I ask uncertainly.

'Yes, please do,' she replies, her eyes skimming her notes again as if my request for a drink means nothing to her, and is simply a minor irritation. I wish my overactive imagination would just settle and focus on the fact that I have done nothing wrong, and in fact should be angered that I'm only here because they requested I come.

Stick to facts, I remind myself internally, taking a long and satisfying sip.

'Better?' Yates asks.

'Yes, thank you.'

'Good. Now, where were we?' She pauses as if waiting for the answer to leap from the page in front of her. 'Ah yes, of course. Can you tell me what you know about the victim, Sir Anthony Tomlinson?'

I cough as spittle catches in my throat. Ultimately, he may or may not be the reason we're all here, I don't say. I'm suddenly conscious of just who else could be listening to this conversation playing out. I'm aware that others may one day listen back to the recording, but that doesn't mean there aren't other officers in this very building listening in. It also doesn't rule out the possibility of unseen faces elsewhere hanging on every word.

Stick to facts, I tell myself again.

'Only what I heard on the news,' I reply. 'I understand he was a former Met Police Commissioner.'

'Yes, indeed, something of a minor celebrity in these parts. Much like yourself in that respect.'

Was that a dig? Maybe a subconscious one if not fully intended.

I don't rise to it, awaiting her next question.

There is a pause before she moves on. 'You didn't know Sir Anthony?'

'Not personally, no,' I reply evenly, the adrenalin still playing havoc with my nervous system.

She frowns as she looks back at her notes before the wrinkles flatten in her forehead. 'So you've never met Kylie Shakespeare or the victim of today's shooting, Sir Anthony?'

'As I've already stated: to the best of my knowledge, I've never met or spoken with either.'

I desperately want to let out the sigh that's building within me, but hold it back for now.

'Okay, let's talk about you next,' Yates continues, still

looking down at her list of questions. 'How long have you been writing for?'

The question is a bit out of left field, but I can't imagine it will lead to anything incriminating.

'On and off since university,' I answer honestly. 'I interned and then worked as a freelance journalist at the *Dorset Echo* for a few years, until I published my first book.'

'Ah yes, the now infamous *Monsters Under the Bed*,' she says. 'Would you say it was the book that put you on the map, so to speak?'

The question is worded very oddly, but I half nod, half shrug.

'For the purposes of the tape, Miss Hunter has nodded in response to the question.'

I simmer inside; I don't need someone narrating my actions for me.

'Yes, *Monsters* was certainly the project that brought me to the attention of the public,' I say loudly. 'And just as well it did,' I add snidely, 'as otherwise the victims highlighted in the book wouldn't have found the justice they deserved.'

I know it's a cheap shot, but I'm fed up of being on the receiving end of police officers that see my work as a general criticism of the role they carry out. It isn't that. I told Freddie, Mike, and Steve's stories because their previous attempts had gone unheard. I wanted to expose Arthur Turgood and those who quashed their victims' complaints. Yes, that did include one or two serving police officers, but they were only a minority, as far as I was concerned. I'd say that more than ninety-nine per cent of the serving police officers I've met and had dealings with were nothing short of angels in Doc Martens. I've never intended to cast them in any other light than that of selfless heroes putting their lives on the line for the sake of humanity.

'Your missing sister never got the justice she deserved, did she?'

I open my mouth to respond, but I don't know how to, as the question is even more bizarre than the last one.

'M-my sister?' I stammer.

'Yes, your missing sister features quite prominently in the books you've published since *Monsters Under the Bed*, hasn't she?'

'Well, yes, my pursuit of the truth about what happened to her goes on.'

'In fact, you've created quite the backstory about her mysterious disappearance, haven't you?'

Her questions are coming in at such speed and at such angles that it's making the room spin in front of me.

'What does my missing sister have to do with any of this?' I ask, reaching for the water again.

I suddenly have the strangest feeling, like when you're asleep and you realise that what you're witnessing is just your subconscious' landscape of the world, and that you are in fact dreaming. I lower my free hand to my thigh and pinch the skin, but the two plainclothes detectives don't disappear in a swirl. They remain very much there, living and breathing in front of me. Maybe it's just the short and frequent breaths I'm taking that are making me feel so lightheaded.

'You were only seven when she disappeared, right?' Yates says, studying my reaction closely.

'That's right,' I reply uncertainly.

'It must have been so hard for you.'

'It was painful for all of us.'

'And you were the last one to see her right before she disappeared, from what I've managed to dig up?'

It troubles me that she would feel the need to do any digging on my background, let alone the moment that has haunted me for the last twenty-one years.

'That's right,' I say again, unwilling to share any of the pain and self-recrimination that followed in the days, weeks, months and years after that fateful day. I don't know why she's decided to ask these questions, but I think I'm just about through with them holding all the cards.

I take a deep breath. 'Are you going to tell me what's going on? I was perfectly happy at home in Weymouth when *you* called me and told me that one of your suspects wanted to talk to me. You were quite insistent that I drop everything and make the five-hour trip up here in heavy traffic, only stopping once for any kind of refreshment. You didn't phone me back at any point to say that plans had changed, yet ever since I arrived, I've been treated like I'm a criminal. I don't know what elaborate game you're playing, but unless you're prepared to explain yourselves, I think I might have had second thoughts about that offer of legal representation.'

'You are of course well within your rights to legal rep—' Yates begins, before Oakley raises her arm in front of her, cutting off the well-rehearsed speech in an instant.

The Detective Inspector reaches into the notepad before her, and extracts a coloured page, sliding it across the desk towards me. 'Do you recognise the woman in this photograph?'

I look down at the mugshot of the shaven-headed woman. The cheek below her left eye is slightly swollen and there is yellow bruising starting to glow beneath the eyelid. There isn't a trace of makeup on the freshly washed face, and whilst there is something quite striking about her, I can't say I recognise her.

I shake my head. 'No, but I'm going to hazard a guess that this is Kylie Shakespeare?' I look from Oakley to Yates. 'You mentioned on the phone that she had a shaved head,' I add for the benefit of the recording.

'That's correct,' Oakley replies, fixing me with a hard stare. 'Miss Shakespeare wasn't carrying any form of identification when she was arrested in the home of Mr Tomlinson. She would only give us her name, but refused to provide a date of birth or home address. Once we'd taken her clothing for forensic examination, and had cleaned the blood from her hands and face, we took a copy of her fingerprints for examination purposes, but there was no match on IDENT1, which I'm sure you know is the national database.'

She pauses to ensure she has my full attention, though she needn't have bothered, as I'm hanging on every word.

'We did, however, find a match to the samples of DNA we collected from her.'

Another pause, and I now sense that she's about to lay the royal flush she's been keeping so close to her chest.

'The woman currently being held in the cells of this very police station is none other than your missing sister, Anna.'

Chapter Four

THEN

Portland, Dorset

'What do you mean she's missing?' Emma's dad turned and looked directly at her, crouching on the staircase. 'Where's your sister?'

'She went to Grandma's house,' Emma replied, no longer certain of her statement, terrified by the gnawing feeling in her gut.

Emma's dad held a hand out to his wife as if presenting an imaginary gift. 'There you go; she's at your mother's.'

Bronwyn swatted the hand away. 'I've just spoken to Mum, and she isn't there.'

'Well, we can collect her on our way.' He turned, satisfied with the resolution he'd engineered, but Emma's mum pulled on his arm.

'That's what I'm trying to tell you: Emma said she left for Mum's ages ago, and she hasn't made it. She isn't at my mum's, and there's no sign of her in the house.'

He looked back down at Emma, who could feel the tears starting to pool and blur her vision. She nodded helplessly, hoping to convince him of the situation.

He opened his mouth to speak, before thinking better of it and throwing his arms into the air in frustration. 'Have you checked out on the road for her? Maybe she's just hiding from her sister.'

Bronwyn shook her head, unsure how she hadn't considered it the next logical step.

Emma's dad left the pair of them at the staircase and marched purposefully towards the front door, pulling down the latch and thrusting the door open in one swift movement. He stepped out, scanning the yard with military precision, before moving down to the pavement and searching left and right, as if he would suddenly spot his daughter and the world would make sense again. But there was no sign of her.

Returning to the house, he crouched down beside Emma. 'I want you to tell me everything you remember. Okay? You won't be in any trouble, Emma, but what did Anna say?'

Emma swallowed her frustration that Anna's selfish tantrum had now landed the pair of them in trouble. She tried to recall the exact moment when she'd last seen Anna, but in truth she hadn't been concentrating, relieved to have the skateboard all to herself, and concentrating on maintaining her balance as she tried to push the board along the uneven ground.

'She said she was going to Grandma's house,' Emma said, unable to look either of her parents in the eye, in case they saw through her self-doubt.

'And when was this?' he pressed.

They kept asking how long ago the argument had occurred,

but she really couldn't say for certain. She had to have been back in the house for several minutes, and it was some time before that when Anna had left, but whether it was ten minutes, or fifteen, or even twenty, Emma had no sense of how long had passed.

Her lip trembled, as she raised her gaze to his. 'I-I'm sorry, Daddy… I-I don't know.'

He straightened and looked at Bronwyn. 'Let's see if we can work this out. We had lunch, and that must have finished at what…? Two? The kids were playing in their rooms for a while—'

'Until you kicked them out for being too noisy,' Bronwyn reprimanded.

'I didn't kick them out,' he snapped back.

'You were the one who told them they should go outside and play.'

The finger of blame had been pointed, and whilst it wasn't beneficial to start analysing the fallout of the afternoon's decisions, Bronwyn would never forget.

'What time was that though? Three-ish? They were outside when the Grand Prix started on the television, and it hasn't finished yet, so they can't have been outside for more than an hour. What time is it now?' He pulled up his shirt sleeve and studied his watch. 'Jesus! It's nearly five already.'

'Where is she, John? It's so unlike her to be out this long without checking in. What if…?' She stopped herself finishing the sentence, her eyes falling on her tearful daughter at her feet.

'She can't have gone far,' Emma's dad said, pulling down his shirt sleeve. 'She might have just bumped into a friend on her way to your mum's and lost track of time. I'll walk to your mum's now, and check the usual haunts for her. You pop next door and see if any of our neighbours have seen her. Okay? She's probably just at a friend's house.'

He didn't wait for his wife to respond, hurrying out of the front door once again, before darting back in and grabbing his anorak from the hook behind the door. 'It's started spitting,' he said. 'She doesn't have her coat on, so if she is outside, she'll soon come running back; you know she doesn't like the rain.'

With that, he was gone again. Bronwyn double-checked the coat hooks, part of her satisfied that both of Anna's coats were where they should be, pulling down her own and helping Emma fasten her cagoule.

'I'm sorry about Anna, Mum,' Emma tried, but she wasn't really listening. Bronwyn snatched her house keys from the dish on the side and grabbed Emma's wrist as she ploughed out into the fine rain.

Emma's cagoule wore a sheen of tiny droplets by the time they made it to Mrs Hammond's house next door. Her mum's grip on her wrist remained firm as she hammered on the PVC frame. Anna would be in so much trouble when they caught up with her. It was one thing for her to have walked to Grandma's without telling Mum and Dad, but to have wandered off and caused such panic would receive some punishment. Emma just had to hope she wouldn't become too entangled in whatever sentence was passed. She'd be angry if the skateboard was taken away as a result.

'Hi, Jill,' Bronwyn now said as Mrs Hammond's door was opened. 'Have you seen Anna this afternoon?'

Mrs Hammond was wearing an apron covered with flour, and had to put on the glasses hanging from the string around her neck before she realised exactly who was speaking to her.

Emma wasn't sure how old Mrs Hammond was, but her short hair was grey all over, and her own children had long since grown up and left home.

'Anna? No I haven't seen her, I'm afraid. I've been in the kitchen baking all afternoon, I'm afraid.'

Unlike the houses across the road, the kitchens on this side all faced the rear garden.

'Is everything okay?' Mrs Hammond asked now.

Emma's mum pushed the fringe back over her head. 'We were supposed to be going away this afternoon and she's wandered off. Can you do me a favour? We're going to keep looking for her. If she comes back while we're out, would you grab her and call my mobile?'

'Of course, of course. Do you want me to keep an eye on young Emma here for you? It's no bother.'

Bronwyn glanced down at her daughter, considering the offer, before shaking her head. 'Thank you, but I'd best keep an eye on this one. Thanks, Jill.'

Mrs Hammond remained on the doorstep, watching as they headed back down the driveway, and moved up along the next one, repeating the brief interrogation with Mr and Mrs Knowles, and then onto the Parsonses' house. The responses were the same: nobody had seen her.

Emma's wrist was tugged once again, as she was dragged back to the yard.

'I want you to show me what happened,' Bronwyn said. 'Where were you standing, what did your sister say, and then which direction did she go in?'

Emma was relieved when her wrist was finally released, and she rubbed it gingerly as she picked up her skateboard, and put it back where she thought it had been when the argument had started. She closed her eyes and heard Anna's voice shouting:

'It's just a stupid baby toy anyway. I don't need it and I don't need you!'

With that, she'd kicked the skateboard back to Emma and had crossed her arms, turned and climbed over the railing.

Emma had asked where she was going, and Anna had given her a snide look. 'I'm going to Grandma's house, so there!'

'And which way did she go?' her mum's voice cut through the memory. Keeping her eyes closed, Emma thrust out her arm and pointed to the left, picturing Anna stomping off. At one point she'd glanced back, but hadn't slowed her pace. Emma had watched until she disappeared, having passed the Jeffersons' house further down the road, her attention then falling back on her skateboard.

'She didn't say anything else?' her mum asked.

Emma shook her head.

'Then where on earth is she? We really don't need this. Not today!'

Emma remained where she was, watching as her mum pulled at her head, pacing the yard as if the answer would suddenly present itself. After three circuits of the small square space, inspiration struck, and she once again reached for Emma's wrist before settling for the cagoule-covered hand. Emma had to hurry to keep up with her mum's strides as they tore out of the yard and back onto the pavement in the same direction she'd seen Anna pursue. They followed the bend in the road, stopping only when they reached the alleyway that cut through to Grandma's road.

The alleyway was lined by the tall fences of the two

properties that bordered it, but both had large trees and bushes which hung over the fences and seemed to come together at the highest point of the path, creating a kind of leafy wooden arch and blocking out the light. Emma shivered as they stepped under the arch, the air suddenly much colder, as if they'd gone through a tunnel and entered a vast cave. Keeping her head bowed, Emma counted the steps as she took two for every one of her mum's. A variety of weeds and grasses shot out from beneath the rotting fences, creating a green trim along the walkway, adding to the sense of foreboding.

At step one hundred and fifty-two, Emma knew they'd reached the midway point, where the alleyway seemed to be at its darkest. The overhead foliage was so thick that it blocked out the sky, meaning the only visible light was the hole directly ahead of them, and the one equidistant behind. Keeping her eyes on the ground, Emma continued to count until they reached the entrance to Bletchley Street, and two minutes later they were standing outside her grandma's house.

'Mum, it's me,' Bronwyn said, as she used her key to enter the old property. 'Is Anna here?'

Emma's grandma was in the sitting room at the back of the house, and promptly lowered her knitting as the two of them entered.

'Still no sign?' Emma's grandma asked.

Bronwyn shook her head. 'John's out looking for her now. She definitely hasn't been by today, has she?'

'No, dear, it's just been me and the wireless.'

Bronwyn studied her mum's face. 'And you're sure, Mum? You know your memory isn't what it once was. It isn't possible that Anna stopped by, and you simply forgot about it?'

Emma saw her grandma's cheeks flush. 'Thank you,

Bronwyn, but I'm not ready to be put out to pasture just yet. I think I'd remember if my granddaughter had stopped by. Besides, look on the windowsill. I always leave two pound coins out for when they come and visit me, and I already checked; both pound coins are still there. If she'd been by, at least one of the coins would be missing.'

Emma eyed the gold coins on the windowsill.

'It's okay, Emma, you go and collect them,' her grandma encouraged, 'but be sure to give one of them to your sister when she turns up.'

Emma glanced at her mum for confirmation, before hurrying to the windowsill and collecting the two coins, securing them in the Velcro pocket of her cagoule. 'Thank you, Grandma,' she said, climbing onto the old woman's lap.

'You're very welcome, my darling.'

'Mum, will you watch Emma for me for a few minutes while I help John look for Anna?' Bronwyn asked.

'Of course I will. Don't worry, darling, she'll turn up.'

Emma's mum didn't look so convinced, but kissed the top of Emma's head before heading back out. For the first time, Emma wasn't so certain this story would have a happy ending.

Chapter Five

NOW

Market Harborough, Leicestershire

I blink at Oakley several times, before my mind tells me she's going to need to repeat her last statement.

'What did you say?'

Oakley nods at Yates to stop the recording. 'You didn't know then,' Oakley says as if I need it explaining to me.

'There must be some mistake,' I challenge, as I feel a burning roar rising in my throat.

'We checked and checked again. The samples taken from Kylie Shakespeare are a definite match to the IDENT1 database. From what I understand, strands of hair from a comb and saliva from your sister's toothbrush were taken, analysed, and added to the database five years after her disappearance. The case was under review and because DNA testing was becoming more prevalent in the UK, it was decided that her DNA be added in the event…'

She doesn't finish the sentence but I assume it was taken in case a comparison to a dead body was required.

Oakley crosses her hands on the desk. 'I'm sorry for the manner in which you found out. We had to be certain that you didn't know, and I can see from how pale your face has turned that this has come as quite a shock. Are you going to be okay?'

I'm not even ready to consider whether I'll ever consider myself *okay* again. I don't know how to feel. A large part of me still doesn't believe what I'm being told. I have spent twenty-one years clinging to the hope that Anna is still alive out there somewhere, but to have it handed to me on a plate like this feels too convenient.

Jack's voice is in my head again: just when we thought they were shutting us down… up pops the key to all our problems.

Oakley pushes her chair backwards, the feet scraping against the tiled floor in anger. 'DS Yates, I think Miss Hunter would benefit from a cup of strong, sweet tea. Would you mind fetching her one, and not the drivel from the vending machine next door?'

Yates stands without question and excuses herself.

'You'll have to forgive my young sergeant,' Oakley says, removing her glasses and folding the arms in, before placing them on the table in front of her. 'She can come across as cold, but she has huge potential. A real go-getter, and one day I think it'll be me referring to her as *Ma'am*.' She smiles at me. 'There's no one better in my team when she has the bit between her teeth, even if you do have to scratch beneath the ice-cold veneer to find her charm.' She narrows her eyes. 'Do I need to get you a bucket to be sick into?'

I open my satchel and pull out a packet of tissues, removing one and dabbing the sides of my mouth. 'I'll be fine.'

'Good. When Ky— Sorry, when *Anna* turned up at the police station and gave her name, all she would tell us is that she wanted to speak to you. It's not the sort of demand I would usually consider, but my superintendent told me to get her confession by any means. Whilst Sir Anthony rose to fame in the Met Police, he was from these parts originally, and when he retired to the town, he played an active part in the local community. I think you'd be hard pressed to find anyone with a bad word to say against him. So you can imagine the pressure that comes with being charged with solving his murder. That's why I asked Sarah to call you and get you up here by hook or by crook. It was about an hour later that we heard the DNA results and realised that the two of you were sisters. It was one of our DCs who mentioned your books and your search for Anna. We couldn't take the risk that the two of you have been in contact, and that you were also involved in what happened this morning. I can't say for certain that you're not involved, but my instincts are rarely wrong when it comes to people.'

So that's why Jack and I had been made to wait in the reception area for Yates to come down: they thought I had conspired with my long-lost sister to murder Tomlinson. My heart races as I process the implications of such an accusation. Given the draft email to Maddie containing the conspiracy and potential links to Tomlinson, the plot outline of my next two books screams motive. It's just as well I haven't mentioned his possible connection to our investigation. That said, the way Oakley describes Tomlinson, it's like we're talking about different people. The man we know is potentially linked to a ring of traffickers and paedophiles; hardly Mr Community Spirit.

But then, maybe Jack and I are wrong about his involvement with the ring. All we have to positively tie him to the conspiracy is that photograph I was anonymously sent showing Arthur Turgood, the Reverend Peter Saltzing, and a much younger Anthony Tomlinson. Just because we know two of the three had nefarious dealings, doesn't automatically mean the third did too. That said, why else would my long-lost sister kill him this morning?

I used to think my instincts were pretty accurate when it came to people, but now I'm not so sure. If you'd asked me five minutes ago, I'd have described DI Marina Oakley as an austere headmistress, but now I'd say she's much more like an aunt who makes a big fuss of you when you visit for Christmas.

'I-I don't know what to say,' I tell her, sipping from the paper cup of water. 'This feels like a dream.'

She cranes her neck and looks at the printed image of the mugshot. 'You'd never know the two of you were sisters,' she says.

My eyes return to the image. When I first saw it, there was no recognition, but blessed with the insight I now have, there is something vaguely familiar about the deep-set eyes. A few years ago I spent a lot of money having a company create aged versions of Anna using a host of images I sent to them. I uploaded them to the site where I post information about her, but in all of the pictures, whether with natural brown locks or with highlights, she always had longer hair. I never thought to have a version of her with her head shaved. Picturing those artificially aged pictures, I can now see how this one might fit in with the selection. But then, maybe I'm just seeing what I want to see.

'D-does she know?' I ask, my eyes remaining on the image.

I see the shadow of Oakley's head shaking on the desk. 'We don't believe so, but as I said, she hasn't said anything other than that she wants to speak to you. We tried to conduct an interview with her, but all she'd offer was a "no comment". She refused legal representation as well.'

In the years that have passed, I've never been able to determine the reason why Anna wouldn't have tried to make contact with me or Mum if she ever managed to escape the clutches of the men who forced her to make that video we found on Turgood's hard drive. Would she have repressed memories like Zara Edwards, and therefore not remembered us, or would it have been too painful to confront her former life, as Aurélie Lebrun found?

I guess there's only one way I'm ever going to know.

'Can I see her?' I ask, but am not surprised when Oakley shakes her head again.

'I'm sorry, but no. Whilst I'm ninety-nine per cent sure you had no involvement in what caused Anna to go to Tomlinson's home this morning, she's part of an active investigation, so I can't allow you to speak to her.'

I'm not surprised, and I should probably be grateful she's shared as much as she has so far.

'I understand,' I tell her. 'Is she okay otherwise? Healthwise, I mean? Is there anything you *can* tell me?'

She stands and opens the door, peering out into the corridor, but with no sign of Yates returning any time soon, she closes it again, turning back to face me.

'Go ahead and ask me anything you want. If I deem it to be operationally sensitive, then I will say as much, and you can move on to a different question. How does that sound?'

It's an olive branch, and I imagine it will be quickly retracted when Yates does reappear so I need to take advantage but be succinct. I run my hands up my face and through my loose hair. I'm sure I tied it earlier, but there's no sign of a hair tie now. I stand and begin to circle the small space between my chair and the wall; I always think better on my feet.

'The bruising around her eye in the photograph,' I say, 'is the wound fresh today?'

She rests her bottom on the edge of the table and considers the question. 'Given the latency of the swelling, we believe that was an existing injury, so not sustained today.'

'The radio said that neighbours called the police when they heard gunshots, but are there any witnesses who saw Anna entering his home?'

She shakes her head. 'I can't provide any details of witnesses or information specifically relating to this morning's operation.'

I figured she'd probably say something like that, but thought it was worth a punt.

'Okay, sorry. Let's focus on Anna herself. Can you tell me what kind of state she was in when she was arrested?'

Her lips tighten. 'I can't go into specifics, I'm afraid.'

'She wasn't injured in the incident though?'

'No specific physical injuries were recorded by the on-call doctor.'

'And her mental health?'

She squirms. 'She was given a full examination when she was booked in, as per procedure. Anything she disclosed to the doctor, I can't tell you about, but we have a duty of care to all in our custody, so that should give you comfort that she's doing okay.'

Hardly surprising. I up my pace, trying to kick-start my journalist's brain.

'Clearly this has been a huge shock to me, finding out Anna is still alive after all this time… Is there any way of finding out where she's been or why she adopted this Kylie persona?'

Oakley shrugs. 'Maybe when she decides to talk to us about what's happened today… but it's too early to say.'

I stop still as a question leaps to the front of my mind. 'You said when she was arrested she asked to speak to me.'

Oakley nods, and I'm sure I can see the faint trace of a smile forming.

'Why?' I say, leaving the question hanging.

'That's precisely what I want to know, Miss Hunter, and the reason we asked to meet with you this evening. Why you? If she knows that you're her sister, why go through the pretence of giving a false identity? There's no logic to it. She must have known we would check her fingerprints and DNA, so the false name just delays us identifying her by a few hours. I don't see that she'd have anything to gain from that.'

She stands and moves behind the chair she was previously seated on, and presses her fingers into the back of it, leaning forwards. 'But if she doesn't know that you're her sister – and there's no way to know for sure – why would she ask to speak to you? What ties you to her being in Tomlinson's house?'

I will the heat not to rise to my cheeks, certain her inner lie detector will pick up on any fluctuation. 'I don't know,' I say.

She studies me for a long moment, before releasing the chair from her grip. 'Nor me. And unfortunately I'll now have to wait until the morning to find out, because it's getting late and we are required to give arrestees beauty sleep when they're in our care. For your awareness, I plan to request to extend her stay with us by a further twenty-four hours to give my team more time to find out what set Anna on this path.'

'Are you planning to tell her about me being her sister?'

Oakley raises her eyebrows but doesn't answer as Yates opens the door and brings in a mug of tea.

Chapter Six

NOW

Market Harborough, Leicestershire

Entering the hotel room, I throw my overnight bag onto the mattress as Jack places the brown bags of fast food on the table next to the wall-mounted television. We both stare at the double bed for too long.

'Listen,' Jack says, clearing his throat, 'I can see if there's another hotel with a room nearby. You need your space.'

I was physically and emotionally drained when I stepped out of the police station, and as soon as Jack got out of the car and came to greet me, I crumpled into his arms. He didn't pepper me with questions, just held me firmly and allowed the tears to flow. I couldn't speak, but he was okay with that, and eventually ushered me back into the car, telling me he'd managed to find us a room for the night, but it hadn't been easy due to a concert being held nearby. I was just grateful he'd even looked. I'd nodded when he suggested we collect a burger and fries on the way here, and it was only the awkward moment at the check-in counter – when we were told the room was a double – that has distracted me from my thoughts.

'It'll be fine,' I tell him, trying to visualise whether there will actually be enough room for the two of us to lie still without touching.

'Are you sure? Worst-case scenario, I can always sleep in the car.'

I cock my eyebrow at him. 'Not with those injuries. If either of us should give up the bed, it's me.'

He waves away the suggestion. 'Not on your life, Emma Hunter! I won't have it. It may be old-fashioned, and I'm comfortable admitting that my viewpoint is out of touch with the new world, but I won't have you suffering for my sake. I can kip on the floor.'

I wish he wouldn't be so stubborn. 'Fine,' I huff, lacking the will to argue over something so pointless. 'We'll just have to share the bed. We're both adults. I'm sure we can figure out a way to share a bed without anything untoward happening.'

I feel like such a grown-up, and that's not a feeling I experience often enough, despite my age.

'You're right, of course,' Jack agrees. 'You're an adult, and I'm an adult, and we're friends, so there's nothing wrong with us sharing a bed. It doesn't mean anything.'

I drop onto the mattress and my shoulders slump.

'And it's not like this is the first time we've shared a hotel room. Do you remember when we were searching for Cassie Hilliard and we had to share that cramped room in Torquay? At least this place is bigger.' Jack opens one of the brown bags, examines the contents, and passes it to me. 'Those are your chicken nuggets and fries.'

I pull out a fry and shovel it into my mouth. I don't have an appetite, but the smell of the fried food wafting up from the bag has the juices flowing in my mouth, and I eagerly reach for another.

'Look, the room even has a mini bar,' Jack says, nudging the glass-fronted refrigerator with his toe. 'The rooms I usually stay in only have a kettle at best. I'd have a beer, but not at those prices.'

He sits on the far corner of the bed, and tucks into his burger. He still hasn't asked me what caused the emotional outburst outside the police station, but I sense he wants to know. Conversation has been stilted since he put me in the car, and that's unnatural for him.

'Anna is alive,' I blurt out, and it's all he can do to keep the mouthful of burger from flying out. 'That's who they have in custody. Kylie Shakespeare is, in fact, Anna Hunter. They have DNA results to prove it.'

He chews quickly and swallows. 'Jesus! I-I don't know what to say.'

'I was pretty speechless too,' I admit.

'Did you speak to her? Where's she been?'

I reach for another fry and shrug. 'Your guess is as good as mine. When Yates took me through to the interview suite, she introduced me to her DI, who said they couldn't let me speak to her in case I'm somehow part of a conspiracy to kill Tomlinson.'

He scoffs. 'They really said that? What a joke! How could you be part of something with someone you didn't even know was alive?'

I roll my eyes and explain that they interviewed me under caution and the nature of the questions they were asking.

'That is out of order,' he says when I'm finished. 'You

should have phoned me; I'd have put them straight about you.'

I appreciate his support, but I'm not sure they would have listened to him even if I had asked.

'You must be delighted though; ever since I met you, you've always had that certainty that she was alive and out there somewhere, and you were right. I'm sorry I ever doubted you.'

'I don't know how I feel about any of it. Yes, she's alive, but when they showed me her mugshot I didn't even recognise her. I've always been adamant that if I passed her in the street I'd know, but her face now lacks the softness I remember. How could the girl in my memory, whose face I've stared at in photographs for as long as I can remember, have become the number one suspect in a murder inquiry?'

I keep replaying that Sunday afternoon over and over in my mind. I've wasted so much time playing the 'what if' game for years and years, hypothesising how differently our lives would have played out had I just listened when she'd tried to tell me how to ride the skateboard properly. How could one such insignificant decision when I was a child have caused so much damage? If only I'd given in to her ultimatum, she wouldn't have stomped off. If only I'd run in straightaway and told my parents that she'd gone to see Grandma.

If only I'd started searching for her sooner. It was only when I was in my twenties and at university that I stared doing anything to try and find her. Why did I leave it so long? Why did I kick up a stink every time Mum wanted us to go into Weymouth town centre and hand out pictures of Anna, asking if anyone had seen her? I should have been championing Mum's effort, but instead I bemoaned the fact that I was less lucky than the other children in my class. I should have realised how lucky Anna and I were to have a mum who spent every waking hour trying to get her little girl back.

'Did Yates say whether they would let you speak to her tomorrow?'

I shrug. 'I guess that will depend on whether Anna continues to insist on speaking to me before she'll speak to them.'

'It probably also depends on how much evidence they have against her too,' Jack ponders, shovelling a fry into his mouth.

I stare blankly back at him.

'All I mean is, just because she refuses to answer their interview questions, if the evidence against her is strong enough, they'll still be able to make their case to the CPS to press charges. Did she say what they're holding her on?'

I shake my head. 'DI Oakley wouldn't share anything operational with me.'

Jack frowns. 'If you're lucky, then all they have is her in his house, which on its own wouldn't be enough.' He pauses, and looks down at his food. 'But if they have her prints on the murder weapon, and traces of GSR on her clothes or person, then…'

He doesn't have to finish the sentence. Pushing myself off the bed, I head over to the table and drop down to the small refrigerator, opening the door and selecting one of the three small bottles of wine inside. I also pass Jack a bottle of lager. Unscrewing the cap on the wine, I press the bottle to my lips and take a long slug, welcoming the cool, spiky liquid as it flows down my throat. I grimace at the bitterness, but take a second gulp.

Jack is watching me, still holding his bottle. 'Are you all right?'

I nod and take the bottle from him, twisting off the cap and handing it back. 'I want to drink to forget tonight, and I can't do it alone. I'll settle the bill in the morning. Cheers.' I hold out the bottom of my bottle and he clinks his against it and takes a sip of his drink.

The voice in the back of my head is relentless with questions and I need to shut it up if I'm ever going to get any sleep. I finish the nuggets and fries and have moved on to the second small bottle when Jack lies back on the mattress.

'Well, I think it's good news that you and Anna have found each other after all this time. Granted, it's not necessarily the circumstances any of us would have wanted, but ever since we met, you've had this drive to find her, and regardless of how it's happened, you've succeeded. I still remember when you first told me about your sister. It was right after Leroy Denton told us about Cassie Hilliard still being alive. I was sceptical to say the least, but not you. You told me there was nothing I could say to make you stop believing Cassie and Anna were still out there. I thought you were just overly optimistic, but once again you've proved me wrong.'

I know he's just trying to offer me the reassurance he thinks I'm craving, but there's more to it than that. I'm not looking for someone to tell me that everything will be okay. I'm too much of a realist to believe in happy endings. God knows I've seen enough stories end in tears.

Freddie Mitchell's face momentarily flashes before my eyes. I need to get hold of him somehow. Our friendship might have become strained in recent months, but he was the only one who never doubted the possibility that I'd find Anna one day.

He'll probably see it as another win against the ring, but is it that? Are there any traces of my sister left in the woman with a shaved head and swollen eye currently locked up in a police cell?

She clearly managed to get away from the men who forced her to make that video when she was thirteen, but how long has she been free? Why hasn't she come looking for me before now? If she isn't aware that we're sisters, why did she ask for me upon her arrest?

I finish the second bottle of wine, and practically fall off the bed as I attempt to stand. I'm not a big drinker, and despite the meal, the alcohol has gone straight to my head. Yet, even with the light-headedness, the voice in the back of my head is as loud as ever. Choosing to stay on my hands and knees, I crawl to the mini bar and open the door, reaching for the final small bottle.

'You want another beer?' I call out to Jack, but he doesn't respond.

Eventually, I turn to look and see the gentle rise and fall of his chest, and hear the rumble of his snoring.

'Lightweight,' I whisper mockingly, opening the new bottle and taking a long sip, slumping back against the side of the bed.

Freddie isn't the only person I'm going to have to break this news to. There's one other person who never gave up hope of being reunited with Anna, but how is Mum going to react when I tell her Anna is back but in prison for murder? With her health worsening, it could be the final nail in her coffin.

Chapter Seven

THEN

Portland, Dorset

The house reminded Emma of gatherings her parents had hosted on New Year's Eve. Pockets of people talking loudly; one conversation drowning out another, which drowned out another. It was impossible to discern any specific topics of conversation, though the subject matter was obvious: the missing girl. She hadn't returned home last night, and so her parents had reported her disappearance to the police. On account of her vulnerability, they'd dispatched two uniformed officers to the property instantly. They'd arrived just before seven last night and had asked about what Anna was wearing, whether she'd ever run away from home before, and whether she had any friends she might have been staying with.

They'd taken the information they'd discovered, and reported the disappearance to their colleagues who had spent the night searching the streets for her, but to no avail. Then, before seven this morning, two new uniformed officers had arrived, swiftly followed by three people – two men and a woman – in the sorts of suits Emma's dad wore to funerals and weddings. And the throng of arrivals had continued throughout the morning. The latest group – dressed in what resembled spacesuits – had been upstairs going through Anna's things and occasionally carrying large brown envelopes down the stairs and out to their large van parked on the road outside the house.

Emma's mum had said Emma didn't have to go to school today, and so she'd been sitting on the sofa, hunched over a colouring book for most of the morning, while the grown-ups had splintered into their groups for their lengthy and noisy discussions. Emma's mum was beside her on the sofa, talking to one of the men in a shirt and tie. He had a black moustache, which resembled a caterpillar crawling above his lip, and he wore the most serious expression. Emma would catch him looking at her every now and then, and as soon as their eyes would meet, he'd offer that sad look her mum usually reserved for when she hadn't come first in one of the races at Sports Day.

'We found some suitcases upstairs,' the caterpillar-wearing man says now. 'Were you and Mr Hunter planning a trip away?'

They hadn't mentioned anything about a holiday that Emma could recall, though she briefly recalled the exchange between the two of them yesterday afternoon when they realised Anna wasn't home.

So, we're agreed, we go tonight and we don't look back?

'No, no trip planned,' her mum replied now. 'They're just out from when we were away for half-term a couple of weeks ago. I've been telling John to put them away in the loft.'

Emma frowned at this statement, and wanted to ask her mum why she was lying to the kind policeman, but thought better of it. She'd been told off for interrupting grown-up conversation before, so remained quiet, and reached for the next felt-tip pen.

Emma spotted her dad standing in the doorway to the kitchen, talking to another man in a suit. The police had insisted on speaking to her parents separately, though Emma hadn't understood the reason why. She couldn't understand why all these people were gathered in her house asking questions, when they should be out on the street calling Anna's name. If she'd got lost while walking to Grandma's house, she could be anywhere out there now, trying to find her way home. If they shouted her name loudly enough, she might just hear it and find her way back. It had rained heavily last night, and Emma had eventually drifted off to sleep hoping Anna had found somewhere to shelter from the rain.

'And how was Anna when you last saw her?' the policeman asked her mum next. 'Was there any indication that she wasn't happy?'

Emma listened intently, waiting for her mum to tell the man about the silly argument over the skateboard, but there was no mention of it.

'She was like any normal, happy girl. She wouldn't run away; I keep telling you all. Someone has to have taken her.'

Emma's pen drifted outside of the black line, and she screwed up her mouth, angry that the picture of the vase and flowers would now carry this mistake. What did her mum mean that someone had taken Anna? Who? Why would someone take her? Did they mistake her for their own daughter, like when

Emma accidentally brought home Suzie Fenster's duffle coat that day after the school trip to Monkey World? In Emma's defence, it wasn't her fault that Suzie Fenster had happened to buy the same coat from C&A, nor that the label had fallen out. It was only when the coat wouldn't fasten up that Emma's mum realised the mistake. But how could someone have mistaken Anna for their own daughter? It didn't make sense.

'What are you colouring?' A woman's question caught Emma's attention.

Looking up from the page, she saw the woman in the jacket and trousers crouching beside the coffee table. It was a silly question to ask, as the picture was quite obviously flowers in a vase. Emma glanced at her mum to check whether she was allowed to speak to the strange woman, but her mum didn't seemed to have noticed.

'It's very pretty,' the woman continued, craning her neck for a better view, and smiling warmly. 'Do you like drawing and colouring?'

Emma nodded. In truth, she preferred reading and writing, but with so many people swarming downstairs, she wouldn't have been able to concentrate on either.

'My little girl loves colouring in too,' the woman continued, her accent reminding Emma of the Scottish lady who reported the weather on the television. 'She's four, so she's not good at keeping within the lines like you are.'

Emma's vision darted to the smudge where her pen had strayed, and hoped the woman didn't notice it.

'I'm Polly, by the way,' the woman said. 'And you're Emma, aren't you?'

Emma nodded again.

'All this must be a bit weird for you, right? Having all these strange people in your house, I mean.'

Emma nodded for a third time, putting the lid on her pen and reaching for the next one in the packet.

'So this is one of those colour by numbers pictures, right? Where you colour shapes based on the number printed inside the shape.'

Emma's grandma had bought her the colouring book for her birthday last year, but this was only the second time she'd had it out to colour in.

'I bet it really helps with maths at school, knowing what all the numbers look like. What's your favourite subject at school, Emma? Art? Maths? PE?'

'English,' Emma muttered, glancing at her mum again, half expecting to be told she shouldn't speak to strangers. But then, the woman worked for the police and had been allowed into the house, so surely that meant it was okay for Emma to talk to her?

'English? That was one of my favourites too. I loved reading books as a kid. I was always dragging my mam to the library to get new books out. I bet you're the same, aren't you?'

Emma loved going to the library in Weymouth, but she'd managed to read most of what they had there, and these days they often had to look books up on the computer and have the library order them in from other local libraries. Nothing thrilled her more than when Mum received a phone call advising a book was available for collection.

'When I grow up, I'm going to be a writer,' Emma said proudly.

The woman looked impressed, and nodded encouragingly. 'What a fantastic job that would be! I must admit I envy anyone with the imagination and ability to create stories like that. I could never do it, which is why I joined the police instead. I love puzzles and mysteries, me.'

Emma enjoyed helping her grandma complete jigsaw puzzles when mum and dad would drop her there for a few hours. They'd even managed to finish a five-hundred piece puzzle while Mum and Dad had been out looking for Anna last night.

'My job is a bit like completing a jigsaw puzzle. Whenever something bad happens, it's my job to find the pieces – the clues – and work out how they all fit together. Do you understand, Emma?'

Emma nodded. She'd caught glimpses of her parents watching Inspector Morse on the television, so she understood how the police solved crimes like murder.

'And so, I'm here to try and understand what happened yesterday, and find out where your sister Anna is. I understand that you were the last person to see Anna yesterday, is that right?'

Emma poked out her tongue as she concentrated on keeping within the thick black lines.

'I know you've already spoken to your parents about what happened, but do you think you could tell me too?'

Emma returned the lid to the pen, but held onto it. 'She told me she was going to walk to our grandma's house.'

The woman produced a small notepad and pen. 'Can you tell me what was happening before that? Where were you both and what were you doing? Think about it like writing a story. Do you know what I mean? We know that you and Anna are the main characters in the scene, but you need to give the audience a setting and a conflict that they're dealing with.'

Emma frowned. 'We were playing with my new skateboard, and Anna was telling me that I wasn't doing it right, and kept trying to pull me off it, so she could show me how to do it right.'

'And how did you react to that?'

'It isn't her skateboard, and I told her that.'

'Does Anna tell you what to do a lot? Is she a bit bossy?'

Emma wouldn't have described her sister as bossy, but it seemed to be what the policewoman wanted to hear, so she nodded along.

'So what happened when you told her you didn't want her help?'

'She wasn't happy, and that's when she climbed over the railing and said she was walking to Grandma's house. I'm not allowed to walk there by myself because I'm only seven, but Anna is nine, so she's allowed.'

'Has Anna walked to your grandma's house on her own before then?'

Emma couldn't remember a specific occasion, but she was pretty sure there had been times when she and Mum had collected Anna from Grandma's house, so she nodded along again.

'Did she tell your mum and dad where she was going?'

Emma shook her head.

'Did she ask you to tell them where she was going?'

Emma shook her head again.

'So how would you describe her attitude when she left?'

Emma frowned at the question, not quite understanding.

'I mean, would you say she was happy? Sad? Upset?'

'She was angry because I wouldn't let her use my skateboard.'

'And how did that make you feel?'

Emma hadn't really thought about it. She'd been glad to get the skateboard to herself, but she'd soon grown bored of the slow judder over the paving slabs. And whilst she resented that everyone was making such a big fuss, she desperately wished her big sister was there to share the experience, and so they could talk about the weird situation. Whatever game Anna was playing, Emma hoped it would soon end, and things would go back to normal.

Chapter Eight

NOW

Market Harborough, Leicestershire

Sleep didn't seem to come until the early hours, and when it did, it was disjointed and filled with anguished thoughts about what the future will hold for Anna as well as myself. If she's found guilty of Tomlinson's murder and sentenced to life in prison, it will feel like I've lost her all over again.

Jack didn't seem to suffer in the same way; I don't think he moved once, and even his snoring wasn't loud enough for me to blame my restlessness on it. I was already up and showered when he finally woke.

'I want to go back to the police station,' I told him. 'I know what Yates and Oakley will probably say, but I have to try. I can't give up on the prospect of speaking to my sister after twenty-one years.'

He looked at me for a long time before sitting up, wiping

the sleep from his eyes, and leaping from the bed. 'Okay. Let's go.'

He looked confused when I didn't immediately make to follow him out of the room.

'It's only seven and the station doesn't officially open to the public until ten. We have time for you to shower and change first.' I passed him one of two steaming mugs of tar-like coffee.

At this point he pulled the creased polo shirt to his nose and nodded at my idea. 'Thanks for the coffee. I can't remember the last time I woke and a beautiful woman had made me a hot drink.'

I think he meant it to sound playful, but I instantly cringe, and by the way he subsequently tiptoes past me and into the bathroom, I'm guessing he realised just how inappropriate a compliment it was.

Three hours later, and after a fried breakfast at an independent café in the town centre, we pull up outside the police station once again. We won't be able to stay parked on the yellow line today, so Jack drives around the nearby residential streets until he locates a space, and then we double-back to the station. Still no sign of any press, which surprises me given how big the story was yesterday.

We head in through the reception area. The uniformed officer behind the desk has closely cropped black hair and casts a suspicious look in our direction as we approach.

'Morning,' I say, as brightly as my fatigue will allow. 'We're here to see Detective Inspector Marina Oakley if possible. My name is Emma Hunter, and this is PC Jack Serrovitz from the Met Police in London.'

I know using Jack's rank as a method of somehow adding

to the importance of our visit isn't right, but I don't want to be fobbed off.

The suspicion doesn't leave her dark-brown eyes. 'Can I ask what it's in relation to?'

'I met with her late last night in relation to the fatal shooting yesterday morning. She took my statement.'

I don't say any more, as I don't want Oakley to send her apologies via the phone. She gave me five minutes to ask her anything and my brain failed me. It hasn't stopped whirring since Jack fell asleep, and now I have a mental list of questions to throw at her.

The woman behind the desk asks us to wait in the reception area while she phones through. The area certainly isn't any warmer than last night, and I'm grateful I remembered my coat this time. Jack seems to be moving with greater ease this morning, and I haven't seen him grimacing as much as before, but I don't know if he's just keeping it from me because of everything else that's going on. I'm also worried that he needs to return to London and work in a few days, and I'm going to miss having him around. I know he'll say I can phone him if I need to speak to him, but I don't know if that will be enough.

He smiles as he sees me looking at him, and I turn in case he can read my mind. I know there are more important things I should be thinking about, but my mind doesn't always listen when I try and change it. I have far too much on my plate – Anna's return, the outline to be sent to Maddie, the official publication of *Trafficked* – that I don't have the energy or strength to deal with my feelings for Jack. I've been putting off dealing with whether or not I can see a future with him, and I'm still not sure whether it's worth wasting time even thinking about it. Jack lives in London, where he has work and parental commitments; I can't leave Weymouth permanently and I'm smart enough to know long-distance relationships are destined to fail from launch. And then there's Rick, who is really sweet, clearly wants things to develop, and local. But he isn't Jack, and I don't want to feel like I'm settling for Rick. I wish I knew how Jack really feels about me, and whether—

'Miss Hunter, good morning,' I hear DI Oakley say. Turning to face her, I hadn't even heard the secured door buzz.

'Hi, good morning,' I stammer. 'I wasn't sure if you would speak to me again.'

'I assumed you'd probably call by,' she replies, smiling, and introducing herself to Jack. 'I returned from sleep a little before seven, and I was surprised to find you weren't camped out on the doorstep. Shall we sit?'

We drop down onto the ripped seats, which are comfier than they look.

'I really don't have much more I can tell you since last night,' she begins.

'I wanted to check how Anna is,' I interrupt. 'Is she well? Is she worried? Is she talking yet?'

'I spoke to the custody sergeant on my way out here, and she says that Anna did sleep during the night, she's eaten the breakfast she's been given, and has been doing push-ups and sit-ups since. I don't believe she has asked for anything specific, and we have yet to re-interview her.'

'Have you…?' I begin, taking a moment to get the words clear in my head. 'Have you told her about me yet? I mean, have you told her I'm her sister?'

She shakes her head. 'Not yet, and I will remind you that I can't discuss details about an open investigation. We are treating Anna as we do anyone in our custody, so she's as well as she can be.'

'And you still won't let me speak to her?'

Oakley shakes her head. 'I don't believe it is in the best interests of the investigation at this time.'

'But what if she still refuses to speak to you until she speaks to me?'

She shrugs apologetically. 'Then we'll put our questions to her as we would any other suspect in an inquiry and record her responses. If she chooses not to speak and tell us what really happened…' She shrugs again. 'That's her right. We will make a decision about whether we have sufficient evidence to press charges, and see whether the CPS agrees. Your friend here should be able to explain the rest of the process.'

Jack doesn't need to explain that if they bring charges against Anna, she'll wind up in court. I can't let that happen; she's been through enough already.

'I want to help her,' I say bluntly. 'Please, tell me what I can do to help.'

Oakley looks at me for a long time without responding. Just when I'm about to repeat my question, she stands. 'Your sister has declined legal representation. If it were me, facing a charge as serious as this, I think I'd rather have someone else on my side, particularly if things progress to a courtroom situation. You could instruct a solicitor on your sister's behalf. Anna is not obliged to agree to being represented, but the solicitor might be able to talk some sense into her.'

'Can you recommend anyone?' I ask, as she turns to leave. 'Neither of us knows the area very well.'

She considers the two of us again, and must take pity. 'There's a firm in the centre of the town called Waltham,

Nesbitt, and Watson. They've been around for decades, and have a reputation for plucking only the best graduates from Leicester University. They'd be worth a punt.'

I try to thank her, but she's already back at the door punching in the security code. As far as she's concerned, she's given all the help she can. I appreciate her coming down to speak to me again; I've met Senior Investigating Officers who wouldn't be so generous with their time.

I strain a smile in Jack's direction. 'What do you think?'

'Honestly, I think we should take her advice. She's not wrong that your sister will fare better with proper legal representation. You've done all you can here, and I don't think there's any way you're going to get to speak to Anna now, not until she's bailed or put on remand. Our window of opportunity closed the moment the DNA results came back.'

It's the answer I was expecting, so I unlock my phone and search for the solicitor's firm Oakley recommended. They answer on the third ring.

Waltham, Nesbitt, and Watson operate out of one of those brown buildings that sings of its history. The sign hanging outside the door claims the firm was established in 1967, and looking at the grime on the windows, and the peeling brown paint on the fascia, I can believe it. If I didn't know it was a legal firm, I could easily have mistaken it for an undertaker's. The glass is translucent but inside hangs a faded net curtain, making it impossible to see inside. It certainly doesn't project a welcome feeling.

A bell rings on the door as we step through into an

unbearably warm office, with more than a dozen doors scattered left and right. A single desk stands at the far side of the room where a grey-haired woman is talking in an indistinct language into the headset she's wearing. Jack and I stand just inside the door until her call ends and she beckons us forward.

'I have a meeting with Saira Mistry,' I say, reading the name I scribbled on the back of my hand.

The grey-haired woman holds up a finger as she accepts a new call through the headset. It isn't clear whether she's finished with us, or whether she has more to say once her call has ended, but we don't get the chance to find out as a door to the left opens. A striking woman steps out and introduces herself as Saira Mistry. Her petite figure is offset by the enormous heels she's wearing, which means I hang just below her eye line. There's no doubting she has the beauty to be a model, and judging by Jack's inability to speak coherently, I'd say he's noticed too.

She welcomes us into her office, which is much cooler, and promptly closes the door.

'It's Emma, right?' she asks, retaking her seat behind the desk.

'That's right,' I say, 'and this is my friend Jack.'

'And how is it I can help you both today?'

I take a deep breath. 'My sister has been arrested on suspicion of murder, and I need someone who can help her.'

Saira whips out a pen and begins scribbling in the open notebook in front of her. Her desk is otherwise clear, save for an open laptop to one side, and a locked iPad to the other. Allowing my gaze to take in the rest of the room, it gives me a feeling of satisfaction to see just how well ordered the office is. Everything seems to have its own space. The longest wall is lined with tomes of legal books of statutes, the sort of thing I've seen in the British Library. On the opposite wall are far more modern-looking books with softer spines, but a perusal of the titles suggests they are all law-related too. There are no family photographs or mementos as far as I can tell.

'She was arrested here in Market Harborough?' Saira asks.

'Yes,' I confirm. 'She was the suspect arrested at Anthony Tomlinson's house yesterday morning.'

The pen pauses on the page and she looks up. At least she knows what I'm talking about.

'I see.'

'They won't let me see her, and so I can only hope that she's okay. She's refused legal representation until now, but I can't sit by and let her face an interrogation alone.'

She scribbles another note in her book. 'Does the SIO know that you are speaking to me, and that they should hold on any interview?'

I look to Jack. 'Well, she was the one who suggested I engage with a solicitor, but I don't know if they plan to wait.'

'Don't worry,' she says offering a tremble-free hand. 'I'm on first-name terms with most of the detectives in the county, so I'll phone and make sure they hold off. Before I do that, can I ask you a few questions about your sister?'

I nod grimly, uncertain how much information I'll be able to give her.

Chapter Nine

NOW

Market Harborough, Leicestershire

The Greyhound has that warm and welcoming feel of pubs that know their place in the community, and don't try to modernise to keep in touch with customers who are only looking for a place to watch the football. There isn't a television anywhere in the place, as far as I can tell, and the patrons already inside the dark oak-lined walls seem only the better for it. The windows are single-pane, the tables a mixture of barrels and non-flat-pack, and even the barman looks like an extra from a soap opera, his thick grey beard so in keeping with the old-fashioned feeling of the place.

Jack returns to our booth, the pews reminding me of childhood trips to church. He places my pint glass of draught lemonade on the table top between us, the ice jangling in the glass like warning bells. After last night's fill of wine, I thought it safer to keep my mind focused on the task at hand. Jack clinks his bottle of alcohol-free lager against my glass, and opens the large bag of cheese and onion crisps he's purchased and offers me one.

'Best I could do,' he says, crunching one between his teeth. 'The barman said the kitchen's closed because of an ongoing dispute with the chef. The fish and chip shop next door should be open in the next ten minutes, and he's happy for customers to eat their takeaway in here so long as they buy a drink.'

I take a crisp and put it between my dry lips, but need a swig of lemonade to help wash it down. I check my watch for the tenth time since we arrived, and then check my mobile still has signal.

'She'll phone,' Jack reassures, no malice in his voice. 'Saira said she'd go straight to the police station and demand to speak to your sister. She'll phone when she's done it. You just need to try to relax.'

I raise an eyebrow in his direction. We both know I'm not going to be able to relax.

'Okay, okay,' he says raising his hands, palms out, 'but there's nothing we can do until she phones, so we need to figure out something to pass the time. Game of I-spy?'

I smile thinly at his attempt to lighten the atmosphere.

'I just wish I could speak to her,' I say after a moment. 'There are so many things I want to know, but it's more than that. I feel like there's so much she needs to know. Like our dad, does she know that he's dead? Or our mum, she should know that the Alzheimer's has taken full control and she doesn't have much longer.'

Jack rests one of his hands on mine in a comforting gesture, but I quickly snatch my hand away.

'I need to know what she's facing, Jack. I know we discussed it briefly last night in the hotel, but I also know you were holding back for my benefit. When Saira eventually calls, I don't want any surprises. In your experience, what is the likely outcome of Oakley's inquiry?'

He opens his mouth to speak, probably to offer a false reassurance that I have nothing to worry about, but he quickly changes his mind. 'Okay, I can be brutally honest if that's what you want, but there are so many variables that I can't control.'

'Like what?'

'Well, for starters, I have no idea what kind of evidence they've got. Do they have the murder weapon? The neighbours said they heard gunshots, so if Tomlinson was shot, would Anna have had time to stash the murder weapon? I doubt it, and if it wasn't on her person when the arresting officers entered the property, they would have searched the place until they found it. As far as we know there is still a crime scene team and experts in recovery of forensic evidence crawling all over the place, so I think it's safe to assume they have the murder weapon.'

He pauses and takes a sip from his bottle. 'So the next question is, what does the murder weapon tell them? Is it Anna's gun or was it already at the property when she arrived? If it's the former that suggests premeditation, which will make a murder charge more palatable for the CPS. She's got a better chance if the weapon was Tomlinson's, but this isn't the US; people owning guns for personal protection – even former police officers – is far less common.

'Then, assuming they have the weapon, what evidence has been recovered from it? Do the bullets in the weapon match those that caused the fatal shot? And is there evidence that Anna was the one who fired it? I said last night the whole thing could hinge on whether her fingerprints are on the weapon and whether any gunshot residue was recovered from her clothing or person.

'Oakley will be desperate to demonstrate that Anna was the one who shot Tomlinson, but she needs to prove it beyond a reasonable doubt. No prints and no GSR don't mean that Anna *didn't* fire the gun. Anna would still have to prove what she was doing at Tomlinson's house at the time of the shooting. And if she's not prepared to answer questions to that effect, that allows Oakley to draw on why Anna isn't prepared to defend herself.'

I feel physically sick and reach for another crisp to settle my stomach. 'I had no idea there were so many moving parts.'

'And we haven't even got to identifying Anna's motive for killing Tomlinson, if she even did.'

It is Anna's potential motive for yesterday's incident that has been troubling me most. Tomlinson wasn't part of our investigation until I was anonymously sent that photograph of him laughing with Turgood and Reverend Saltzing. That was what set us off pursuing possible links between Tomlinson and the ring of traffickers, but as far as I'm aware, Jack has yet to find any evidence to support such an allegation. Does that mean that Tomlinson has been good at covering his tracks, or that there is no evidence to cover because the allegation is false? We don't know who sent that photograph, nor the pictures of Faye McKenna and Cormack Fitzpatrick. What if it was the ring that sent the pictures to throw us off their scent? Jack and I haven't really considered that possibility, but as time has progressed I think I've started to believe more and more that Tomlinson is involved, with no evidence to support the assumption.

What if we've got it terribly wrong?

I have to remind myself that despite the success I've enjoyed in helping Freddie, Cassie Hilliard, and Sally Curtis, I am *not* a professional detective. I'm an amateur sleuth at best, and amateurs can make mistakes. It hangs around my neck like a great weight.

But whether he has a connection to the ring or not, what the hell was Anna doing at his house yesterday? I think back over the detail I gave to Saira in her office ahead of her agreeing to go and meet Anna. I told her all about Anna disappearing that day in Portland, the police investigation that turned up nothing, and my eventual decision to reignite interest in her case while I was at university. It broke my heart when I told Saira how Jack and I inadvertently stumbled upon the video of thirteen-year-old Anna on Turgood's confiscated hard drive. That video all but proves that Anna was being abused by the same ring responsible for the abuse inflicted on Faye McKenna, Aurélie Lebrun, and Freddie Mitchell.

Freddie once told me that Turgood would offer them rewards to appear in those videos, but whether or not Anna was persuaded to appear or forced to, it's still abuse. No thirteen-year-old is able to rationally decide that she wants to appear in that kind of filth. It was abuse whether she was a perceived willing participant or not. But what happened in those intervening years that drove her to Tomlinson's house yesterday morning?

Should I draw the conclusion that Tomlinson *was* one of her abusers and her confrontation with him yesterday was driven by a desire to get revenge for the abuse he'd inflicted? It feels too simplistic an explanation, and whilst a part of me would feel he got his just deserts, I can't condone that kind of reaction. And how did she find him so many years after?

I raise my glass to my forehead and roll the condensation around my temple.

'Headache?' Jack asks.

I nod. 'Give it to me straight, Jack: is Anna going to prison?'

He begins to shake his head, before finishing in a shrug. 'As I said, there are too many—'

'Worst-case scenario,' I interrupt.

He sighs, and his eyes dance around the room as he tries to find the words that he knows are going to sting, but that I'm demanding regardless. 'Okay, okay. Worst-case scenario, they have her prints on the weapon, GSR was recovered from her person, and they manage to determine a motive for her wanting him dead… She'd be charged with murder, and would go to court for a plea hearing. If she pleads guilty, the judge might be kinder in his sentencing; if she pleads not guilty and it goes to trial but a jury still finds her guilty, then it's life imprisonment.'

It's like he's plunged an ice-cold knife into my chest. I can't breathe, and it's all I can do to get to my feet and stumble blindly towards the toilets. Bursting in through the door, I make it to the cubicle before I expel the remains of my fried breakfast.

I find Jack waiting for me outside the door. 'I'm sorry,' he says. 'It doesn't mean that's what will happen.'

I take his arm and he leads me unsteadily back to the booth. I'm conscious that my breath probably stinks, but I find a packet of mints in my satchel and place three on my tongue, welcoming the sting of mint and the sweet taste.

'Can I get you anything?' Jack asks, his face a picture of anxious concern.

I shake my head, but my T-shirt is clinging to my clammy

body, and all I want is another shower. I look at my watch again. It's been almost an hour since we left Saira's office. I'd half expected her to phone apologetically and tell me that Anna had still refused her support, but no phone call might mean that my sister is listening to Saira's advice, which I suppose can only be a good thing.

There's so much I wasn't able to tell her about Anna. I don't know where she lives – is she local? Did she travel far to reach Market Harborough yesterday? Is she living under the Kylie Shakespeare identity or was that just a name she plucked from obscurity when forced to provide one at the police station? Is there a significant other in her life who should be notified of her arrest? Presumably the custody officer would have asked if she wanted to phone anybody and advise them of her arrest, but did she take them up on that offer? Or was I her phone call? And wherever she lives, does she have pets that might need feeding if she's going to be away for a long time? Here I am assuming that I'm the only one who could possibly care about the mess she's in, but I don't know what network of friends and family she has developed without me in her life. Even someone as introverted as me has friends I can rely on in difficult times.

These are the sorts of questions I should have told Oakley to ask her last night when my brain was stuck in the fog, but none of them presented themselves.

I've almost finished my lemonade when Saira arrives, but she declines Jack's offer of a drink. She's even prettier up close, her skin smooth and her makeup sparingly applied, and yet she seems to wear her beauty as a chip on her shoulder. Maybe she's just fed up of people making assumptions based on her appearance, rather than her skill and intellect.

'Did you speak to her? Is she okay?'

Saira nods. 'Yes, she agreed to speak to me, and yeah, overall I'd say she is well. She's obviously worried about what she's facing, but was willing to allow me to sit with her when they brought her in for a second interview.'

'Did she agree to answer their questions?'

She shakes her head this time. 'I advised her not to, as they weren't willing to disclose their evidence yet. They ran through a series of basic questions, to which she refused to comment, and then she was bailed, pending further investigation.'

My mouth drops. 'Bailed? They've let her go?'

'Of course. They're only allowed to hold her for twenty-four hours before they must make their case. I think DI Oakley had requested an extension, but it must have been declined. They will go away and continue their investigation, and as and when they're ready, they'll recall Anna to the station, at which point I imagine they'll disclose what they've got ahead of the interview, and allow me to advise Anna of her options.'

I'm suddenly conscious of the fact that Anna isn't with Saira. 'Where is she then?'

Saira's face is devoid of emotion as she speaks to me. 'As far as she tells me, she isn't aware that she has a sister, and when I advised that her sister had reached out to me to contact her… she didn't react well. You know better than anyone how difficult it would be to process the reality of a long-lost sister coming out of the woodwork.'

'So where is she? Is she staying locally? I need to speak to her.'

'I'm sorry, Emma, but she doesn't want to see you right now. I know where she is, and will continue to work with her for as long as she wants me to, but for now there's nothing more I can tell you.'

'But I'm the one who hired you.'

She shrugs. 'My conversation with your sister is protected by client–attorney privilege, and I'm not at liberty to divulge what she told me.'

I open my mouth to interrupt, but she raises a placatory hand to cut me off.

'Your sister is fine, and she's no longer in police custody. Give her some time to get her head together, and I'm sure she'll contact you when she's ready.'

This doesn't feel right. After twenty-one years, my sister comes back into my life, but now disappears just as quickly. I feel adrift.

'Go home, Emma. I have your address and phone numbers. There is nothing more you can do for now.' She looks at her watch. 'I need to go. I will keep you updated as best I can.' She slides out of the booth, and collects her bag from the floor. 'It was a pleasure to meet you. I'm a big fan of your books.'

With that, she spins and departs, leaving Jack and me with nothing to do but start the long journey back to Weymouth.

Chapter Ten

THEN

Portland, Dorset

Four days and no Anna. Four days of perky Polly – who was now being referred to as the Family Liaison Officer – sleeping on the downstairs sofa. Four days of microwave dinners and meals whenever boredom struck. Four days of strained smiles, and jumping at the sound of every telephone call. Four days of being woken by her mum's sudden cries of anguish in the middle of the night. If this were some kind of practical joke, seven-year-old Emma certainly wasn't laughing.

It had also been four days being kept off school, which ordinarily would have had Emma bouncing off the walls with excitement, but because it wasn't half-term, there weren't any cartoons on the television to watch.

'Do you fancy helping me make your mam a cup of tea in the kitchen?' Polly asked, though from her tone it was clear she already knew what the answer would be.

Emma nodded and clambered off the sofa, following Polly

into the kitchen and watching as she moved effortlessly from cupboard to cupboard, selecting the apparatus she would need as if it were her kitchen. It might as well have been, as Emma wasn't sure she could remember the last time she'd seen her mum leave the sofa.

'Think of me as a handy helper,' Polly had said when it had been confirmed she would be temporarily moving in with the family. 'Anything you need, you're only to ask. Best to leave your mammy and daddy to deal with everything they've got going on.'

Polly hadn't alluded to what activity that included, but as far as Emma could tell, it meant drinking lots of tea, crying, and answering the questions of whichever police officer turned up next.

'Would you like a chockie bicky?' Polly asked, reaching for the tin from the top shelf of the cupboard above the microwave.

Dad's secret stash – Emma didn't tell her, just accepted the chocolate-covered digestive.

'We're running out,' Polly said, biting into one of her own. 'Maybe you and I could go to the local shop this afternoon and pick up some supplies. What do you think?'

Emma didn't mind. At least it meant she'd be able to escape the claustrophobic cloud that had descended in the aftermath of Sunday afternoon. It felt odd having Polly in the house; she'd said she had joined the police because she liked solving puzzles, but all she'd done so far was cook and babysit. Was that really a role in the police force? Polly didn't seem to mind though, and was a ray of sunshine every morning when Emma emerged from her bedroom.

Emma brushed the crumbs from her hands into the bin

before looking at Polly and trying to summon the courage to ask the question that had been playing on her mind.

'You look like you've got something on your mind,' Polly commented as the kettle whistled on its stand.

'You said I can ask you anything, right?' Emma began.

'Aye, anything you like. I promise I will always be honest, and if it's a question I can't answer, I'll tell you why.'

That sounded fair enough, so Emma took a deep breath. 'How long will I be off school?'

Polly's anxiety evaporated into a thin smile and a waggling of her eyebrows. 'Oh, I see. Well, I suppose that will be up to your mammy and daddy to decide. Are you missing school?'

Emma nodded. In truth, she'd finished the book she'd borrowed from the school library and was eager to swap it for the next in the series.

'I bet you're missing all your friends, aren't ye?'

Emma nodded again. She enjoyed the routine of school, and time certainly seemed to go much quicker between the sounds of the school bell than it did stuck in the house with nothing to do. Mum hadn't let her out in the yard to play on her skateboard since Sunday, and the grass in the back garden was too wet and muddy to play on.

'I bet they're all missing you too. I'll ask your mam in a bit and see whether she's happy for you to go back tomorrow. How does that sound? I can always drop you in and collect ye if she thinks it will be too much for her.'

It wasn't like her mum had anything better to do, but Emma just nodded and followed Polly back into the living room, climbing onto the sofa beside her mum, who didn't react to the movement.

'Emma helped me fix you a cup of tea, Bronwyn,' Polly said.

Emma looked up at her mum, but it was as if someone had frozen her in time. Her hair was poking out at all angles, in need of a brush, and her face looked as though someone had rubbed white chalk all over it, save for the dark circles beneath her bloodshot eyes. She looked as though she was crying, yet her cheeks were dry as a bone; no more tears left, Emma supposed.

'And if it's okay with ye and Mr Hunter, I might take Emma to the shop with me this afternoon to pick up a few supplies.'

Emma's mum's head turned to look at her daughter, but her face was devoid of any emotion. Emma gave her brightest smile, resting her hand on top of her mum's, jarring slightly at the cold touch.

'We could buy you some flowers to brighten things, Mummy,' Emma said, squeezing the hand slightly.

Her mum always seemed to smile whenever her dad returned from work with a fresh bouquet, though Emma wasn't certain what type of flowers were her mum's favourite.

Emma's mum continued to look at her daughter, before returning Polly's gaze, and nodding ever so slightly.

'Good,' Polly acknowledged. 'I'll have a rummage through the kitchen and make a list of bits and pieces to pick up: bread, milk, cheese, and that sort of thing.'

Emma watched her leave, slightly annoyed that Polly hadn't asked the question about her returning to school, when it had felt like the perfect opportunity. She was about to ask herself when the phone rang and her mum snatched away her hands, standing and hurrying to where it hung on the wall.

'H-hello?' she stammered into the device.

Emma remained where she was, watching as Polly joined her mum, and secretly hoping that it was Anna on the end, finally revealing where she'd been hiding all this time. It didn't once cross her mind that Anna probably wouldn't even know what number to dial to get through to them.

Emma's mum's eyes widened at whatever was said down the phone, her face finally gaining some colour, before she thrust the phone at Polly.

'You're speaking to PC Polly Wells, whom am I speaking—? No, you'll have to go via the media relations team for any comments on the current investigation, as I'm sure you know only too well. No, neither Mr nor Mrs Hunter are available to comment on your story. Do not call here again.'

'Did you hear what they asked?' Emma's mum said, incredulous. 'They wanted to know whether we were being charged with killing Anna. How can they just phone up and bowl out with such a vicious allegation?'

Polly offered her hands, palms out, in a calming gesture. 'Just ignore the phone. If it's anything about the case, the DI will phone my mobile.'

'But how did they get our number? How do they know Anna's name? There hasn't been a public appeal made yet.'

Polly opened her mouth to answer, but thought better of it, and shrugged instead. 'Unfortunately, these things always have a way of getting out. Somebody somewhere lets something slip, and a journalist gets wind of it. The DI is due to make the public appeal tomorrow lunchtime, so it could be as simple as reporters from the local news outlets being contacted, and people putting two and two together. I'll mention the call to the DI and see if we can put some kind of caller ID on the line so we can pre-empt who's calling you before answering.'

Emma had stopped listening at mention of the allegation the journalist had made. Was that really what people thought? That her mum and dad had killed Anna? It was a preposterous idea as neither of them had been there when Anna had wandered off. Emma felt angry that people out there could be judging her family in such a way, and wished she had a means to correct them all.

'Try not to let it bother you, and in the meantime, why don't you leave me to answer the phone for you? If it's a friend or relative, I can screen the call, and then hand it over. After tomorrow's press conference, you can expect to see an increase in the volume of calls and the attention that will come your way. Ultimately, the more people talking about Anna, the more people will be looking for her, but there is a trade-off required.'

Polly caught Emma looking over and offered her a bright smile, as if it would be enough to wipe any memory of what she'd just witnessed. 'I'll go and make that shopping list, and then you can show me where the nearest shop is, Emma. How does that sound?'

Emma nodded from the safety of the sofa, and with Polly returning to the kitchen, Bronwyn returned to her place on the sofa.

'It will be all right, Mum,' Emma offered. 'The police will find Anna and bring her home, and then everything can go back to normal.'

Bronwyn's eyes welled as she took in her daughter's naivety, and she pressed a hand to her cheek.

'I hope you're right, my darling.'

They both started as the front door opened and Emma's

dad entered the room. He looked exhausted, as he always did when he'd worked the night shift. His belly looked as though it was fit to burst from the seams of his navy jumper, and there was a strange white scuff mark on the cuff of his trousers, but he otherwise didn't look any worse than when he'd left last night. Emma had heard the two of them arguing when Polly had stepped outside to make a personal call, but she hadn't heard exactly what about. It had been the same since Sunday; it was as if they'd forgotten how to be civil to one another, and all exchanges ended in shouting or tears. Then whenever Polly returned to the room, they would both fall silent.

John took one look at his wife and daughter, and sighed. 'There's no news then?'

Bronwyn shook her head, fresh tears escaping.

'They'll find her,' he said glumly. 'It's only a matter of time.'

Emma's mum looked as though she might say something but thought better of it. Emma looked from one to the other, positioned at opposite ends of the room, but neither able, nor maybe willing, to bridge the gap.

'I'll go and have a shower and get some shut-eye,' he said after a minute.

Bronwyn nodded, but didn't respond.

Emma watched as he continued to stare for a moment longer, before crossing the room and taking the stairs quietly. He hadn't asked them how they were feeling, and he hadn't told them how his day had been. Was this all the future held now? Why couldn't they both see that Anna would be back soon, and then everything would go back to how it should be?

Chapter Eleven

NOW

Portland, Dorset

Back home, with the sand between my toes, the sound of laughter nearby, and the smell of salt in the air, there is nowhere I'd rather be than checking on my mum. Jack parks us outside the care home, as if reading my mind. He unfastens his belt but looks at me, waiting for my agreement rather than assuming I will submit to his request.

'You want to come and meet her?' I ask.

'The way you speak about her, I feel like I already know her… I can wait in the car if you prefer? I just thought you might need the moral support.'

My eyes pool instantly at his offer, and I'm grateful to feel his arms embrace me. I quickly dry my face in his shoulder. Where do I begin telling her about Anna?

When I'm composed again we break apart, and I take a deep breath before opening the car door and swinging my legs out into the cold air. The horizon glows orange with the sun setting behind the building as we approach, and I'm suddenly conscious that visiting hours are almost up. I hadn't realised it was so late in the day.

Entering, I sign us both into the guest book, and lead Jack along the corridor towards my mum's room. Knocking twice, I open the door, but she isn't inside. Checking my watch again, I can only assume she's already headed to the dining room for supper when the door to the care home manager's office opens and Mum steps out.

'Ah, there you are,' she says, looking me up and down, 'we were just trying to call you.'

The care home manager Pam Ratchett, appears behind her. 'I was phoning to see if you wanted to come up,' she quickly explains. 'She's quite lucid since waking from her afternoon nap.'

Mum is already in through her door.

'Take as long as you like,' Pam says, touching my arm. 'Make the most of her as she is. I'll have her supper kept warm.' Her eyes fall on Jack, and she waits for me to introduce him.

'This is my friend, Jack,' I say quickly.

Pam shakes his extended hand. 'It's nice to meet you. I'll have some tea sent to you all.'

She closes and locks her door, before following the throng towards the dining room at the back of the building.

'Sorry about the smell,' I warn Jack in advance. 'You'll become accustomed to it in no time.'

He doesn't reply, following me in through Mum's door, where we find her in the process of opening the door into the enclosed garden.

'Mum,' I call over, 'I'd like to introduce you to Jack. He's my…' I'm uncertain how to finish the introduction.

'We work together,' Jack finishes, as Mum strides across the room and kisses his cheeks.

Mum rests her hands on his arms, and stares at him for a long time. 'I can see why she likes you.' She leans closer, and my mouth drops when I hear her whisper, 'If I were thirty years younger, she'd have a run for her money.'

Jack smiles awkwardly, but she quickly releases him, and comes over to kiss me. 'How are you, Emma?'

My eyes well instantly again, but I bite down on my lip to keep them at bay. 'I'm well, Mum,' I say, the emotion hard to restrain.

She doesn't seem to notice how painful it is for me to speak and steps out into the darkness, scraping a chair as she sits.

There is a knock at the door a moment later, and one of the nurses enters backwards, carrying a small round tray with a pot of tea, a jug of milk, and three cups. Jack takes it from her and carries it outside to the small round table. I encourage him to sit in the remaining chair, while I drag Mum's armchair over to the doorway so I'm as close to the table as I can be.

'How are you, Mum? Everything okay? Is there anything you need me to pick up for you?'

She ignores my question and I'm concerned that her lucidity has already waned, when she reaches for Jack's hand across the table. 'And are you a writer too, Jack?'

He chuckles gently at the question, and glances at me. 'No, I don't have the way with words that your Emma does. It amazes me how anyone can have the patience to write so much and in such a coherent manner; I struggle to write a postcard, if I'm honest.'

Mum places a frail finger to her dry lips, pondering. 'So you work with Emma, but you're *not* a writer… Given your build and obvious strength, I'm going to hazard a guess that you don't work in a normal office…'

He doesn't answer, encouraging her with raised eyebrows and subtle nods of his head.

'You don't bear a middle-age paunch, so I imagine that whatever you do you're fairly active, so probably not a doctor… A fireman perhaps?' She studies his reaction, before clicking her fingers. 'If I had to guess, I'd say a policeman.'

Jack applauds. 'I'm impressed, Mrs Hunter, and I see now where Emma inherited her deductive reasoning from.'

I'm not going to lie but even I'm impressed. I never understood why my brain works the way it does, but I've never had reason to attribute it to Mum before.

She waves away the praise. 'You must call me Winnie. When someone calls me Mrs Hunter, I automatically assume my mother-in-law is lurking nearby.' She leans closer to Jack and speaks in a loud whisper. 'Now there was a woman who could freeze water at fifty paces. I won't lie, it felt like a relief when she eventually… you know…'

'Mum!' I gasp. 'You can't say that about Granny!'

She looks over to me, as if only just realising I'm sitting at the table too. 'You only knew her when she'd mellowed a bit. She used to spoil you and your sister rotten with sweets and comic books, but mark my words, she was formidable in her day. Even your father was terrified of her.'

'Okay, *Winnie,*' Jack says, 'what other attributes did Emma inherit from you – aside from your natural beauty of course?'

She feigns embarrassment like some Parisian courtesan, and turns to me. 'You want to watch this one, Emma. It looks like he's trying to sweep me off my feet and steal your inheritance.' She winks at us both. 'And I'm quite prepared to let it happen.'

She and Jack both laugh, and the earlier tears I was trying to resist fall freely, but in happiness rather than sorrow.

'Biscuits,' Mum blurts out. 'They've forgotten the biscuits!' She touches Jack's hand again. 'Jack, my dear, would you be a sweetheart and go and find one of the nurses and ask for some biscuits?'

'Mum, there's really no need,' I begin to say, but she shushes me.

'We can't drink tea without something to dunk into it,' she says, smiling at Jack again.

He stands and offers a playful salute. 'I'll see what I can rustle up.'

Mum waits until she hears the door close, before leaning closer to me. 'You've got yourself a good one there,' she says conspiratorially.

'Oh, we're not together,' I correct. 'We're just friends.'

She looks shocked at the statement. 'What's wrong with him?'

I frown. 'Nothing's wrong with him, but—'

'Then I don't see what the trouble is,' she interrupts. 'Handsome, in good shape… He's not gay, is he?'

'No, he's not gay, Mum,' I confirm, trying not to allow the frustration to play through my voice.

She gives me a funny look. 'You're not gay, are you?'

My cheeks burn. 'No, Mum!'

She frowns at my discomfort. 'It wouldn't be a problem if you were, you know. Barry who lives upstairs has a gay daughter. I could ask him to pass on your number if you want me to?'

'I'm not gay, Mum,' I say through gritted teeth, willing a hole to appear in the ground to swallow me up.

'What are you blushing for then?'

I can feel my hands fidgeting beneath the table cloth. 'Because… I don't like talking to you about things like that.'

'Like what? Sex? Don't be such a prude, Emma! What goes on between a man and a woman, or a woman and a woman, or a man and a man for that matter, is nothing to be ashamed of. It's perfectly natural! Not so much in my day, but you can't turn on the television these days without seeing sex being thrust at you.'

I can't meet her stare.

'All I'm saying is you could do a lot worse than Jack.' She continues to stare me down until I manage to raise my eyes to hers. 'Anyway, that's not why I sent him away. There's something else I wanted to speak to you about. That's why I asked Pam to phone you. Though how you got up here so quickly is beyond me.'

Does she know? Has my body language inadvertently told her that Anna is back? Or has her true identity now been revealed on the news and I'm not aware of it because we were listening to Jack's Spotify in the car ride home?

She lifts the lid from the teapot and stirs the bags around inside before replacing the lid. 'I don't have long,' she begins, lifting the pot and starting to pour. 'I've been having strange dreams – flashbacks to my earlier life, if you will – and it terrifies me that this disease which is robbing me of my sensibilities will take full control before I've managed to fix things.'

I'm not following her train of thought, but I don't interrupt, sensing that she may have already rehearsed this speech.

She finishes pouring the tea and returns the pot to the tray. 'I know I wasn't always there for you after your sister went missing. You don't have children yet – wait, you don't have children yet, do you?'

I shake my head, suddenly feeling guilty that I haven't yet provided her with a grandchild to dote on.

She breathes a sigh of relief. 'Anyway, where was I?' She pauses, replaying her words in her head. 'Oh yes, I wanted to apologise to you for not doing more to support you. I know it's all water under the bridge, but if I don't tell you now, I worry that I never will.'

My chest tightens at whatever is eating away at her. Should I just tell her about Anna and the arrest? Doesn't she have the right to know that she's been found after all this time? What if it's too much of a shock and causes her to suffer another heart attack? I'd never forgive myself.

'I have taken care of all the arrangements,' she says.

I frown. 'What arrangements?'

'Funeral service and cremation. I remember when your father died, and it was such a horrible experience having to organise it all while mourning his passing. I don't want you to have to worry about any of that. So I took out a plan many moons ago, and all the details are with my solicitor, as well as my final will and testament. I know I don't have much to show for my name, but he said it was probably best to formalise the minutiae so you don't have to go through probate and legal proceedings to get what should rightfully be yours.'

This is it: my chance to tell her that her years of appealing to the public weren't a waste; that Anna has been alive this whole time. Yet, as I open my mouth to speak, the words won't leave my lips.

Fresh tears fill my eyes. 'Mum, you've got years left; you shouldn't be thinking about things like this yet…'

'There, there,' she says rubbing my arm. 'There's no need for you to be upsetting yourself. Death is just the next chapter of life's journey for us all. Not to talk about it would be a greater crime. When the time comes, you don't need to worry about anything, okay? I've even booked a venue for the wake, and a prospective guest list – though you may need to check that they're all still alive first.' She chuckles at this.

I quickly wipe my eyes as I hear the bedroom door opening and Jack enters. He has draped a white cloth over his wrist and carries the plate of Hobnobs like a waiter from Downton Abbey. I remove myself from the table so I can fix my face in Mum's private bathroom. When I return, I can hear her laughing at something Jack has just said. I hang back, revelling in the sound of her laughter; it's been too long since I heard her truly celebrating life.

'I like you, Jack,' she tells him, and I can see him squirming at the compliment. 'Emma needs someone in her life like you, to take care of her when I'm gone. Don't leave it too long.'

Chapter Twelve

NOW

Weymouth, Dorset

'Sorry about Mum's matchmaking,' I say to Jack when we've driven back to Weymouth and parked up outside my flat. 'I know you probably don't need reminding, but she is losing her mind.'

He laughs. 'You do realise if I were a gold-digger and took your mum up on her offer, you'd have to call me Daddy.'

I slap his arm in playful shock. 'I think I was just a bit sick in my mouth.'

He laughs again. 'Sorry. Listen,' he pauses, 'it's been a bit of a crazy few weeks, and yesterday was... I don't even know how to describe it. And the weeks to come are probably going to be even more stressful for you... What do you say, for tonight only, we put it all aside, and just go for a meal somewhere and pretend like we're not who we are. I think I could do with a bit of normal, even if just for a few hours. What do you say?'

It really has been a trying start to the year, and I feel like I don't know if I'm coming or going. Saira made it clear that Anna would make contact when she's ready, so in reality there isn't a lot I can do until that happens.

'Okay,' I say, returning my overnight bag to the back seat of the car. 'We can wander into town for a walk.'

He looks like the cat that got the cream, quickly locks the car, and joins me on the pavement. 'Lead on.'

The moon is enormous in the virtually cloudless sky, and I snuggle into the warmth of my jacket as a chill wind bites at my cheeks. I love my home town at this time of year, when the air is fresh with spring around the corner, yet not spoiled by the disruption the summer sunbathers bring with them. At the height of summer you can actually smell suntan lotion in the air the second you step outside, even in the built-up town centre away from the beach. But right now, with the worst of winter behind it, the area is refreshed. Even the seagulls sound happier as they prepare for the fish and chip attacks they undoubtedly have planned for next season.

Jack asks me questions about my childhood and I do my best to answer truthfully, though I probably paint the memories in a kinder light. I don't want him thinking ill of me or my town. Yes, growing up wasn't always easy, especially after Anna disappeared, but experience tells me others had it much worse. I never went hungry, and always slept under a roof. Neither of my parents physically or mentally abused me, and my life now is testament to the good job they did in raising me to count *my* blessings rather than envy others.

Jack tells me about growing up in London, and how busier and more threatening it now feels to be raising a child there. I've only met his daughter Mila a couple of times, but she seems a sweet girl, and I can see from the way he speaks of her that she is his proudest achievement. It does make me wonder why he hasn't been snapped up by another prospective beau. Mila's mum, Chrissie, is married and has recently welcomed a new child to her brood, but from the way Jack speaks of her, I don't sense that he's ready yet to move on from the end of their relationship. Maybe he's just the typical policeman: married to his job.

Maybe I should stop ignoring Maddie, Rachel, and now my mum when they tell me I could do a lot worse than someone like Jack. But whenever I allow myself to think about the possibility of a future with him, I realise how ridiculous it is. Jack won't ever leave London to move down here – he wouldn't want to be so far from Mila – and I couldn't move to London permanently, so what chance would we have? He means too much to me as a friend to risk a long-distance relationship destined to fail.

When he was driven off the road and left in a coma a couple of days ago, I was terrified I'd never have a chance like this again: to hear his voice and goofy laugh. It reminded me how much I care for him, and how I wish things were a bit easier so that maybe we could see if friendship could develop into something more, but there are still just too many moving parts. Anna's return was unexpected, and I need to be available for when she decides she's ready to talk. I've missed not having a big sister, but I'm not sure she even remembers having a little sister, or whether she'll ever want to broach the subject of what happened to her, and how she might end up facing life imprisonment for murdering Tomlinson.

What troubles me most is that with Tomlinson now gone, Jack and I no longer have a way of tracing the other corrupt individuals running the ring. Once again, their interference has left us dead in our tracks. It feels like they've been there watching in the background, closing doors when we want to go through: the break-in and fire at Rachel's flat; Saskia's hit and run; the theft of the foundation's accounts books; Jack's accident. And now Tomlinson's murder? Just how far will this group go to stop their illicit deeds being exposed? Am I putting everyone's lives in danger?

'What are you thinking about?' Jack asks, and I start at the question. 'It's just… you suddenly went very quiet.'

I'm about to respond when I realise where our random walk has brought us: the homeless shelter and canteen. I suppose on some subconscious level, my mind identified this place as the 'normality' it was craving.

'Have you heard from Freddie recently?' Jack asks next, as he spots the queue of people waiting by the door.

I shake my head. 'Not since…'

'You can go inside and see if he's there, if you want? Probably best if I wait outside. He's not my biggest fan.'

It's such an odd dynamic in my life. Before *Monsters* was published, Rachel and Freddie were my closest confidantes, and since its success, Maddie and Jack have become good friends, yet the past and the present are always at odds with one another, like repelling magnets. I wish there was a way I could get them all together and show them that there's no reason for animosity. I love them equally.

The queue for the former church hall with the leaky roof is already down the road and around the corner. Dragging Jack around to the rear entrance, I spot Barbara stirring a large pot and she waves as I head inside.

'Hello, my dear,' she says warmly, 'what brings you down to our neck of the woods?'

'I'm looking for Freddie,' I respond. 'Is he working tonight?'

Barbara shakes her head. 'We really haven't seen very much of him at all recently. I was going to ask you whether you'd heard from him, or whether you knew if he was unwell.'

I don't tell her that I haven't been able to reach Freddie since I pushed him to reveal the truth about what happened to him at Pendark Film Studios. That night, I saw in his face that we'd crossed a line from which our friendship would never recover, but a naïve part of me had hoped he might be willing to listen to my apology.

This place means so much to Freddie, and I don't want to believe he's given it up just to avoid seeing me.

'When was the last time you saw him?' I ask.

Barbara stops stirring for a moment, and her eyes wander as she trawls through old memories. 'I really can't remember. A few weeks easily. One of the regulars mentioned spotting him out and about on the other side of the town, I seem to recall. Have you been by his flat?'

'Freddie has a flat now? I didn't…' My words trail off.

There's me considering myself a good friend of Freddie's and yet I didn't even know he'd secured himself a flat. What else has been happening in Freddie's life that I've been oblivious to because I've been chasing ghosts and criminals? Have I really become so single-minded that I've closed doors on others?

'If you see him, will you let him know I'm keen to speak?' I ask, and Barbara nods.

'You take care of yourself, Emma. There've been a few

muggings around here of late. Not safe for a young lady like yourself to be walking alone so late at night.'

I haven't heard anything about a small crimewave, but appreciate Barbara's concern and reassure her that I'm not alone.

My heart sags as I step back out into the cool evening air.

'No luck?' Jack asks, and I shake my head despondently.

'Do you mind if we head home?'

Jack reaches for my hand but I pull it away and move forwards, unable to escape the realisation that I'm putting his life in danger by keeping him close. We walk the lanes in silence, the salt in the air a reminder of a time when life was simpler.

From nowhere, we're cast in a beam of bright light that has us both shielding our eyes, and I'm grateful when I feel Jack's arm around me and he drags me to the safety of the pavement as a dark van accelerates past us.

'Bloody delivery drivers,' Jack curses, but my pulse is racing too quickly to even look back at the van.

'W-we could have been killed,' I gasp.

'Not with me around,' he replies, his voice far calmer, and I can no longer keep my fear and frustration at bay. Leaning into his chest I don't stop the tears flowing, and I pray for a solution to all our problems.

Chapter Thirteen

THEN

Portland, Dorset

Be careful what you wish for!

That was the warning Grandma always gave before Emma blew out the candles on her cake. She'd say that Emma could make one wish, which the fairies would try to make come true if she managed to blow out all the candles in one go. Anna said it was nonsense and that there was no such things as fairies. But then Anna also used to say that Santa Claus wasn't real, and yet he brought them presents every year, so it wasn't like she was always right.

But this was the second time this week that Emma had made a wish that had come true and that she'd subsequently regretted. Maybe there *was* more to Grandma's warning. The school bell finally sounded, and Emma was able to put the last ten minutes in the playground behind her. Ten minutes of silent stares; ten minutes of pointing and whispering; ten minutes of none of her classmates coming to see her to ask if she was okay. She hated being the centre of attention, and for the last ten minutes it had been a living nightmare. Yet this return to school is what she'd wished for last week when she'd asked Polly when she would be returning, and Polly had said she'd have a word with her mum and dad. It had been boring being trapped at home, but right now she'd swap it for her current conditions.

Polly had walked her to school this morning, and the twenty-minute journey hadn't been too bad. They'd talked about the book Emma had been reading. Polly said she hadn't read it, but could remember watching a BBC television series about it which her little girl had watched. Emma asked Polly about her daughter, and her face had brightened significantly as she'd talked about her. Her name was Caroline, and she was aged fifteen, so now in secondary school and preparing for her GCSEs. Emma had asked whether Polly missed her, on account of the fact that she'd been living with them for the last week. Polly said she did, but that Caroline was lucky enough to live with her dad and his new wife, so she probably hadn't even realised that Polly was away from home. This had saddened Emma. There were a couple of children in her year group whose parents had separated, and Emma didn't want to picture what life would be like if her parents were to separate. They seemed to be arguing more and more, and although Polly had told Emma it was nothing to worry about, neither her mum nor her dad had offered any such assurances.

Since the police officer with the black caterpillar on his lip had made the appeal on television, Mum and Dad were famous. Emma and her mum had walked to the nearby petrol station to pick up a loaf of bread yesterday afternoon, and they had been approached by six different people before they'd returned, all asking questions or offering their condolences. It had left Emma's head in a spin, so when Polly had suggested she walk Emma to school this morning, Emma and her mum had both leapt at the chance.

At registration, Mrs Murray formally welcomed Emma back to the class, and warned the other students to remember to be kind and check how Emma was doing throughout the day. Mrs Murray then asked to speak to Emma privately, and said how sorry she was to learn about Anna's disappearance, and that if it all felt too much today, Emma was to come and find her to talk. Emma had appreciated that, and had been tempted to tell Mrs Murray that she'd changed her mind about returning to school, until Mrs Murray told her that she was welcome to go to the library at lunchtime if the thought of the playground was scary.

'I imagine most of the other children saw the police appeal,' she added, 'and if they didn't, I'm sure their parents did, and would have spoken to them about it. There's no way to hide from the truth, but what I have learned about schoolchildren is that they soon forget. I bet by the end of the week, none of them will even be talking about your sister.'

This alarmed Emma, although she didn't say so. Her mum had said that the more people who were talking about Anna, the more people would still be looking for her. It was now a week since she'd stomped away from the yard, and there was still no sign of her. When they'd gone to Brighton on holiday a couple of years ago, they'd shared a double bed in the hotel room they'd stayed in. Her dad had won the holiday through work, and the girls would stay up late, talking about what they wanted to do the next day, and inevitably what they wanted to be when they were older. Emma had talked about becoming a writer or a journalist, but Anna had said she wanted to be a vet, even though it did mean extra studying at university. Emma couldn't help but wonder whether that was where Anna was now, though she hadn't said as much to her mum and dad. But if there was still no sign of Anna by the weekend, she was determined to tell them.

Maths class passed without incident, though Mrs Murray came over and asked if she was okay three times, and three times she said she was fine, even though she could feel twenty-plus pairs of eyes staring at her for most of the lesson. That was followed by writing practice, and then drawing class came. Emma tried to draw the lion from her book, but she couldn't get Aslan's mane right, and ended up bursting into tears when she'd rubbed out the pencil lines so many times that the paper ripped. Mrs Murray took her out of the classroom to the sick bay where she could sit quietly and compose herself. Mrs Cross – a funny name given she oversaw the sickbay, and was supposed to offer the students care – said it wasn't unusual, but agreed to watch Emma for a few minutes.

When the bell sounded for lunch, Emma told Mrs Cross that she was feeling better and that Mrs Murray had told her she could go to the school library to change her book. Mrs Cross looked relieved that she wouldn't be late getting to the teachers' lunch queue, and locked the door to the sick bay behind them.

Emma loved the musty smell of the library, and felt comforted for the first time that morning as she stepped in and took a deep breath. Some of her classmates complained about the smell of the books, but Emma saw it for what it was: the breath and wisdom of hundreds of writers who had slaved to craft their words into worlds of wizards and dragons, and princesses and potions. Hundreds of thousands – maybe even millions – of children had been entertained by the books squeezed into these shelves, and what finer profession was there than to entertain the world?

Emma was already reading above her age group, a fact that Mrs Murray strongly encouraged. 'The more you read, the better your writing will be,' she would tell the class. And so, if Emma wanted to be the best writer she could, it meant she'd have to keep pushing herself.

Disappearing to the back of the library, where fewer of the students dared to go because of the dark shadow overcast by the tallest of the freestanding book cabinets, Emma scanned the shelves for the next in C. S. Lewis's series. She'd torn through the pages of *The Lion, the Witch and the Wardrobe*, and she knew from the back of the book that the next instalment was called *Prince Caspian: The Return to Narnia*. But although searching high and low, she couldn't find the right spine.

She was about to go and search for one of the library assistants – older students who were chosen to 'work' in the library as a reward for good work – when she heard two loud girls enter the library, clearly unfamiliar with the formality of silence in such a place

'Did you see her standing all alone before school started this morning? I always used to think there was something odd about her… Do you know what I mean? Always had her head buried in a book when she could be running about in the fresh air. I mean, Anna was all right – a bit of a square – but her kid sister? Something not right about that one, if you ask me.'

Emma fell back against the bookcase, listening intently.

'My parents forced me to watch the police appeal on the

news, using it as an example of what can happen if I don't listen to them,' the second girl said.

'Oh, I know what you mean. Mine are like *this is why we always told you not to talk to strangers*. I'm eleven for crying out loud!'

'My dad said that their dad works up at the old prison at the top of Portland. A prison guard or something. Anyway, I heard Dad telling Mum that all that time spent with criminals was bound to rub off at some point.'

Emma's chest tightened and her breaths came in shallow bursts.

'He reckoned the police will probably find her body buried in their garden,' the second girl continued. 'Probably picked up tips from the prisoners he's supposed to be guarding.'

The first girl erupted into a fit of giggles. 'Gamekeeper turned poacher? Maybe. I just feel sorry for the parents. If you had to lose one of the sisters, you wouldn't have chosen Anna to be the one to be taken. They should have snatched the weird one instead.'

'The mum was probably in on it. That's why the police haven't checked the garden yet.'

The two girls turned the corner and suddenly came face to face with Emma. Their mouths dropped and their eyes widened, but neither acknowledged her, quickly turning and heading back to the exit of the library.

'See what I mean?' the first girl whispered loudly. 'What kind of weirdo hears that and doesn't speak up?'

'You think she heard then?'

'Duh, obviously! Come on, let's get out of here before she starts plotting our disappearances.'

Emma felt the sting of tears at the edges of her eyes, but bit down on her tongue to keep them at bay. She'd never cried inside the library before, and she didn't want to start now. Blinking to clear her vision, she took several deep breaths, trying to clear her mind of their words, but each sentence echoed louder and louder, as if someone had recorded the conversation and was now playing it back over a loudspeaker.

The police will probably find her body buried in their garden.

Emma covered her ears with both hands.

Probably picked up tips from the prisoners he's supposed to be guarding.

Emma dropped to her knees and closed her eyes, willing the voices to stop.

The mum was probably in on it.

Emma's mouth dropped open and she silently screamed. They didn't know her parents like she did. They wouldn't hurt a fly. They loved her and Anna equally, and they'd been inside when Anna had left, so they couldn't have anything to do with her disappearance. And yet…

Emma shook the troubling thought from her head.

No, their arguments had nothing to do with them being involved in what had happened, and were simply a matter of neither being able to deal with the feelings of guilt and regret they were experiencing. That was what Polly had said on the way to school that morning. She'd said it was nothing for Emma to worry about, and Emma so wanted to believe her.

But if the Year 6s thought Anna was dead, how long would it be before the police reached the same conclusion? And when they did, how long would it be before they realised that Emma had ignored her grandma's advice on Sunday afternoon and cast another wish she now deeply regretted?

Chapter Fourteen

NOW

Weymouth, Dorset

Jack is in the shower when I wake, but has left me a mug of tea in the kitchen. Last night he insisted he was fit enough to sleep on the sofa bed, meaning I was back in my own bed after a quick change of the sheets. It made a huge difference to my sleeping pattern, and although it took a while to switch off my brain and drift off, once I did, I didn't wake until just now. I'm not one who usually sleeps past seven, so to see it is just after nine tells me I must have needed the additional rest.

Outside, the seagulls are calling me to get out of bed and to welcome the promise of a new day. Last night, Barbara told me one of the regulars had spotted Freddie hanging out on the other side of town, and something is telling me if I go searching, I'll find him. Life's too short for regret, and I desperately want to patch things up with him. I know how thrilled he'll be to hear of Anna's return too.

Leaping out of bed, I dress quickly and leave Jack a note telling him I've popped out to buy us some pastries for breakfast. I sign the note with a heart after my name, but stare at it for a long time, before screwing it up and rewriting the note, this time without the heart.

The air is electric when I step outside, and the pavement and road are wet from fresh rain, but tentatively sticking out my hand, the rain seems to be through. The sky over the town has glimpses of blue, and the heavier light-grey clouds are blowing eastwards, so I leave my umbrella in its stand and step out. Across the road, there are several dogs racing along the beach, sending up clouds of sand like mini volcanoes as they go. I remember running along that same stretch of beach when I was younger, and how it always managed to ground me. But I don't feel the urge to hare along it today. Despite everything that's up in the air, I feel calmer than I have for a long time, and optimistic that today is going to be a better day than yesterday.

Following the road into town, there are plenty of others milling about from shop to shop, and the occasional one catches my eye and nods or smiles in my direction. There are times when such gestures would have me heading for the nearest hat shop or even returning straight home, but today I greet each one with a huge smile, and none of them bother to ask for an autograph or selfie.

I keep my eyes peeled as I walk along St Thomas Street, until I make it to Town Bridge, crossing over the water and into the old end of town. I head along Trinity Road, stopping when I arrive at a narrow alley that leads up to the residential properties beyond. There used to be access to a bar and clothes shop up there, but both have long since been closed up, the businesses abandoned. For as long as I can remember the tiny gap between buildings has been used as a makeshift residence for some of the homeless who refuse to take up much-needed beds at the hostel. Instead, they brave all weathers and hunker down, out of sight and out of mind of most of those who pass by. It was where I saw Freddie the first time, and followed him to the hostel where I felt compelled to offer my support.

The alleyway is empty, but I can see from the damp, flattened cardboard boxes that line the concrete that it has been used as a resting spot by someone recently. I turn slowly in a circle, looking for anyone who might be able to tell me if Freddie's been by, but whoever was sleeping there is long gone. I continue onwards,

The smell of fish is overpowering here, being so close to the water, and I stop for a moment, looking out at the bobbing boats. This was my dad's favourite part of the town. He used to tell me it was because it was far enough from the bustle of shoppers and beach dwellers, and how the lapping of the sea against the wall almost sounded as though it was applauding our efforts to contain it. I wonder what he'd make of all the council's attempts to attract more tourists to the town.

'Give me your purse!'

The deep baritone voice is so sudden that I instantly freeze, and my neck slumps below my shoulders. The breath catches in my throat, and it's like my body has decided to play musical statues.

I didn't notice anyone approaching, but I can feel their shadow hanging over me now, and how the breath suddenly bears the scar of tar and stale beer. I don't dare turn.

'Give me your fucking purse!' the voice yells again.

Suddenly there's a hand on my shoulder and I am yanked

back and spun around. A spindly kid of about fourteen or fifteen is standing there, his face a scowl of anger and menace. Light bounces off the blade in his hand and temporarily blinds me. I know if I were braver, I could club him around the head with my bag, and follow it up with a knee to his groin, but that part of me is in hiding. I can't speak and I can't move. There is nobody in my immediate periphery, so I don't think shouting or screaming would help anyway.

My eyes fall on the blade as he moves it closer to me and reaches for the strap of my satchel. I don't resist as he slips it from my shoulder. All I can think about is how unfair it would be if I were to die right now when my sister has only just returned to me. Then I picture Jack stepping out of the shower and seeing my note and not realising how much I wish I hadn't screwed up the version with the hand-drawn heart.

The kid wrestles the strap over my trembling wrist and unzips the satchel. Why won't he just go? He has what he wanted, and I haven't caused him any trouble.

His eyes rise from the contents of my satchel up to my face. 'Is this it? Ain't you got a tablet or anything?'

I literally only grabbed my purse and phone this morning, neither of which have any particular value. I shake my head in answer to his question, aware that my flat keys are in my coat pocket. What if he isn't satisfied and goes to my house to search for more stuff?

'P-please,' I whisper. 'I have nothing else.'

He narrows his eyes and his gaze lowers to my coat pockets, but then a noise to my left distracts him. A heavyset man in a high-visibility jacket is walking in our direction, laughing uproariously at something he's just heard on his phone. The kid takes one look at him and scarpers.

My legs go, and I crash to the wet floor.

The man in the high-vis jacket calls 999 to report the crime, and waits with me until the PCSO arrives. I've never been so relieved and embarrassed to see Rick Underwood. He takes a description from the man with me who then departs, leaving me leaning against the railings and Rick's uneasy gaze on me.

'You're pale as a sheet,' he says. 'Are you sure you're all right?'

It's lucky he hadn't seen me twenty minutes ago; at least some of the blood is starting to return to my cheeks.

'I'll be fine,' I tell him.

'Can you describe your attacker, including any distinguishable features that might help us identify him?'

I try my best, but already his face is fading to little more than a blur, as the adrenaline begins to slowly subside.

'Sounds like one of a dozen of the kids around here,' he admits sombrely. 'Could be motivated by any number of factors: drugs, alcohol, boredom. Sorry, I know it isn't any consolation, but it wasn't personal.'

Something stirs in the back of my head. The attacks on Rachel, Saskia, and Jack float nearby. Was this really just a random act of violence, or was there another reason somebody wanted to take my purse and phone? Yet further obstacles in the way of the truth. Or am I just being overly paranoid in light of everything that's happened these last few weeks?

'I'll give you a lift home if you like,' Rick offers.

I think about the look on Rick's face when I saw him two days ago when Jack and I were on our way to Market

Harborough. How has it only been two days? It feels like a lifetime ago.

'I'm surprised you're back in town,' he says, less casually than I think he intended.

The last time he saw me I was clutching my passport and overnight bag, so I suppose he must have assumed Jack and I were off on a short break away. I wish we had been, rather than how things played out that day.

'Listen, Rick,' I begin, conscious that now isn't the time for a conversation about my personal life, 'I'm sorry about the way we left things. There's so much going on that I don't even know where to begin.'

'It's okay, Emma. You don't need to apologise.' He leans closer, lowering his voice. 'We never agreed what we were. We went on a couple of dates, which I really enjoyed, and I think you know how attracted I am to you, but we never had the conversation about where things were heading.'

The blood is rushing back to my cheeks in earnest now, but he won't stop speaking for long enough for me to interject.

'I've read *Ransomed* and *Isolated*. I know you and Jack are close, and the last thing I want is to get in the way of that... When I saw the two of you at your place, I was disappointed, as I'd planned to have *that* conversation with you and had worked it all out in my head. I went home and saw Mum and was in a bit of a mood. She told me that anything worth having is worth fighting for, and it made me realise something: I'm not ready to give up on the possibility of us.'

I don't know what to say. Verbalising my emotions has never been a strength, and although my mouth opens to reply, my brain has yet to queue up any words to come out.

'Listen,' he says, 'now isn't the time to be talking about any of this, and it isn't fair for me to put you on the spot. All I ask is that you think about what I've said. I like you, Emma. I *really* like you, and if you'd give me the chance, I'd spend the rest of my life trying to brighten yours.'

He moves back to his car before I can say anything else. Jack must be wondering what's taking me so long, but without my phone I can't even message him to let him know where I am. The last thing I need is for Jack and Rick to run into one another again.

'Thanks, but I think I'll walk,' I tell Rick, brushing some of the sea mist from my jacket. 'It'll help clear my head.'

He doesn't argue, but waits in his car until I'm safely back over Town Bridge before driving away. The walk home is quieter, and I keep my eyes on my feet, now overly aware of my surroundings, and silently questioning everyone around me. It's why I'm shocked as I near the flat to see a car parked outside my flat, and DI Marina Oakley glaring at me from behind the wheel.

Chapter Fifteen

NOW

Weymouth, Dorset

'Where is she?' Oakley demands, thrusting her door open and rolling out towards me.

'Where's who?' I ask absently, uncertain why Oakley would be at my door here in Weymouth.

'Time is of the essence, Miss Hunter, and I would have thought, given your previous experiences, *you* would know just how important that is.'

A couple have stopped walking to watch the drama unfold. I can just imagine Maddie ticking me off for allowing myself to be videoed having an argument with a senior police figure.

'I genuinely don't know what you're doing here,' I say calmly, putting my hands up in a not too dissimilar way as I did for the gunman, 'but please come into my flat, and then we can discuss it like rational people. Okay?'

I extract my house keys from my coat pocket, and hold them out so she knows they aren't a weapon, before climbing the stairs to my front door and unlocking it. Bored, the couple who'd stopped move off again, as Oakley follows me inside.

'Finally!' I hear Jack exclaim. 'I was beginning to think I should send out a search…' His words trail off as he steps out of the kitchen and sees me with Oakley.

I don't have time to get into a detailed explanation about how my morning's turning into a nightmare, and spin to face Oakley. 'Would you like a cup of tea or coffee?'

She shakes her head. 'No, I just want to know where your bloody sister is.'

My brow furrows. 'Anna? I don't know. I haven't seen her. Why? What's going on?'

Oakley stares at me for a long time, and I sense she's trying to read my body language for signs of deceit. Satisfied, she moves past me and into the living room, looking left and right, before completing a full review of my flat. She hasn't asked if I'm comfortable with her searching my property, nor has she given any reason why she'd want to, but I let it slide as I know I have nothing to hide.

She returns to the living room, where Jack is whispering to me, asking what the hell is going on.

'Your sister is in a lot of trouble, Miss Hunter,' Oakley says, moving to the window, and staring out at the crashing waves across the road, 'and if you don't want to join her, you'd better start talking fast.'

I scratch my head, trying to think of why Oakley has driven all the way to Weymouth, and why she might think Anna is here. I suppose she may not be aware that Anna refused to see me after she was bailed yesterday, so if I were in Oakley's shoes and looking for Anna, my flat seems a logical enough first stop. But why drive four hours to check, when she could have just as easily requested the Weymouth and Portland police stop by? And more importantly, what has happened that means she's suddenly hunting for Anna again? Have they turned over new evidence and want to pick up where they left off? Surely she would have had to provide them with residence details to be bailed. At the very least they could try phoning Saira and checking, rather than me.

Oakley turns to face me. 'When did you last speak to your sister?'

I look at Jack for corroboration. 'I haven't spoken to her. You wouldn't let me see her, and then she refused contact once you released her.'

'I want to see your phone,' she says, eyeing the satchel I'm still holding.

'I don't have it,' I reply apologetically.

'Where is it?'

'You're not going to believe this, but it was stolen this morning.'

'What?' Jack speaks up. 'Where? When? Is that why you took so long?'

'I was mugged,' I tell him. 'We can discuss all that later.' I fix Oakley with a hard stare. 'I'm happy to provide you with my mobile number so you can check with my provider that I haven't been in contact with Anna. I haven't made or received any phone calls or text messages since your DS Yates phoned me two days ago. Phone my provider and they'll confirm.'

'Ma'am,' Jack says, 'if you tell us what's going on, Emma and I will be only happy to help in any way we can.'

Oakley moves across to the armchair and perches on the edge of the cushion, while Jack and I sit on the sofa.

'Just before half-past seven this morning, a child was

abducted in Southampton. A girl, aged fourteen, who was waiting at a bus stop. A witness who was out walking her son to school said she saw a white Hyundai i20 pull up and the driver speak to the girl, who then climbed into the front before the car sped away. The girl never made it to school.'

My eyes narrow. 'With all due respect, what does any of that have to do with me or Anna?'

Oakley interlocks her fingers. 'The i20 was stolen from a residential street five minutes from where the girl was taken. A dog walker reported a woman in her early thirties with a shaved head smashing the rear window of the car with a brick, before speeding away with it.'

My chest tightens and the air evaporates from my lungs.

'We have traffic camera images of the i20 heading from that scene to the abduction site and then onwards onto the A31, heading west. We lost track of the car just west of Ringwood.'

'You think Anna abducted this girl? That's ridiculous. Why would she?'

'You tell me, Miss Hunter.'

I glance at Jack, who looks equally gobsmacked.

'Ma'am, if I may? A woman with a shaved head stole a car and then supposedly abducted this fourteen year-old girl? I appreciate how serious a crime that is, but what I don't understand is how you're involved.'

She considers the statement, but chooses not to answer it. 'Where would your sister go, Emma? She's already in enough trouble because of the shooting without adding child abduction to her list of crimes. I need to find her ASAP.'

I can't believe this is happening. It's like a nightmare that I can't wake from.

'Have you spoken with her solicitor?' I try. 'The last thing she said to me was that Anna needed time to clear her head before dealing with the prospect of a long-lost sister. I haven't seen Anna for twenty-one years, and I have no idea what she's been up to, or where she might go.' I pause, and try to gather my thoughts. 'Just because a witness said a woman with a shaved head stole the car, it doesn't mean it was Anna. Surely you must have more to go on than that?'

'The witness also said she was wearing a charcoal-grey sweatshirt and light-grey joggers; the exact outfit Anna was wearing yesterday when she was bailed.'

'That's still not enough to leap to the conclusion that another woman with the same taste in threads and haircut isn't responsible,' I counter.

'Nor why you have any involvement in the hunt for her,' Jack echoes. 'Do you seriously expect us to believe that in,' he looks at his watch, 'under four hours Hampshire Constabulary have managed to rule out all other suspects, and have narrowed it down to the woman who is your chief suspect in the shooting of Anthony Tomlinson?'

She considers Jack for a moment, and I imagine she's weighing up how she would deal with such a challenge from one of her own team.

'Who is the girl who's missing?' I ask, desperately trying to control my own rising temper.

'Her name is Daisy Beauchamp.'

The name means nothing to me, and Jack's face shows no recognition either.

'Who is she?' I ask.

Oakley narrows her eyes. 'On the face of it, she's just an ordinary teenager, with parents who are worried sick about her.'

'And is there anything you've found to tie Anna specifically to her? What I mean is, are you saying that after she was bailed yesterday, Anna made her way to Southampton and snatched this girl at random, or is there more to it?'

'The team in Southampton are checking Daisy's phone records and messages, and examining her computer thoroughly. If there is a connection, they'll find it.'

There's more she's not saying, I can sense it, but I can't decide if she's deliberately toying with me, or whether it's simply that she doesn't trust me.

'I swear to you I know nothing about any of this,' I say earnestly. 'Thirty-six hours ago I didn't know for certain that my sister was still alive. I'd like to argue that she couldn't be responsible for abducting a child because it is so out of character, but the truth is,' and I sigh as I say it, 'I don't know anything about her character. Before you told me otherwise, I would have said no sister of mine could murder anyone…' My words trail off, and for the first time I'm relieved I didn't mention any of this to Mum last night.

Oakley pulls a phone from her pocket and checks the display, before looking at the two of us again. 'Daisy Beauchamp is the great-niece of Ian Beauchamp. Does that name mean anything to either of you?

I shake my head but see Jack nodding in my periphery.

'As in *the* Ian Beauchamp? Former Tory backbencher?

Oakley nods, her eyes still narrowed. 'And one-time party leader candidate, after John Major stepped down in the mid-90s.'

'His name came up in connection with my work at the NCA,' Jack whispers, 'but he was ruled out of any involvement.'

'I've been doing some research of my own,' Oakley continues, uninterested in what Jack has just uttered. 'After we bailed your sister, I asked DS Yates to find out more about the two of you. I had no idea you were so instrumental in locating Cassie Hilliard, Sally Curtis, and Aurélie Lebrun.'

Technically, we didn't help find Aurélie, but I'm loath to correct her. Jack remains silent too.

'I also spoke to a contact of mine at the NCA where you were recently seconded, PC Serrovitz, and he told me – off the record, of course – that you've been investigating a trafficking ring. So it just makes me suspicious that I have a suspect accused of killing one prominent member of society, and abducting the great-niece of another, who just happens to be related to you.'

You and me both, I don't say.

'You still haven't told us why you're so certain that Anna Hunter is the person you're looking for in relation to the abduction,' Jack says evenly.

'An anonymous tip was phoned through to the 999 switchboard reporting the abduction,' Oakley replies, 'naming Kylie Shakespeare as the kidnapper, and specifically mentioning the Tomlinson shooting. I was informed about that call just before eight o'clock this morning while I was on my way to London, and diverted here.'

I'm incredulous. 'An anonymous phone call? That's what has you ready to judge and sentence my sister? Have you even traced who made that call?'

Jack must sense how frustrated I'm growing because he attempts to put his arm around my shoulders to calm me.

'No, Jack,' I say, shrugging off his arm. 'You know as well as I do how hard *they've* worked to shut us down. And just as we're getting closer to the truth, they produce my missing sister from out of the woodwork and set her up as some crazed avenger.'

Oakley stands and hands me a business card. 'There's a lot of pressure coming from above to recover Daisy as quickly as possible. If you want to help your sister, Miss Hunter, I'd suggest you find her and have her hand herself in. Otherwise, I don't see how this ends any way but with more pain for all concerned. This is my number. You can reach me any time, day *or* night.'

She moves out of the living room and I show her to the door.

'There's just one more thing, Miss Hunter,' she says, stepping out and onto the doormat. 'When Anna was arrested at Mr Tomlinson's house two days ago, she was carrying a copy of one of your books. You asked me whether she knew the two of you were related, to which I don't have an answer. But one thing's for sure: she knows who you are. If she gets in touch, please let me know.'

Chapter Sixteen

THEN

Weymouth, Dorset

Emma watched her mum in awe as she moved from person to person, forcing them to take one of the homemade leaflets bearing Anna's angelic face and their home telephone number. How anyone could withstand so many rejections and uninterested acknowledgements was beyond her. And yet it didn't seem to matter how many shoppers politely declined her advances, assuming she was trying to sell them something, still she pursued. It was as if somebody had told her that the only way she would find Anna was to make sure that she'd spoken to every visitor to Weymouth.

Emma was standing alongside the wooden board her dad had hammered together. It too bore a picture of Anna's face, her school photograph from last year, along with the words: HAVE YOU SEEN THIS GIRL? Emma also had a handful of the leaflets that her mum had designed on their home computer and subsequently printed off. Each leaflet was A5 in size. Polly had lent Bronwyn a paper guillotine so she could save paper by printing two to one page. That only encouraged Emma's mum to print double the quantity needed. They'd already walked the lengths of all the roads within a five-minute radius of home, fastening the leaflets to every available lamppost and telegraph pole with Sellotape. They'd then had to retrace their steps and replace every one after it had rained and the ink had run. The new laminated versions wouldn't weather so easily.

Whilst Bronwyn had been sad and distraught the first few days after Anna's disappearance, she'd been resolute ever since, going out every day to pester anyone who was willing to listen. Because it was now Saturday, and her dad was working at the prison, Emma had been dragged along, which is why she was now standing in the middle of the street, one hand firmly gripping the wooden board with the A3 print-out of her sister's face. It had barely stopped raining all morning, and so most of the shoppers her mum approached quickly hurried on past. Most accepted the leaflet, but Emma had witnessed more than one of them then depositing it in the waste bin fifteen metres along the road when they thought nobody was looking. Emma didn't like to think how many copies of the leaflet were now in bins across the town.

'If anyone has any information, you be sure to send them over to me,' her mum had said shortly after they'd arrived in the town centre, and set up base on St Thomas Street, the main pedestrianised strip. 'I have a good feeling about today,' she'd added with a deep breath.

Emma had hoped she was right, but as the day dragged on, it didn't seem like her mum's optimism had been well placed. Emma thought about the other children in her class, and what they were probably doing at this very moment. Most probably would have slept in, and would be gorging on cartoons and books. Emma would love to have been home reading about Lucy, Edmund, Susan, and Peter's adventures in Narnia, but instead she was trapped in the fine rain, beside the public bench. She would have sat down but the seat was all wet.

She'd asked why she couldn't have gone to her grandma's house while her mum came into Weymouth town centre, but her mum had refused, saying Grandma was in no condition to watch her all day. She'd asked whether she could stay with Polly instead, but Polly had said she was going home to get fresh clothes and see her daughter for the day, so that hadn't been an option either.

Emma gripped the edge of her hood and gave it a shake to clear the latest puddle of rainwater before brushing the side panels. It wasn't fair that she had to be standing out here, where she could easily catch a cold. She'd complained about the conditions about an hour after they'd arrived, but hadn't been prepared for the snappy rebuke her mum had delivered.

'Don't you want to find your sister?'

Emma hadn't been able to answer. Of course she wanted Anna to be found and brought home, but if most of the people who accepted a leaflet weren't even bothering to read them, what was the point in them being out here? Was it all just for show? Emma could still hear the words of the Year 6 girls in the library: *The police will probably find her body buried in their garden.*

Was all of this – the tears, the arguments, the public appeals – was it all just to push the spotlight away from the possibility that Anna could already be dead? Emma hated to think such thoughts, but her mum would never discuss it with her. That night after the first day back at school, she'd tried to talk to her mum about what the other girls had said, but she'd instantly dismissed the possibility that Anna was anything but fit and healthy.

Emma had thought about asking Polly about what the girls had said, but she didn't want to get her mum and dad into trouble, so when Polly had asked how school had been, Emma had said everything had been fine. She'd dreaded going in every day since, and had made a point of keeping her head down in class, and her breaktimes hidden away in the library. Mrs Murray had been right; by Friday the stares of the other children had stopped, and Emma was no longer the hot topic of discussion.

Emma's stomach grumbled, and she clutched her hands to it. All this fresh air and drizzle had built up an appetite, and although Polly had made her a bowl of porridge for breakfast, she was desperately craving a pasty from the bakery a stone's throw away. She watched as person after person emerged from the shop, the paper bags rustling in their hands as they opened and devoured their purchases. Steam erupted from their mouths as they tucked in and carried on with their lives without another care in the world. What she would give to swap places with them for only a minute.

Looking up the road, Emma saw her mum was now engaged with a blond-haired man grasping an umbrella. He was holding the A5 piece of paper, studying it closely, and listening intently as Emma's mum spoke with him at length. Was that a positive sign? He hadn't simply walked on by like so many of the others, and he was now speaking to her as well, though Emma was too far away to hear what they were talking about.

Emma imagined how good it would feel if her mum came trundling over to say that the blond-haired man had spotted Anna hiding out somewhere and could now lead them to her. Wouldn't that be the best news they could receive today? It would mean Polly and her colleagues could leave them in peace, and she'd be able to prove to the world that her parents had nothing to do with Anna's sudden disappearance. It would certainly shut up those girls from Year 6.

'What's all this about then?' a gravelly voice said, startling Emma.

She looked to her left and quietly gasped as her eyes fell on the owner of the voice. He was wearing a green and brown camouflage jacket, like she'd seen soldiers wearing on the television. But that was where the resemblance to military personnel ended. His grey hair was long and straggly, resembling a mop head that had been chewed and spat out by moths. His long and pointy nose reminded her of how she'd first pictured Mr Tumnus when she'd read about Narnia.

There was a disgusting smell starting to claw its way around the two of them, and although she didn't like to think it, she was pretty sure the smell was coming from him. It reminded her of the smell that cloaked the walls of the public toilets down by the beach. Whenever her mum had taken her in there before, Emma had always insisted on pinching her nose, and she desperately wanted to pinch it now.

'What's that you're holding?' the man spoke again, sniffing and wiping the end of his nose with the back of his hand.

Emma didn't move, glancing back to where her mum was still talking to the man with the umbrella. She could shout out but didn't want to interrupt the prospect that the man was telling her where Anna could be found, but more so because the fear wouldn't allow any sound to escape her throat.

'You don't need to be so scared,' the man said to Emma, 'I won't bite. Who's the girl in the picture? Your sister? Your friend?'

Emma's eyes slowly returned to the man. 'M-my sister.'

She noticed now that he had a rolled-up sleeping bag beneath one arm and a four-wheeled shopping trolley, not dissimilar to the type she'd seen her grandma use on occasion. The T-shirt beneath the camouflage jacket was torn and faded, and the longer he stood so close, the more she could smell the stale pong of tar and tobacco.

'And what's she done then? Run away?'

Emma nodded as it was easier than trying to explain.

'Let's have a look at her then,' he said, thrusting out his hand for a leaflet.

Emma reluctantly handed him one, taking a slight step closer to the wooden board, so at the very least she could kick it to make noise if he lunged at her.

The man pushed the leaflet up so it was barely an inch from his face. 'That's better. I can see her now. Pretty young thing, isn't she?' He lowered the image once again, and fixed Emma with a look. 'My eyes ain't what they once was, you see?'

Emma remained where she was, willing her mum to hear the silent call she was making.

'What's your sister's name then?'

'A-Anna,' she stammered.

'And you? What's your name?'

'Emma,' she said, finding confidence she hadn't expected.

'I bet you'd love to find your sister, wouldn't you, Emma?

What if I told you I think I've seen her? Here in Weymouth. Not far from here as it goes.'

Emma's hands stopped trembling. Was it possible that her mum had been right and today would be the day they'd find her?

'W-where?'

'As I said, not far from here. I could take you to her now if you like? We could be there in a few minutes if we go now?'

Emma looked back to her right, but her mum still had her back to her, now handing the blond man a handful of the leaflets. Maybe he wasn't giving her good news after all, but had agreed to help hand out leaflets.

She thought about her mum's words when they'd arrived: if anyone has any information, you be sure to send them over to me.

'Can you take my mum to Anna?' Emma asked, turning back to the man with the shopping cart and sleeping bag.

'We haven't got the time,' he replied, cautiously looking up the road. 'Come with me now and we could be back here with Anna before your mum even realises you've gone. Imagine how pleased she'd be to see that you'd found Anna all on your own.'

She could almost picture her mum's look of joy and surprise, but instinctively she knew better than to go anywhere with this perfect stranger.

'But if we could just tell Mum where Anna is, I'm sure she'd be just as happy,' she said, raising a hand and waving frantically in her mum's direction.

The man began to move away.

'No, please wait. If I can just get her attention, I know she'll come. Please, mister, don't go.'

But he was no longer listening, screwing up the flyer and dropping it to the floor, as he pulled the shopping cart behind him.

'I need some more of your flyers,' her mum said, suddenly by Emma's side. 'The nice man I just spoke to is the vicar at St Mary's Church and he's agreed to speak about Anna at tomorrow's services. He's going to leave some leaflets at the back of his church too. See, I told you today was going to be a good day!'

Chapter Seventeen

NOW

Weymouth, Dorset

Jack is already on his feet when I return to the living room.

'She wouldn't do this,' I say to him, pushing the hair out of my face with my hands.

'I know, I know,' he agrees, but I sense it's more to placate me than because he believes it.

He comes over to try and offer a hug, but that isn't what I need right now and I bat away his efforts. Why isn't he as angry as I am? Can't he see what's going on here?

'It's the ring,' I say pointedly. 'It has to be. They're terrified we're getting close, and because they can't see and hear what we're up to since removing that hacking software they installed on our phones, they're trying to discredit us. Running you off the road was to try and scare us, and now they're upping their efforts. If I write what I know, who's going to believe the sister of a convicted murderer and child abductor?'

Jack is nodding, but his frown is telling quite a different story.

'You don't agree, Jack?' I ask, tilting my head.

He takes an unsteady step backwards. 'No, it's not that, it's just… I don't know.'

But I'm not going to let him get out of this hole so easily. 'It's just *what*, Jack?'

He closes his eyes and tilts his head upwards. 'It's just… Do you realise how paranoid you sound right now? I don't doubt that the ring are beavering away to cover their tracks, but…' He stops himself to spare my feelings.

'I'm a big girl, Jack. If you have something to say, just spit it out.'

He sighs, bringing his gaze back to meet mine. 'Playing devil's advocate for a minute, what if you're wrong about Anna? Putting the ring to one side for a minute, what if Anna really did murder Tomlinson, and has now gone after Beauchamp's great-niece? What if these two actions aren't as a direct result of the ring?'

I'm about to snap my response, but the question replays in my head, louder this time. I clamp my eyes shut as the voice grows unbearably louder.

'What would her motive be?' I say for my benefit as much as Jack's.

'I don't know. Remember when you spoke to Aurélie, and she said how the group forced her to participate in the abduction of others? What if *this* is something like *that*?'

My eyes fly open in shock. 'You think she's still working for the ring?'

He shrugs pathetically, but I can see from his face that I've hit the nail on the head.

'So she killed Tomlinson because *they* wanted him dead?' I clarify.

'Maybe, who knows? All I'm saying is – and the last thing I want to do is upset you – but we have to keep an open mind. The woman you almost met at the police station yesterday is *not* the Anna you remember. She's twenty-one years older and has been through God knows what kind of tests since. If I were you, I'd stop thinking about her as your sister, and think of her as Kylie Shakespeare instead.'

My brow furrows further. It may be easy for him to compartmentalise his life, but finding Anna has been the driving force in my life for as long as I can remember, and I'm not going to give up on her just because it isn't the heart-melting reunion I dreamed of.

'Tell me about Beauchamp,' I say, changing tack. 'You said his name had come up, but had been dismissed. Why?'

Jack runs a hand over his patchy beard. 'Um, it was near the beginning, to be honest, so you'll have to bear with me while I try and remember. I think it was when we were first going through the filing cabinets from Pendark. We found initials on some of the lists of crew who had been present at filming locations, suggesting some kind of effort to protect real identities, but couldn't be certain. I think we managed to identify one film report that we were pretty sure was something… less than legal, and in some other notes we found references to senior figures. Not names specifically, but things like "Lord such and such", or "MP"… I wasn't heavily involved in chasing that down as it felt like a dead end.

'One of the team was charged with comparing initials with lists of MPs and peers from the time. I think Beauchamp's name came up as matching initials, and he'd been involved in some kind of marital scandal, which I don't have the details on, but I think when checked he was abroad at the time of filming, so his name was removed from the inquiry. To be honest, if I could log on to the NCA portal, I could search. Can I borrow your laptop?'

I nod and point to the desk in the corner. 'Help yourself.'

He rubs my arm before taking his leave. 'If anyone can figure out what's going on here, it's us, right? Your sister couldn't have asked for a better team behind her.'

Something tells me she's going to need a lot more help than I can provide on my own. Jack kneels down beside the desk, leaving the chair vacant for me, but I remain standing where I am. I don't want to rest until I find Anna and help bring her home. He stops when his phone starts ringing, and looks at the screen, placing it to his ear.

'Hello? Oh, hi… No it's fine, I'm with her now… Her phone was stolen… No, hold on, you'd better speak to her.' He lowers the phone and looks at me. 'It's Rachel. She says she's been trying to phone you all morning, and was worried that something had happened to you.'

I go across and take the phone. 'Hi, Rach, everything okay?'

'All good here, but what's this about your phone getting stolen?'

I still haven't explained the incident to Jack yet, and it doesn't feel right for him to overhear it in conversation. 'Oh, it's nothing. I'll have to cancel the SIM card and get another one, I suppose. What can I do for you?' There is a distant hum in the background, and I'm sure her voice is carrying an echo, as if I'm on speaker phone. 'Wait, are you driving?'

'You're on Bluetooth,' she clarifies, 'but, yes I'm driving. On my way to you, as it happens.'

My heart quickens. 'You're coming down to Weymouth? That's so good to hear.' My gaze falls across the room where Jack's sports bag is open on the floor, clothes strewn around it. It'll be a tight squeeze, but to hell with it. 'When can we expect to see you?'

'I'm about an hour away, I think. The thing is,' she pauses, 'I was hoping you might be able to help me with something.'

Her reluctance to speak instantly makes me paranoid about what favour is about to come, but she is my best friend, so I brace myself instead.

'I've got an audition of sorts,' she explains. 'The short of it is, I applied for a position at an online journal, and despite my credentials they want to know whether I can write something to drive traffic to their site. They're small but growing by the day, and I've been wracking my brains for something punchy, and then I saw this morning's news, and hey presto, I'm on my way.'

I haven't watched any news yet, but I already sense what she's going to say before I ask. 'Today's news?'

'Haven't you seen? Some woman has abducted the niece of Ian Beauchamp in broad daylight. It's the number-one trending topic on Twitter. And so I thought… I know you usually work cold cases, but given your instincts, and how close it is to home… you might be willing to help me get the inside scoop?' Her pace quickens. 'I know it's a lot to ask, but I need to find a new job, and I haven't told Daniella that I was forced out of the *Telegraph*; I'd prefer to wait until I have something new before I tell her. And you're my best friend, and I wouldn't ask if I wasn't desperate… Please?'

Jack is trying to signal my attention.

'Hold on, Rach,' I say, lowering the phone, and covering the mouthpiece.

'They've blocked my access,' Jack says, straightening. 'I was hoping they wouldn't have taken me off the system yet, but it looks like they have.'

'Okay, never mind,' I begin to say, but he cuts me off mid-sentence.

'I do have another idea. One person who is certain still to be able to review the case notes is DCS Rawani. I know when we last spoke to him he washed his hands of the case because of his retirement, but I'm sure if I could speak to him one to one he'd help. We need to be able to determine whether Beauchamp could somehow be entangled with the ring, and the notes should help provide some context. I don't want to abandon you, but…'

'You want to return to London?'

'Only to help move things along. My new role starts on Monday, but I can see if I can take a couple of days' leave before I start, and then I could come back.'

I don't like the idea of being here alone, but with Rachel coming down today, it shouldn't be too long.

'There's something else,' Jack continues, cringing as he speaks. 'I'm meant to be collecting Mila from school this afternoon and having her overnight. I meant to say something to you this morning when I got out of the shower – I was going to see if you wanted to come back with me – but then you weren't here, and then Oakley arrived, and…'

Despite my own desire to keep him close, I refuse to keep him apart from his daughter, and quickly nod. 'It's fine, Jack. You go back and take care of Mila. If you get the chance to speak to Rawani too, then great. I'll be fine.'

'Are you sure? You're more than welcome to still come with me. My flat is a bit cramped, but not much smaller than this place. It could help take your mind off things.'

I can see from his face that he knows how I'm going to respond. 'Anna is down here somewhere, and you heard what Oakley said: she could reach out. I need to stay put, Jack. But I'll be fine; Rach is coming down, so…'

Jack nods and an awkward silence descends before he points at his sports bag and begins to throw his clothes inside. I put the phone back to my ear.

'Hi, Rach, sorry about that. What were you saying?'

'I was about to thank my best friend for agreeing to help me find the girl who's been abducted, and breaking the story exclusively with my new employer. Seriously though, it could be fun; the two of us back together again. It'll be like when we were trying to figure out what happened to Sally Curtis. We make a great team.'

My work with Jack has always been allowed because the cases were cold, and not subject to the parameters of an investigative team. This is a live case, and we'll have to tread carefully, but Oakley practically demanded I get involved, so how can I refuse? It's in Anna's best interests to figure out what's going on.

'There's a lot more I need to tell you,' I say, 'but that can wait for when you arrive.'

'Thank you so much, Em. Why don't you take a look at the latest news so you're up to speed when I arrive? They've flashed up a picture of the prime suspect, and she's a real GI Jane-looking sort. The kind of woman you wouldn't want to get on the wrong side of, if you know what I mean? Anyway, I'll see you in a bit. Thanks again.'

She disconnects, and I reassure Jack that I'll be fine as he zips up his sports bag.

'If you need anything, just give me a call,' he says, before slapping his palm against his forehead. 'I forgot, you lost your phone… I don't like the thought of leaving you without a phone.'

'I have the landline,' I say, pointing at the old device hanging from the wall. I can't remember the last time I had to use it, but as I lift it from its bracket, I'm relieved to hear a dial tone. 'I'll be fine. Go and spend some time with Mila, and let me know what Rawani says.'

'I will,' he says, smiling. 'And you keep me informed about how things progress down here. If you need *anything*, just call me. Okay?'

I move towards him and give him a squeeze hug, but as we separate, there's a moment of electricity where our faces are so close I can smell his cologne. We stay like statues, until he shakes himself out of it and steps backwards.

My heart is racing so hard that I'm certain it's the loudest noise in the room. If Jack can hear it he makes no indication, and he lets himself out of the door.

Chapter Eighteen

NOW

Weymouth, Dorset

Rachel arrives within the hour, while I'm staring out of the window at the sand and the sea. My mind is elsewhere.

It's like someone has kicked me in the brain, and everything inside has been stirred up into a cloud of dust and the memories are settling in a randomised order. I can't help wondering if this is what it's like for Mum every time she wakes up these days. Memories of Anna float behind my eyes, memories from before all of this. Glimpses into a fragmented world where we were all happy; naïve enough to believe that the creation of such memories would continue to occur until the end of time.

I see Anna and me sitting beside a Christmas tree, dressed in long pyjamas and wrapped in thick cotton dressing gowns. It is dark, the only light coming from a lamp Anna turned on in the corner of the room that was furthest from the living room door, so as not to disturb our parents. Anna has pressed a finger to her lips to remind me of the covert nature of the operation. I recall now that it was me who woke her and suggested we go and open our presents from Father Christmas. She told me we should wait until Mum and Dad tell us it's okay to be awake, but she must see how sad that made me, and says it would probably be okay if we only opened one; one little present wouldn't be noticed.

So, we'd put on our dressing gowns and snuck through the house on tiptoe, closing the living room door behind us, our eyes widening at the shiny boxes at the foot of the tree that impossibly hadn't been there the night before. Our presents had been so carefully stacked, mine in silver paper and Anna's in rose-coloured paper, as they always were.

Despite her advice, my eyes had been instantly attracted to the biggest of the boxes at the bottom of the tower, but Anna had deterred me, pointing instead at a pyramid-shaped box at the top, taking a small book-shaped box from the top of hers.

'Just these, and then bed,' she'd reminded.

Good old Anna, always sharing the best of her experience with me. Her present had been a book of Elinor Wylie poems, *the* book that hadn't left her side until that day; the same book that keeps pride of place on my desk, serving as a permanent reminder of the sister she once was. I can't remember what my gift was, but I remember it doing little to satisfy my urge to tear into all the presents. So we'd opened another, and then another. Soon we'd been surrounded by brightly coloured packaging, and our parents had emerged through the lounge door, questioning what we thought we were doing. I'd been terrified they'd tell us we couldn't have any of the toys because we were awake too early, but now all I can see is Mum smiling, and Dad tottering in carrying a big bowl of sausage rolls for us to eat.

It's funny now because at least twenty minutes must have passed between our excited mutterings waking them to allow Dad to make the sausage rolls, but I don't recall any cross words or return to bed. And I don't recall Mum letting her mask slip and allowing us to think anyone but Father Christmas was responsible for the arrival and careful placement of the gifts. Parents lie to their children all the time – Father Christmas, the Tooth Fairy, and the Easter Bunny – and yet when we find out the truth, we don't hold them accountable. And when it's our turn on the merry-go-round, we automatically repeat our parents' lies with a clear conscience. Okay, so I don't have children of my own yet, but I have no doubt that I will do everything in my power to prolong the magic, even though it is a deceit contrary to the honesty I will be trying to instil into him, her, or them. How many other parental lies will I claim as my own in the name of love? How many more did *my* parents tell me for my own good?

Another memory settles somewhere in the back of my mind: the first Christmas after Anna's disappearance, when I only found one stack of presents beneath the tree, the paper somehow less glossy than before, the stack not looking quite as high without a second stack to compare it to. I remember asking Mum why Santa hadn't brought Anna presents? Was it because he knew she wasn't home? Would he still deliver her presents to wherever she had gone, and if so, did that mean he knew where she was? Couldn't the police ask him her new address so they could bring her back? I can't remember what lie was spun in response, or whether they even answered the question.

A third memory plays out in my head as Rachel climbs out of her car and waves at me through the window. This time, Anna and I are on a beach of beautifully golden sand, but I know in my heart we aren't in Weymouth. The texture of the sand in the memory feels different to what I'm used to. The grains as they fall from my open toes aren't as sharp as Weymouth sand; they're softer and more forgiving, forming stronger sandcastle structures. I don't know how old we are, but presumably I'm aged somewhere between six and seven, but I can't recall us going away then; surely Mum would have reminded me had we been on holiday in that period.

I close my eyes and try to concentrate my mind's power on recalling further detail. I can't focus on anyone around us, but the whiff of suntan lotion is strong in the air. That, and the salt in the sea, only a few metres away from us. We are walking now, Anna clutching my hand tightly as she leads me along the soft sand towards the wide open green sea. The surf is thicker than we're used to as our feet hit the warm water. Instinctively, I don't think the memory is UK-based, yet I don't recall us going anywhere foreign on holiday.

I sense now too that Anna and I shouldn't be in the sea unaccompanied, which is why she is gripping my arm so tightly, as if she believes I will float away if she loosens her hold on me even a fraction. She stops us when the water is splashing against our ankles, and the sand beneath is claiming our feet for its own. There are so many people around us splashing in the surf, so many screams of joy. Anna stoops and fills her bucket with water, and urges me to do the same. My bucket feels heavy as I pull it back out and stare into it. The water looks so brown and cloudy up close, but Anna is already pulling us back out and up the hot sand, until we arrive at the enormous pit we've dug. She sits me down at one side, while she sits opposite, and then on the count of three we tip the warm water we've stolen over our feet, squealing in delight as it doesn't instantly dissipate beneath our toes. Anna is pleased with herself, because we've dug deep enough – and close enough to the water's edge – that the water is retained for long enough for us to splash our toes in it, before the sand eventually reclaims it.

Looking back on the memory, I can now see that Anna had built us our own kind of foot spa, but I don't remember exactly when or where the memory was formed, or why it's suddenly come back to me now.

The doorbell sounds and I pull myself away from the window, then go and answer the door to Rachel. She starts talking immediately, telling me how pleased she is that I've agreed to help her, and how if she can just get enough views on the site then she's certain it will lead to bigger and better things. She tells me the site makes money by selling advertising space to third parties and that the bigger the viewing numbers the site claims, the more they can charge the third parties, and the bigger cut of the profits she can share.

'It works out as pennies per line rather than per word, but with the right story, it could be an untapped gold mine,' she adds excitedly as she dumps her small suitcase where Jack's sports bag was less than an hour ago.

'Are you all right?' she questions, when I'm unresponsive to anything she's said.

To be honest, it feels like a protective sheet has been thrown over me, and when I hear her words they sound further away, as if being received via a wireless transmitter rather than being spoken in the same room.

'A-Anna's back,' I manage to stutter before my legs give way and I collapse into her arms.

Half an hour later, and with a mug of hot, strong, sweet tea in my hand, I have caught Rachel up on everything I've learned in the last couple of days. As always, she listens intently, offering words of encouragement whenever there's a slight pause in the conversation, and passing no judgement.

'I can't believe you've found her, after all this time,' she says when I pause to take a sip of the tea. 'I'm just so pleased for you, Em. You're a testament to never giving up on your dreams.'

But I can't share in the smile spreading across her lips because this doesn't feel like a dream come true. It's a nightmare from which I can't seem to wake. I'm thrilled Anna's still alive, but not even in my wildest imagination did I ever think she'd return as a murderer and child abductor.

'I have to say though,' she concludes, 'that DI Oakley is a bit out of order rocking up here and expecting you to do her work for her. The cheek of it! As if you wouldn't tell them if you knew where she'd go.'

'How could I know?' I say glumly. 'It's been a lifetime since I saw her. How many experiences has she lived through that I can't even begin to imagine? If she's on the run, I can't know where she'd go.'

'Presumably if she *has* snatched this Daisy Beauchamp, it'll only be a matter of time before she'll contact the authorities and makes her demands anyway.'

Typical Rachel, refusing to outright point the finger of blame because she knows how much it'll sting me. She won't accept Oakley's words as fact until I'm ready to do so too. But what choice do we have? There was no doubt in Oakley's mind that Anna was responsible for taking the girl; the only question that remained was why, and what her intentions towards the girl were. Oakley hadn't said it, but the implication had been there: Anna had already killed once, so what would stop her doing so again?

'I'm here for whatever you need,' Rachel adds, coming over to the sofa and wrapping her arms around me. 'No question; no judgement.'

I already feel calmer just having her here with me.

'I don't know where to begin looking,' I say, my shoulders dropping in resignation. 'She didn't even want to see me yesterday, so despite Oakley's belief, I can't see that she'd come down here or reach out to me.'

'What about places you went as kids? Did she have a favourite place she might revert to in her desperate hour of need?'

The image of the beach-made foot spa flashes into my head, but I can no longer be certain it's an actual memory or a dream I clung to after her disappearance. I have no frame of reference for when or where it was.

'I just don't know,' I sigh.

The landline ringing has us both turning and staring at my desk. Rachel offers to go and retrieve it, but I put my hand out to keep her where she is and head over, finding the handset beneath the upturned Elinor Wylie book.

'Hello? Jack?' I say, anticipating his gravelly tones.

'Emma? No, it's Pam Ratchett. Sorry, I tried your mobile, but it was switched off. It's about your mum; she's had another heart attack and is on her way to Weymouth Community Hospital. I'm sorry, Emma, but I think you need to go there now while there's still time.'

Chapter Nineteen

THEN

Portland, Dorset

Almost two years had passed since Emma had last seen or spoken to her sister, and yet Anna's disappearance was still the dark cloud that hung above the Hunter family. That Sunday had been like any other until the moment Anna had chosen to walk out on them. The Sundays that had followed had been filled with desperate hope and anticipation, until even that had abandoned them.

Polly had stopped turning up first, choosing to phone them once a day instead of visiting, but then the telephone calls had become less frequent. Every other day at first, and then every couple of days, before eventually they were once a week, and then once a fortnight, once a month, and now non-existent. Most of the laminated posters that Emma's mum had meticulously stuck to lampposts and telegraph poles had been removed or blown down. It was as if the only traces of Anna that remained were in the heads of the three people sitting in the living room of the house where she'd once lived.

Emma was curled up on the sofa, head once again buried in a book because it was easier than confronting the pain of reality. The television played in the background – the post-*EastEnders*-omnibus slot reserved for straight-to-video movies. This one was from the early 90s and featured a cast of faces familiar to those used to watching such drivel. The opening credits had suggested it was 'based on a true story' but none of the main characters' decisions suggested they could have been made by anyone with any common sense.

Emma's dad was dozing in the armchair, the gentle rhythm of his snoring the only evidence that he was still alive. The navy sweater that had once barely managed to contain his beer belly hung limply over his frame. Emma hadn't realised just how much weight he'd lost in the years that had passed.

Emma's mum was hidden behind the ironing board as she worked her way through the pile of fresh laundry taking up the remaining armchair. Nobody really cared whether the pile was ironed, hung over the radiators to dry, or just left to fester and crease. The shirt she was currently running the hot iron over for Emma's dad would be hidden by the overly large navy sweater he donned each day, so nobody would see the effort she'd gone to anyway. But it kept her hands and mind busy, which was probably the point.

She looked exhausted. Emma couldn't remember the last time she'd seen her mum wear makeup or do anything specific with her hair. The grey had taken total control, despite her relatively young age, but she hadn't made an appointment at the hair salon for colouring in what seemed like forever. The flannel shirt that hung from her thin frame did nothing to accentuate her femininity, nor did the loose leggings. If Anna were to suddenly return, she probably wouldn't recognise the family that had been left behind.

Bronwyn lifted a fresh shirt from the pile, holding it between her fingers as she shook it, before laying it on the ironing board, running her hands the length of the side, manually flattening the creases, before grasping the plugged-in iron and repeating the process, as a cloud of steam acknowledged her action with a satisfactory, synchronised whooshing sound. Reaching for the pot of water, she squeezed the trigger twice over a stubborn crease before running the iron over it a couple of times. She returned the hot device to its cradle and adjusted the shirt, before repeating the process.

Emma watched her from the safety of the rim of her *Point Horror* book. She would have offered to help, but she already knew her mum would have declined the offer. Since giving up work so that she could concentrate her efforts on maintaining the public appeal for information, the housework had become her *joie de vivre*. Emma's dad continued to work all available overtime at the prison to keep the bills paid, and she ensured there was food on the table every morning and evening and that the clothes on their backs were clean and pressed. It had become their pantomime show for the world to see how 'normal' they were, even if they were anything but.

The iron hissed again as Bronwyn began on the first of the sleeves, pulling on the cuff to flatten the cotton and to avoid the hurdle of the button. She was an automaton, her eyes barely leaving the TV-movie as she lifted the shirt sleeve, gave the shirt a gentle shake, gathered up the second sleeve, and squashed it out flat against the hard surface. Her arm shot out and her fingers coiled around the end of the water bottle without her even looking for it. She depressed the trigger with two sharp bursts and mist exploded from the nozzle, falling slowly onto the sleeve. This was followed by another hiss of the iron as it danced merrily along the cotton. And then the shirt was pulled up, and shaped around the wire hanger before being hung with the others on the brass handle of the kitchen door.

Bronwyn's eyes caught her daughter's and although Emma tried to bury her face quickly behind the pages of her book, it was too late.

'Have you finished all your homework?' her mum asked, pressing both hands on top of the ironing board, as if she might topple onto her face without the support.

Emma lowered the book, pushing the index finger of her left hand between the pages so she wouldn't lose her place. 'Yes, I did it on Friday night.'

'Good, good,' Bronwyn said, reaching for the next shirt and flattening it against the surface.

No check to see what the homework had been, how challenging Emma had found it, or any effort to make sure it was actually completed ahead of school the next morning. In Bronwyn's defence, she'd never been called into the school because of late homework or any question over the quality of Emma's work, but Emma couldn't help thinking it would have been nice for her to take slightly more interest in her academic studies.

The assignment had been a basic reading comprehension exercise: read a couple of paragraphs of a set text, and then answer questions about it. Nothing that had stumped Emma, though she had had to look up a couple of words in the dictionary to check their meaning; words she'd now committed to memory should they be required in future assignments. School was nearing the end of term and as such the teachers were less precious about setting complicated homework that might require more effort on their part to mark and correct.

'What's for dinner?' Emma dared to ask, her stomach starting to grumble with dissatisfaction.

'I haven't thought about it yet,' her mum replied, eyes once again firmly fixed to the love story playing out on the screen.

John snorted suddenly, waking himself from slumber, his eyes snapping open in panic and only relaxing when he saw his wife and daughter staring back at him.

'If you're that tired you should go up to bed,' Bronwyn sighed. 'You know you won't sleep later if you doze down here.

'I wasn't asleep,' he fired back, reaching for the newspaper that had fallen from his lap. He flapped it loudly in disgust, his eyes widening and narrowing as he tried to shake the sleep from them and work out what he'd been reading before.

'Oh, well if you weren't asleep, you might need to check the double glazing because something was making the windows rattle. I'd put it down to your snoring, but—'

'Leave it, Winnie,' he warned, glaring at her. 'You know how hard I've been working. If a man can't rest on a Sunday afternoon, I don't know what the world's coming to.'

Emma quickly raised her book, re-reading the same page she'd been on.

'And I suppose the rest of us aren't entitled to rest because the work we do isn't nearly as important,' Bronwyn snapped back without missing a beat.

Emma's dad lowered his paper. 'Poring over maps and praying for divine intervention hardly puts food on the table though, does it?'

'It's not like the food magically appears though, is it? You might be the one who pays for it, but it takes more than magic to turn the scraps I can get hold of into something edible. It doesn't cook itself, you know.'

He folded the newspaper and removed his reading glasses. 'Well, why don't we swap roles then? You go out to work all hours and bring home the bacon, while I do the laundry and cook the meals. How about that?'

The iron hissed as she pressed it against the material. 'Ha! I'd love to see that. You seem to forget what your mum said to me when I first met her: *he doesn't know one end of a frying pan from another.*'

'Ironic considering the only meal she knew how to cook was spaghetti bolognaise or toast.' He sighed. 'I really don't think you appreciate what I have to deal with day in, day out at that place. The shit I see and hear from those under my guard... enough to turn your hair grey! And then I come home and have to put up with your snide comments too.'

She snorted. 'You don't have to come home. When you *are* here, all you do is eat and sleep and moan about the conditions up there. It's not like you do anything to help maintain the upkeep of this place.'

'Maintain the upkeep?' he roared. 'We wouldn't have anywhere to maintain if it wasn't for me, and you'd be wise to remember that every now and again.'

Emma jumped as the iron was slammed into its cradle. 'You

think it's easy for me? Balancing housework with taking Emma to school, and trying to work out where Anna is? You think that's easy? I'd give anything to find a job that would take me away for hours at a time, allowing my mind to concentrate on something that isn't our missing daughter! You don't know how lucky you are.'

'How lucky I am? Winnie, I haven't had a break from work in over two years! You wake up in the morning and don't have to think twice about what your day is going to look like. My routine is such a slog and all I ask in return is for you not to judge me when exhaustion takes control.'

'You want to talk about exhaustion? Imagine what it's like trying to get through each day on the few minutes of sleep my body allows me to take at night. I haven't slept properly in years, John! Insomnia is the curse mothers bear. Night after night I lie there listening to you snoring and you've no idea how envious that makes me!'

He stood and threw the newspaper in her direction, but it fell well short. He didn't check to see whether his wife had anything more to say. He simply marched up the stairs and banged about in their bedroom before emerging at the foot of the stairs, carrying a sports holdall.

Emma's mum opened her mouth to speak, but closed it again, folding her arms in the process, ready to call his bluff. Emma looked up from her book, trying to force eye contact with her father. She looked from one parent to the other, but neither seemed prepared to back down and admit that they needed the other.

'Where are you going, Dad?' Emma tried, but though his eyes were watering, he didn't meet her gaze.

'Mum? You can't let Dad go. Say something. You have to stop him.'

But her mum didn't budge from her stance. The two of them remained where they were, staring each other down, before he took his leave, slamming the door behind him.

Chapter Twenty

NOW

Weymouth, Dorset

It feels like I'm outside of my body, watching as Rachel gets me up and into her car, assuring me that everything will be fine; Mum's recovered from a heart attack before, and she will do again. I don't argue – I can't, as my brain isn't able to process any of what's going on.

I recall how panicked I was the last time Pam called and broke the news. I ran around like a headless chicken, grabbing a camera so I could record just one last moment with her. But this time it feels different; despite Rachel's attempts at reassurance, in the back of my mind, I somehow know that the grains of sand are slipping from the timer, and there's no way to stop the inevitable.

We arrive at Weymouth Community Hospital, and my pragmatism takes control, finding a parking space that's equidistant between the barrier and ticket machine, yet not a long walk from the building's main entrance.

'It's this way,' I tell her; no need to read the signposts pointing us towards the Emergency Department.

I should be upset. I should be screaming at the world that it isn't fair; that I'm not ready. Mum's early Alzheimer's diagnosis was cruel, but at least we knew this moment would eventually come. How many go through life ignoring the spectre of death, only to live with regrets? But not us. Every time I've left Mum at the home, I've hugged her tightly and told her how much I love her, as if it would be the last time. And now I seem to know deep down that this really will be the last time. It's like I've been granted the gift of hindsight early, but it doesn't make it any easier to bear.

There's a queue at the check-in desk. In front of us, a little girl is seated in a wheelchair, one plastered leg suspended out in front of her, a plastic tube beneath her nostrils also connected to a metal canister on the back of the chair. She looks up at my watering eyes and smiles. She can't be much older than seven, but how much pain has she already experienced in her short life? It puts Mum's sixty-five years of relatively decent health in perspective. Sixty-five seems too young to be saying goodbye, but I bet this little girl would swap places in an instant.

The girl's father thanks the woman in white behind the desk and wheels the girl away. She's still smiling, and offers a little wave in my direction, as Rachel ushers me to the desk.

'Bronwyn Hunter,' my lips say involuntarily. 'I'm her daughter, Emma.'

'She was brought in with a suspected heart attack,' Rachel adds for me.

The woman in white types something into the computer, before asking us to take a seat in the waiting area, promising someone will be out to help us shortly. Rachel leads me away, seating me before disappearing to find a vending machine.

'I had a fall,' a quiet voice says, and as I blink back my own tears, I see the little girl in the wheelchair is parked across from me.

'Oh,' I reply instinctively. 'I'm sorry to hear that.'

Her dad looks up from his phone to check who she's speaking to, before returning his gaze to the screen.

'I have brittle bones,' she continues, with a roll of her eyes that I sense she is mimicking from one of her parents.

'Sounds painful,' I reply.

'It's not too bad,' she replies, but I realise now she is tenderly holding her left wrist in her right hand. 'My mum says I need to be more careful,' she adds, with a small sigh that also feels like an imitation.

'You should listen to your mum,' I tell her, wiping the itch from my right eye. 'And your dad. It may feel like they don't understand at times, but they know a lot more than we realise.'

'Why are you here?' she asks next. 'Did you fall too?'

I shake my head and strain a smile, figuring she's probably already experienced enough pain and sorrow for today.

'No, I didn't fall. I'm here to see my mum because she isn't very well.'

The little girl nods as if she understands. 'My mum has a cold too; that's why my dad had to bring me in.'

Despite the pain in my heart, her misunderstanding makes me chuckle.

Rachel returns and hands me an energy drink. 'The tea machine was out of order. Drink this; it might help.'

I open the can and take a long gulp, grimacing at the sweet

fizz as it gushes down my throat. 'Eurgh, that's disgusting,' I say apologetically.

Rachel takes the can and necks a gulp of her own, but there is no discomfort evident on her face. 'It's fine; we just need to get you out of this backwater and living in the city. I wouldn't make it through most days without one of these.'

She offers me the can again, but I shake my head as a young man in a blue shirt and navy trousers appears at the secured double doors beside the reception desk and calls out my name. Rachel waves and helps me up.

'I hope your mum feels better soon,' the little girl says, as we leave the waiting room and approach the waiting attendant.

He takes us through the doors and along a maze of corridors, explaining that Mum has been taken up to the Intensive Care Unit for monitoring. The air here feels much lighter and cooler, to the point where I'm regretting not wearing a coat. The light overhead feels so artificial, and my own health already feels worse from being beneath it.

Squirting sanitiser onto our hands, the attendant leads us into the ICU ward and to a large room containing six beds. My heart leaps when I see Mum is sitting up in bed, looking sprightlier than I was expecting. For a moment I want to question whether there's been some kind of mistake, but then I see the wires leading from her chest to the beeping monitor beside the bed. The nurse explains that the heart attack was a mild one, but they want to keep her under observation. I know the drill; it was only a couple of months ago that I was receiving the same explanation from a different nurse. He leaves us, and Rachel collects a chair from beside one of the other beds where there is a woman snoring contentedly.

'Hello, Mrs Hunter,' Rachel says, sitting down. 'How are you feeling?'

Mum's head turns, and she eyes Rachel suspiciously. 'Who are you?'

'This is my best friend Rachel, Mum,' I clarify from the seat on my side of the bed. 'We were at university together. Remember?'

She now looks at me, but her eyes narrow further. 'And who are you?'

If I hadn't been presented with this question a dozen times before, it would be harder to bear. Given her present condition, it isn't surprising that her memory isn't firing on all cylinders as it was last night when I brought Jack to see her.

'I'm your daughter Emma, Mum. Do you remember? You have two daughters – Anna and me – but you don't remember things as well as you once did.'

Her gaze flits between me and Rachel, but her concern only grows.

'It's okay if you can't remember, Mum.'

She doesn't answer, fumbling around on the bed until she locates the pad she's looking for, jabbing at the orange nurse call button.

'Is something wrong, Mum? Are you in pain?'

Still she ignores me, jabbing at the button again.

A nurse arrives, her hair swept up into a messy bun, and she gives Rachel and me a funny look.

'I don't know who these people are,' my mum tells her.

'I'm her daughter, Emma,' I say quickly, 'and this is my friend Rachel. Her memory isn't what—'

'That's okay,' the nurse interrupts. 'We're aware of your mum's health issues.' She then resets the call pad and speaks to my mum directly. 'It's okay, Winnie. This lady is your daughter, Emma. Now, are you in any discomfort? Do you want me to fetch you a drink?'

'I want to go home,' she says sullenly.

'As soon as the doctor says you're well enough to go home, you will,' the nurse tells her empathetically. 'You just focus on getting better.'

She has such a soft tone that even I believe her. She leaves us, but I don't think Mum believes we are who we say. In these situations I know it's best just to behave normally as her memory could re-fire at any moment.

'You had us all worried, Mum,' I say evenly, keeping my tears at bay. 'Is there anything you need? Something to read?'

Her eyes harden. 'You're the reason I'm here.'

'I don't understand, Mum. You're in the hospital because you suffered a heart attack. As the nurse said, as soon as you're better they'll let you go home.'

She scoffs. 'Don't come at me with all that. I know what you're after, and let me tell you, you won't get your hands on any of my money.'

Her mood has definitely shifted, and with everything else that's going on, my brain is struggling to keep up.

'Mum, nobody is trying to take anything that belongs to you.' I don't add that there is no money left as we had to sell the family home to pay for her care home fees. 'We all just want you to get better.'

'You're not having any of it! Not a single penny.'

I reach for her hand, but she snatches it away, almost yanking the cannula out in the process. 'I'm not after your money, Mum, I promise,' I try to say, but I can see she's not listening.

'You thought if you had me locked up you'd get one of those power of attorney things, and you'd get it all. Well, I'm telling you I've hidden the lot, and you won't ever see a penny of it! Ha! What do you have to say to that?'

I glance at Rachel to see if she has any ideas, but she frowns back at me.

'I'm sorry you're feeling so off today, Mum,' I try again, but it's a struggle to keep my frustration at bay.

'No you're not! If you had your way you'd have me locked up permanently. You think I don't know that this was your plan all along? You're just like your father, always trying to steal whatever you can.'

This isn't the first time she's been abusive towards me, and I have to remind myself that this isn't her; it's just her mind's way of dealing with the illness.

'Let's talk about something else, Mum. What were you doing this morning before you were brought in?'

Her hand shoots out from nowhere and slaps me hard across the face. My hand flies up to my cheek. I'm in shock.

'For years I've wondered whether I made the right choice, but now I've seen your true colours, I can see what a tremendous mistake I made.'

Rachel sits forward and tries to interject, but Mum's anger continues to boil.

'I thought you needed greater protection, and that you wouldn't survive without me, but all along you've been planning this, haven't you? Get the old bat locked up in a home so you can steal my money.'

I open my mouth to argue that financial gain was never my motive for taking her to the care home, but her shouting has now caught the attention of the woman in the bed across the room from us.

'It was bad enough your father getting us in the situation where a choice had to be made – I could never forgive him for that – but to think I made the wrong choice... How different things could have been for us... I bet Anna wouldn't have betrayed me in this way.'

I lower the hand from my cheek. She's talking so quickly that I wasn't properly listening to the words, just allowing her to rant and rave at me, but now my interest is heightened. But before I can question any of it, she is suddenly clutching at her chest and her head drops to one side. The room erupts into a clamour of noise as the heart monitor alarm sounds loudly and the room suddenly fills with nurses in varying shades of blue tops. They ask us to move back so they can help Mum.

The back of the bed is lowered and they pull down the hospital gown she's wearing. The skin on her chest looks so dry, grey, and wrinkled, not pink and vibrant as I remember it.

'Mum?' I call out over the clamour of hurried voices. 'Mum? Anna is still alive. She's alive, and I found her. Please don't die. You need to see her.'

Rachel places an arm around my side, though there's nothing we can do but watch as the heart monitor delivers a long-drawn-out, monotone cry.

Chapter Twenty-One

NOW

Weymouth, Dorset

Six and a half minutes. That's all it takes for the doctors and nurses to determine that no amount of heart massage and oxygen will bring my mum back to life. It feels so surreal watching them fuss and work over her, like engineers desperately trying to get a Formula 1 car ready to return to the race.

'I'm so sorry, Miss Hunter,' one of the nurses says, and that's all it takes to tip my restrained emotions over the edge.

I crash to the floor, my legs no longer able to support me. Hot tears sting my cheeks and slip over the edge of my lips as my entire body refuses to accept this conclusion. No amount of screaming or shouting will bring her back, but it's as if my soul refuses to listen. I am wailing against just how unfair it is that she's been taken from me, just when I was starting to piece our family together. Only I could find a sister and lose a mother in one day.

Rachel doesn't say anything, but she drops to her knees beside me and I don't resist as she folds her arms around my shoulders and attempts to stop my shuddering. The faint trace of eucalyptus plays on my nostrils, and suddenly I can't remember what my mum used to smell like. She must have worn the same perfume every day when I was growing up, and already I can't recall what it smelled like, or what it was even called. How many more memories of our time together are now simply going to fade away because she is no longer there as my constant? She was the lighthouse keeping me away from the rocks.

The nurses and doctors step away from her bed one by one, those brave enough to make eye contact offering little more than a solitary bow of the head. I don't blame them; I know they gave it their all, but sometimes there's nothing that can be done. Maybe I should have done more. How many times did I leave her at that care home, and put her out of my mind? How many times did I bite my lip to keep my frustration in check, when I should have been holding her and telling her how much I loved her? With her Alzheimer's, did she even know she was loved in those final moments?

It is Pam Ratchett suddenly appearing in the doorway of the ward bay that snaps me out of my sobbing. She crosses the room in an instant and extracts me from Rachel's embrace, lifting me back to my feet, but holding me tight so I won't fall.

'This won't do,' she whispers into my ear. 'This isn't what Winnie would have wanted. She hated public shows of emotion. I know you're hurting, and my heart goes out to you, Emma, but not here.'

Rachel pulls herself up and tries to protest, but deep down I know Pam is right. If Mum were watching me now, she'd be telling me to straighten up and brush off the pain. I can hear her voice in my head: crying is reserved for the darkness and safety of bed where it won't be seen or heard.

Pam passes me a tissue from a packet and holds it to my eyes until I take it from her and dab the tears.

'Winnie never stopped telling us how strong you are,' Pam continues. 'She was so proud of the woman you've grown into.'

My eyes well again; I've never heard anyone tell me she was proud of me, and I would give anything to hear it come from her lips, but it's too late now. Patting Pam on the back, I step away and shuffle unsteadily to the side of the bed. She looks so peaceful, as if she has simply dropped off and will wake at any moment. The nurses have covered her chest with a white sheet, so all I can see is her face. I lift her hand and press it to my lips. It's still warm, and for the briefest of moments my brain questions whether they haven't made a tremendous mistake and she is in fact still alive. Yet the sheet doesn't rise and fall as it would need to.

Releasing her hand, I bend forward and kiss her forehead. 'I love you, Mum, and I'm sorry I couldn't bring Anna to you in time. I promise I'll do whatever I can to help her, and I'll tell her all about how hard you worked to try and find her. I'll make sure she knows she was loved.'

One of my tears lands on her cheek and I brush it away with the tip of my thumb. If I am strong, then I inherited my strength from this woman. I remain at her side for another twenty minutes, and with each passing second, I feel fractionally stronger. When one of the nurses returns and asks if it's okay for her to take the body, I don't resist.

Half an hour later, Rachel and I are sitting in a coffee shop on the ground floor, neither of us ready to leave the hospital, and yet nothing is keeping us here but grief. There are maybe a dozen small round tables around us, most occupied by single diners, and the artificial light overhead is suffocating. Rachel doesn't speak, but there is no awkwardness in the silence between us. She is giving me the space and time to adjust to this new state.

'Do you want another coffee?' she asks eventually, draining the remains of her latte.

I shake my head, even though that will mean it's time to leave and take the first tentative steps of a life without my mum in it.

'Can I ask you something?' she says next, picking at a biscuit crumb on the table.

'Sure,' I say quietly.

She squashes the crumb flat. 'Did you know?'

My brow furrows. 'Know what, sorry?'

'What your mum said in there… Did you know?'

For years I've wondered whether I made the right choice.

Deep down, I know what Rachel is getting at, but I'm not ready to even consider how much truth there could have been in that dying confession. Mum was confused, she was dying, and she couldn't have known what she was saying. Her body was rebelling against death's knock, and she was lashing out. There's no way it could have been more than that.

How different things could have been for us.

I watched as the police investigation faded into obscurity; the effect it had on my parents' marriage. I witnessed the desperation in her eyes every time someone would accept one of the flyers.

I bet Anna wouldn't have betrayed me in this way.

Rachel is still staring at me, awaiting a response.

'She was just confused,' I settle for, but feel like I'm having to defend her.

'Em, I've known you for years… You're my best friend, and I love you like a sister… But I have to ask: were your parents involved in Anna's disappearance?'

'What? No!' I shout.

The pharmacist in a green uniform at the table beside us gives a cursory glance.

'Anna left home of her own accord,' I say, quieter now but more assertive. 'I watched her walk away. My parents were in the house, so they couldn't have been involved. Do you realise what you're asking?'

Rachel holds her palms out in a pacifying gesture. 'I'm sorry, but you heard what your mum said. What else could she have meant? What choice did she make where she was protecting you over your sister? She even said your dad had forced her into making the choice. I know you were a child when Anna disappeared, but can you remember anything now that might lead you to think that they could have been involved?'

I shake my head vehemently. 'No. There's no way my parents were involved. She was probably misremembering a film or programme she once watched. She was very ill.'

Rachel nods her concurrence, but there is still doubt in her eyes, or maybe I'm just seeing doubt, reflecting my own uncertain feelings. I was heartbroken when my parents split up, and I hated having parents who lived in different postcodes. For a long time I assumed that Anna returning would somehow throw them back together, like the last piece of a jigsaw puzzle. But was there more in the undercurrent between them that my young mind couldn't fathom?

I look back to Rachel, ready to face more questions, but her attention has been captured by something over my shoulder. Turning, I see she is watching the television screen hanging from the wall. The screen is flickering with camera flashes, but as I focus on what I'm seeing, my heart skips a beat. The camera is focused on a podium outside a police station that I recognise as the headquarters of the police station in Southampton. A notification appears at the bottom of the screen announcing the broadcast is live.

A white-haired man in full uniform steps up to the podium, his flat cap angled so low, I can't see his eyebrows, but I can only guess they're as white as the closely cropped beard and moustache he wears with pride.

The television is muted, so although his lips are moving, it isn't clear what he is saying. The notification at the bottom of the screen reveals the man speaking is Chief Superintendent Mike North, and below his name the word *ABDUCTION* is in bold. I look back to Rachel, but she has risen and is at the counter asking the barista to turn up the volume as the mugshot of Anna fills half the screen.

'…It is believed Daisy was taken by the woman on the screen now. Her name is Anna Hunter, but she goes by the alias Kylie Shakespeare, and we are keen to speak to her as a matter of urgency.'

It's as if the rug has just been ripped out from beneath my feet.

'We are coordinating with forces in Dorset and Wiltshire to bring this matter to a swift resolution, and we believe she is still in the local area. If you spot either Daisy or Anna, please do not approach them, but dial 999 and report their whereabouts. Let me reiterate, we believe Anna Hunter is armed and extremely dangerous.'

I can't listen to any more. Standing, I push myself away from the table, and hurry from the coffee shop, out into the bright light of the hospital's thoroughfare. NHS staff, patients, and visitors pass by left and right, but I don't see any of them. My head feels as though it will explode.

Rachel catches up to me. 'Whoa, whoa,' she says, 'you've turned decidedly green. Are you going to be sick?'

I shake my head uncertainly. 'I need to find her, Rach. I promised Mum I would help her.'

'Okay, okay, then that's what we'll do.'

'But how? I don't know where to begin.'

Rachel bows her head towards mine until our foreheads meet. 'This is what you do, Em. Come on, put yourself in Anna's shoes. Where would she go?'

'I-I don't know.'

Rachel places her hands on my cheeks. 'She's on the run, and her face is plastered all over the television. She'll probably be panicking, so what would you do if it was you?'

'I wouldn't abduct a child,' I snap back.

'Maybe not, but she's your sister and you knew her for seven years. Where would she go if she was panicked?'

I'm racking my brain for any kind of memories of Anna. But all I can see is the moment she stomped away from the yard in the direction of Grandma's house.

'She'd want to go somewhere she'd feel safe,' I say.

'Good, and where would that be?'

I'm about to tell her I have no idea again, but then a thought hits me, and I know exactly who might know where she'd go.

Chapter Twenty-Two

THEN

Portland, Dorset

It wasn't clear to Emma whether her mum, who was wrapped in a thick overcoat and head scarf, was planning to brave the colder weather and head into town, or whether she was planning a heist and didn't want anybody to recognise her. She didn't appear to have any such qualms about Emma herself.

'But it doesn't fit anymore, Mum,' Emma complained as her mum pulled her arms into the plastic sleeves of the cagoule, which creaked and groaned in complaint.

'Of course it does; you've not grown that much.'

It had been almost a year since she'd last worn the cagoule, and as much as her mum hated to admit it, Emma was growing all the time. Her mum pushed Emma's second arm into the rattling plastic sleeve, but stopped when she saw the hunchback her daughter was being pressed into.

'Oh, it really doesn't fit, does it?' she finally admitted. 'Must have shrunk in the wash.' She yanked it off with the same steadfast force with which she'd been pulling it on her, and then perused the remaining options on the pegs, where once Emma's dad's overcoat had hung. His flat cap was still there, but no other traces that he'd ever lived here.

'We're going to be late,' Bronwyn sang to herself, rifling through what were essentially her own coats, looking for anything that would pass for today.

'I don't want to go anyway,' Emma moaned for the third time since she'd woken an hour or so ago. 'Can't we just pretend we forgot, and stay here instead?'

'No, we certainly cannot,' Bronwyn snapped, without looking back at her. 'You know I have important things to do today. Today's meeting has been in the diary for weeks.'

Her eyes widened as they fell upon the only real option that wouldn't require her to head back up the stairs to Emma's room and commence the search again. She pulled it down and held it up to the hallway light, before comparing it size-wise to Emma.

Emma shook her head as she realised what her mum was holding. 'No, Mum, that's... That's Anna's cagoule.'

But her mum wasn't in the mood for arguing. 'It's just for today, until I have the chance to go into town and get you a new one. It says it's a size nine–ten so it should fit perfectly.'

Anna's bedroom, next to Emma's room, had remained untouched from the Sunday she'd stomped off from the yard just over two years ago. Bronwyn went in and dusted and hoovered it every week as part of her routine, but the bedding, the way in which Anna's books had been stacked, and the CD in the small stereo system all remained untouched. The wardrobe was packed full of clothes that could have been handed down to Emma, but both had agreed that they shouldn't take anything without Anna's permission, and so Emma made do with what her mum could find in the host of charity shops around Weymouth and Portland. Not that she minded; often the clothes her mum returned with were virtually unworn, and were far more fashionable than anything Bronwyn could have afforded new. Emma actually quite liked the idea of breathing new life into someone else's unwanted goods. It was certainly better than seeing a perfectly good garment winding up in a landfill.

'Put it on,' her mum said, handing it over. 'One day won't make a difference.'

Emma wanted to outright refuse, but there was no point. Her mum had made up her mind, and it would only make things worse later if they had a full-on argument about Anna's cagoule, which ultimately Emma would end up having to wear anyway.

It still smelled like Anna, Emma noticed, as the material passed her nose, and for a split second it was like Anna was there with them in the room. Sliding her jumper sleeves into the coat, and fastening the zip, it almost felt like Anna was hugging her, and suddenly Emma had no qualms about wearing the cagoule on today of all days.

'Ready?' her mum checked, as she opened the door, maybe expecting further dispute.

Emma nodded and the two of them stepped outside, which was the moment Bronwyn snatched up Emma's hand, gripping it tightly and marching down the road towards the veterinary practice that had sprung up six months ago and past the playground where children squealed and cheered as they climbed the apparatus and glided through the air on the swings. Emma tried to pull her hand free, having to take two steps to every one of her mum's, but Bronwyn's grip remained firm and fixed.

'Mum, you don't need to hold my hand,' Emma pleaded, certain there would probably be at least one child in the park who knew her.

She didn't want to have to put up with the embarrassing chatter on Monday morning when it was announced to the playground that Emma's mum didn't trust her to walk unaided to the bus stop. She was nine now and understood the dangers of main roads, and how she had to stop and wait and look before crossing the road. She was a sensible young lady who knew what the rules were, and why they had to be followed.

Still, Bronwyn's grip remained resolute. They arrived at the bus stop just after the blue Sureline bus to Dorchester had departed.

'Damn!' Bronwyn cursed. 'You see what's happened now? We've missed it because of that silly fuss you made over your jacket.'

Emma wasn't disappointed that they'd missed the bus, but resisted the urge to point out that it was probably a sign that they shouldn't be making today's journey. She hoped her mum would realise this all on her own.

Bronwyn studied the timetable through the bashed plastic covering. 'The next bus due will take us into Weymouth, which I was hoping to avoid because of all the weekend traffic. From there I suppose we can catch a bus to Dorchester, and then a third bus on to Swanage. That of course will make us late, but my mobile doesn't have any credit, so I can't let your dad know we'll be late. I could try and buy some in

Weymouth, *if* the next bus isn't late, and message him, but I won't have time if the bus is late. Of course, he's sure to blame all of this on me, like I haven't got enough on my plate already.'

She shushed as two new travellers arrived at the bus stop, knowing better than to air her dirty laundry in public. Emma's cheeks reddened the moment she recognised the two girls from her class. They hadn't been accompanied by their mother, and from the way they were dressed, Emma sensed they were probably going into Weymouth to peruse the shops, or go bowling. In that moment she wished the ground would open and swallow her whole. She tried to pull her hand free again, but that only seemed to tighten her mum's grip. She saw the two girls whisper and snicker, occasionally glancing over, and for the first time she regretted that they hadn't managed to catch the blue bus to Dorchester.

The bus to Weymouth eventually turned up, and Bronwyn didn't release Emma's hand as they clambered on and paid the man at the window. Bronwyn pushed Emma into one of the seats about midway along the bus, and Emma had to look on with envy as Cindy and Terri with an 'i' hurried past, giggling at her as they nonchalantly made their way to the back of the bus as if they owned it. There was no way Emma would live down the ignominy come Monday morning.

Cindy and Terri with an 'i' departed the bus as it arrived on St Mary Street. 'See you on Monday, Emma,' Cindy cooed as they passed – the modern equivalent of striking her around the face with a glove.

'Friends of yours?' Bronwyn asked, observing the two of them in their short denim skirts and thin anoraks.

'Not exactly,' Emma replied, knowing no matter how much

she tried to distance herself, her mum would still tar her with the same judgemental brush.

'You know it's beyond me how blasé some parents can be about the whereabouts of their children. They're what, nine, ten at most? How quickly people forget the dangerous world we live in.'

They exited the bus near the Community Hospital, but didn't have to wait long for the bus to Dorchester. By the time it reached its stop in much sunnier Swanage, more than an hour had passed since they'd debated the cagoule situation by the front door. Emma felt exhausted, even though they'd largely been sitting down for the whole commute.

'There she is,' Emma's dad cheered as they disembarked, holding his arms out wide, and scooping Emma up as she ran to greet him.

Despite her earlier reservations, she was now pleased that her mum had insisted they make the trip here.

'I've missed you,' he whispered into her ear.

'I'm sorry we were late,' she whispered back. 'It wasn't Mum's fault, so don't blame her.'

'Understood,' he said conspiratorially, kissing the top of her head.

He straightened and took in his wife's appearance. 'How are you, Winnie?'

She offered no smile. 'Fine. And you?'

'Mustn't grumble, you know. You're looking well.'

Any hopes Emma had held that the two of them would forget the last months of disruption and share a loving embrace were quickly dampened.

Bronwyn brushed and flattened her overcoat. 'I'll be back here to collect her at 5 p.m. sharp. I appreciate we're half an hour late arriving here, but if you could be prompt, it will mean we can catch the necessary connections to get home swiftly.'

'Sure. I understand. These things can't be helped.' He winked at Emma, before looking back to his estranged wife. 'And you? Do you have plans for the day?'

She adjusted the lining of the headscarf. 'I have an appointment with the manager of the bank in town, and a few other errands to take care of. Nothing that need concern you.'

'Could I give you a call later? There's something we need to discuss, but away from prying ears.'

They both looked at Emma as if to make a point, even though she'd already determined that hers were the ears to which they were referring.

'Of course,' Bronwyn replied, not dropping her guard. 'Shall we say after eight?'

'It's a date,' he smiled, though she made no attempt to reflect his warmth.

'I will see you both back here at five. Emma, be a good girl for your father.'

With that, she straightened her overcoat again, turned and made her way towards the centre of town. Emma's dad remained where he was, watching her leave, and allowing her the distance she clearly craved.

'And what shall we do today?' he asked, stooping to meet Emma's eye line. 'I'd say we could go crabbing, but you can do that sort of thing at home. There is a cinema in town, but I'm not sure what they're showing. My place isn't very big, so although I'll show you what it looks like, it's not very practical for us to spend the day in.' He straightened again, and took in the shops ahead. 'I tell you what, why don't we have a burger and some fries for lunch? And if you're lucky, maybe I'll even let you have a milkshake; just don't tell your mother I took you to Wimpy, or she'll have my guts for garters!'

She squeezed his arm and nodded excitedly. At least he seemed pleased to see her.

Chapter Twenty-Three

NOW

Weymouth, Dorset

When DI Oakley appeared on my doorstep and first informed me that Anna had taken Daisy, she told me I had a small window to find my sister and bring her in. From what Rachel and I witnessed in the televised press conference moments earlier, I sense that window is rapidly closing. For them to publicly announce that Anna is armed and dangerous serves two purposes: firstly, it will make the public think twice about helping her, and secondly, it will help explain should Anna not survive this endeavour. If the ring is trying to tie up loose ends, then today's incident just put them a giant step closer to achieving that end.

I don't know why Anna decided that abducting a fourteen-year-old child was a good idea, and I can't yet see what her endgame is. Instinct tells me that Daisy was targeted for a reason, even if I can't see it. Jack said her great-uncle's name came up in the investigation, which sets off a major alarm bell in my head. The fact that he was cleared of any wrongdoing would ease my alarm, but for the fact that Jack also said it was someone else in his team who made the decision to clear Beauchamp. Maybe I'm just being cynical, but I'd feel less sceptical if it had been Jack himself who had cleared him. Is it really that difficult to believe that the ring could have infiltrated our investigation at ground level? How else did they manage to hack our phones and computers?

Rachel drives us back to the town centre, and it pains me leaving my mum's corpse there alone, but I don't have a choice. I can only hope she'll forgive me. I feel like she would want me to find Anna before the knot tightens, but how do I find someone who doesn't want to be found? It's not like I haven't been searching for the last eight years without success. Searching for my missing sister has been my reason for living for so long, but what's going to make this time different? I suppose at least I know for certain she *is* alive. It's all the additional impetus I need.

'Can you park up here?' I ask Rachel, as we near the former church hall.

It's not yet midday, but there's already a small queue at the door to the homeless kitchen and shelter. There's no sign of Barbara or Judith, but they're not who I'm looking for. I haven't seen Freddie Mitchell for weeks, ever since I demanded he confront a part of his life he'd buried deep. He'd looked at me with such hurt in his eyes, but I needed him to go back to that place to help us learn more about the ring. If anyone can shed light on where one of their victims might run to in a panic, then surely it's Freddie. He understands the pain I've been through in my desperate hunt, and although he claims never to have met Anna, he has probably experienced some of the same atrocities as her. I'm working on the hypothesis that the abduction of Daisy Beauchamp was anything but random, and that Anna is searching for a way to get revenge on her abusers. It's the only theory that makes sense in my head. Why else kill Tomlinson? What I'm hoping is for Freddie to tell me some of the places they might have taken her on the off chance she would return to them to continue her plan.

Rachel kills the engine. 'He wasn't here last night; what makes you think today will be different?'

I shrug as I pull on the door handle. 'It's where I first interviewed him. He feels safe here, and it allows him to make a difference. I have to try.'

Rachel climbs out, but I stop her with a shake of my head. 'I need to do this, but Freddie isn't great with an audience. I know the two of you have met, but if I'm going to get him to open up, it might be best if I'm alone.'

Rachel opens her mouth to tell me she doesn't want to leave me alone in my grief, but she thinks better of it. 'I'll go back to your place and check on the latest news. Keep in touch with me, please? And I'll let you know if there's any progress from my end.'

My irises burn, but I strain a smile. I don't know what I'd do without her. 'Thank you.'

She pulls away, and I head past the small queue and around to the back as Jack and I did last night. Barbara is surprised to see me as she opens the door.

'Back so soon? I have two volunteers already, but you're welcome to stay if you—'

'I need to find Freddie,' I interrupt, rubbing my hands

together against the cold wind blowing down the narrow enclosure.

'He isn't here, I'm sorry,' she offers.

'Where would he go? Please, Barbara, I need to find him urgently.'

'I-I don't know, my sweet, I'm sorry. It's been weeks since he made an appearance here, and he doesn't carry a phone, as you know.'

I look back along the narrow pathway. 'Will you call me if you do see him? I can't stress how important this is, Barbara.'

She nods apologetically. 'Of course I will. Good luck!'

I head back towards the queue, but stop as I near the front. 'Good morning. How are you all doing?'

There are nods of acknowledgement, as the small group of men huddle close to the door.

'I'm trying to find Freddie,' I say. 'Have any of you seen him about recently?'

Freddie is a well-known figure in the homeless community in Weymouth, such is his energy and hard work. A couple of them exchange glances, but nobody comes forward.

'It's really important I find him,' I say. 'Please, have any of you seen him today?'

'Try the top end of town,' a voice says from behind the group.

I look through the gathered group and spot a woman wrapped in a tight rose-coloured sleeping bag. Her once blonde hair is straggled and poking out from beneath the hood of the sleeping bag.

'Have you seen him there?' I ask, hope surging into my chest.

She shrugs, bearing the weight of the glares of the rest of the group. 'If I was looking for him, I'd start there.'

I reach into my pocket. I don't have much by way of cash, but pull out the only note I have and hand it to her. 'Thank you. Thank you, so much.'

Hurrying away from the queue, I can't ignore the glares that the others gave the woman. Has Freddie specifically told people not to speak to me? Did I hurt him so much that he's built a wall of silence to keep me away?

With this thought pricking at my conscience, I hurry through the town, head down, not wanting to think about the kid with the knife who confronted me only hours earlier. Surely he wouldn't be stupid enough to strike twice? Crossing the road, I find the sheltered gap between the buildings where I first found Freddie, but as far as I can see, there's nobody in there now. I suppose it's possible the woman in the sleeping bag was just telling me what I wanted to hear, but I'm certain in my head that Freddie would never turn his back on this community.

I continue up the road and over the water, looking left and right as I go. The shops here are few and far between, but there are a couple of bars for those mooring in the marina. Heading further forwards, I feel like I'm wasting my time, but unless I can find him…

I stop still as I see a hooded figure ahead. He's leaning over a person in a doorway, and seems to be handing something over. I can't see the face of the hooded figure, but the height and build are right. I duck out of the way, sheltering behind a column of one of the bars. The hooded figure straightens and moves away from the doorway. I wait until he has walked past me, before I approach.

'I knew you wouldn't be able to walk away totally.'

The figure freezes and his head bows slightly.

'How have you been?'

I move around him and force my gaze beneath the hood, recognising his blue eyes, even if they're almost hidden by greying hair. I can see now he's carrying a lined box on his back, and in his hand is a stack of paper cups.

'Soup,' he explains, as he catches me looking at the contraption. 'I distribute to those who can't make it to the canteen.'

I'm not surprised that Freddie has taken on a delivery service in order to keep away from the shelter to avoid me, but I don't have to guess who's been supplying the soup. It's so great to see him, even if he doesn't look as well as I had hoped.

I take a deep breath. 'Freddie, I owe you—'

'I'm sorry, Emma,' he interrupts, staring down at the ground. 'I should have said it a long time ago. You were nothing but kind to me, and I… I betrayed that trust. I don't expect you to forgive me, but I want you to at least know how sorry I am.'

'It's me who owes you the apology, Freddie. I never should have pushed you to dig up the past for my own gains.'

His head snaps up and meets my gaze. 'You don't owe me anything, Emma. I knew you were desperately searching for your sister, and I should have told you there was far more to Turgood's abuse than what I did.' He looks out to the marina. 'I can't explain it, but in my head it was like, if I don't acknowledge it, then it's like it didn't happen. I realise how immature that sounds, but I spent a long time repressing those memories with booze and drugs.'

I step forward and embrace him. 'I'm sorry,' I whisper.

I feel his head press into the crook between my neck and shoulder. 'I'm sorry too.'

The smell of tomato and basil wafts around us, and my stomach grumbles, but it only reminds me that time is slipping away through the egg timer.

I pull us apart. 'Anna is alive,' I tell him. 'It's a long story, but I've found her.'

His mouth drops as he studies my face for any hint of a smile. 'She's… Oh gosh, Emma, you have no idea how happy that makes me.'

'She's in trouble, Freddie. I need to know where she might go if she was panicking. I'm certain she'd go somewhere familiar to her, but I don't know where.'

He stares blankly back at me. 'I-I don't know, Emma.'

'I need you to access those memories again, Freddie,' I say assertively. 'And I'm sorry to ask, but I need to understand what she's been through, where she's been, and how she's survived. You've been close to the people who had her. Can you think of anywhere that she'd be familiar with? The police believe she's somewhere in Dorset, Wiltshire, or Hampshire, but I don't know where she'd go, and it's too large an area for me to search alone.'

Freddie's eyes dance about as he searches for answers. 'I just don't know. Turgood didn't take us anywhere but the film studios. Most of the time, he was abusive at the boys' home. The trips to the film studios were few and far between. We never came this far south that I can recall.'

This isn't what I was hoping to hear, and all I can visualise are the grains of sand slipping away.

'Can you remember anything else about that time? Maybe something that you overheard, or somewhere others said they'd been or came from? Anything, Freddie. Please? I'm desperate. If I don't find her, I'm worried they'll have her killed.'

'I wish I could help, Emma, God knows I do, but I can't think of anywhere. Would she go to the film studios?'

'It's just a building site now though. There's nothing there for her.'

My hands fly up to the side of my hair as a headache grows. It's like I can see her across a gorge, and she is crying out for my help, but is just out of reach. I need a way of crossing but I can't find a bridge.

'What about that other girl?' Freddie says. 'You know, the French one you interviewed. She was held prisoner for thirteen years, right? Maybe she can shed some light on the subject.'

It's as if Freddie has just lit a bulb in my mind. Of course, all these years I've been striving to find Anna I've been doing it alone. I have contacts now, and research is the key to great writing.

Chapter Twenty-Four

NOW

Weymouth, Dorset

We decamp to my place. With no phone, my only chance of getting in touch with Aurélie Lebrun and Zara Edwards is via my laptop. Rachel's mouth drops as Freddie and I come in through the door. Dropping my satchel on the sofa, I grab my laptop from its usual place on the desk and carry it through to the central table in the living room.

'Make yourself comfortable,' I tell Freddie, who lifts the straps of the soup warmer from his back and rests it against the wall behind the door.

'What's going on?' Rachel asks, her reporter's nose twitching at the adrenaline fumes filling the room.

I don't look up from the laptop screen as it whirs to life and I wait to type in my credentials. 'I'm going to set up a video call with Aurélie Lebrun and Zara Edwards. The two of them and Freddie all had dealings with the ring as far as we're aware. Maybe between the three of them, and what I know about Anna as a child, we can narrow down where she might run to.'

I catch Rachel nodding in my periphery. 'There've been no updates on the news, though I did re-watch that Chief Superintendent's announcement. He also said they've checked Daisy Beauchamp's computer and found evidence that Anna may have been in contact with her via chatrooms. They're saying there are a variety of conversations between Daisy and someone anonymous who encourages her to run away. I assume there's something to make them think that Anna is behind the anonymous account, but he didn't elaborate.' She pauses. 'Em, I don't believe it, but the way he sounded... there was no sense of innocent until proven guilty. Anna is very much the only person in the frame for this, and it sounded like they were trying to swing public opinion ahead of any potential trial. As it finished, I found myself thinking she sounded guilty as hell.'

I don't want to think about the machinations going on behind the scenes. If I were looking to run a smear campaign against someone I feared could expose dirty secrets, this is precisely the sort of route I'd want to follow.

'We have to find her first then,' I say vehemently. 'She needs her family.'

'I'll put the kettle on,' Rachel says, with just a hint of self-reproach. 'Tea? Coffee?'

I glance up and mouth *thank you*. As always, she doesn't judge or criticise, just offers her support and encouragement. I don't deserve a friend as loyal as Rachel.

'Coffee, please,' I tell her, returning my attention to the screen and looking for the Zoom app.

'It's good to see you, Freddie,' I hear Rachel saying. 'Tea or coffee?'

'Tea, no milk, please.'

We both look at him at the same time.

'I decided to become vegan,' he says with a nonchalant shrug.

Rachel heads out to the kitchen and I can hear her filling the kettle.

'Do you have a map of the area in question?' Freddie asks, joining me on the sofa. 'It might help to see the names of the towns under consideration.'

It's a good point, and I open an internet search window, typing in Hampshire, Wiltshire, and Dorset. A moment later, the screen fills with the three counties, but it isn't easy to read the names of the largest towns. It is such a huge area; no wonder the police haven't found her yet, even with three forces hunting. Someone who's managed to keep herself hidden for twenty-one years must have picked up a few tricks along the way.

Aurélie is the first to join the call I've set up, and I introduce her to Freddie.

'I tried to phone you,' she says straightaway. 'Have you seen the news? Police are looking for someone called Anna Hunter in connection with a child abduction in Southampton. Do you think she could be your sister?'

I'm amazed at how natural Aurélie's English comprehension now sounds. A French accent is slowly returning to her voice after spending several months back in her homeland, yet when I first met her it seemed as though she understood nothing of what I said to her. She's subsequently explained why she hid so much on those first days after she escaped from the bolthole where she'd been held for thirteen years.

'That's why I'm calling,' I explain, as Zara's face appears next on the screen.

'Emma? Hi, is everything okay?' she asks, concern darkening her eyelids.

'I need both of your help,' I begin. 'My sister has finally appeared, but is in trouble. The police are seeking her in connection with the murder of Anthony Tomlinson in Market Harborough yesterday, and this morning's abduction of Daisy Beauchamp. Whilst I can't say for certain, my gut tells me these two acts are not born out of malice, but are some attempt to expose the ring for all their nefarious activities over the years. I'm gathering the three of you together because you each suffered at their hands, and I need your insight to help me better understand my sister's mindset.'

I share my screen so they can all see the map. 'Anna was identified stealing a car here, in Highfield, Southampton,' I hover the cursor over the area, 'which is at the northern point of the city, close to the M3 motorway. The car is next seen at the bus stop where Daisy was waiting for a bus to school. There are no reports that Daisy was forced into the car, and given that the police have now suggested prior communication between the two of them, it is assumed Daisy went willingly, whether under false pretences or not.'

Rachel comes into the room and places our mugs on the table beside the laptop before sitting in the single armchair just off screen.

'A traffic camera saw the car joining the A31 in a westerly

direction, but it then disappears. Given the number of minor roads leading to areas of the New Forest, I suppose this isn't too much of a surprise. But the question is: where is she now? Put yourselves in her shoes; if you were seeking revenge against the men responsible, but you needed a place to hide, where would you go?'

Nobody speaks.

I just hope that means they're thinking.

A minute passes.

'Aurélie, when we spoke last month, you said you remembered being taken to a building in London with a bronze statue of a lion outside of it.'

'Oui.'

'Have you had any memories return of other places you might have been taken to?'

Her brow furrows on the screen. 'I don't know… Before I arrived in Poole, I have flashes of places I lived before, but we were blindfolded when moved from place to place. As far as I know, they could have taken us out of one building, driven us around, and then returned us to the same building. We wouldn't know.'

'We?' I press.

'Yes, I vaguely remember there being other girls held with me.'

'I remember there being other girls too,' Zara chimes in. 'When I was first taken, I was kept in a dark cell, but each mealtime I would be led into a large hall with other girls; they would sit us in a big circle and make us eat rice or pasta, and then we would be returned to our cells. None of us were allowed to speak, but I don't know where we were.'

'I don't know about any of that,' Aurélie challenges, 'but I remember there being lavish parties, and being in rooms with other boys and girls who would then be taken away by older men.'

I feel Freddie tense beside me, and I rest a hand on his knee.

'The day I was bought by my captor,' Aurélie continues, 'I'm sure I recognised Big Ben on the horizon, but we were near water. I think we were by London docklands, but I can't be certain.'

'I'm not worried about London,' I interrupt, the irritation seeping through my words. 'I just need to know about possible locations in these three counties.' I sit back and let out the sigh that's been building in my chest. 'Please? I need to find her, and you three are my only hope.'

'You said she was spotted heading west on the A31,' Freddie says quietly. 'Are you sure she isn't headed down this way to see you? Does she know you're her sister?'

I think back to Saira Mistry's revelation yesterday. 'She knows, but according to her solicitor she has no interest in a reunion… At least, not yet.'

Aurélie scoffs. 'That doesn't mean she wouldn't come to you in desperation. Why would she tell anyone her true intentions? If she was always planning on abducting Daisy Beauchamp, she would surely leave a trail of breadcrumbs to mislead the authorities and the ring?'

It's a fair point. I'm only assuming she's in one of these three counties because DI Oakley said that's where the police are focusing their attention. Heading west on the A31 could just as easily be a smokescreen, and maybe that's why there's been no trace of her on traffic cameras since. This could all be a waste of time. My heart sinks.

'Pendark studios is in Newbury in Berkshire,' Freddie says

next, 'and that seemed to be something of a hub, so maybe there are places near that area that were used for holding children. Can we look at the map and see what places are close to that?'

I drag the cursor over the map until Newbury appears on the right of the screen, before zooming in slightly.

'How many girls would you estimate were in the feeding hall with you?' Freddie asks Zara.

'Um, I'm not sure,' she replies. 'Twenty? Maybe thirty? It's hard to remember.'

'Okay, so we'd be looking for somewhere twenty to thirty girls could be held where nosey neighbours wouldn't oversee or overhear what was going on,' Freddie continues. 'And it would need to be relatively close to the studios in Newbury for convenience. Turgood used to drive us from the St Francis Home in Banbury down to Newbury for those parties. Maybe there were other similar sites is what I'm saying.'

Rachel sits forward. 'But why would she go anywhere like that? I'm sorry, but in my mind that makes no sense. We're assuming these actions are her efforts to expose the monsters responsible for her captivity, but what if she's just trying to lie low? Maybe she didn't expect the police to know she was responsible for taking Daisy. Em, I don't think you should be thinking about places she's been since she disappeared. Think about places *your* sister would go where she'd feel safe. Maybe she is coming to Weymouth, but if she has any sense, she would avoid anywhere associated with you. If she knows her name has been shared on the news, surely she'd expect the police to come here first? What can you tell us about the Anna *you* remember?'

I open my mouth to speak, but I've already been down this route. When Oakley was here earlier I tried to think of anywhere Anna would run to, but drew a blank. The laptop beeps, warning that the battery is running low. Standing, I move to my desk to fetch the charging cable, but it's buried beneath papers and I have to shuffle things about to locate it. The book of Elinor Wylie poems drops open.

Anna's favourite book of poetry. I've lost count of the number of times I've subsequently read each entry, searching for answers, but have found none. I hold the book up for Rachel and Freddie to see.

'I don't suppose Elinor Wylie ever came to the UK, did she?'

Freddie shrugs while Rachel unlocks her phone and searches. I drop the book back on the desk and drag the cable back to the laptop.

'According to Wikipedia,' Rachel says excitedly, but rolls her eyes at her choice of source, 'following the death of her father in 1910, Elinor Wylie eloped to England with her future husband Horace, and spent a couple of years here. She was married at the time, and her life was littered with scandal, but yes. she did come here for a period... The site doesn't state where in England she was based, but I'll keep searching.'

Something is stirring in the back of my mind, but I can't quite connect the pieces. Moving the cursor over the map, I search the other towns printed in bold on the screen. Reading, Basingstoke, Winchester, Alton, Andover, Salisbury, Warminster, Dorchester, Bournemouth. I freeze as something else stirs in the back of my mind. My interest in reading and literature started before I can remember, but as I picture young

Anna, I can't imagine her now without one book or another in her hands. It was she who encouraged my passion for reading. Whilst she loved Elinor Wylie's poetic voice, she devoured Jane Austen over and over, despite her relatively young age.

Six months before her disappearance, Mum and Dad took us to a large country house estate with enormous green lawns that Anna and I ran around while my parents ate the picnic lunch Mum had packed. Something in the back of my head tells me that Jane Austen was connected with this place, and that we'd come as part of Anna's birthday present. Had Austen lived there? The answer is so close; it's on the tip of my tongue.

'According to this site, Wylie spent part of her time in London and part in Winchester,' Rachel continues, reading from her screen. 'And whilst her exact location isn't known, there are references to Chawton House in the letters she sent back to family in the US.

My eyes widen. 'That's it! My parents took us to Chawton House before Anna disappeared. She was obsessed with Elinor Wylie and Jane Austen.'

Rachel doesn't look convinced.

'Think about it,' I say, playing the idea through my head, searching for doubts. 'When she was arrested, she gave the name Kylie *Shakespeare*. She was carrying one of *my* books, even though she didn't know we were related. She headed west on the A31 to mislead the police, so that she could double back and follow camera-free roads to Alton in Hampshire.'

'It's two hours away,' Rachel tells me. 'Are you sure? It's a long way to go if you're wrong.'

I fix her with a certain stare. 'What's the alternative? Sit here and wait to hear that she's been arrested, or shot on sight? You heard what that Chief Superintendent said. He claimed she was armed and dangerous; do you really think she'll be arrested and brought in quietly? Please, Rach, drive us to Alton. I might be wrong, but I have to try something.'

Chapter Twenty-Five

THEN

Swanage, Dorset

Emma turned to a fresh page, but paused when she realised it was the start of a new chapter. Glancing over to where her dad was gently snoring in his faux leather armchair, she let out a quiet sigh of dissatisfaction. He'd refused to bring her back here that first day her mum had taken her over to Swanage for a formal visit, but six months on, he was less concerned about putting on airs and graces. Every visit now started the same way: a trip to the local Wimpy restaurant for a burger and fries, followed by an ice cream on the way back to the one-room bedsit.

It had felt exciting the first time she'd come here. Although it was small, she'd gasped when he'd shown her how his bed pushed up so that it became part of the wall. She'd never seen anything like it before, and had thought how much extra space it would give in her room if her own bed could be pushed into the wall. The kitchen area was small, yet large enough for a microwave, kettle, and small sink, and whilst her dad had seemed embarrassed by the meagre possessions, she'd been proud that he was managing to survive despite the upheaval of the separation from her mum.

Bronwyn hadn't seen the place, and when asked how it was, Emma kept her dad's secret and only mentioned the positive aspects, namely: it was on the ground floor, within walking distance of a park and playground, and there was a stray cat that would visit whenever she was there. She didn't tell her mum that there was a horrible smell in the bedsit, that it was up a very steep hill, or that she had to sit on a cushion on the floor because there was only one chair, which her dad sat in.

He was trying his best, and wouldn't benefit from her mother's critical eye. It couldn't be easy, Emma figured, to cover the rent on two properties, and he hadn't ever complained about the state of his digs, or that he received no financial contribution from Bronwyn's part-time job. He always asked after her, whether she was happy, whether she was struggling for cash, and whether she was taking good care of her. Emma responded resolutely every time that life at home was fine; Mum was trying her best to feed and clothe her while continuing her search for Anna. He never asked about Anna, and whenever Emma would mention her name, he'd look away or start a new topic of conversation. After her fourth visit, she stopped mentioning Anna too.

She'd been surprised to learn that her parents weren't the only ones to have separated, and after Bronwyn had told Emma's teacher, she'd admitted that her parents had divorced when she was a child. And it turned out that Cindy's parents had both remarried and shared custody of Cindy, with her dad having her at weekends. Emma didn't like to admit that she only saw her dad once a month, and avoided sharing details of what their visits amounted to.

He grunted suddenly, waking himself in time to catch the brown bottle that had nearly slipped from his grasp. He raised it now and drained the rest of the beer. Rubbing his eyes, he only realised Emma was still there when he happened to glance around the room.

'You made me jump,' he said, smiling at her. 'What are you up to?'

She lifted the spine of her *Point Horror* book and showed him the cover. 'Just reading my book. You fell asleep.'

He rolled his eyes in silent admonishment of his behaviour, before mouthing *sorry*. He'd looked tired when he'd collected her from the bus stop, and she'd overheard him telling her mum that he'd pulled an all-nighter at work, but was fine to still look after Emma for the day. The weight he'd lost in the aftermath of Anna's disappearance had returned with a vengeance and he'd been quite breathless as they'd made it up the hill to the bedsit, but he'd waved away her concern when she'd mentioned it. Judging by the bags of crisps and takeaway dinner packets she'd spotted in his outside dustbin, he wasn't taking proper care of himself. If ever there was someone who would benefit from a warm bed and a home-cooked meal it was him, but he was too proud to admit he was struggling. Emma couldn't understand why he couldn't just move home with them. He'd have been closer to work, and with the money saved on the bedsit rent, probably wouldn't have had to work such long hours. He'd also be able to take care of her when her mum was handing out flyers to anyone who would spare her two minutes to listen. Not that she went out as often as she once did, but it had become their Sunday morning ritual after the church service.

Her dad suddenly looked at his watch, exhaling in relief that he hadn't slept through the time he should be taking her back to the bus stop to meet her mum. Emma was all too aware that they had to be back by five, and that they'd need to leave by quarter to at the latest. She would have woken him when the time came.

'My race is on in a minute,' he said, sitting up straighter and raising the volume of the television. 'Are you going to come and cheer her on with me?'

This was another of their monthly rituals, but based on the familiar way he spoke with the woman behind the counter at the bookmakers, Emma sensed he didn't only go in there when she visited. It had started that first visit. Having devoured the burger, fries, and milkshake, they'd wandered around the small town centre like a couple of tourists, and as the sun had begun to set, he'd suggested she help him pick a winner in the four o'clock horse race. She'd never been in a bookmaker's before, and as he'd read out the names of the horses to race, she'd chosen Mother's Helper as that was the name of the *Point Horror* book she was reading at the time. She hadn't expected it to actually win, but the smile on her dad's face when it had come in first was a memory she'd wanted to repeat. Alas, the three horses she'd subsequently picked didn't fare so well.

'I have a good feeling about this one,' he said, reaching into his pocket and pulling out the ticket. 'Come and watch it with me, and bring us some luck.'

Carefully inserting the bookmark at the present page, she placed the book on her cushion and moved across to the armchair. In her eyes, she was too big to sit on his lap now, but he patted his knee, and wrapped his arms around her when she climbed on. She turned her face away as the pong of the beer on his breath assaulted her nostrils.

'She was a seven to two shot so she has a chance of coming in the top three,' he explained. 'What made you pick her out of the crowd?'

When he'd read out Soeur Perdue, she hadn't hesitated, understanding the translation from French better than him.

'I just liked the sound of her name,' she fibbed. 'It kind of rhymes.'

'Well, let's hope she's in form today.' He paused. 'Would you do me a favour and fetch me another beer from the fridge?'

She hopped down and took the empty bottle from him, dropping it into the dustbin and counting at least three other bottles it clattered against. Pulling open the small fridge door, she selected the final bottle from the door, ignoring the obvious lumps in the plastic carton of milk beside it. She carried the bottle back to him, where he proceeded to open and sip from it.

Soeur Perdue finished third, which meant he was in a good mood when the time came for them to leave. Exiting the bedsit, she was disappointed that the stray cat wasn't there waiting for her like usual, but didn't like to think about what could have happened to her in the last month. She was already missing one eye and walked with a limp, which suggested she hadn't had much luck in life.

She looked away as he lit up a cigarette.

'Don't tell your mum,' he said, exhaling a huge cloud of smoke. 'I know she doesn't like it.'

Emma bit her lip, uncertain whether to admit that she

didn't like him smoking either. They'd been shown a video in school which explained what happened to the lungs of people who smoked, and how it could cause cancer, and ultimately death.

She was about to tell him as much when she felt his arm move across the front of her, as if shielding her from some oncoming threat. He continued to manoeuver her around until she was standing directly behind him, and when he stopped suddenly, she jolted into the back of him.

'Johnny boy, just the man I was looking for,' a young man's voice said from somewhere in front of them.

'Not now, Sean,' her dad replied. 'I've got my daughter with me, and I'm taking her back to her mum. I was going to come and see you afterwards.'

'Was you now?' the first voice challenged, with a northern accent. 'That's good to hear, Johnny boy, because I was starting to think you was trying to avoid me. And we can't have that now, can we?'

'Please, Sean, let me just get my daughter to the bus stop and then you and I can go for a pint and chat through things. Yeah?'

Emma tried to peek out from behind her dad's legs, but his hand pushed her back in.

'And who do we have here then?' the second man asked, moving around the side of her dad until he was staring directly at Emma.

He didn't look how she'd expected – much younger than her dad – and if she was forced to guess, probably barely ten years older than her. He was wearing a white Adidas tracksuit top with black wavy lines, making him resemble a zebra. His hair was covered by a red baseball cap, and he had holes in the knees of his designer jeans. Definitely not the sort of friend she was used to seeing her dad engaging with.

'What's *your* name, little girl?' he asked, but before she could even consider the merits of replying, her dad's hand once again shepherded her behind him.

'None of your business, Sean.'

Her dad turned to face her, and gave her some change from his pocket. 'Why don't you run along to the newsagent's up the road and buy yourself a bag of crisps for the bus ride home?'

She counted the money in her hand.

'Buy your mum a bag too,' her dad encouraged, pushing her to move forwards and away from their conversation.

'Pretty young thing,' she overheard Sean comment as she moved away, but she didn't hear how her dad responded.

Turning into the newsagent's doorway, she stopped herself entering the shop fully, instead peering out round the edge of the doorway, instinct telling her to keep an eye on her dad for his own safety. She was too far away to hear what they were talking about, but from the way Sean's hands were moving, jutting out and gesticulating, she sensed he wasn't happy about something. Her dad just stood there, head bowed, eyes on his shoes, as he accepted the reprimand. She guessed this would probably be another little secret she needed to keep from her mum.

Chapter Twenty-Six

NOW

Alton, Hampshire

I can tell Rachel is less than convinced that our trip to Jane Austen's house is a worthy use of two hours in the car. Not that she's said as much, but as she circles the car park, looking for a space as far from the entrance as possible, I can hear her attempts to suppress her irritation.

'You don't have to stay,' I tell her, as she pulls in on the other side of a classic VW camper. 'I understand if you want to get back.'

'Nonsense,' she says, with a short shake of her head, but avoiding looking at me directly. 'If you think *this* is where we'll find Anna, then I'm all in.'

To be honest, I'm no longer convinced either, but as the car park empties around us, we don't have much time to find out. According to the Alton House website, they'll be closing in the next hour, so we may already be too late to catch up with Anna even if she is here.

Exiting the car, I'm about to hand Rachel her phone back, when I see Jack's name appear on the screen next to a green phone icon.

'Answer it,' Rachel says, when I show her the display, and so I put the phone to my ear.

'Hi Jack, it's Emma,' I say, as Rachel pays for a parking ticket at the machine.

'Great, I was hoping you'd still be with Rachel. I tried your landline but there was no answer.'

'What's up? What's going on?'

'I'm on my way to collect Mila from school, but I thought I should update you on what I've found. I drove straight to DCS Rawani, and he agreed to speak to me. His access to the NCA server has also been removed, but he was able to share some of the documents he'd downloaded and printed prior to his access being revoked. There's not a lot about Ian Beauchamp, however what I have found is how his name came up in the investigation. According to the notes, his name was flagged because of a scandal he was involved in during his bid for leadership of the Conservative party back in the mid-90s.'

This rings the tiniest of bells in my head, but I allow Jack to continue speaking. Rachel returns and sticks the parking ticket to the inside of the windscreen.

'Beauchamp was the frontrunner in the campaign after John Major decided to step down, having lost the General Election to Tony Blair and the Labour party. In fact, Beauchamp was the bookies' favourite to take control of the party until he voluntarily stepped aside and withdrew his nomination from the race. It was all very sudden and mysterious and he publicly claimed his decision was influenced by family illness. He disappeared from the public eye, only returning to the party several years later, but in a backbencher capacity.'

'I don't understand what any of this has to do with our investigation,' I say when Jack stops talking.

'Rumour has it that the sudden change of heart had nothing to do with a family illness as Beauchamp claimed, and everything to do with the death of a rent boy in Battersea Park. What brought his name to our interest was an interview with another male prostitute that never saw the light of day in court. According to the statement, the victim was hired by Beauchamp the day before his body was discovered, and when the team to whom the statement was made chose not to pursue charges against Beauchamp, the witness took his story to the tabloids. The story was never published, but the timing with Beauchamp's sudden withdrawal from the election shouldn't be overlooked.'

'You think he was blackmailed into withdrawing from the leadership race?' I conclude.

'Bear in mind that at the time, there was still stigma attached to being openly gay in the public eye, and in 1997 only a handful of MPs had formally come out during their time in office. Things are more relaxed now, but not back then. It's perfectly feasible to assume that the pressure or threat of exposure would have been enough to see Beauchamp step away.'

'But that doesn't mean he had anything to do with our investigation.'

'Which was the conclusion drawn by the NCA agent who was investigating this time around. That's not to say your sister hasn't found something to contradict that conclusion, or has personal eyewitness testimony to directly tie Beauchamp into the ring, which could be why she targeted his great-niece. Ian Beauchamp and his wife Hilary have no children of their own, and from what I've managed to find, they pay the fees for the school Daisy attends. If they have a vulnerability, it would seem Daisy is it.'

Rachel ushers us out of the car park and towards the signs for the museum and the house where Jane Austen lived in the early nineteenth century.

'She targeted Tomlinson, who we believe is linked to the ring, so there must be more to Beauchamp than we've found so far,' I say, hurrying to catch up with Rachel.

'Assuming Tomlinson *is* in fact tied to all this,' Jack says, and I can hear the doubt in his voice. 'Playing devil's advocate, the only thing that we found to tie Tomlinson to any of this is that photograph of him with Turgood and the vicar, right? But we don't know who supplied that image. What if it was sent to us by your sister?'

I stop still as my brain works overtime processing the possibility. 'That would mean she also sent us the pictures of Faye McKenna and Cormack Fitzpatrick,' I say.

'It's not against the realms of possibility,' Jack says. 'What if she knew them, and her sending us the pictures was to help us connect the dots? Do you remember the bunch of flowers at Ribery's grave, left in the memory of Cormack? What if Anna has been trying to expose the ring all this time, and has been feeding us breadcrumbs to follow?'

It never sat easy with us that there seemed to be some mystery person helping us along, and I've hoped it might be an insider keen to tear down the organisation.

'Well, what if it is?' I say, chasing after Rachel again. 'If Anna *was* the one leading us to Tomlinson, and is now targeting Beauchamp, what are her intentions towards Daisy? Tomlinson was killed, but surely she wouldn't…?'

Chief Superintendent Mike North's words fire to the front of my mind: *we believe Anna Hunter is armed and extremely dangerous.*

'It explains why Beauchamp is putting so much pressure on the police to get Daisy home. But that doesn't mean Anna is right. Either way, I think we need to speak to her. If she's the one who's been trying to help us, we need to know everything she does. We may be the only ones who can help her. Where are you now?'

We stop outside the small wooden fence wrapped around the orange brickwork of Jane Austen's house. There are four upstairs windows, plus two in the roof, and a large white door at the front. A small group of tourists exits the property via the door, but as Rachel and I move forward towards it, a woman in a beige gilet blocks our path.

'I'm sorry, but the last admittance was at three twenty. We're closed for the day now.'

I lower the phone to my chest. 'No, we need to go inside. I'm sorry, but I'm expecting to find something there. Please?'

She shakes her head, the large round glasses reminiscent of a style popular in the 80s. 'I'm sorry, you'll have to come back tomorrow. We're open from half ten.'

'You don't understand,' I try. 'I'm Emma Hunter, maybe you've heard of me?'

The heat rises to my cheeks, and I hate that I'm relying on the fame I've shirked for so long, but if Anna is the one who's been feeding us these clues as Jack has suggested, then I'm certain I'll find another one inside that will reveal where she's gone.

'I'm sorry but I don't know who you are, and it doesn't make a difference today. We are able to arrange special out-of-hours private parties, but you'd need to phone ahead to organise something like that.'

'Please, we'll only be ten minutes, and I'm willing to make a generous donation to the upkeep of the museum, if you'd just let us in. Please?'

She doesn't budge; doesn't even consider the request. 'I'm sorry, but we're closing.'

I don't step away either. 'Can you at least tell me how many people are inside? I was supposed to be meeting my sister here, and she may still be inside. Can I wait and see if she appears?'

She gives an irritated nod of her head, but doesn't object, clearly bored of the conversation.

Two minutes pass, but nobody emerges. The woman – her badge identifies her as Gwen – pokes her head in through the door and has a brief conversation with someone inside, before turning back to Rachel and me.

'There's nobody left,' she says pleasantly enough. 'I'm afraid if your sister was here, she isn't anymore. There's a pub just along the road; perhaps she is waiting for you in there. They do a wonderful afternoon tea.'

I look up the road where she has indicated, but I don't feel like Anna would wait in a pub full of people who might identify who she is.

'Thank you,' I say to the woman, returning the phone to my ear. 'Jack? Sorry about that.'

'No worries, what's going on?'

'Rach and I came to Alton in Hampshire following a gut instinct, but it seems the lead has gone cold. Are you able to call in any favours and get an update on progress from the team coordinating the hunt? I hate to ask, but I'm worried about what's going to happen if the police catch up with her first.'

'I can reach out to Zoe Cavendish if you want? I think she's still a DI in the Bournemouth and Poole area.'

I shudder at mention of Cavendish's name, remembering our two previous encounters with her. She's certainly no fan of mine, and I doubt she'll be willing to help us in our quest.

'Sure,' I say, deflated. 'If you think it will help, I'll try anything right now.'

Jack says he'll phone back as soon as he knows more, but I'm more certain than ever that we've missed our window to catch up with Anna.

'You know, afternoon tea doesn't sound like an outlandish idea,' Rachel says, mirroring my disappointment. 'We should probably get something to eat at some point.'

I shake my head. 'I'm sorry but I have no appetite at the moment. Would you mind if we headed back? And Rach? I'm sorry to have wasted your time coming here. I was so certain…'

She links her arm through mine as we follow the path back to the car park. 'Hey, don't worry about it. What are friends for?'

The car park is a lot emptier now, though there are still half a dozen vehicles parked up and empty, including the VW campervan blocking sight of Rachel's car. From the entrance to the car park you wouldn't even know it was there.

I freeze, dragging Rachel to a stop, as my eyes fall on the

figure leaning against the campervan, smoking a cigarette. The shaved head and grey tracksuit top are identical to those I saw in the image Oakley and Yates showed to me the other night.

Unless my eyes are deceiving me, we've found her.

Chapter Twenty-Seven

NOW

Alton, Hampshire

I don't hesitate. Breaking into a sprint, I tear off across the car park. Rachel struggles to keep up. I don't want to frighten Anna, but I also don't want to give her the chance to get to whatever vehicle she's arrived in and make her escape. She doesn't notice me at first, which gives me an advantage, but flailing arms in a bright-yellow overcoat aren't exactly subtle, and it isn't long before our eyes meet and I see her flick the cigarette away. I can't be certain she realises who I am at first; I see her tense, and immediately look to the opposite side of the car park, as if anticipating seeing a troop of police cars moving in to block her exits.

My thighs and lungs are burning in equal measure as I swallow up the distance between us, and although she remains coiled like a spring, she maintains her position at the front of the campervan. I'm breathless as I pull up, and as much as I want to tell her I can't believe I've finally found her after all these years, I can't get a single word past my lips. Who knew I was so out of shape? If she were to take off now, I don't think I'd have the energy to give chase; I'll just have to hope that her standing by our car is more than coincidence.

Rachel catches up with me while I'm bent over, hands pressed into my legs, trying to compose myself. It irks that she's not so out of breath.

Anna hasn't spoken a word, but is eyeing the pair of us carefully; I imagine with everything she's been through, she doesn't welcome trust and faith without a full cavity search.

I straighten, ready to speak, and yet the time it's taken to catch my breath has also filtered fresh doubt into my mind. I've never been much of a hugger, aside from Rachel and Mum. Given how long it's been since I last saw Anna, I don't instinctively feel like hugging her is the right move. Throw into the mix the fact that for all I know she's murdered two people in cold blood in the last few days, and maybe I should be a bit more wary of mine and Rachel's safety.

'I can't believe you're here,' I settle for, now resting my hands on my hips as the adrenaline continues to flood my system.

She continues to eye us warily, while her other eye remains on the two possible escape routes from the car park. 'They said… they said you're my sister?'

Her voice is deeper, grittier than I'm expecting. There's an edge to it that would suggest an upbringing in maybe London or Essex, though the smoking could also be the cause of the gravelly echo.

'That's what they told me too,' I reply, offering a passive smile, trying to put her at ease, but now I'm questioning whether Oakley and Yates could have lied to the pair of us, and in fact this woman's DNA *doesn't* match my sister's. I never actually saw the DNA test results.

I push the thought to one side. I know those eyes, though they're much darker than I remember. And that nose, although it is more bent out of shape – I'm guessing it's been broken at least once – still resembles what I picture in my mind when I see her stomping off from the yard that day.

'Do you remember me?' I ask next, wanting to move closer but my legs refuse to cooperate.

She shakes her head instantly. 'I don't remember anything from before… I didn't even know I had a sister.'

I try to keep the disappointment from my face, as I remember my recent conversations with Zara Edwards – the Brighton Rock Girl – who'd also managed to repress much of her past prior to her abduction. I can't blame Anna for not remembering.

'Well, I'm Emma,' I say, in case she isn't actually aware who I am. 'And your name is Anna. Anna Hunter. Unless you're married?' I correct myself. There was me assuming she'd adopted the surname 'Shakespeare' when she could just as easily have taken her partner's surname.

'I'm not married,' she confirms. 'You?'

'No.' I shake my head, chuckling, but uncertain why.

This all just feels so odd. In all the years I've been searching for her, so many times I've pictured the moment we'd meet, and what we'd discuss: old memories, love-life disasters, favourite movies and books. None of those topics feels appropriate right now.

Rachel clears her throat, and I quickly introduce her. 'Rachel and I met at university, and have been best friends since.'

Anna nods at her. 'I read about you in Emma's books. It's nice to put a face to the name.'

Rachel smiles, but for the first time in her life appears to be lost for words.

Anna's stance suddenly changes and she thrusts a hand out, snapping her fingers. 'I need your phones. Now.'

'I don't have one,' I reply quickly. 'Mine was stolen this morning. Rach, give her your phone.'

Rachel looks reluctant, but eventually hands it over. I know it's still relatively new, and the doubt in her temple suggests she's worried it's about to get trampled on.

Mentioning my own phone has suddenly reminded me that I should check in with Rick at some point and find out whether he was able to recover it. The last we spoke, he was haring off after the thieves, trailing the signal. I don't think Rick has my landline number, nor Rachel's contact details, so I may just have to wait until he makes contact at home.

Anna studies Rachel's phone screen before asking for her PIN. Again, Rachel gives it reluctantly, and once the screen is unlocked, Anna lights a fresh cigarette and taps at the screen.

'No tracing software,' she concludes, reaching into her pocket and extracting a paperclip, which she straightens out, before inserting it into Rachel's phone and removing the SIM card. 'But if they're monitoring your number, they'll know you're here.' She looks back to me. 'Promise me you're not lying about not having your phone with you.'

I fix her with a hard stare. 'I swear. I will never lie to you. You're my sister, after all.'

She passes the phone back to Rachel but keeps the SIM card, pocketing it along with the paperclip. We've clearly not established any trust yet.

'How did you know we'd be here?' I ask next.

She inhales deeply, before exhaling a cloud. 'I didn't. I needed somewhere to lie low, and figured hiding in plain sight was better than a layby. You'd be surprised at the number of people who are so unobservant in a car park. I was parked here when you arrived, and couldn't believe my eyes when I saw you hurrying towards the house. I thought I'd imagined it at first, and figured if I waited long enough by your car, you'd eventually come back and I'd know for sure.'

'We came here as kids,' I tell her. 'It was a birthday present for you, I think. Mum knew how much you loved Jane Austen and Elinor Wylie, and figured…' I stop speaking as her eyes narrow. Have I just triggered a glimpse of a memory? If I keep talking, will I unlock more?

'We shouldn't stay here,' she says, stretching her arms over her head as if preparing to sprint away. 'If they've been tracking your phone, it won't take them long to figure out what you're doing here.'

'I don't think anybody would track my phone,' Rachel says, looking at me for reassurance. 'Nobody knows the two of us are together today.'

She raises a single eyebrow, a trick I remember my dad doing from time to time. 'Are you fucking kidding me? Haven't you read any of her books?' The cigarette bounces up and down as she speaks, as if nodding in agreement with her. 'You two are like Tweedledum and Tweedledee. Where one goes, the other follows.'

She probably has a point. If Oakley learns that my phone was stolen this morning, it wouldn't take a huge leap of imagination to consider checking Rachel's phone. Maybe I shouldn't have been so explicit about our relationship in my other books. But ultimately, would it be so bad if Hampshire Constabulary rocked up here now? Ultimately, the woman before me is under suspicion of murder and child endangerment.

'Where's Daisy Beauchamp?' I ask, as casually as my racing pulse will allow.

Anna takes a long and deep inhale again, before exhaling the big cloud. 'She's perfectly fine. Don't worry.'

I was secretly hoping she'd say she had no idea what I was talking about; that she'd never heard of Daisy Beauchamp and had nothing to do with her being taken. I'm again questioning just how much trust I can place in the broken woman before me. She might be my sister by birth, but this isn't the same person I remember.

She steps forward, as if to move away, but I take a sideways step to stop her. We're not going anywhere until I know Daisy is safe.

'Where is she? Her family are worried.'

Anna blows smoke into my face. 'I told you not to worry. She's close by, and is perfectly safe.'

'Why did you abduct her?'

She snorts with derision. 'I didn't abduct her. She was a willing participant.'

I frown. The witness said that Daisy had willingly got into the stolen car, but that doesn't mean it wasn't under false pretences. There's so much going on behind those eyes; I need to understand her intentions, but I doubt she'll tell me if I ask her outright.

'I'm sure she didn't realise you were going to stop her going to school so you could use her as a means of getting back at her great-uncle.'

There's a twitch of her head. 'Good, so you figured out who Daisy is, and how Uncle Ian fits into all of this.'

'Not exactly, no. Is Ian Beauchamp connected to all of this? Jack's team investigated him, but he was cleared of any involvement.'

'I wondered when you'd mention Jack,' she smiles. 'I'm surprised he isn't tailing along too.'

'He's back in London trying to help find me find you. If you're worried that the police won't listen to what you have to say, let me take you to Jack. He won't judge. He'll listen, and will look after you.'

She throws the cigarette away. 'Not yet. There's more I need to find before I take it to the police. If your intention is to try and convince me otherwise, you're wasting your time.'

'You killed Tomlinson and abducted Daisy; the police will catch up with you eventually. Your best means of getting through all this is to turn yourself in.'

'I never killed Tomlinson,' she snaps, the first real emotion she's shown today.

'You were found at his house, when he was shot. You were arrested on suspicion of his murder.'

'He was already dead when I got there.'

'You were seen breaking into his house before the shot was fired.'

She shakes her head. 'It was staged.'

'Staged? By who?'

'If I knew that, I wouldn't be searching for answers.'

'What were you doing at his house if it wasn't your intention to kill him?'

She sighs loudly. 'I went there to ask him what he knew about the ring of traffickers I've been trying to expose for the last five years. I have reason to believe that he knew the likes of Arthur Turgood and that bastard Peter Saltzing. You know all of this: I did send you the picture I found.'

My heart skips a beat. 'So it was you who sent those pictures? You knew Faye and Cormack?'

Her anger quickly subsides to an expression of remorse. 'I knew Precious and Chesney, but later learned their real identities. They died because of me, and the bastards responsible need to answer for that; for all their crimes.'

'Then let me help you,' I plead. 'You've read my books, right? You know I only want to expose the truth.'

'I sent you those photos months ago, and you've done nothing with them. Your next book – from what I've read online – is about some missing French girl. Why aren't you telling Faye and Cormack's stories?'

'I will, but they're not ready yet. There's so much more I need to know before I can do that.'

'Like what?'

'Like, who are the ringleaders? Jack searched for ties to Tomlinson, but couldn't find anything.'

'Tomlinson wasn't involved… at least, not in that way. I thought he was, after I found that picture in Terry Brown's filing cabinet, but I then discovered that they were just using it to blackmail him into silence. He told me as much before they killed him, framing me in the process. All Tomlinson was guilty of was not pursuing the bastards.'

I don't know whether to believe her or not. In theory, if Oakley could prove beyond a reasonable doubt that Anna was guilty of murder, she never would have allowed her to go free on bail. That doesn't mean she isn't guilty, but I want to believe she was framed, and so I'm choosing to trust her now.

'Even if you didn't kill Tomlinson, you *did* abduct Daisy.'

'No, I didn't. I collected Daisy from the bus stop this morning because she asked me to. Ask her yourself if you don't believe me.'

'I will if you take me to her.'

She pauses, considering the suggestion, before eventually nodding and spinning on her heel. She disappears behind the campervan. I hurry after her, finding her gripping the handle of the sliding door. A moment later, she drags it open, allowing Rachel and me to peer inside to where Daisy Beauchamp is propped up against the side.

Chapter Twenty-Eight

THEN

Portland, Dorset

'Right, my bag's packed,' Emma told her mum, coming down the stairs, and immediately heading for the coat rack. She'd been dreading the weekend visit to her dad all month, but knew there was no point in arguing with her mum about going. Instead, she'd packed three new books, a bag of her favourite sweets, and the MP3 player she'd been given for Christmas. Even if Dad planned to spend the afternoon getting drunk in front of the horse racing, at least Emma wouldn't be bored.

The first few times she'd visited him in Swanage, she'd clung to the hope that it was only a temporary situation, that both of her parents would eventually see sense, that her mum would welcome him home and they'd find a way through all the post-Anna mess. He'd now been living at the bedsit for nineteen months, and Emma wasn't prepared to waste precious brain fodder on impossible dreams. Her family life was over. Her dad was gone, Anna was gone, and neither was likely to return any time soon.

That had been a monumental moment in her young life: finally accepting that her sister wasn't coming back. For a long time she'd wanted to believe her mum was right, that Anna was simply lost and that if they kept searching for her, she'd eventually be found and come back. But Emma had eventually caved and actually listened to the mutterings of her classmates. If Anna was simply missing, there would have been some clue to what had happened to her. But nobody knew. Not even the police after their extensive investigation could truly say what had happened. It was as if she had just disappeared off the face of the earth that day. One moment she'd been stalking away from the yard, and the next, poof! Gone.

If only Emma's mum would finally accept the certain truth, maybe she'd find a way to move on with her own life. If her future wasn't to be with her husband, wasn't it time she started finding new love? Emma knew enough about what happened between a man and a woman (or a woman and a woman) from the sex education classes they'd had to endure at school. While the boys had giggled at mentions of penises and vaginas, Emma had listened and learned. Whilst she wasn't looking for a new brother or sister, her mum deserved some kind of companionship. There were dating websites now where single people could meet other single people and form friendships and more. Emma had broached the subject once, and her mum had quickly dismissed the idea out of hand, but that hadn't stopped Emma creating a profile for her mum in secret, and in the ten days since it had gone live, Bronwyn Hunter had received several requests for dates. Emma would have to vet the applicants carefully before confessing what she'd done, but she was hopeful of persuading her mum to consider it.

Emma pulled on her coat before turning to see whether her mum was any nearer to joining her at the door, only to find she hadn't moved from the spot in front of the television.

'Mum, we're going to be late,' Emma said, fastening the zip.

Still, Bronwyn remained where she was, a hand at her mouth. Emma finally joined her to see what had so captured her attention, freezing when she read the words at the bottom of the screen.

'A riot at the prison? That's where Dad works, isn't it?'

Bronwyn nodded, dropping into the sofa and beckoning Emma to join her. 'Apparently it started right after visiting time yesterday afternoon,' she explained. 'Several of the prisoners barricaded themselves inside the visiting suite, threatening staff and two members of the public with weapons they'd made from various implements.'

Emma's dad had often claimed that his job was more perilous than he ever let on, but when Emma had tried to get him to open up about the types of dangers he faced, he always refused to say.

'Best you *not* know,' he would say time and again.

'Is Dad there now?' Emma asked, sitting beside her mum.

'I don't know,' Bronwyn replied. 'I thought he'd said he was supposed to be off yesterday, but you know what he's like with overtime. I've tried phoning him, but his mobile is switched off.'

'Do you think they would have called him in on his day off after the riot broke out?'

'I don't know. Maybe? I don't think we should go traipsing to Swanage without hearing from him though.'

Emma immediately regretted the joy this statement brought her, and silently chastised herself. This wasn't about her avoiding the crummy bedsit; this riot was a serious incident, likely affecting more than just her dad. Even if he hadn't been there when things had started, many people he knew probably were involved in what was happening.

'Is there anyone we can phone to check?' Emma asked. 'Can we phone the prison directly? Would they tell us?'

Bronwyn considered the question. 'I don't know. Maybe. I'm not sure what the number is.'

Emma steered her towards the dust-covered computer in the corner of the room. 'You could google it.'

John had bought the computer second-hand so that Emma could use it for her studies. Bronwyn hadn't been keen on the idea, saying, 'The internet is a dangerous place. You never know *who* is watching.'

She stared at the keyboard on the desk, but the look of anxious concern said more about her inability to operate the device than it did about any fear she had about the dangers of online stalking.

'I'll do it,' Emma said, motioning her away, and dropping onto the wobbly chair in front of the screen. She loaded up a search window before tying in the prison's name. The first results generated were for the BBC News website, and an article talking about the very thing they were watching. Checking that her mum's eyes were once again back on the television set, Emma clicked on the link and began to read. Why wait to hear someone tell her what had happened when she could read it for herself?

According to the article, which was somewhat limited in factual detail, authorities had been alerted to the incident shortly after 5 p.m., when three to five inmates made their move. Prison guards managed to get four members of the public out of the visitors' centre before the inmates took control, but three prison guards and two visitors became trapped inside with the inmates. Tables and chairs were moved in front of the two exits to the hub centre, and officers had to remain where they were due to the threat to the lives of the guards and visitors inside. News of the incident quickly spread to the rest of the prison, and although there was some disruption within, lockdown was sanctioned and the main body of the prison was brought under control. The prison governor was now in dialogue with the rioters, with a view to protecting those trapped inside in as peaceful a manner as possible.

The article continued by citing concerns presented by prison governing bodies previously, suggesting that reforms were needed at HMP Portland following a similar incident in the Youth Offender section of the prison three years earlier. That incident didn't involve danger to any members of the public, but questions had been raised as to whether the category of the prison should be reviewed. Despite calls for further reform, no action had been taken, as a result of cuts to funding.

'Have you found the number yet?' Emma's mum asked, and Emma quickly exited the BBC site and located the contact details, scribbling them on a scrap of paper, and handing them to her mum, who dialled the number and placed the phone to her ear, moving over to the window where the signal was strongest.

Emma turned up the volume of the television, but the news anchor moved to a different story, so Emma switched off the set.

Bronwyn lowered the phone, and cancelled the call. 'It's engaged,' she said, the anxiety making her voice come out in shuddered breaths. She redialled, but shook her head sorrowfully. 'They're probably receiving lots of calls from worried families,' she acknowledged, rejoining Emma on the sofa. 'I'm sure they'd have phoned if there was anything for us to be worried about,' she added, though it did little to offer the reassurance that was intended for her daughter's wellbeing.

It was the most concern Emma's mum had shown for her dad in a long time, and it stirred a memory in the back of Emma's head, a time shortly before Anna's disappearance, but as Emma's mind tried to pick at the memory it faded just as quickly. Even so, if her mum was this worried about him, didn't that mean she still cared for him? And if she cared for him, wasn't there a chance that she still loved him? If her life were one of those TV movies her mum loved to watch so much then an incident like this could be the spark to reignite the flame of passion. Or maybe she was just allowing her imagination to get the better of her.

'Yes, I'm sure everything is all right,' her mum continued, more for herself than for Emma. 'I'm sure he specifically said he was having his day off on Friday this week.'

A fresh thought pierced Emma's brain, and slowly spread like a web: what if he was one of the guards trapped inside the visitors' centre? She'd been dreading going to the bedsit today, but she hadn't considered the prospect of not seeing him again. Part of the reason she'd been so against going was because of the argument they'd had last month when she'd dared to criticise his drinking and poor diet. She'd told him he needed to start taking better care of himself, and he'd flown off the handle at her. He wasn't a dad who shouted, but his face had turned a deep shade of purple and he hadn't held back. He'd hugged her at the bus stop when Bronwyn had arrived, but it had lacked his usual warmth.

What if she didn't get the chance to tell him she was sorry and that the only reason she'd criticised him was because she was worried about him? What if her last words to him had been spoken in anger?

'Can you try and phone the prison again?' Emma asked, trying to keep the trepidation from her own voice. 'If he isn't there, I'd hate for us to be late and leave him waiting, not knowing where we are. That wouldn't be fair on Dad, would it?'

Bronwyn reached for her phone, jumping when the screen lit up as it received a call from a withheld number. Snatching up the phone, she moved back to the window.

'H-hello? Yes, this is Bronwyn Hunter… I see… Yes, we've just been watching it on the news… I didn't think he was supposed to be working today… Oh, I didn't realise… He's what…?'

Emma watched on, trying not to think about all the terrible things her mum could be listening to, but was unable to keep the tears from pooling in her eyes.

Bronwyn ended the call and slowly turned to face Emma, her own eyes betraying her emotions. 'That was one of your dad's colleagues at the prison. It seems he was there when the incident broke out. It's okay, he's alive, but they've taken him to the hospital as a precaution. Grab your things and we can go there now to see him.'

Emma didn't need telling twice, standing and grabbing her bag as she moved to the door. 'Dad always said his job was dangerous,' she commented as they stepped out. 'I wish he could find something safer.'

Her mum paused as she locked the door. 'That was the strange thing. When I told the woman I didn't think he was working today, she said he wasn't. Apparently he was there visiting one of the prisoners.'

Chapter Twenty-Nine

NOW

Alton, Hampshire

I'm relieved that Daisy looks in perfect health. She's leaning against the side of the van, but there's a laptop screen she's working at, connected to a mobile phone for internet access. She briefly glances up from the screen as she feels our eyes on her.

'Hi,' she says, offering a simple nod before returning her gaze to the screen.

I don't know how I feel to learn that Oakley was right and that my sister has indeed kidnapped Daisy. At first I'd wanted to believe it was just another part of the smear campaign set up against Anna, but seeing Daisy in the flesh puts paid to that. And if I was wrong about her abducting Daisy, what else have I been wrong about? It's all very well Anna saying that she *didn't* kill Tomlinson, but she has yet to offer any explanation of what she was doing at his house, or how exactly he died. I so desperately want to trust what my sister is telling me, but I need to try and cling to some kind of objectivity in all of this.

'Daisy, this is Emma Hunter – the woman I told you about – and her friend… Sorry, what was your name again?'

Rachel clears her throat. 'Rachel Leeming. I'm a journalist. Let me tell your story, Anna, and there might just be a way out of all this mess.'

Anna turns up her nose at the suggestion. 'I'm not looking for a way out of anything. I'm on a mission to cripple the bastards responsible for killing Precious and Chez, and I'm not going to let *anybody* stop me.'

I look past Anna into the van. 'Daisy? Are you okay?'

She looks up from the screen and frowns as if I'm speaking in a foreign language. 'What? Yes, I'm fine, or at least I would be if I could figure out the bloody password for this thing.' She looks to Anna. 'He must have changed it after we took off.'

Anna clambers into the van and peers at the screen. 'Can you break it? We need to get access to those files.'

'I only get three attempts before it locks me out for good. Each time a wrong entry is recorded it will trigger an email to him, and he'll figure out what we're up to.'

'Maybe I should just put a gun to his head until he gives us the password,' Anna muses, and I genuinely can't tell if she's joking or not.

'Anna, you can't keep Daisy here like this,' I try. 'She's a minor, and you're committing a crime that could result in a custodial sentence.'

She rolls her eyes in my direction. 'How many times do I have to tell you? She's here of her own volition. Daisy, would you mind explaining to Emma that you found me, rather than the other way around?'

Daisy pushes her glasses up her nose and dips the laptop lid. 'It's true. We met in a chatroom after I went looking for other victims of my uncle and his friends.'

I'm conscious of how carefully I need to tread here to avoid becoming an accessory after the fact. Now that I've found the pair of them I should immediately contact DI Oakley and let her know so she can reunite Daisy with her frantic family. However, I don't have my phone, and Rachel's won't work without the SIM card, so my options are limited. If I go off in search of a phone in a village I'm not familiar with, there's a chance Anna will up and leave with Daisy before I get back, and then I'll lose any limited trust I've so far managed to garner. The best thing I can do right now is keep as close to the two of them as I can, and ensure no harm comes to Daisy while I await an opportunity to get hold of Oakley.

I take a step forward, concerned about Daisy's use of 'other victims'. 'Are you saying that you've witnessed your uncle abusing others?'

'Duh!' she retorts, with an eyeroll as insipid as my sister's.

'Daisy, this is important,' I say, softening my tone. 'Did you suffer abuse at the hands of your great-uncle?'

She looks to Anna, as if seeking a parent's approval to speak. Anna nods gently.

'Not first-hand, no, but I was at his house when one of his friends tried to do something… Ian stopped him immediately, but when he came to speak to me about the incident afterwards, he made it very clear I wasn't to mention it to anyone. He described it as a drunken misunderstanding, and bought me this laptop as a formal apology – or bribe as I prefer to think of it. But it got me thinking about all the other times something had felt off about him – the times I caught him looking at me a little too long. And then I remembered a girl called Sandrine who had been an au pair who'd lived with us when we went to stay at his house in France. It was four years ago, and everything had seemed fine, but then this one night she burst into my room in the middle of night in tears. I was too young to understand what she was saying – she was speaking in French – but I never forgot the look of terror in her eyes. That was the last time I saw her, and when I joined Facebook last year, I looked for her, because we'd got on so well, and that's when I found the stories about her suicide the week after I'd last seen her.'

I'm struggling to keep up with how quickly Daisy is talking, though I sense this is a story that Anna has heard countless times, as she is nodding along despite the giant leaps in the dialogue.

'I started searching for stories about Ian, but it was only when I managed to get into his computer at his house three months ago that I realised just how much of a lie he's been covering up.'

'Tell her about what you found in his files,' Anna encourages. 'Tell her about the dark web.'

To be honest, I'm not sure I want to listen to any more, but I don't interrupt. I just wish I had my phone so I could record the interview.

'I couldn't believe how easy it was to find his password: he'd written it on a Post-it note in his desk drawer. I didn't know what to look for, but then I found a folder marked "Private" and that's when I found a shortcut to an external hard drive on his network. I opened it, and found close to two thousand video files of various lengths. There didn't seem to be any logical filing system to them, other than the date they were recorded, and I felt sick when I chose one at random, and saw what the men in it were doing to the girl. She couldn't have been much older than ten. I didn't have the courage to watch any others, but I found a folder of still images too that made me want to throw up. What kind of sick pervert would hold onto such things? I wanted to call the police, but he returned home, and I had to scarper out of his office, and then I never seemed to be left alone at his house when my parents would take us to visit. I know that hard drive is in that house somewhere, but I don't know where, and without proof I can't go to the police. That's why we're trying to access it remotely now. If we could get some screenshots, as well as the location of the drive, we'll have what we need.'

I have to remind myself that Daisy is just fourteen years old as she speaks with an eloquence far beyond her years. And yet, because of her immaturity, I don't feel comfortable that Anna is using her in this way. Attempting to hack the credentials and private hard drive of a former MP is serious enough, without throwing currently unfounded allegations of child abuse at him. As much as I too want to get to the truth about the ring I believe Arthur Turgood was a part of, there are ways and means, and there is also a time to step back and allow the police to do their job.

'Oh, and he had a shortcut to a Tor site saved amongst his favourites,' Daisy continues, 'which he obviously uses to go on the dark web, and I'm sure you don't need me to tell you the sorts of things that go on there.'

I clear my throat. 'Anna, could I have a word with you a second? Outside.'

She eyes me warily, before sliding back out, lighting a fresh cigarette as her feet hit the stony ground. 'Happy now? I told you she was perfectly safe, and she's not in any danger with me. If anything, I've taken her out of harm's way.'

'Or you've painted a giant target on both your backs.' I sigh, if only to buy myself time to get my thoughts clear. 'You have to take Daisy back. Right now your faces are plastered all over television and social media. There is an active manhunt for you both, and if you're not careful, you're going to give them all the ammunition they need to put you away for a long time, or bury you for good.'

She exhales a big cloud of smoke in my direction. 'Do you have any idea how long I've been fighting to get at these bastards? They took me when I was barely old enough to know anything about life, and they did things that you cannot even begin to imagine. After they killed Precious, they got me hooked on methadone, as a means of controlling me and forcing my obedience. They smuggled me out of the country to Spain where I was forced to sell my soul for a hit. Then, when I thought I could take no more, they dragged me back to the UK and made filthy videos they could sell en masse. I had to fight tooth and nail to escape, and I was ready to end it all, but I knew deep down that I couldn't go until I'd stopped them by any means necessary.'

My heart is breaking for her, but she needs me to be her conscience. I rest my hands on her shoulders. 'I'm sorry for all of that, Anna. And I understand your desire to identify those responsible. I'm fighting the same fight, but going this way is not the answer—'

'Don't lecture me,' she interrupts, brushing my hands away. 'You have no idea what I've been through, and I'm not about to stand here and take advice from someone who was brought up in a loving home, in a perfectly picturesque life. I sent you those pictures because having read your first book, I believed that if anyone could help me, it was you. I had no idea we shared parents, but I have to say I'm disappointed at how different we've turned out to be.'

Her eyes mist over, as do mine.

'Let me help you, Anna. Let's take Daisy back home, and then you and me, and Rachel, and the police can work together to uncover the truth.'

'Don't be so naïve, Emma! Don't you realise that these people – these *monsters* – have their claws in all levels of power? You think I haven't tried to go via the police before? It doesn't work! Inquiries get shut down all the time. Come on, you saw how they treated your friend Freddie. Do you really think anyone would be willing to listen to me without any evidence? Especially after what happened to Tomlinson?'

Now my frustration reaches boiling point. 'Well, what did happen to Tomlinson? You've told me you didn't kill him, but you still haven't said exactly what occurred this morning. If he wasn't guilty of abuse, how come he ended up dead? What aren't you telling me, Anna?'

She doesn't answer, simply shaking her head and stomping the cigarette into the ground. 'You either want to help us, or you don't. Either way, we can't stay here any longer. If they were tracing your mate's phone, then they're already on their way. So what's it to be, sis? Are you coming with us, or not?'

Chapter Thirty

NOW

Chichester, West Sussex

Some would say it was against my better judgement to clamber into the back of my sister's potentially stolen campervan, but in my defence, I don't feel I had any other choice. Rachel certainly wasn't impressed with the decision, but she couldn't leave her car where it was in Alton, and there wasn't space for a fourth person in the campervan, so I took her to one side and asked her to drive back to Weymouth and wait for me there.

'I don't like the thought of leaving you with this woman, especially without a phone,' she said.

'But you forget,' I replied, loudly enough for Anna to hear, 'this woman is my sister, and she's asked me to trust her, so the least I can do is listen.' I then lowered my voice and added. 'There's a card with DI Oakley's contact details on it. Give her a call when you get back and explain the situation. I'll keep working on Anna to see if I can get her to give herself up.'

That was the moment Anna had leaned out of the van window and told me to get in or miss out. I was relieved when she returned Rachel's SIM card to her, with the added warning not to use it until she was far enough away from the area.

We've been driving now for almost an hour, and the sky ahead is starting to darken, like a portent of what might be about to befall us. I've kept my eyes on the window ahead, and although we've taken a somewhat circuitous route, it looks like we're on our way to Chichester, an area I'm not overly familiar with, save for the fact that it is along the coastal road that runs from Devon to Folkestone. Is it really so surprising that our next stop should be in the centre of the coastline where the ring have been operating for so long unchecked?

'So, what's in Chichester?' I ask her as casually as I can, but also to show her I'm not stupid and have figured out where we are.

She glances over, even more casually, and simply says, 'The truth.'

It almost makes me laugh how dramatic and ominous the words sound, as if she's rehearsing for a poorly written play.

She has elaborated very little since we left Alton, and although I believed Daisy was still working at the laptop, I glimpse her in the vanity mirror, and as the glow of the passing street lights catches her face, I can see she is fast asleep. It's probably been as harrowing a day for her as any of the rest of us. To think, my morning started with a trip to the Tesco Express to buy pastries for my and Jack's breakfast. I never pictured this is how I would wind up.

'So, do you remember me from before?' I ask next, now that I know Daisy isn't listening in.

She doesn't answer initially, and I'm tempted to ask again

in case I said it too quietly, but I catch her looking over. 'Not really. It was a long time ago, and so much has happened since then.'

'You don't remember the last time we saw each other then?'

She shakes her head. 'Maybe if you tell me what happened, it might trigger… I don't know.'

I've pictured this conversation a hundred times or more, but now that the moment's arrived, I don't know how much I should or shouldn't say.

'It was a Sunday afternoon,' I begin. 'I can almost remember it like it was yesterday. You and I were in the yard of Mum and Dad's house in Weymouth, playing with my skateboard, but we had an argument, and you left because I think you were upset, and said you were going to walk to our grandma's house.'

'Did I?'

'Yeah, you were older than me, so Mum and Dad trusted you to go there alone; it was only five minutes around the corner, but you never made it.'

'Figures.'

'You don't remember what happened to you? Can you remember anything about the day you went missing?'

Another long silence descends, before she finally, and with a quiver to her voice, says, 'No.'

I can't tell whether that's the truth, or just a convenient truth that she's managed to convince herself of all these years. I remember having a similar conversation with Zara Edwards earlier this year about her memories of her abduction, but it soon became clear they'd been repressed for her own mental security. I wonder just how much Anna has repressed for the same reason.

'Anyway, that isn't technically the last time we saw each other,' she says next.

I can't keep the surprise from my voice. 'It isn't?'

She shakes her head, smiling crookedly. 'Do you remember back in January, you were doing a book signing at the Waterstones in Weymouth? I think it coincided with the release of your book *Isolated* in hardback. You arrived with a police escort, which I thought was such a cool entrance. The others in the queue were suitably impressed, let me tell you.'

I do remember the signing she's talking about, and how Rick gave me a lift from Portsdown police station because I was running late. I remember feeling flustered and panicking that Maddie would be cross about me being late, but surely I hadn't been so blinded that I'd signed an autograph for my sister.

'You were really there?' I ask. 'Did we speak?'

She shakes her head. 'No, I came along because I was going to ask you whether you'd received the picture of Precious that I'd sent to your agent, but then I bottled it at the last moment and left the queue. I was worried you would tell me to leave you alone, and that you weren't interested in their stories, but then when I saw you turn up at Chez's grave on Hayling Island, I knew I'd piqued your interest.'

'You were following me?'

'Not intentionally. I'd gone to lay flowers at the grave where I figured they'd buried Chez, and was leaving the graveyard when you and some guy turned up. Who was he, by the way? Your boyfriend? I can't imagine that he's the Jack Serrovitz you write about as he's much taller than you've suggested. Unless that's just a bit of artistic licence on your part.'

Rick must certainly be wondering where I am by now. Knowing him, he's recovered my phone, and has been waiting on my doorstep to give it back to me heroically.

'No, he's just a friend,' I reply. 'I can't believe I could have found you sooner, if I'd just looked hard enough.'

'Don't beat yourself up. Had I known you were my sister, I might not have avoided coming forward on those occasions. I was in awe of your writing and the determination you showed in bringing the likes of Arthur Turgood to trial. I figured if anyone could help me with my situation it was you.'

She said *could* rather than *can*: does that mean she's having second thoughts about me helping her, or have I finally managed to convince her that this vigilante-esque plan is destined to fail?

'Do you still write?' I ask, attempting to keep the conversation light.

'Did I ever?'

'Yes,' I nod, 'you were the reason I got into it. I idolised you as a child, and when you disappeared, I thought if I started writing like you used to, that somehow… I don't know, it sounds silly now to say it out loud, but I thought it would give us a connection. I read so many books as a means of escaping the drama at home, and that fuelled my imagination. I never thought I'd end up choosing fact over fiction though.'

'What do Mum and Dad think about your writing? Are they proud of you?'

A lump fills my throat as my chest tightens. I haven't told her about Mum's passing, nor Dad's, and it reminds me just how cruel the timing of all this has been. If only she'd come forward back in January, there might have been a chance we'd have connected the dots sooner and she could have met Mum.

After a lifetime of searching for Anna, Mum never learned the search was finally over; she deserved to know.

'We don't really discuss my writing… The thing is, Anna, Dad died many years ago. I'm sorry.'

The steering wheel jerks momentarily, but she quickly regains control. 'I suppose I shouldn't be surprised. A lot of time has passed, right? In fact, you'll know better than me; how long has it been since I was taken?'

'Twenty-one years now. A heck of a long time. You should know that Mum never gave up. She used to drag me out to town centres every weekend to hand out leaflets with your picture on, stopping anyone in the street who wasn't running away. She always believed she would find you, and never gave up hope that you were still alive; I guess it's what drove my belief too.'

There's another jerk of the steering wheel, and the air around us in the front cabin suddenly feels decidedly cooler. There are fewer street lights around us, making it more difficult to read Anna's features.

'You spoke about her in the past tense… Is Mum dead too?'

My eyes instantly fill as I think back to the nurses and doctors fussing over her in that bed. 'This morning' is all I can muster before my heart explodes with grief.

'Oh wow, I'm sorry,' she says, and although I can feel her eyes on me, I look away.

'I suppose I should be sad too,' she continues, 'but it's difficult when I don't even remember what she looked like. I guess, in my mind, she died a long time ago. Or at least, I'd resigned myself to the fact that I wouldn't ever see her again. Was it sudden?'

I wipe my eyes with the back of my hand. 'She'd suffered

with Alzheimer's for a number of years… She was in a care home, but had suffered a minor heart scare earlier this year. I suppose it was only a matter of time before her heart packed up again. I tried to tell her that I'd found you, but I don't think she heard me.'

I hear Anna sniff, but I can't see whether her eyes are shining. 'Probably for the best. She didn't need to hear about everything that's happened since they took me. I'm sorry for you though. Losing a parent is never easy.'

That's when it hits me: my only family left is sitting in the driver's seat beside me. No matter what hair-brained scheme she's concocted, she's asked for my support, and I can't simply turn my back on her. I'm all she has left, even if she doesn't remember me.

Her shoulders tense. 'We're nearly here.'

'Can I ask where we're going? Is this where you live?'

'Not exactly, but it's a place I know. You wanted to know the truth, right? Well, I'm taking you to somewhere that has the proof you so desperately crave. And when you've seen the evidence with your own eyes, maybe you'll see why I've done the things I've done, and realise just how much danger Daisy was in when she reached out for my help.'

The road narrows, and but for the headlights, outside is pitch black. I can just about make out large trees either side of the road – conifers, unless I'm very much mistaken. They stretch up so high that I can't even see the tops with my forehead pressed against the ice-cold glass of the window. Although I've lost my bearings since we left the last road, I can understand how she has evaded detection for so long. To say this road is off the beaten track would be an understatement. And then we arrive at a sign marked 'Private Road', but she doesn't hesitate, lurching the campervan along it. The first house we pass on the left has a long driveway, and must be at least a six- or seven-bedroom detached property, about a hundred metres from the edge of the road. But it is just the first of many such elaborate properties. Something doesn't feel right, but as I try and catch Anna's gaze, I can see it is rooted firmly on the road ahead. The properties here must be worth seven figures or more each, and I can't see how Anna would have got her hands on that kind of money, given what little I've learned about her.

She finally pulls over as the end of the road looms, parking by a large expanse of chalk-like wall. Darkness envelopes us as she kills the engine and the beam of the headlights evaporates.

'We walk from here,' she says, opening her door, grabbing at the bag beside my legs, and quickly slipping it over her shoulders.

'What about Daisy?' I ask, turning to search the back but finding nothing but shadows.

'She'll be fine where she is. She needs the rest. Come on, we won't be long.'

I exit the vehicle, gasping at just how cold it is outside, and even though I zip up my jacket, it provides little warmth. I too slip on my satchel, not that it contains anything of any use. Certainly nothing I can use to let Rachel or the police know where we are. And as I follow Anna along the pathway, keeping less than a foot behind her in case the darkness swallows her up for ever, I can't help thinking there's a lot she's still to tell me.

Chapter Thirty-One

THEN

Dorchester, Dorset

It was all Emma could do to keep up with her mum as they bustled into the hospital, past the flurry of cafés, restaurants, and shops, only stopping briefly to read the directory of departments hanging overhead. According to the prison governor, John had been taken to the Accident and Emergency department at Dorset County Hospital as a precaution because of injuries sustained during the fourteen-hour siege. Bronwyn had relayed this information on the bus ride into Dorchester, and the knot in Emma's stomach hadn't stopped growing ever since.

He's still alive, she reminded herself. That meant her final words to him – whenever they might be – wouldn't be the silly argument they'd had last month. She had to be grateful for that; grateful for the chance to tell him how sorry she was, and how she'd only criticised him because she was worried about losing him. Because she hadn't told her mum about the argument, she'd have to wait for the right opportunity to apologise, but as soon as it presented itself, she vowed to take it.

Turning left, her mum once again picked up the pace, doors and hand sanitation units passing them in a blur, and it was once again all Emma could do to keep up. They eventually reached the Accident and Emergency department through a maze of corridors and came to an abrupt halt by the main reception desk.

'John Hunter,' Bronwyn said urgently. 'He was brought in from Portland prison.'

The woman behind the desk tapped her fingers across the keyboard, studying her screen. 'And you are?'

'Winnie – sorry, Bronwyn – Hunter. I'm his... I'm his wife.'

The woman's eyes didn't leave her screen. 'Okay, he's being assessed at the moment. If you'd like to take a seat, someone will come and find you when you can see him.'

Emma could barely see over the top of the reception counter, and pushed herself to her toes. 'Is my dad going to be okay?'

The woman looked at her, and something softened in the focused glare she'd been diverting at her screen. She smiled reassuringly at Emma. 'That's what we do here, my love. We're the best at making mummies and daddies better. Take a seat with your mum and we'll let you see your dad as soon as we can. Is that okay? If you ask your mummy nicely there's a vending machine around the corner; maybe if you're super good, she might buy you a treat.'

Emma wasn't convinced, but as Bronwyn led her daughter from the desk, she headed straight back to the corridor, locating the vending machine. 'Okay,' she said, 'I don't have much change, but what would you like?'

At home, there was usually a 'no sweets before mealtimes' policy, but even though it wasn't even midday, the rule had been relaxed.

Emma selected the least expensive chocolate bar, and was surprised when her mum chose two, handing one to Emma, and swiftly tucking into the other.

'Our little secret,' she said as they found two free seats and plonked themselves down.

The chocolate bars hadn't lasted long, but eventually a nurse called their names from the desk and led them through the secured doors, past the emergency department, and up to a ward designated for outpatients.

'He's had stitches to the laceration on his neck, and we'll keep him in overnight for observation due to a likely concussion,' the nurse explained to Bronwyn. 'He's awake and in good spirits at the moment.'

They stopped at a closed door, and the nurse waited for them to sanitise their hands again, before allowing them to enter. Emma couldn't prevent the gasp escaping her throat when she saw her dad beneath the white sheets. His face was purple and swollen, resembling a gobstopper; his neck was surrounded by a thick scarf-like bandage, with obvious droplets of blood smeared against it, and one of his arms was held against his broad chest in a sling. She broke free of her mum's grasp and hurried to the side of the bed.

'There, there,' he croaked. 'I'll be all right. There's no need to make a fuss.'

Bronwyn closed the door behind her, but maintained her distance at the foot of the bed.

He hugged Emma close with his free arm. 'You didn't need to come all this way to see me,' he said to Bronwyn, 'but I appreciate you coming. I'll be out of here by morning hopefully.'

'What h-happened?' Emma stammered as the tears escaped her eyes, and she blotted them with the corner of his starched blanket.

'Nothing that need worry someone as innocent as you, my love,' he said, resting his bruised cheek on the top of her head. 'Sometimes bad men feel the need to do bad things to be heard. That's all that happened yesterday. You remember I've told you that there are some bad men that I have to watch over at work?'

She nodded, and he winced as her head bobbed against his cheek.

'Well, some of those men didn't feel that they were being treated well enough by my some of my colleagues at the prison, and so they caused a big old fuss so that they could make their complaints heard by the prison governor. He's my boss and is in charge of decisions that affect the prison and those imprisoned.'

'Will the bad men be punished?'

'Yes, I imagine they will have to remain in prison for longer than originally planned, and they'll probably find some of their home comforts are taken away because of what they did.'

Emma couldn't really understand why anyone would risk staying in prison for longer, but simply nodded, dismissing her dad's words as nothing more than complicated adult things.

'What were you doing there, John?' Emma's mum bristled from her post at the end of the bed. 'And don't lie to me; I know you weren't working.'

He opened his mouth to respond, but closed it again. 'I was visiting one of the inmates,' he said, raising his head from Emma's and straightening in the bed.

'Who?'

'A new lad; he's only been there for a couple of weeks, and he's been struggling to adjust. This is his first time inside, and he'd been expecting his fiancée to visit him this week, but I heard on Thursday that she was a no-show and I was worried about what he might do, so I stopped by to check on him. That's all. Perfectly innocent.'

'Nothing's ever perfectly innocent where you're concerned, John,' Bronwyn scoffed.

They exchanged a silent glare before both remembered Emma was still in the room with them.

He looked up at the grey clouds framed in the windows. 'I don't know what else to tell you. I went in to see him, and that all went perfectly well, but then as I was leaving, and chatting to one of my friends, suddenly all hell broke loose and three of the inmates charged us, and threatened us with shivs they'd made from toothbrushes and combs. We should have been better prepared, but they took control of the room, and used me and Josh as shields. We were never really in danger, and it was only a matter of time until the governor negotiated with them and we were released.'

She snorted with derision. 'Never in danger? Look at your neck, John. How do you explain that?'

He shifted uncomfortably. 'Do we have to do this now? In front of Emma? Hasn't she been through enough already?'

'All *she's* been through? What about *me*, John? When are you going to accept accountability for what you've put me through?'

Emma didn't like that her mum had decided to pick a fight when he was in such a bad way. She'd seen how worried her mum had been since receiving the phone call: how she'd devoured the chocolate in no time; how she hadn't been able to keep her hands still while they'd waited for news. Why couldn't she just admit she still loved him, and then they could all go back to the small house in Portland?

'This isn't the time for any of that,' he grizzled.

She looked at her watch. 'Great! Now I've missed my appointment, and I'm going to have to rearrange it.'

'What appointment?'

She glanced at Emma before shaking her head. 'That's the problem with you, John, you never think about anyone but yourself. Heaven forbid that I might use your monthly visitations for myself.'

He looked confused. 'What appointment? Your hair looks fine.'

She shook her head. 'Not for my hair… Oh, never mind. What's the point anyway?'

'Listen,' he said calmly, 'will you give me and Emma a bit of alone time so I can apologise properly for missing our visit today?'

Bronwyn ran her tongue across her teeth in disbelief, before stamping her feet. 'Fine, you can have as long as it takes for me to go and buy a cup of tea.' With that, she turned and headed out of the door, closing it behind her.

Emma's dad raised his eyebrows and he pulled a guilty face. 'Looks like your old man is in the dog house again.' His face softened into a smile. 'Sorry you had to see that. There's a lot of things about your mum and me that you don't know, and it isn't right for the two of us to carry on like that in front of you.'

Emma sighed. 'I just wish the two of you could show how much you still love each other and get back together.'

He frowned sadly. 'There's nothing I'd love more, squirt, but I don't think that will ever happen now. As I said: too much water under that bridge. But listen, there were two things I wanted to talk to you about, and we probably haven't got much time before your mum comes back and takes you away. Firstly, I wanted to apologise for how we left things last month. I know—'

'I'm so sorry about that too,' Emma interrupted. 'I only said what I did because I was worried about you.'

His lips pulled into a thin smile. 'I realise that now, and how I reacted was immature, and I'm sorry. You're such a bright and clever girl, sometimes I forget which of us is supposed to be the grown-up. I shouldn't have shouted at you, and then given you the cold shoulder. I'm sorry.'

She gingerly wrapped an arm across his chest. 'I'm sorry too, Dad.'

He patted her head with his free hand, before resting it on her shoulders. She wished she could have stayed like that for ever, but he withdrew his hand and lifted her chin.

'There's something else... I need you to do me a favour, but you can't tell your mum, whatever you do... Can you promise me?'

She thought about all the promises he'd made her keep since she'd first been shown the bedsit, but nodded anyway. 'Okay.'

'Before I moved out, I left something in the garage. It's a box of sorts, a green case but small. It contains something very important and I need you to get it for me.'

She frowned. 'What is it?'

He shook his head. 'That isn't important. Listen, we don't have much time. I need you to find a moment when your mum isn't going to catch you and start asking questions, and go into the garage. If memory serves, you'll find the green case on the shelving unit at the back of the garage. You know, behind where the shovel and fork hang, where I have shelves that contain things like my tool box, and all those tins of paint?'

She could picture the dusty shelving unit he'd always insisted she stay away from and which he'd once chastised Anna for climbing.

'I know where you mean,' she said quietly.

'Well, it's on the top shelf, right at the back. You might need to climb up to see it. I need you to get it down and hide it for me; then, once you have it, use your mum's phone to call me and let me know, and I'll work out how to collect it from you.'

Emma couldn't shake the feeling of doubt clawing its way over the knot in her tummy. 'But what is it? Why can't you ask Mum to get it for you?'

He took a moment to think. 'It's… it's a present for your mum's birthday, and I don't want her to know about it. If you can get it to me, I can wrap it and give it to her. You see? That's why you can't tell her about it.'

Emma might have been young, but she wasn't stupid, and the way he was avoiding eye contact and shuffling awkwardly told her that whatever was in the case *wasn't* a gift for her mum.

'Will you do that for me, squirt? Please?'

She hated to disappoint anyone, least of all her dad. 'Okay,' she nodded.

'And promise me you won't mention any of this to your mum, yes?'

'I promise.'

He pulled her into his body with his free arm and squeezed her tightly.

'I need the toilet,' she told him.

'That's okay, sweetheart, there's one through that door in the corner of my room.'

She looked to where he was pointing and headed over, closing it to and flicking on the light. She didn't like that he was asking her to keep more secrets from her mum, but she couldn't begin to think what else could be in the case aside from a present, and decided she would try and open the box to check the contents before determining whether she spoke to her mum about it.

Finishing on the toilet, she couldn't reach the flush, so focused on washing her hands in the sink. She was about to push the door open and tell her dad that she hadn't managed to flush the toilet when she heard him speaking.

'I know you don't believe me, Winnie, but I'm doing everything I can to fix things.'

'As am I, John,' her mum replied, apparently back from buying her tea.

'There's something else I haven't told you, Winnie… About the real reason I was at the prison yesterday… The guy I went to visit, he reckons he knows where she is. He's going to tell me if I can just get him what he wants. We're so close, Winnie.'

Chapter Thirty-Two

NOW

Chichester, West Sussex

Anna has increased her pace, and as I turn back to check on the campervan, I can no longer see it, such is the darkness of night surrounding us. I don't like the idea of leaving Daisy alone in the campervan. Yes, she's fourteen, and based on what Anna has told me, I don't doubt that she's a very capable girl, but that's the point: she's still a child. Maybe I should have insisted on staying with her, but I'm not sure I'd be able to find my way back through the trees we've cut through. The ground is so uneven, yet if anything, Anna's pace has only increased, as if this is a route she's taken multiple times.

I'm relieved when she suddenly stops and begins running her hands along a solid surface. Moving closer, I push out my hands, and feel the rough grain of the wood pressed against my skin. A fence of some kind, though what it leads to and what it is protecting are questions currently beyond my imagination.

'What are you looking for?' I whisper as I hear Anna continuing to run her hands over the wood.

I'm not entirely sure why I felt the need to whisper, but Anna whispers her response back. 'There's a gate here somewhere.'

A second later, a flash of light erupts before my eyes as she uses her cigarette lighter to brighten the area immediately in front of us. She spots what she's looking for and moves onwards, reaching into her pocket and extracting a key that she places into the handle of a gate, turning it until we hear the click. She pushes the gate open. She hurries me through and quickly closes it behind her, relocking it.

The garden we now find ourselves standing at the end of is better lit, with a series of lights stuck into the ground beside a pathway of paving slabs. To the left of the path, steam shimmers from the Olympic-sized pool, and beyond that there is a covered hot tub and area of decking. To the right of the path is a large shed and glass greenhouse. The garden is well tended, and as we head up the path a large detached property comes into view. I haven't quite got my bearings, but it must be one of those we drove past on the private road.

Is this her place? It doesn't feel likely, and I'm now starting to worry about why she's brought us in via the garden fence, rather than up the driveway and in through the front door.

'What is this place?' I whisper again, hurrying after her. 'Where have you brought me?'

'Relax,' she says, with more than a hint of nonchalance, 'it belongs to a friend of mine. I figured it was safer to come in the back in case the police are watching the front.'

I suppose there is some logic in her response, even if the voice of paranoia in the back of my mind is shouting. After all, she did have a key to the gate, which would lend itself to the property belonging to a friend.

The path continues all the way to a conservatory, with lawn either side of us, but as we get near, an overhead security light floods the garden and Anna ups her pace, throwing herself against the wall beside the conservatory and dragging me with her. Alarm bells are ringing inside my head.

Anna presses a finger to her lips, preventing me asking any further questions, and then she appears to mime something that leaves my face in wrinkles of confusion. She eventually rolls her eyes and indicates for me to stay put. I watch on as she shimmies along the ground, her body remaining pressed against the wall like something from those old prisoner-of-war movies our dad would watch on television on a Sunday afternoon. And then she's up a small flight of brick steps to a raised patio, leading to more stairs that lead up to an extended balcony on the first floor.

Every muscle and sinew in my body is telling me that Anna is about to gain illegal entry to this house, and, remembering the promise I made myself to be her conscience, I hurry after her up the stairs where I find her crouched down at a patio door on the upper balcony.

'I told you to stay down there,' she chastises in a fog of breath.

'You're breaking in here, aren't you?' I fire back in an angry whisper.

She rolls her eyes again, but doesn't answer the question, reaching inside her coat and extracting a small leather pouch, which she proceeds to unzip. It isn't much bigger than a purse, but as I look inside, I know precisely what tools I'm looking at. I press my hand over the selection of picks, shake my head, and mouth the word 'no', but she bats my hand away and extracts two thin spiky shards and places them into the lock of the door.

'What is this place?' I demand, raising my voice a fraction over a whisper so she'll hear the urgency in my voice.

She pauses momentarily. 'Whose place do you think it is?'

I think back through everything we've discussed since meeting in the car park in Alton, and then my eyes widen in panic.

'This is Ian Beauchamp's estate, isn't it? The one where Daisy accessed his computer.'

A broad grin breaks out across her face, and it's my turn to feel disappointed by how much we've grown apart.

'I cannot allow you to go in there,' I say. 'It is against the law, and you are already facing enough charges without adding burglary to the list.'

She doesn't stop fiddling the picks in the lock, leaning one ear close to listen while she works. 'What's your problem anyway? We both want the same result: to stop the paedophiles and traffickers operating along the south coast, right?'

I nod, defeated, knowing nothing I say or do is going to stop her going through with her ridiculous plan.

'Well you have your ways,' she says, her grin widening as she hears the lock pop. She quickly returns the picks to the pouch and hides them back inside her coat. 'And I have mine. We need the external storage device that's inside this house.'

'But what's the point?' I try one last time. 'If you take it, it won't be any use to the police. Stolen evidence is inadmissible in court. They'd need to locate the drive here with proof that Beauchamp is the only one with access. Even if you phoned the police now and told them, your picks have probably left scratches inside the lock allowing a defence team to question the evidential value of anything recovered in the property.'

'I'm not planning to give the drive to the police,' she snipes. 'I've already told you that all police intervention will do is allow the group to cover their tracks quicker. Tomlinson said as much to me on the phone before I went to his place. For all I know, he knew they were going to kill him and his inviting me over was one last favour for them. This entire business is covered in manure, and the only way to get to the bottom of the mess is to get your hands dirty.'

'I'm not going in there with you,' I tell her firmly.

She lowers the door, and there's a part of me praying an alarm will sound, forcing her to abort her mission, but our ears are only greeted with silence.

'That's your choice to make,' she says, crawling through, 'but if I were you, I'd hurry up and think how I'm going to explain my presence here to the guard patrolling the perimeter.'

She nods at a figure who has emerged on the lawn below the security light, the large black and tan dog beside his feet already sniffing the air.

I have no choice but to follow Anna in through the door on my hands and knees, but everywhere my palm touches feels like another year they'll add to my sentence. I can already picture the headlines:

BESTSELLING AUTHOR CAUGHT REDHANDED

Anna closes the door behind us, so as not to attract the security guard's attention. I can only assume he must have been alerted when the security light came on, or perhaps there was a silent alarm triggered when we opened the gate. Either way, he's blocking our escape, so we're trapped here until he moves away.

'Come on,' Anna whispers, still crawling, but now away from the patio door and past a low-slung leather sofa.

We must have come into a living room of sorts, as there is a flat-panel television on the wall across from the sofa, and a small refrigerator humming beside it. I'm angered that Anna clearly always had the intention of breaking in here, and was just stringing me along in the campervan with her talk of showing me evidence to quash any doubts. Presumably Daisy gave her the key to the rear gate, and the real reason for mounting an attack from the rear of the property was to avoid attracting the attention of the security guard.

There is no noise in the house, and as we crawl out onto a carpeted landing, there isn't any obvious light from anywhere else in the house. It's not long after five, so wherever Beauchamp is, I can only hope he isn't planning on returning any time soon.

'Daisy said his office is on the second floor,' Anna whispers, leading me to a staircase and crawling up it.

I follow because I don't know any better, and I'm resenting myself for ever daring to believe I could trust my sister not to get herself into more trouble. If I had my phone, I'd call Jack and let him know what's going on, but that isn't an option. The best thing that can happen from here is for Anna to either find what she's looking for, or to give up, so we can get out of here before we're discovered.

At the top of the stairs, there are two doors, both of which are closed. Anna stands, and tries the handle of the door to the left, which opens into a large double bedroom, smelling of fresh flowers. Closing the door, she tries the second, undeterred when she finds it locked, immediately reaching for her picks again.

I step to block the door as she's unzipping the pouch. 'We could phone the police now. We could speak to my friend Jack, or to the Detective Inspector who interviewed you in Market Harborough yesterday. We can certainly trust Jack, and he could put us in touch with someone who will take our claims seriously. We can tell them about Daisy's input, and then a professional team of detectives can search for this hard drive.'

Anna makes no effort to be soft as she pushes me out of the way, and I have to reach out for the wall to correct my balance. She doesn't offer an apology as she crouches and goes to work on the lock with her picks.

Rubbing my arm gingerly, I remain on the small landing as she unlocks the door and heads inside the room, leaving the door open. I watch on as she moves immediately to the large wooden desk in the centre of the room, dropping into the black leather chair in the room and trying the drawers, finding all locked. She doesn't bother trying to pick the locks; instead, she stands and moves around to the front of the desk, pulling out her lighter to give her a better view of what else is inside the office.

I can't tell what she's looking for, but she crosses the room quickly, looking behind the frame of a large landscape portrait before lifting the frame down from the wall.

'Bingo!' she says triumphantly.

As she moves the lighter over the wall, I see there is a metal safe door, no bigger than forty centimetres wide, by twenty tall. A numerical pad and thumbprint sensor reflect the flame's glow.

'Just because he has a safe, doesn't prove anything,' I challenge, but she isn't listening. She's studying the number pad.

'There are ten thousand possible combinations, assuming the passcode is four digits,' she observes, focusing on the pad. 'But there is grease on the numbers four, three, two, and eight, which certainly improves the odds for us.'

I'm about to argue that there are still fifteen possible combinations, assuming she's right that the PIN is only four digits long, but she's already started typing in guesses. I head into the room to try and stop her, which isn't the only mistake I've made all day, but potentially the most costly. Because that's the moment an ear-splitting alarm sounds overhead, and metal shutters drop inside the door and windows, trapping us like sardines in a can.

Chapter Thirty-Three

THEN

Portland, Dorset

Emma kept her eyes on the television as she heard her mum open the front door and immediately huff.

'Mrs Hunter?' the young woman's voice enquired, staring in through the door.

'Yes?' she replied, as if she had no idea who the woman was, nor why she had darkened the doorstep.

'Oh good,' came the reply. 'I wasn't sure if I had found the right house as there's no number on the door.'

Emma had lost count of the number of delivery men and women who'd made similar comments when they'd come searching for the address.

'Well, that one beside us is number thirty-seven,' her mum began, as she always did, 'and the one the other side is number thirty-nine, so obviously we're number thirty-eight. You do count, don't you?'

Emma could only assume her mum didn't realise just how rude this response was. Either that or she simply didn't care.

'Oh yes, of course,' the young woman replied, sounding flustered. 'That's what I assumed, and why I knocked. You were expecting me, weren't you? I know I'm a couple of minutes early, but I figured it was better to be prompt than late.'

Ordinarily, good timekeeping would have won the poor woman a brownie point, but Bronwyn wasn't in a generous mood.

'Yes, yes, of course,' Bronwyn replied, stepping to one side, allowing the young woman to enter so she could get a better look at her under the light beside the front door.

Putting on her glasses, Bronwyn took in the woman's appearance. Long blonde hair, hanging loose, but at least recently cleaned; clear skin and no obvious makeup; the thick coat she was wearing bore a sheepskin lining, which was practical for the cold temperature but unlikely to resist rain.

'How old are you exactly?' Bronwyn asked.

'Nineteen,' she replied evenly. 'I'm just back from university over the summer and looking to earn some money for books.'

'And what are you studying at university?'

'Child psychology, but I'm planning to convert to a PGCE when I graduate.'

Bronwyn wasn't impressed by her credentials, and Emma could tell she was looking for reasons to dismiss the girl and change her mind about going out for the evening. The last thing Emma needed was for her to change her mind about going out, and she quickly sprang from the sofa, introducing herself to the potential babysitter.

'I'm Emma.'

'Hi, Emma,' she responded warmly. 'I'm Paula. It's nice to meet you.'

'I like your hair,' Emma commented.

Paula instantly ran her hand down the locks. 'Thank you. Yours is nice too.'

Bronwyn's shoulders relaxed slightly with the exchange, but that didn't stop her biting the tip of her finger as she once again considered whether she could justify leaving Emma here so that she could attend the appointment she'd been forced to rearrange after John had been admitted to hospital on Saturday.

'Do you have much experience babysitting children?' Bronwyn asked next.

'Oh yes, loads,' Paula replied, meeting her stare. 'I have a younger brother and sister that I regularly watch for my mum and stepdad. I can see you're concerned, Mrs Hunter, but I assure you I know what I'm doing. Your daughter will be perfectly safe with me.'

'It's fine, Mum,' Emma echoed, keen to seal the deal. 'I'll be fine with Paula. You don't need to worry.'

Bronwyn hadn't been keen on the proposed Tuesday evening appointment, and was now regretting agreeing to it. She crossed the room to the sideboard where she scooped up the list she'd spent most of the afternoon writing. Handing it to Paula, she carefully recited each item.

'That's my mobile number at the top. It will be switched on all evening, and you're to call me if you have any questions or worries. The next number is for Emma's dad, but I don't know if his phone will be switched on, as I'm not sure what time he's being discharged from the hospital. He might already be out, but I haven't heard yet. Given his condition, he probably won't be any use, so I'm your best bet. The third number is for my friend Hayley. She lives five minutes away, but has a family of her own. Only phone her if you can't get hold of me for any reason.'

'I'm sure I won't need to phone,' Paula replied evenly, 'but I will keep the list handy. There really is no need for you to worry.'

Bronwyn did look reassured, but pressed on with the list. 'I've left instructions on how to operate the central heating system. I tend to keep the thermostat on twenty-two degrees, but it can be turned up if Emma complains of being cold. I've checked the weather forecast for this evening, and no cold front is expected in Portland tonight; however, it isn't like the BBC weathermen haven't been wrong before.'

'Understood.'

'I've also left instructions about where you will find cups, tea bags, and the kettle. You're welcome to help yourself to any beverages in the fridge, but please do not drink any alcohol. I know there is an open bottle of wine in the door of the fridge, but I will know if any has been—'

'I'm teetotal anyway,' Paula interjected with a smile. 'I have a sort of allergy to alcohol-based drinks, so I tend to avoid them. I promise you, Mrs Hunter, your daughter will be in great hands. I'm a qualified first aider too, and if you want to phone my mum and stepdad to check, I'm happy for you to do so.'

Bronwyn looked down at Emma and then back to Paula, her eyes welling up. 'I'm sorry, it's just I haven't… This will be the first time of me leaving Emma with someone who isn't a relative or at school, so I'm a little nervous.'

Paula didn't seem put off by Bronwyn's neuroses. She scribbled something on the bottom of the list and tore it off, handing it to Bronwyn. 'This is my mobile number. I'm happy if you want to phone and check how things are going once you arrive at your destination. If that will make you feel better, then it's okay.'

Bronwyn clutched the note to her heart. 'Thank you for this.' She turned and lifted her coat from the peg. 'Emma has some homework to complete, and I put her to bed by eight o'clock because it's a school night. I probably won't be back before that, but I will definitely be home before nine.'

'Understood.'

'Emma, be good for Paula while I'm out, won't you?'

Emma mock saluted. 'Of course, Mum. Go out and have some fun. Everything will be fine.'

'Fun is the last thing on the agenda,' Bronwyn said, straightening her coat, but her finger was soon back in her mouth as she looked from one to the other, uncertainty returning and knocking her off balance like one of the large waves that always made the beach look so threatening during storms.

'I'll see you at nine,' Paula offered encouragingly, nodding for Emma to offer something equally supportive.

Emma hugged her mum. 'I'll see you in the morning, Mum. Love you.'

Bronwyn squeezed her tightly. 'I'll check on you as soon as I'm back. You know my number by heart, so if anything is wrong and you need me, you are to use Paula's phone to call me. I mean absolutely *anything*.'

She eventually released her daughter and headed out the

door, with Emma and Paula waving reassuringly until she was out of sight.

'Oh look, *Hollyoaks* is just starting,' Paula commented, closing the door and nodding at the television. Do you fancy watching it with me?'

Emma shook her head, pleased to finally have her mum out of the way and remembering her dad's words in the hospital: *before I moved out, I left something in the garage… I need you to get it for me.*

'Thanks, but I'm going to go and finish my homework in my room. Mum doesn't like me watching *Hollyoaks* anyway.'

'I'm surprised that didn't make the list,' Paula muttered under her breath, before quickly smiling, as she caught herself. 'You're not missing much. Do you need me to make you a drink or snack before you go?'

Emma patted her tummy. 'No, I'm still full from dinner. I have an essay to finish, and would prefer to get it done before I come back out.'

Paula settled onto the sofa. 'Okay, well, I'll be out here if you need anything.'

Emma checked she was watching the screen before making loud stepping noises as she approached her bedroom, leaving the door ajar and counting to sixty in case Paula immediately came to check on her. When she heard no movement, Emma slowly opened the door and crept out, closing her door to again, and tiptoeing towards the back of the house. She'd left the back door unlocked in preparation for this moment, and ever so quietly pulled the handle down, holding her breath as it slowly opened. She didn't immediately step out, once again counting to sixty and straining to hear any movement from Paula. Satisfied that she was now engaged with the television,

Emma squeezed through the small gap, quietly closing the UPVC door behind her.

The bulb in the outdoor security light had blown months ago, and her mum had yet to brave a trip up the ladder to replace it, meaning Emma had to do less sneaking to get to the garage. There was just enough light still in the sky for her to follow the stepping stone path across the lawn. Reaching into the pocket of her jeans, she pulled out the long, rusty key. She'd hidden it earlier, and pushed it into the lock of the weathered wooden door. Before he'd moved out, her dad would remove the door from its hinges on an annual basis, sanding and repainting it before screwing it back in. But it had suffered in the years since he'd left, and was now crumbling with each passing day.

It creaked open, but she was confident Paula wouldn't be able to hear it on the other side of the house. Closing it behind her, she resisted the urge to flick on the light just in case Paula happened to head into the kitchen and glimpse it from the window. Instead, Emma switched on the small night light she'd taken from her bedroom. It cast a dim and eerie glow over the stacked boxes immediately in front of her, and the years of cobwebs that almost looked as though they were bearing the weight of the memories buried within.

The night light's two double-A batteries weren't strong enough to brighten the shadows at the back of the garage, and for the first time Emma questioned whether she was really making the right choice coming in here so late at night. The rational part of her brain told her that she had nothing to fear, that the garage had been locked from both ends, and yet the cynical side of her mind reminded her that Anna had probably been equally naïve when she'd headed to their grandma's that day.

It would be easier for Emma to leave the garage, return to the house and her room, and just pretend none of this had happened. When her dad eventually asked where the case was, she could simply say she'd been unable to find it. He'd have no way of disproving it, but if he was telling the truth, and it really was a present for her mum, her not finding it might be the final nail in the coffin of their marriage. For that reason – and only that reason – she took a deep breath, and stepped around the tower of boxes. Holding the nightlight out in front of her, she peered through half-closed eyes, taking baby steps forwards towards the engulfing shadows, praying the night light would find more power.

The garage had been used for storage, but she couldn't recall her mum coming in here any time in the past year, which suggested that the boxes either held nothing of value, or items too painful to keep close by. Anna's room still remained untouched, but as Emma ran the night light over the scrawled writing on one of the boxes by her feet, she spotted her sister's name. Pausing her search, she crouched down and unfastened the interwoven panels on the top and peered inside.

She was surprised to find two large photo albums, a small round box labelled 'teeth', a christening candle, and a metal tankard inscribed with Anna's name. Appalled by the thought that her mum had been squirrelling away baby teeth under the guise of the tooth fairy, she heaved one of the albums out of the box, and, resting it on the ground, opened it up. She was immediately repelled by the mustiness of the pages, but couldn't help smiling as she saw her sister for the first time in years, albeit much younger than she could recall. There were photographs of Anna as a baby, as a toddler, and then holding baby Emma in her arms with the widest gap-toothed smile. She continued turning the pages, trying to ignore the stabbing in her chest, before returning the album to the box and refastening the panels.

Wiping her eyes with the back of her hand, she coughed as dust tickled her throat, but felt less scared as she moved further through the garage, as if Anna's spirit was there by her side. Locating the shelving unit attached to the wall, she held the light overhead, searching for the small green case her dad had described, but nothing obvious leapt out. He'd mentioned it was hidden, but that didn't mean her mum hadn't already previously found it.

It's on the top shelf, right at the back. You might need to climb up to see it.

If her mum knew that she'd snuck out here and was now considering climbing the shelves, she'd go ballistic, but Emma had made a promise to her dad, and she wasn't prepared to break it. Placing the night light at the highest point she could reach, she gripped the ledge tightly, and stretched her right leg up until her foot rested on the first piece of wood. Hoisting herself up, she made sure to plant her left foot on the same shelf, before lifting her right again and moving it to the next one. It was so dark and dusty up here that it was all she could not to sneeze and alert Paula to the fact that she'd snuck out. Moving up to the next plank, her eyes were now in line with the items up here. She saw a couple of cobweb-covered bricks, a box of galvanised nails, a plastic pot of fence paint, and just behind it a small grass-coloured metal case. She gasped and coughed as the dust tickled her throat and nose again.

Keeping her feet still, and her left hand clinging to the shelf, she reached out and pulled the green case clear of its hiding place. It weighed less than she'd expected and, pulling it clear, she was able to keep hold of it as she carefully lowered herself back to ground level. Reaching for the night light, she ran the beam over the case, studying it for any clues as to what it might contain or how long it had been hidden up there. Had she not climbed, she never would have known it was up there, and, given the height, she doubted her mum would have seen it without a ladder either. But why would her dad have hidden a birthday present in such a small box, and – judging by the rust-covered hinges – such a long time ago?

Her mum's words at the hospital reverberated through her head: *nothing's ever perfectly innocent where you're concerned, John.*

Grasping the case by its sides, she attempted to lift the lid, but the small padlock remained firm. Lifting the box she shook it violently, even allowing it to drop to the floor, hoping the impact would break the case and allow her to look inside. She wouldn't have an issue telling her dad she'd accidentally dropped it and it had opened, but it remained sealed, along with the secret it was protecting.

Conscious that Paula might be tempted to check on her, Emma switched off the night light and returned to the garage door, creaking it open. She locked it behind her before hurrying across the now almost invisible stepping stones. Making it back inside, she tiptoed along the corridor, daring to peek into the living room, and shuddering when she saw Paula was no longer on the sofa. Emma's eyes widened as her imagination immediately played out a scene where Paula had wandered into her room and was waiting for her to return, Bronwyn already on the phone demanding answers.

'Oh, hi, I was just fixing a coffee,' Paula said, her head

popping out from behind the kitchen door. 'Can I get you anything?'

Emma kept the case hidden behind her back, her heart so loud in her chest she was certain her mum would be able to hear it no matter how far she'd ventured.

'No, I'm fine,' Emma managed to croak, the words sticking in her throat.

'How are you getting on with your essay?'

'Nearly done,' Emma lied, willing Paula to disappear back into the kitchen so she could hide the case in her room.

Paula continued to watch her for a moment, before boredom took hold and she ducked back behind the door. Emma didn't wait to count to sixty this time, spinning and sprinting to her room where she buried the case in the bottom of her satchel. She no longer cared what it contained; she just wanted it gone as soon as possible.

Chapter Thirty-Four

NOW

Chichester, West Sussex

'Name?'

The custody sergeant behind the hardened plastic panel must be in his fifties, judging by the grey patches of hair just above his ears, the wrinkled face reminiscent of a dry chamois, and the thin moustache that looks more like a hairy worm. His gruff tone and unforgiving demeanour remind me of an old headmaster I had at school. Back then, I only ever had to see him for positive reasons, but his dour expression and disposition had remained as emotionless as if he had been giving me detention. The irony that the custody sergeant is about to detain me isn't lost.

'Emma Hunter,' I say reluctantly.

In the back of the police car on the way here I had considered whether I should try and come up with a pseudonym to protect my real identity, but it probably wouldn't have taken them long to go through my personal effects and find my driving licence and bank cards.

When the alarm was reset and the metal shutters lifted, I'd half expected to see an angry Ian Beauchamp standing on the other side, rather than three officers in Kevlar pointing automatic weapons at the two of us. The fight had left me instantly, and as soon as they'd barked at us to drop to our knees and put our hands on our heads, I'd obeyed. Anna hadn't tried to fight either, though there'd been more of an air of nonchalance about her submission.

'Don't say anything,' was the only advice she'd offered when the alarm had ceased. A casual, throwaway line in keeping with her previous experience of a similar situation two days before. I remember Oakley and Yates saying Anna (or Kylie as she was back then) refused to comment when interviewed about Tomlinson's shooting.

I never should have followed her in through the gate, and I definitely shouldn't have crawled in through the balcony door. While my motivation was to try and help keep her from getting herself in more trouble, it seems she wasn't so concerned about my wellbeing. I feel like a prize fool for trusting her.

'Do you understand why you've been brought here today?' the custody sergeant asks, his eyes not leaving the screen.

The officer who has her hand on my shoulder has already explained to him that I've been arrested for attempted burglary, and am to be detained while they carry out further investigation and prepare to interview me about the allegation.

'Yes,' I mutter, feeling very sorry for myself, and desperately hoping this is just a nightmare from which I'll wake in a minute.

I was relieved there were no reporters or camera crews outside Beauchamp's house when we were led out with our wrists tightly secured behind our backs. But I doubt my anonymity will remain much longer. At least one of the uniformed officers we passed on the way in here gasped when she saw me, and I wouldn't blame her for cashing in on that sweet titbit of information; probably worth several thousand pounds to the right editor.

'Are there any underlying medical conditions we should be aware of?' the custody sergeant asks, finally looking straight at me, his eyes looking as tired and arid as mine feel.

I shake my head.

'No anxiety, diabetes, respiratory illnesses?'

I shake my head again. 'No.'

'And apart from being here today, how are you feeling?'

I feel like the rug has been pulled from beneath my feet, I don't say. I feel like someone took my dream of finding Anna, turned it on its head, and is now forcing me to wish I hadn't found her. I feel ashamed for being so stupid, for putting my career on the line over something so stupid. I can see my entire life being flushed down the toilet and there's nothing I can do to prevent it. I can hear my father's voice – a prison guard exposed to criminal life for more than twenty years – constantly reminding me to keep my nose clean. How disappointed he would be if he could see Anna and me here now. I can see Jack's face the moment the news is bestowed on him, and how frustrated he'll be that I didn't find a way to contact him the second I found Anna in Alton. I feel like I've let everyone down, and I just want to bury my head between my legs and sob.

I don't say any of these things, just fight to stop my bottom lip from trembling. 'I'm fine.'

The custody sergeant finishes updating his computer file, and then explains that I am now under his care, and that I will be taken to a cell where I will be held until the officers in charge are ready to speak with me again. He tells me my fingerprints will be taken, and I will be asked to give a voluntary DNA swab.

This cannot be happening! They're the only words turning over and over in my mind. I've watched so many real-life documentaries about criminals being arrested and going through these exact steps, and yet most of the time they look so calm and casual. All I want is to reach for my mum and dad and tell them how sorry I am, and for one of them to tell me everything will be okay. But with them both gone that isn't even an option anymore.

I am taken to the cell, like I'm being escorted to a hotel suite by a porter. I'm almost surprised when the woman in the stab-proof vest doesn't proffer her hand for a tip.

'Make yourself comfortable,' she advises. 'Can I get you a drink? Cup of tea or coffee?'

A large glass of Pinot Grigio would be more appropriate to the occasion, but I thank her and order a sweet tea, only because I know it's supposed to be good for shock. I shudder as she closes the door and raises the screen, shutting out the outside world. Is that a sound I'm going to have to grow accustomed to? Being shut in every night?

I can't see any way this ends in anything other than a scrupulous interview, court appearance, and custodial sentence. We were caught red-handed trying to break into Beauchamp's safe, in his private home to which we'd gained unlawful access. Anna's pouch of picks was placed in a clear plastic evidence bag, so there really is no defence for either of us. And worse still – well, worse for us – is that as the police car was driving me from the scene, I saw the campervan surrounded, which means they also discovered Daisy. It's good that she's now safe, but there's every chance I'll also stand accused of conspiring in her abduction or illegal detainment.

I look around the small cell space. A concrete block jutting out from the wall has been lined with a wipe-down mattress and pillow. The place certainly wasn't designed with comfort in mind. I can see there is a small camera housed in the corner of the ceiling pointing down at me; all of my movements are being recorded and documented for posterity. A small gap in the wall leads to a doorless toilet, and I can only hope that there is some kind of mask on the lens so they won't see me totally exposed when I use it.

Presumably they'll allow me to make a phone call at some point, but I don't know who to phone. One call just doesn't seem enough. I suppose I should contact a solicitor for legal advice, but I'm not sure whether Saira Mistry would be able to represent me *and* Anna, or whether she'd even be willing to come down all this way to do so. I want to phone Rachel and explain what happened and where I am so she doesn't worry. I want to phone Maddie and warn her that she will probably have to start fielding calls from journalists about this whole sorry escapade. And I want to phone Jack and apologise for being so stupid, and to ask whether there's anything he can do to soften the blow of the charges I'm facing.

I've just thought: what if I'm not released, and therefore unable to plan or attend Mum's funeral? Imagine the shame of having neither daughter at the funeral because they're both serving custodial sentences. Dad would turn in his grave.

I drop down onto the mattress and stop fighting the pain that's growing in my heart, and then I cry until the tears dry up.

I can't say how long passes before the shutter on the door is slid down and a pair of eyes stare through the gap at me. The door opens a moment later and I see a woman with the words 'Detention Officer' plastered over her uniform.

'You have a visitor,' she says. 'Would you like to follow me?'

I stand and put on my shoes before heading out of the room and following her along the corridor, until we arrive at a brown wooden door. I wipe my face as best I can, but without a mirror and makeup bag, I'm going to look like a panda no matter how much rubbing I do with the sleeves of my jacket.

She opens the door and holds it there so I can enter. I immediately recognise the hunched shoulders and stocky frame of DI Marina Oakley, standing with her back to me against the far wall of the interview suite. The detention officer closes the door behind me.

I'm confused, as I'm sure it isn't common practice for detectives from other forces to be granted access to detainees, certainly not without some kind of explanation. I haven't been advised that this is an interview about my crimes, and the fact that Oakley isn't sitting at the desk ready to start recording the exchange has me rubbing at my temple.

I'm about to ask what's going on when she suddenly turns,

unwilling to mask the despondency in her expression. 'You should sit,' she says.

Against my desire to pace the room, I follow her advice, dropping into the nearest chair – the one traditionally reserved for the interviewer in such occasions.

'What a mess,' she sighs, as she moves closer and slips into the seat across the table from me. 'When I told you to find your sister, I didn't actually think you'd manage it.' She laughs slightly to herself. 'But it seems I should have given you more credit.'

Has she come here to gloat? If so, I'm not in the mood, and would prefer to be sitting in my cell awaiting the inevitable conclusion to this story.

'Daisy is safe and well, by the way,' she adds, 'so I guess I should thank you for that. Apparently, the Beauchamp family are so relieved to have her back in their care and want you to know how much they appreciate what you did for her.'

My brow furrows instantly. 'What I did?'

'Yes. Daisy was interviewed once she'd been examined by the medical team in Southampton, and she gave a statement explaining how you'd found her with Anna, and were unwittingly taken hostage by your sister. Daisy was full of praise for the way in which you selflessly took care of her throughout the horrific ordeal, and how it was you who insisted Anna leave her in the campervan, knowing that she could contact the police once the two of you were gone. She said she owes you her life.'

I blink several times, unable to process the words I'm hearing. I'm about to open my mouth and correct her on what really happened, but something stops me, and I bite my tongue instead.

'It's lucky I received the call from your friend Rachel, explaining how you found Anna in Alton. Unfortunately, you were already gone by the time we got there, so then it was just a matter of waiting for you to resurface. Daisy's statement corroborates Anna's account of what happened, and how she forced you to come along with her as she broke into Ian Beauchamp's house in an effort to steal jewellery that Daisy had led her to believe was stashed in the safe, knowing that the alarm system would engage, trapping the two of you inside.'

I can't believe what I'm hearing, nor how Anna and Daisy have managed to concoct such a story when they can't have spoken since we left her in the campervan. The only conclusion I can draw is that they fabricated this account prior to my arrival in Alton, but I don't know how they could have foreseen this is how things would turn out.

'You're to be de-arrested momentarily, but I just wanted to personally thank you for helping us get Daisy back. Even though it wasn't my case, I felt personally responsible as we were the ones who allowed Anna out on bail in the first place.'

'She didn't kill him,' I say earnestly. 'She told me he was killed by someone else.'

Oakley strains a smile and holds up her hand to cut me off. 'Thank you for everything you've done today, Miss Hunter. I'm sure without your intervention things might have gone a lot differently and both Daisy *and* your sister owe you a debt of gratitude.'

I feel I need to correct her, and to advise her that Anna's and Daisy's accounts aren't wholly accurate, but as I'm starting to process their motivation for doing what they've done, the only conclusion I can draw is that they want me out so that I can help expose Ian Beauchamp for his crimes, though how

I'm supposed to do that without the hard drive of files they spoke about is beyond me.

'There's something else I feel you should know. I considered telling you when we first met. At the time I wasn't sure it was in your best interests, but now I feel like it might help put all of this mess into a bit of context. Are you aware of Anna's recent medical history?'

I frown at the question. 'No, how would I be?'

'So she didn't choose to mention her referrals for mental health issues, nor the name of the prescribed medication she's taking?'

Given everything she's been through, it doesn't surprise me that she's receiving support to deal with matters, but I shake my head.

'Sertraline is a strong SSRI used in the treatment of anxiety, but it can have side effects including paranoia, anger management issues, and, in some, mild hallucinations.'

I think back to the limited conversation we had in the front of the campervan, but at no point did it feel like Anna wasn't in full control of her faculties.

'How do you know all this?' I ask, now not certain whether I can totally trust Oakley's motivation for coming to speak with me. Maybe I'm the one now being overly paranoid.

'When she was arrested at Sir Anthony Tomlinson's house, the bottle of pills was on her person. The label on the bottle was in the name of Kylie Shakespeare, and after some further digging, it appears she has been living under that identity for a number of years. She was registered at a clinic not far from Reading in Berkshire.'

It feels like I'm only now being informed about this as a means of influencing how much credence I give to my sister's story, but my brain is so tired, I don't have the strength to argue.

'What happens next?' I ask, trying to keep the obvious relief from my voice.

'There are a few formalities to go through. You'll be asked to make a statement confirming what happened today, but then you'll be free to go home.'

'And Anna?'

'I don't know for certain, but I imagine she'll face a bail hearing in the morning, and will probably be remanded in custody for the foreseeable future.' She pauses and rests one of her hands on mine on the table. 'You shouldn't feel guilty about any of this. You did your best to find her, but you weren't to know what life choices she'd decided to make.'

She's wrong about Anna, but I'll be wasting my breath trying to convince her otherwise.

'Do you have any means of getting home?' she asks next.

I'm about to say I could phone Rachel, but by the time she's driven all the way here, and then back again, it would be just as quick to take a taxi and train.

'I don't mind driving you back to Weymouth, if that would help? I'm unlikely to be able to speak to Anna again about Tomlinson's murder until the morning, so I'm at a bit of a loose end until then.'

My instinct is to decline the offer, as I don't want to put her out, but maybe the journey will allow me to convince her of Anna's innocence. Yet, once we're in the warm car, and her radio is playing classical music, it's only a few minutes until I fall fast asleep, waking as she kills the engine outside my flat.

Thanking her for the lift, I bail out of the car and head inside, trying to stay quiet so as not to wake Rachel, but I shouldn't be surprised to find she is still awake and wearing a hole in the carpet. The moment I'm through the door, she is at my side, throwing her arms around my shoulders.

'Oh, thank God. I was terrified about what might happen to you. Even when Oakley said she'd get you out, I wasn't totally convinced.'

I want to tell her everything, and yet the relief in my system is just too great and I crumple into her arms, burying my head in her shoulder. The feel of her hand rubbing my back reminds me of how close I came to losing everything.

'I've been so worried,' I hear her mutter, before she pulls away slightly. 'Oh, but I got you a present.'

She moves away and searches for something on my desk, before producing a mobile phone that she hands over. 'It's got a temporary SIM card in it until you speak to your provider and have them send you a new one out. I've input my number, Jack's number, and Maddie's numbers, and I've messaged the two of them to let them know they can reach you on this until further notice. That way, if you tear off on another hare-brained scheme, at least I'll be able to get hold of you.'

I don't know what to say. It's such a simple gift, but it means so much that she'd go to that much effort for me. Fresh tears leak out, and I hug her again. Turning the phone over in my hands, I allow her to explain its basic functions, and she shows me how to set my security so that my thumbprint can unlock it. Maddie will be so proud when she sees me embracing technology for a change.

'Oh, and before I forget,' Rachel adds, 'there's an answerphone message for you from some guy.'

'Ah, that's probably Rick,' I conclude. 'Did he say he'd recovered my old phone?'

Rachel frowns. 'No, I don't think that's what he said his name was. He said he's a private investigator and that it has something to do with your mum. I called him back, but he wouldn't give me any further information. He said he'll phone again to make you an appointment.'

I'm too exhausted to consider why a private investigator would want to speak to me about my mum, and I retire to bed, my eyes closing the second my head hits the pillow.

Chapter Thirty-Five

THEN

Swanage, Dorset

Emma clutched the satchel tightly on her lap as the bus trundled along the road, bouncing, and causing her knee to knock against her mum's. Despite packing the small green case at the very bottom of the satchel, she was certain her mum would work out what she'd taken. She'd kept it hidden under her bed all week, checking it was there every day when she returned from school. To now be so close to Swanage… If her deceit was discovered now, she would have wasted the week walking on eggshells and being on her best behaviour.

'Your father has asked to see you this weekend,' her mum had declared matter-of-factly on Wednesday after school, as if it was odd for a father to want to spend any time with his offspring. 'It's his fault he couldn't have you over last weekend, so I'm within my rights to refuse him. What do *you* want to do?'

Since their separation, neither parent had asked Emma to

outright choose between them, but the question had sounded loaded. She hadn't wanted to upset her mum, but her paranoia about the green case had driven her response.

'I'd like to see him too. I want to check he's okay after what happened,' she had quickly added, to avoid any potential fallout.

Her mum had agreed to phone him and make the necessary arrangements, before adding that he would probably be in no condition to do anything too strenuous. Emma hadn't told her that he rarely strayed from the bedsit when she visited anyway. But all week she'd kept waiting for her mum to change her mind and to say that she didn't want Emma to go, or that it wasn't convenient. Even that morning, she'd half expected to hear that something last-minute had cropped up and the visit would be delayed until the end of the month.

'Why must you clutch the bag so tightly?' Bronwyn asked now as the bus flew too fast over a speed bump. 'Why not put it on the floor between your legs?'

Emma didn't respond, keeping her arms wrapped around the bag on her lap. In truth, because the case was at the very bottom of her bag, she was concerned that her mum would recognise the sound of metal if it were to bash against the bus's floor. She couldn't wait to hop down off her seat and hurry to the exit as the bus pulled over at the regular bus stop, and she spotted her dad's yellowing face, as he sat and waited inside the shelter.

Bronwyn followed her excitable daughter off the bus, asking the driver to wait while she said goodbye to Emma.

'I'll be back here at five,' she hollered over the clackety-clack sound of the idling engine. 'If there are any problems, call me.'

John's eyes hadn't left the navy-blue satchel in his daughter's arms, but he raised his hand and waved in acknowledgement. The two of them remained inside the shelter until the bus had pulled away.

'How did you get on?' he asked.

Emma nodded eagerly, lowering the satchel and fiddling the drawstring open. 'It was where you said.'

He put his hand over hers, stopping her fiddling. 'Don't get it out yet. Not here. We'll go for some lunch, and then you can show me when we get back to my place. Okay?'

She didn't like the shifty way he was tottering from one foot to the other, his eyes scanning the street immediately in front of them, as if he was half expecting a swarm of police officers to appear from nowhere and cart them both off.

Tightening the drawstring, she held the satchel out to him. 'Do you want to carry it? It's heavy.'

He shook his head, feeling for the satchel's two straps, before feeding one over her left arm, and the other over her right. 'Put it over your back like this, and it won't be so bad. You can take it off when we get to the restaurant.'

She didn't argue, though was more than a little put out that she seemed to be the one who'd gone to the most effort, and he hadn't even thanked her yet.

'What do you fancy for lunch?' he asked, his eyes not leaving the satchel. 'Wimpy like usual, or perhaps some fish and chips? I know a great place by the water. You like scampi, don't you?'

She nodded.

'They do a great portion of scampi and chips for kids your age. Includes a free drink. What do you say?'

She smiled and accepted his hand when he held it out, and

then the two of them moved off together. They walked through the town centre, following the bend around to the left, and into the small square, lined with three different fish and chip outlets, but only one with seating. He held the door open for her, and they waited to be seated, the smell of frying batter and fresh fish feeding their appetites. The waiter offered them a table by the window, but Emma's dad insisted they be seated upstairs, where it would be quieter, or so he claimed.

The waitress showed them to a table for two, but her dad declined it, asking whether they could be seated at the larger table with four chairs overlooking the sea. The waitress looked uncertain, but acquiesced when John told her it was a special occasion.

'But it isn't my birthday,' Emma whispered to him once they'd been handed their menus.

He simply put a finger to his lips and winked. She winked back and scanned the menu, finding the children's meals, before deciding that the scampi and chips was the most appetising option.

'We probably should talk about your birthday soon, shouldn't we?' her dad said, once their orders had been taken and their menus collected. 'It's a big one this year, isn't it?'

She couldn't work out whether he was gently teasing her, or trying to cover for the fact he couldn't actually remember her age.

'Go on,' he encouraged, 'if you could choose anything – no matter the cost – what would it be?'

She couldn't tell him what she longed for more than anything else, as she knew it was a gift beyond cost; no amount of money or desire could bring Anna home, and to mention her name now would quickly sour his mood.

'My very own library,' she answered after a moment.

He rolled his eyes playfully. 'I should have known your dream gift would involve books somehow.' He straightened in his chair before leaning in closer. 'You haven't had it easy, Emma, and I know I'm partly to blame for that. It might be that I have a bit of money coming my way in the not too distant future, and I'd like to spend it on getting you something really special. God knows, you deserve to be treated better than you have been.'

She opened her mouth to object, but he continued speaking before she had the chance.

'I haven't been the dad I wanted to be, and it's about time I did something about it.'

She reached across the table, and rested her hand on his. 'You're too hard on yourself, Dad. I haven't had a bad life. There are plenty more people out there who've had tougher upbringings than me. I don't need some elaborate gift to know that you and Mum love me. If you're about to win some money then you shouldn't waste it on buying me a present I'll ultimately forget. I'd far rather you use it to get yourself back on your feet, or donate it to charity. I promise you I have everything I need.'

She covered her mouth as she saw his eyes quickly filling. She hadn't meant to speak out of turn and upset him. She'd never seen him cry, even when Anna hadn't come home. She was certain she'd heard him sobbing late at night when she should have been asleep, but he'd never allowed his emotions to come to the surface in front of her.

'I'm sorry, Dad,' she offered quickly, but he blinked away the tears.

'How did I get so lucky?' he croaked, dabbing his eyes with

the paper napkin that his cutlery had been resting on. 'You're such a sweet girl, and I don't know where you get that from. It certainly isn't me.'

'You're not angry with me?'

'Oh God, no. How could I be angry? These are happy tears, Emma; proud tears. You're the most kind, caring, and resilient person I know. I can't tell you how lucky I feel to have been a part of your life.'

Emma felt her cheeks flush and quickly looked away, pleased when the waitress appeared at the side of the table and lowered their drinks. She reached for the thin glass of lemonade and put the straw between her lips. Her dad left his pint of beer where it was.

'I still remember the moment when the doctors handed you over to me, and I couldn't believe how little you weighed.' He paused and dabbed at his eyes again, before dropping the napkin on the table. 'I made a promise that I would do everything I could to protect you no matter what, but I haven't made sure you and your sister were my number-one priority, and I'm sorry.'

Emma lowered her glass, her cheeks burning even brighter. 'It's okay, Dad, you don't need to apologise.'

'Yes, I do, Emma, because I shouldn't have allowed things to get so... complicated. I'm going to do whatever it takes to fix things, I promise.'

Neither spoke again until the food arrived, and even then conversation was stilted. He asked how she was getting on at school, what her favourite subjects were, whether she hated PE as much as he had, and what kind of career she wanted to pursue when she was older.

'So you're planning to go to university one day?' he asked as they neared the bedsit after lunch.

'Maybe. I want to write, but I don't know whether I'd have what it takes to write a book.'

'I think you'd be surprised,' he said, placing an arm around her shoulders. 'If you were to ask me – and I'll admit to more than a little bias – I'd say you could do anything you put your mind to. So you should think long and hard about what industry you want to go into, because whatever it is, those who see you in action won't know what's hit them.'

She huffed excitedly and hurried along the road when she spotted the black and ginger cat with two white paws waiting for her on the kerb.

'Oh, it looks like your friend has stopped by to say hi,' her dad said, joining her on the pavement and stooping to stroke the top of the stray's head.

'Can we take her inside?' Emma asked, her voice full of hope. 'Just until it's time to go.'

Her dad studied her for a long moment, before chuckling. 'Well, I suppose I did say you could have whatever you wanted, and if that's a few hours playing with a cat, then how can I say no?'

Emma's eyes widened and she quickly whispered into the cat's ear, explaining that she could come inside where it was warm and dry for a few hours. When she stood and beckoned, the cat willingly followed them to the front door, but something wasn't right.

John held his arm out, stopping Emma proceeding. The green door was hanging from its hinges. 'Wait here,' he said, lifting the door out of his way.

Emma had never witnessed a burglary, but knew enough to recognise that a door kicked in was a sign of danger.

'Wait, Dad, don't go in. They could still be inside.'

He waved away her concern, stepping in through the doorway and flipping on the light in the main room.

'Bastards,' he muttered under his breath, before turning back to Emma and offering an apologetic shrug.

'I won't tell Mum,' Emma reassured him, stepping onto the inside doormat and gasping when she saw the state of the room.

'Don't come any further,' he warned, 'there might be broken glass. I think we'll have to go somewhere else. I'll get this all cleaned up once I've dropped you with your mum.'

'I don't mind waiting while you phone the police,' she said, placing her hand into his.

'There's no point in phoning the police,' he replied. 'They didn't find what they were looking for.' His eyes fell on the satchel. 'I think it's time for you to give me that case.'

She released her grip on his hand and slid the satchel from her shoulders, releasing the drawstring, and holding it open for him to extract the case.

'And your mum has no idea you took it?'

She shook her head.

'Good girl.'

He scanned the room with his eyes, heading into the open-plan kitchen and dragging the hob-oven across the tiles, until it jutted out at an angle. Emma strained to see what he was doing, but then spotted the small square hole that had been chipped away in the wall, into which he now pushed the case. The hob-oven made an awful squawking noise, as he dragged it back into place.

'There, it should be safe there until I get back. They won't return today.'

What's in the case, Dad? she wanted to ask, but the words couldn't get past the terror bulging in her throat. She also wanted to ask whether the burglary was related to the contents of the case, but deep down she already knew the answer.

'Come on,' he said, holding out his hand for her to take, and then moving her back towards the broken front door. 'It's almost time for us to go and meet your mum anyway. We'll take the scenic route—'

But he didn't finish the sentence as a screech of tyres outside was followed by the sound of smashing glass. Emma instinctively ducked and hid behind the armchair, as her dad stumbled into the room, throwing himself in front of her. An engine revved just beyond the window outside before speeding away, leaving them both on the floor, staring at the large jagged rock in the middle of the floor. Emma was first on her feet, running over to the rock and peeling the elastic band from it, and handing her dad the note.

She looked at him studying the words. 'What does it mean, Dad? What happens in two days?'

He didn't respond initially. Blinking back tears he pulled her closer and kissed the top of her head. 'I won't let anything happen to you or your mother. I know what I need to do.'

Chapter Thirty-Six

NOW

Weymouth, Dorset

I must have slept through the night totally undisturbed, as I'm woozy when I wake. For a split second I think I'm still in that prison cell, until my eyes adjust and I see Rachel carrying a tray of fresh toast and coffee into the room.

'Lucky you've woken,' she says with a wry smile, 'as I was about to fetch a ladle of water to tip over your head. Welcome back to the land of the living. How are you feeling?'

I sit up as she passes me the tray and, stifling a yawn, I thank her. 'Glad to be home. You didn't need to fix me breakfast in bed.'

'I know, but I woke up an hour ago and thought you might be in need of refreshment.'

'What time is it?' I ask.

'Just before nine, but I figured you could do with the extra sleep. I decided to get up and make a start on writing the piece about Daisy. I'm a bit disappointed not to get the exclusive story of her being found and returned – that's all over the breakfast news – but have drafted something I wanted to run past you. All the reports I've seen this morning name Anna specifically, but nobody has formally stated that she's your sister. I don't want to put you in an awkward position, but—'

'It's okay,' I interrupt. 'The world will find out she's my sister soon enough, so if it will help earn you a bit of kudos to announce it first, then I'd rather get something positive out of it. Have they mentioned anything else about her return yet?'

'No, the details seem to be hazy at best. They've said she was found after she was left in a campervan and able to phone police to rescue her. They've said Anna is helping them with their enquiries, but haven't confirmed her arrest as yet.'

'Then you should break the news. If it helps you get the page hits to secure you a slightly more permanent position, then go for it.'

'You should probably read it first, before I submit it.'

I take a bite of the toast, and offer her the other half of the slice. 'I trust you, Rach. I know you wouldn't write anything to deliberately hurt me or jeopardise things. Go ahead and send it, and then you can help me figure out why Anna left Daisy with a phone to report her whereabouts. I couldn't concentrate last night, but now I can't stop thinking that it wasn't an accident. The fact that Anna and Daisy had concocted a story to ensure I got out must mean something, but I just can't figure it out yet.'

Rachel finishes her toast. 'Happy to play Watson to your Holmes once again. Let me go and send the article, and then we can make a start. Oh, and don't forget, that private investigator might phone back today to make that appointment with you. He said his premises are just outside Wareham, but I don't mind driving you.'

She leaves the room and I turn on the new phone she bought, instantly receiving messages from Maddie and Jack. Maddie's is just a confirmation message that all the legal wrangling over *Trafficked* is complete and the hardbacks are due to hit shelves in under five weeks. I must remember to get hold of Aurélie and thank her for squaring everything with her politically minded father. I know he was applying pressure to have the ending rewritten, but we appear to have won the day.

Jack's message sounds more anxious, especially as he has also left a voicemail overnight, advising me about Anna's arrest, and checking if I was aware. I'm all set to phone and update him on yesterday's events when I hear knocking at my front door.

'Do you want me to get it?' I hear Rachel call out, but I'm already on my feet and slipping on my dressing gown as I pass her on the way to the door.

I'm assuming it's going to be either Rick with an update on my stolen phone, or a postman with a parcel that won't fit through my letter box, but I choke on my own spittle when I see the white hair and rosy cheeks of the man on my doorstep. He is wearing a tailored grey coat over a pinstripe suit, a striped tie, and a white shirt. My mouth opens, aghast, but no words emerge.

'Emma Hunter? Please allow me to introduce myself. My name is Ian Beauchamp, and I wanted to personally stop by to thank you enormously for helping oversee the safe return of my dear niece.'

I still don't know what to say; my mind is leaping from one

conclusion to another, and I can't pick a clear course through. On the one hand, I don't want him anywhere near me, based on what Anna and Daisy said about him. But then again, I don't know whether I can wholly trust what Anna and Daisy said about him, particularly given my sister's current prescription regime and mental health concerns. Could he just be an innocent bystander in all of this? After all, she had thought Tomlinson was directly involved with the ring, until changing her mind.

'I must apologise for calling around unannounced,' he continues, signalling to the suited chauffeur standing in front of the long black Mercedes, which is blocking Rachel's car in. 'I was told about what you did to track down Daisy and keep her safe until the police arrived, and I just wanted to show my appreciation.'

The chauffeur appears at his side, carrying an enormous bunch of flowers and a box marked Moet et Chandon.

'I know these don't do nearly enough to reflect my appreciation, but I hope you will accept them regardless.'

He seems genuinely sweet, and there is a kindness to his eyes that I didn't expect to see. I know appearances can be deceptive, a lesson I learned only too well with Aurélie, but I can't leave him on the doorstep, so I accept the gifts and allow him to enter. I don't think I'd be so brave if Rachel weren't inside with me.

'Thank you,' he says, rubbing his gloved hands together, as if he's just stepped out of a snow blizzard.

I show him to the living room, which is barely half the size of the office Anna and I were trapped in last night. I can't help wondering how much he really knows about last night. Presumably he will have been alerted to the fact that Anna and

I had triggered the alarm on the safe, but there isn't anything in his demeanour to suggest he's aware of my complicity in the break-in. It troubles me that he knows my address, and that he'd have the audacity to come here in person if he truly was guilty of the things Daisy accused him of.

'How is Daisy today?' I ask, sitting on the sofa, allowing him the armchair.

He too sits. 'Slept like a baby from all accounts, the poor thing. But she was keen to return to school this morning, despite her guardian's suggestion to stay off, given the media interest in her story.'

I can only assume she's told her family the same tale she spun for the police, but I still can't get over what he's hoping to achieve by coming here today. If he wanted to give me flowers and champagne, he could have had them delivered.

'You're a writer, or so I understand?' he says next, his eyes casually taking in the small space.

'That's correct,' I respond. 'Well, I'm more of an investigative journalist, but have produced accounts of my work in novel form.'

His gaze meets mine, and he smiles warmly again. I can't say why, but my nerves are on edge, and there's something I simply don't trust about this man.

'It truly is a fine skill to have. Writing, I mean. I've had publishers chasing me to produce my memoirs, but I just don't have the discipline to sit and write. I have such admiration for those who can.'

All this positivity and schmaltz is making me feel nauseous, but I remain gracious, trying to play my cards close to my chest.

'Well, it pays the bills,' I self-deprecate. 'Have you travelled far today?'

'We were in Southampton – my wife and I, that is – having been waiting for news on Daisy.' He stands suddenly. 'We're due back in London this afternoon, so I won't take up any more of your time.'

I stand too, tightening the belt around my dressing gown, ready to show him to the door, but he takes a step forward and thrusts out his hand, which I nervously shake.

'If there's anything I can do for you in return for your endeavours, then please get in touch. A donation to the charity of your choice perhaps? Think about it, and if there's anything I can do, you've only to say.'

He promptly moves to the door and opens it himself, signalling for the chauffeur to open his door without turning back to say anything further. I remain on the doorstep, waving as the car pulls away, before closing the door and returning to the living room.

Rachel appears from behind the bathroom door a minute later. 'Who was at the door? Delivery?'

I don't respond, slowly playing the scene through my head once more. I don't understand why he went out of his way to drive ninety minutes down the road to deliver flowers and then immediately return. It's a kind gesture, and maybe that's just in his nature to be that way, but I'm not convinced. I know my own thoughts are sounding as paranoid as Anna, but I can't help thinking this morning's charade was nothing more than him testing the water to see how much I know about his potential involvement with the ring. Maybe he was hoping that turning up unannounced would catch me on the back foot and I'd accuse him outright. Or maybe it was his subtle way of telling me they know where I live.

I wish I could just see what's really going on here, but before I can face Rachel again, there is a second knocking at my door, and part of me isn't entirely surprised to see Daisy Beauchamp beneath a baseball cap.

'We need to talk,' she says.

Chapter Thirty-Seven

THEN

Portland, Dorset

The moment Emma stepped out through the school gates, she knew something wasn't right.

'Auntie Hayley?' Emma frowned, approaching the woman whose eyes were puffy behind her thick-rimmed glasses. 'What's going on? Where's Mum?'

Hayley didn't respond at first, her lips straining as she resisted their tremble. 'She's at my house, love.'

In the years and months since Anna had disappeared, one thing had been constant: her mum collecting her from school. It had even become a cause for resentment. Emma had lost track of the number of times she'd asked whether she could walk home with her friends, or at the very least that her mum wait further along the road, rather than waiting in the playground like the mums of the children in Year 3. It was embarrassing to be the only student collected from the playground.

At least Hayley had waited at the school gate, but the pain and upset on her face was gaining odd looks from the other parents standing nearby.

'Why's Mum at your house? Why isn't she here?'

Emma thought back to the morning, trying to recall whether her mum had said her best friend Hayley would be collecting her instead, but there'd been no mention of a change in plans. Even if something had come up last minute, Bronwyn wouldn't have allowed it to stop her collecting Emma from school. She was obsessive about knowing where Emma was at all times of the day, and the only time she would ease up was when Emma was in school or with her dad. Even then she had to be the one to drop and collect Emma. It was as if she feared Emma following in Anna's footsteps if given even a few minutes of freedom.

Hayley's lips wobbled again, and the tears in her eyes were magnified by the lenses covering them. It didn't take a rocket scientist to work out that something was very badly wrong.

'I'm not going anywhere until you tell me why Mum isn't here,' Emma said, planting her feet, her overactive imagination already conjuring up worst-case scenarios.

'Sh-she had some bad news, that's all. Sh-she asked if I would collect you and bring you back to mine.'

More of the parents were starting to stare at the two of them and, hating being the centre of attention, Emma reluctantly eased her stance. It wasn't like Auntie Hayley was a stranger. She wasn't an official auntie, but that was how Emma's mum always referred to her, and Emma had seen enough of the two of them together to know she didn't represent any kind of danger.

She followed Hayley along the grass verge, the two of them

walking in silence, Hayley struggling to keep her emotions at bay. They stopped at her car – a silver Ford Fiesta – and Emma waited for Hayley to get in and lean across to pull up the locking mechanism.

'Oh, I don't have a child seat,' she said. 'Oh God, I didn't think… Maybe we'll have to leave the car and get a taxi…' She looked as though she was about to release a tidal wave of sobbing.

Emma clambered in, and pulled the door closed. 'I'm sure it'll be fine. Just drive slowly, and I'll sit up straight.'

Hayley's face brightened momentarily; she quickly nodded and fastened her belt, helping Emma to do hers. She started the engine and pulled forward, narrowly avoiding a Mercedes coming the other way. Emma braced herself for impact, but the Mercedes managed to swerve and avoid them, sounding a blare of its horn. They were on the receiving end of an angry glare from the driver, whom Emma recognised as Cindy's dad.

Hayley allowed the car to roll back to its space at the kerbside, before crumpling onto the rim of the steering wheel, her face buried in her arms and her shoulders rocking as she sobbed long and hard.

Emma's overactive imagination was playing havoc with her nervous system. For the bad news to have upset fun-loving and easy-going Auntie Hayley this much, it had to be catastrophic. A conveyor belt of possible causes moved swiftly through Emma's mind, each slightly worse than the previous. And then her mind focused on one scenario that terrified her more than anything else: it had to be about Anna.

Since Anna's disappearance, their mum had ploughed all of her free time and energy into searching for her: time spent researching other missing-children stories; weekends spent handing out flyers to members of the public in Portland and Weymouth, and other neighbouring towns in Dorset; hours spent writing to MPs and local police authorities, begging them not to give up on Anna's case. More than three years' effort, ignoring the cynics who said she was already dead. To learn that all that struggle had been wasted was the only thing that would have kept Bronwyn from coming to collect Emma from school, and the only thing that could have resulted in Hayley being inconsolable at the wheel.

'Please don't cry, Auntie Hayley,' Emma tried, gently rubbing her hand across the older woman's back, and feeling the sting of tears biting at her own eyelids. 'Please just tell me what's happened. I'm a brave girl; I can take it.'

Emma couldn't believe the words tumbling from her mouth, but her grandma had always said that when receiving bad news it was better just to rip off the plaster, and hear it as soon as possible.

'Only once you know what has to be accepted can you figure out how to deal with it,' she would have said if she were with them in the car now.

Emma had been devastated the day her mum and dad had broken the news that Grandma had passed away in her sleep. She'd overheard her mum telling Hayley that Grandma had died of a broken heart, following Anna's disappearance. Even though her grandma had no involvement in what had happened, she'd blamed herself for Anna not making it to her house.

'I should never have encouraged her to come alone,' she'd said to Mum when they hadn't known Emma was listening in.

'Please, Auntie Hayley,' Emma tried again, 'tell me what's going on.'

Hayley started at the sound of Emma's voice, and it seemed to be the impetus she needed to push herself up off the steering wheel and quickly dry her face with the sleeves of her woollen jumper.

'I'm sorry,' she muttered over and over. 'What must you think of me? I'm supposed to be setting a good example. I'm sorry, Emma.'

It didn't bother Emma that Hayley had cried in front of her, but she wasn't happy at her lack of information.

Putting the car in gear once more, this time Hayley checked both ways to make sure there were no cars coming before pulling away from the kerb. They'd been sitting in the car for so long that most of the school traffic had already moved away from them, and they didn't see another moving vehicle until they approached the traffic lights at the bottom of the hill. Emma continued to watch her, but Hayley looked as though she was deliberately avoiding making eye contact, on the assumption that she wouldn't have to speak to Emma if she didn't acknowledge she was even in the car.

'Let's have some music,' she said, fiddling with the dial of her radio, just as the news bulletin was finishing.

'And in local news, police called to HMP Portland in the early hours of this morning are—'

Hayley slammed her hand against the stereo, switching it off. She glanced nervously in Emma's direction, before quickly focusing back on the road as the traffic lights transitioned to green.

A fresh item appeared on the conveyor belt in Emma's mind, and her palms became clammy instantly.

What does it mean, Dad? What happens in two days?

She pictured the look of fear in his eyes as she'd asked the question, the shards of glass on the carpet from the broken window reflecting sunlight back on his face like a chandelier. He hadn't answered, claiming he had no idea why anyone had targeted his home with such a message fastened to a brick, and even tried to claim they'd probably targeted the wrong house. Emma hadn't believed him then, and now all the pieces of the jigsaw were starting to hover in the air before her eyes.

The guy in the white Adidas tracksuit top with black wavy lines, who'd seemed to be threatening her dad in some way; the apparent riot at the prison that had ended with her dad bearing a scar to his neck; the burglary at the bedsit; the green case. It all had to be connected, and now the police had been called to the prison. Emma wouldn't have thought anything of the news bulletin if it weren't for Hayley's determination to shut it off before Emma heard the full report.

Her mum's words now played through her mind on a loop: *nothing's ever perfectly innocent where you're concerned, John.*

He'd told her not to mention the green case to her mum, and he'd refused to phone the police when his home was burgled. What had he got himself mixed up in that now had the police visiting him at work? Had they arrested him? Was that why her mum had stayed away from the school and Hayley had come instead?

And if he had been arrested for whatever that green case represented, did that mean she was in trouble too? Handling stolen goods was a crime; they'd learned that at school when a uniformed police officer had talked to them at assembly earlier in the year. Her tummy felt uneasy, and the clamminess had now spread to her neck. The panic only worsened when she saw the blue and luminous yellow chequered pattern on the police car parked two doors away from Hayley's house.

'Your mum's waiting for you inside,' Hayley said, killing the engine, but making no effort to exit the car.

'Aren't you coming in?' Emma asked, unstrapping her belt.

Hayley shook her head, but couldn't speak as her eyes filled in an instant.

Emma's breathing was shallow, and bile bubbled in the back of her throat as she climbed out of the car and moved towards the uPVC door, pulling down the handle, and stepping through. She took one final glance back at Hayley, whose head was buried in the palms of her hands. A seagull squawked somewhere overhead as if trying to warn Emma not to proceed.

Taking a deep breath, Emma hurried along the hallway, finding her mum huddled up on the three-seat sofa in the bay window. Her eyes were red raw, and the tissue she was clutching was soaked through. She looked up as Emma fell into her side.

'What's happened, Mum?'

Emma avoided looking at the policewoman who was seated in the armchair, a cup and saucer in her hands.

Bronwyn took a long, hard look at her daughter, using both hands to brush the hair away from her face, and then to just gently hold her face. 'I'm so sorry, my darling. It's your dad… He's… He's died.'

Emma blinked over and over again, her brain unable to process the words. It was as if her mum had got the script wrong. She was supposed to say he'd been arrested for doing something wrong, something involving that infernal green case!

'Did you hear what I said, Emma?' her mum asked gently, her eyes glassy.

Emma's internal voice was screaming and yelling, telling her she'd got it wrong, but the message hadn't spread to her face, as she reacted unexpectedly: she laughed.

'This isn't a joke, Emma,' her mum said, barely keeping her face from scrunching in on itself. 'He's died.'

The internal voice took control of Emma's body, but rather than erupting in the shower of anger and denial, it dragged her up from the sofa, sending her satchel crashing to the laminate flooring. Before she knew it, she was through the hallway, out of the door, and tearing across the road, not caring what others had to do to avoid her. Her feet hit the sand a moment later, and her arms pumped and legs bounced as she thundered across the beach, not wanting to look backwards, desperate to put as much distance as possible between herself and the news she refused to accept.

Chapter Thirty-Eight

NOW

Weymouth, Dorset

Daisy doesn't wait to be invited in. Instead, she pulls the baseball cap lower over her eyes and barges past Rachel and me, and into the living room. She proceeds to close the curtains Rachel has not long opened, thrusting the room into darkness.

Turning on the overhead light, I join her on the sofa. 'Daisy, what on earth are you doing here in Weymouth? Your great-uncle was just here.'

'He's many things, but I wouldn't describe him as great. And yes, I know he was just here; why do you think I waited until now to knock on your door?'

She's speaking quickly, there is a shine to her cheeks, and her fingerless gloved hands are fidgeting rapidly. She's either nervous about being here, or perhaps suffering similar withdrawal symptoms to Anna's yesterday.

'Well, how did you get here?' I ask next, suddenly

conscious that if DI Oakley or even Jack turned up here, I'd have a helluva lot of explaining to do.

'I pretended to go to school,' she begins, wiping grubby fingers across her chin, 'but then caught a train down here. I had a change of clothes in my bag,' she says, removing the sports bag from her shoulders, and sliding the strap to the floor, 'and now my uniform's in here.'

'But you shouldn't be here, Daisy. What if the school contacts your guardian or uncle?'

'Relax,' she says, breathing slowly for the first time since she arrived. 'School thinks I'm taking a few days to recover… It's only my guardian who thinks I've gone back to school.'

She lifts the peak of the cap so I can see her eyes better, but I don't share her cheeky grin.

Rachel is watching from the other side of the room, and I'm not entirely sure Daisy has spotted her there, until she looks directly at Rachel, and nods.

'What are you doing here, Daisy?' Rachel tries this time.

Daisy opens the sports bag between her legs and pushes clothes to one side, until her fingers tighten over the edge of something which she then proceeds to grapple out. A glossy box of black plastic peeks out of the bag, and as she continues to pull, a large square of plastic emerges in her hands. She looks up at me before handing over the external hard drive, and then extracts a black power cable and USB cable from her bag.

'Here,' she says, 'you need to plug these into your laptop.'

I accept the cable and study the hard drive she's handed over. I plug in the cables, before carrying them over and attaching them to my charging laptop. Switching on the screen, I allow the device to download software, before a window opens on the screen. I already know what I'm staring at before the filenames begin to sort on the screen.

'How did you get hold of these files?' I ask, mesmerised as the screen fills.

'I wasn't sure how much Kylie would tell you last night,' she begins, 'but I'm guessing by the looks on your faces that it wasn't a lot… Probably safer that way, so you wouldn't have much you could let slip to the police.'

'We didn't manage to get into the safe,' I begin, playing last night's scene over in my mind again, looking for how Anna could have got hold of Beauchamp's files and kept them away from the police.

'I downloaded the files on my computer, and backed them up to this external drive,' Daisy now explains.

'Yeah, but I thought you didn't know his password?' I challenge.

'I didn't, which is why we needed the alarm system to be triggered, so it would reset itself. Your sister really is a sly old girl, you know,' she adds, smiling. 'I wasn't convinced it would work, but sure enough, as soon as the alarm sounded, the system rebooted itself and asked me to save a new password. As soon as I was in, I made a copy of everything and brought it to you.'

I daren't click on any of the files, but I need to test the authenticity, and use my finger on the trackpad to hover the cursor on a date-named MP4 file. I try and read Daisy's face as the cursor flashes on the screen, but she can't quite bring her full gaze to remain on the screen.

A new window opens with the video, and I immediately have to close it as I realise what has opened.

'Oh God,' I stammer as a face fills the screen, before I can close the window.

'I can assure you the rest of the files are similar,' Daisy warns.

'W-why bring this to me? You should take it to the police.'

Daisy shakes her head. 'Are you having a laugh? Do you realise what we have here? This is all of Ian's involvement with his traffickers here. It isn't just video files.' She steps forward and turns the laptop towards her, her finger darting across the trackpad, as she searches for specific files. Excel and Word files now fill the screen as she opens one folder after another. She double-clicks one such file, and a Word document opens. 'There are names, and addresses, and descriptions of what they've bought. This is everything you need to bring him down.'

No wonder Anna kept this a secret last night, as I absolutely would have told Oakley about the real reason we were at Beauchamp's estate, had I known. I feel used by Anna, but suddenly her reckless stabbing at the safe pad makes a little more sense. She *wanted* to get caught, so that the security system would trigger and then have to be rebooted so that they could get the two of us out of the room, but little did anyone realise that Daisy was waiting in the van to harness all the files she was trying to copy.

'The police can't do anything with stolen files,' I point out, as I had tried to reason with Anna when she'd broken into the house in search of the safe.

'Maybe not, but it will show them the sort of detail that's available *if* they go looking for it. Kylie said you had friends in the force you could trust. *Those* are the people you need to get this to, but I'd suggest making a back-up copy before handing it over. I know it's not the sort of thing anyone would want to make duplicates of, but it's important to keep the evidence safe.'

I have to remind myself that she's only fourteen, and her view of the world is probably based on poorly researched books and TV shows, but I do admire her optimism in the face of such wickedness. And she does have a point about me taking this to Jack. Despite the illegal way in which the data was obtained, he might know how the intelligence could be used to our advantage. At least I hope he can.

'We could publish the list of these files online,' Rachel suggests, looking at the filenames. 'That would prevent a cover-up. Force these people into the spotlight, and let the shit land where it falls.'

I shake my head. 'And probably see us mired in civil suits for years to come.' I sigh. 'No, we have to tread very carefully… Presumably your uncle doesn't know you've made a copy of all of this?'

Daisy smiles. 'I covered my tracks. He'll have no idea what we did, I promise.'

I don't like placing such faith in the words of a child, but my technological knowhow is so little that I can't argue. It makes me wonder whether he does know, and his little surprise visit this morning was to check whether the drive was here.

My finger returns to the trackpad, and I look back through the dates of the video files. There are so many files, and amending the metadata filters, it shows there are three versions of some of the files. The lengths of the files go from thirty or so seconds to five minutes in some cases, and worse still, up to an hour in others. In my head I'm picturing trailers, previews, and then full-cut movies. I want to retch, but this is not the time for self-pity. Potentially what I'm staring at is the entire back catalogue of the work undertaken at the Pendark Studios, but maybe it stretches further than that. But if someone – I don't think I have the courage to do it myself – were to watch each one, how many more victims would be identified in addition to those we already found from the much smaller collection on Turgood's confiscated computer? Ultimately, that's more important than bringing those responsible to justice. How many victims are there out there – just like Zara Edwards – who have repressed the abuse they suffered?

The mouse hovers over the first file, dated 14 February 1974. I remember when Jack and I first started going through the paperwork Freddie rescued from Pendark; this was the first record on file. I feel sick to the stomach at what might appear on the screen, but I double-click the link anyway, and watch through gaps in the fingers covering my eyes. I have to know if this really is what we believe, even if I'll never be able to look at the world in the same way again.

A scared little girl walks into a child's bedroom and picks up a spinning top, which she proceeds to play with, while sitting on a frilly pink rug. She can't be much older than seven or eight. The scene cuts away to the door to the bedroom opening, and a pair of feet entering. The scene cuts back to the little girl's face, and her eyes well with sorrow and terror. I have to close the file. I wipe my own eyes.

'Kylie told me we could trust you to do the right thing,' Daisy says, placing a protective hand over the hard drive. 'She sacrificed herself for this information, so the question is, Emma, what are you going to do?'

I head back to my room and collect the new phone Rachel

bought, opening the contacts app, and finding Jack's number. It connects on the second ring.

'Have you seen?' are Jack's first words. 'They've arrested your sister for abducting Daisy Beauchamp.'

'I know, Jack,' I say quietly into the phone. 'I was there when they arrested her.'

'Oh, I see,' he replies, confused.

'Listen, Jack, there's something I need to show you.'

'O-kaaay,' he says, drawing out the vowel sound.

'Yeah, but it's a little bit… sensitive.'

'Ooh, now I'm intrigued. What is it?'

I'm conscious that anyone could be listening at his end, so I need to tread carefully.

'Do you remember what was found at Turgood's house when he was arrested?'

He doesn't immediately reply. 'Sure.'

'I may have come across something similar… but I'm reluctant to say any more over the phone. Can I meet you somewhere safe where I can show you what I have?'

'Is everything okay, Emma? You're speaking cryptically and don't sound like yourself.'

Given everything that's happened in the last week, that should hardly surprise him, but then I haven't got him up to speed with last night's fright yet.

'I'm fine, Jack, but it's really important that I see you. Today.'

'Okay, but I've just arrived at work having taken Mila to school. Can you come to me instead? I'm not sure what time I could get to Weymouth today.'

I lower the phone to relay the message to Rachel and Daisy. 'He wants us to come to him.'

'I can drive you,' Rachel offers without a second's thought.

'I should head back to Southampton,' Daisy interjects, already eyeing the front door. 'I've delivered the drive like I promised Kylie I would. What you do with it from here is down to you.'

I put the phone back to my ear. 'Okay, Jack, we'll come to you,' I tell him, 'but it can't be your new office. As I said, this is *sensitive*.'

Chapter Thirty-Nine

THEN

Weymouth, Dorset

Emma had already been awake for hours when her mum knocked gently on the door before pushing it open and poking her head through the gap. She didn't speak at first, instead staring at Emma, maybe trying to sense just how much comforting would be required this early in proceedings. She was already terrified by the maelstrom of emotion that was going to devastate them before the day was through.

'Morning, my darling,' she said softly, straining to keep her emotions in check. 'The kettle is on if you want a cup of tea?'

Emma remained where she was on the bed but offered a simple nod, more for her mum's benefit than her own; at least making tea would bring Bronwyn a small distraction from the spectre hanging over them.

'Do you fancy a bit of toast too?' Bronwyn asked.

Emma nodded for a second time, despite her lack of appetite.

'Good girl. The car will be here to collect us in about an hour, so you should probably think about getting dressed. I've left your dress hanging on your wardrobe handle, but it looks like it's going to be too warm for the cardigan. Just leave it on the end of your bed, and I'll put it away later. I've cleaned and polished your shoes, and they're by the front door drying.'

Emma still didn't move, almost as if the signals from her brain couldn't get past the wall of emotion so delicately created since that day on the beach when she'd run until her chest and legs burned, and had only stopped when her body could move no more.

Both Bronwyn and Hayley had tried to give chase but neither was in peak physical condition, and they'd kept going just so that Emma's sprinting body was kept in sight. They'd finally caught up with her when Emma's legs had given up and she'd crashed into the sand, unable to cry, so short of breath was she. Bronwyn and Hayley had dropped down beside her, scooping Emma into their arms, telling her it would be okay; offering promises of how they would get through it together; how they could never replace Emma's dad but they would do everything in their power to limit the feeling of his loss.

They'd stayed there on the beach until the sun had eventually set, and Hayley and Bronwyn had listened as Emma had told them it wasn't fair; how they'd already suffered enough with Anna; demanded to know what they'd done wrong to be punished in this way. Bronwyn had offered no excuses, save for the certainty that it was all part of God's plan, and though they couldn't understand it now, it would all make sense one day.

'The kingdom of heaven is reserved for those who've

suffered the most,' she'd added, though it hadn't had the soothing effect she'd intended.

Bronwyn returned what felt like a minute or so later, carrying a tray of tea and toast, but with greater urgency in her voice this time.

'Come on, Emma, you're still not dressed! The car will be here soon, and we don't want to be late, *not* today.'

The glowing red digits on Emma's alarm clock revealed just how much time had passed since the first disturbance, though she couldn't believe it had been twenty minutes. Pushing the duvet back, she moved over to her bedroom window, opening it so she could breathe in the fresh ocean air and listen to the seagulls gossiping. If she could bottle both the scent and sound she would, so she could keep it with her wherever the wind took her. Stepping up to the window, she lifted the hanger from the handle, and held the dark dress to the light. It was so black that not even a speck of the rising sun reflected from it. She hated the colour usually, but today it seemed so emblematic of the shadow hanging over her heart. Slipping the nightdress over her head, she dressed quickly, considering herself in the mirror built into the wardrobe door.

Would Dad prefer she wear her hair up or down? She'd never asked him which way he liked it best, and as she tried to rack her memory for any expression of favour he might have bestowed on one way or the other, she was bereft. She watched as the tears pooled in her reflection's eyes, the deep sense of loss swallowing her whole. She'd never now know whether he thought she was prettier with her hair tied or hanging over her shoulders as it was now. But how many other things would she never know about him? His favourite colour was brown, and he preferred curry over pasta, but there had to be more to him than two salient facts.

She wiped the tear from her cheeks and looked up to the ceiling to keep the rest at bay. Not yet. There would be plenty of time for tears later. She didn't want to make today any more difficult for her mum. Taking a deep breath and wiping her nose, she composed herself in the mirror, instinctively reaching for the cardigan and slipping her arms into it. Like a warm hug, it still smelled like him, and regardless of what her mum said about how warm it was likely to get this spring morning, she needed it today.

The Weymouth Crematorium was situated outside Weymouth in nearby Westham, and in the car it took fifteen minutes to get from home to the site. Thankfully her father wasn't travelling with them, as the people at the crematorium needed to prepare the body ahead of the ceremony. Emma had overheard her mum talking to Auntie Hayley about it, before they'd heard her hovering on the creaking floorboards and had promptly changed the subject. There'd been a lot of sudden changes of conversation whenever they sensed Emma lurking nearby. It was so obvious that they'd switched topic, as their voices would go from low and rumbling to squeaky and positive. Did they really not think she could notice the difference?

That night on the beach, she'd eventually asked them what had happened; what freak turn of fate had caused her father to die. Had it been another riot? Had the same bad men rebelled again? Her mum had promised to elaborate at a later time, telling her the how wasn't important. She'd looked too upset to push on it, but as the days had passed, she'd still not ventured any kind of explanation as to what had happened.

So Emma had been listening at every opportunity. Phone calls at strange hours of the day and night; Hayley and her mum whispering in corners of the living room; strangers at the door offering condolences for their loss. Mum had kept her off school all week, so she couldn't even rely on the usual gossips at school to let something slip. But Emma was resourceful, and references to depression, anxiety, and never truly recovering from Anna's disappearance told her more about his final hours than she'd ever garnered from their monthly visits.

The police officer who'd been waiting at Auntie Hayley's house had stayed until the three of them had returned from the beach, before offering her heartfelt condolences to Emma and her mum. Her final words, 'Let me know if you want any further information about coping mechanisms,' hadn't been what Emma had expected. Where was the team of detectives deployed to solve whatever had happened? They'd come in droves when Anna had gone missing, so why weren't they hard at it trying to figure out who'd killed her dad? The question had troubled her into the early hours of the morning, until the pieces had slotted together. There were no detectives looking for a killer, because he'd killed himself.

Emma blinked as she followed her mum out of the car once they'd arrived, the sun disproportionately bright for the time of the year. And barely a modest breeze blowing. This was the sort of day her dad would have loved. Before the separation, this was the sort of day he'd have spent on the beach from dawn till dusk, only leaving to fetch fish and chips, which they'd then eat out of the paper with little wooden forks. She smiled at the memory, her lips wobbling as she desperately longed to go back to that moment and relive it until the end of time.

'There, there,' Hayley said, offering her a tissue, one hand on her shoulder. 'We'll make it through today together.'

The crematorium was part of the larger estate of Weymouth Cemetery, and Emma followed the signs to the crematorium, dabbing at the tears on her cheeks. She allowed Hayley to lead her in through the double doors to find a wall of black either side of them, most crying or offering solemn nods of condolence to Bronwyn as she passed them. Emma couldn't count the number of strangers who'd all decided to descend on the crematorium to pay their last respects to her dad. She'd had no idea he'd touched so many lives. Standing at the front, she dared to look around only once, where a number of mourners were having to stand against the wall as all available seating had been taken.

She'd never attended any kind of funeral service before, although her mum had tried to brief her on what to expect. When her grandma had died, Emma had spent the day at Hayley's, only being returned to her mum as the wake had neared its end. There had to be at least a hundred mourners around them, many of whom seemed to be dressed in their prison officer uniforms; a show of solidarity for a fallen comrade.

Emma's mum was clutching a small cream programme containing the order of service; on the front was a picture of Emma's dad smiling and wearing a paper Christmas hat. He looked happy and peaceful, a side of him Emma hadn't seen for a number of years. Allowing her eyes to wander to the gables, she wondered if he was up there now, smiling down on them. But then a thought jarred at her mind, and no matter how hard she tried to shake it, it remained: Anna would never know he'd died. It was possible she was up there with him now – father and daughter finally reunited – but Emma's gut told her that simply wasn't the case. Deep down, she couldn't ignore the feeling that out there somewhere, her sister was still alive, but totally oblivious to the fact that she'd never again hear their dad tell her he loved her.

And with that thought, the tears quickly began to fall, and they didn't stop until after the coffin had disappeared behind the curtain.

Chapter Forty

NOW

Chiswick, London

Jack is sitting in his car outside the property when Rachel and I arrive. Neither of us has spoken much on the journey from Weymouth, such is the weight of the discovery resting on our shoulders. I'm worried I will never find happiness and joy in the world again. How can such pain and horror have been allowed to go on unpunished for so long? How can such monsters live and breathe the same air as me?

Jack climbs out of his car and trots over to where Rachel has parked, and it breaks my heart a little that once I share the news with him, he will lose a little more of his innocence as well. It's like a thick tar that spreads once it touches, and will never be removed. There's a part of me that wants to just turn and drive back to Weymouth, destroying the drive in the process. The more who see it, the greater the infection of negativity will spread, and I will be the catalyst that caused it.

How is Jack ever going to be the father Mila deserves once he sees the proof of how evil the world is?

Jack hops from one foot to the other as he waits for Rachel and me to get out, but neither of us has any enthusiasm for what's about to happen. I can see him staring in through the window, trying to work out if we've even removed our seatbelts yet.

'It's going to be okay,' Rachel tells me, sensing my reticence. 'Handing over the drive is the right thing to do. You're just an investigative journalist; you can't possibly bring these men to justice. And you can't hold yourself responsible for what they did.'

I meet her gaze, and even though my vision is misting, I want to tell her how grateful I am to have a friend who always seems to know the right thing to say in any given situation. I don't think I would have held things together for as long as I have without her at my side. I haven't yet started to contemplate how much our relationship will change once she marries Daniella, and whilst I wouldn't ever begrudge her a happy ending, I do fear that things between us will never be the same again, and I need to make the most of our remaining time together. If these last few days have taught me anything, it's that the sands of time are always slipping away, and if we don't embrace the present, we'll soon run out of grains.

Jack taps his knuckle on my window and then shrugs in confusion when I look out at him. Rachel squeezes my hand, and it's the strength I need to open the door and climb out.

'Everything okay?' Jack asks, the confusion spreading from his shoulders to his dark eyes.

I can't answer, but offer a less-than-reassuring nod instead. 'Mum died yesterday morning,' I tell him, though it's hard to get the words out of my mouth without a little sob carrying on them.

It's only the second time I've uttered those words, and it still isn't easier. Somewhere in the back of my head I'm still expecting a call from Pam telling me Mum's having a good day and I should hurry to see her. But the good days are over, and all that remains is the memory of the good days we spent together. I'm so glad that Jack and Rachel got to see her at her best, so I can continue to remember those happier times.

Jack is lost for words, and I don't fight him as he pulls me into him, and wraps his arms around me. 'Oh, Emma, I'm so sorry.'

And that's when the tears come, and despite clamping my eyes shut, I can feel them leaking out and my shoulders gently bobbing as the grief takes over. Jack holds me tight, and doesn't offer false platitudes; he is the rock I need in this moment, and I know in my heart I don't ever want to let him go. If I could freeze time, then this would be the moment I'd choose, even though it was born out of such sorrow.

But as I hear Rachel's door closing, reality crashes through the moment, and it is time for us to move on and bring an end to people whose names are listed on the drive.

Jack keeps his arm around me and leads us to the front door of a four-bedroom detached property, where I recognise DCS Jagtar Rawani's navy Jaguar parked in the driveway.

'How much did you tell him?' I ask, but Jack doesn't answer. He knocks on the frosted window.

Somewhere inside a deep bark sounds, and as a shadow appears behind the door, we can hear the scuttling of claws on a hard wood door as the bark's owner is manhandled into another room and the door closed. Rawani answers the door a moment later in a shirt and tie, his turban as pressed and tight as ever. He looks from me to Jack to Rachel, and his brow furrows.

'What are you all doing here? My retirement party isn't until next week.'

Before any of us answer, I reach into my bag and pull out the hard drive, thrusting it towards him, but he takes a nervous step backwards, shielding himself behind the door.

'What is that?' he asks, as if I might be holding some kind of incendiary device.

'It's the names, addresses, and credit card information of everyone involved in the ring, including those who have bought the filth these monsters pedal. It's everything you need to bring down the operation once and for all.'

His eyes don't leave the drive. 'Where did you get it from?'

'It was stolen from the home of Ian Beauchamp late last night,' I reply, without missing a beat.

Jack, who didn't know exactly why we'd come up today, lowers his arm, and I can see him now giving me a questioning glare, but I ignore it.

'I believe he is one of the leaders – if not *the* leader – of the whole thing. We've spent so long trying to link all of this together, and now here it is, practically gift-wrapped with a bow on the top.'

Rawani makes no effort to invite us in, almost as if he can sense the virus nearby, and he wants to protect himself from infection.

'Why would you bring this to me?' he asks. 'I'm on gardening leave, ahead of my retirement from the Metropolitan Police. I can't help you.'

'You're the only one who can help us,' I counter. 'Jack

doesn't have the seniority to launch the investigation this needs, and right now you are the only other detective in the world I trust. Please, Jagtar, don't shut us out now. You were there in the beginning, and I can't do this without you. *We* can't do this without you.'

The dog behind the door offers a solitary bark, and I can see Rawani weighing up his options. He's always been pragmatic, but also one who follows the rules to the letter. Given his impending retirement, he's going to need a lot more convincing, and the fact that he hasn't invited us inside tells me he wants nothing to do with this drive.

'There are thousands of video files on this drive,' I continue. 'Even more than what was found on Arthur Turgood's computer. I could leak the names and addresses of the conspirators, and let the police forces across the south coast face questions about why action wasn't taken to tighten the net around this group, but I don't want to do that. I still believe in the police force. The vast majority of serving police officers do it for the right reasons, and just because there is the occasional bad apple, it doesn't mean the whole force is tainted.'

'Sir, it was my idea to come here,' Jack offers. 'I'm sorry, I should have phoned you, but I hadn't realised exactly what Emma had found. This is what we spoke about so many times, sir, the keystone that will bring down the whole operation. It isn't ideal that the intelligence within the drive was obtained by illegal means, but it doesn't mean we can't use it to broaden our original investigation. We owe it to Jemima Hooper, Aurélie Lebrun, Faye McKenna, Cormack Fitzpatrick, Zara Edwards, Freddie Mitchell, Anna Hunter, and all the other victims we've yet to identify on these files.'

Rawani is frozen, the only movement the subtle bounce of

his eyes. There are other avenues open to us if he refuses to help, but he was the one who first set Jack and me on this road, and it won't feel right continuing without him.

'You'd better come in,' he eventually relents, and holds the door open, allowing us to enter, before taking a glance outside as if checking to see if anybody is watching.

He asks us to remove our shoes as the carpets in the rest of the property have just been cleaned, before he opens what turns out to be the kitchen door and lets an enormous, long-haired German Shepherd dog sniff each of us, before it trots happily away, curling up on the hearth in front of the fireplace in the main room. I'm not surprised that Rawani's house is as pristine as his turban and office: the picture frames on the walls; the cushions on the three settees; the matching curtains hanging either side of the bi-fold doors, which open out into one of the largest residential gardens I think I've ever seen – almost as long as Beauchamp's last night. It is a beautiful room, but I don't feel comfortable, almost as if my being here is making the place look untidy.

'Tell me again how you got hold of that drive,' Rawani instructs, as Rachel and I sit together, while Jack and Rawani sit on separate settees.

I proceed to explain to him how I was contacted by Yates and Oakley and how that led me to finding Anna, who in turn broke into Beauchamp's house, while working with his abducted niece. By the time I've finished, he looks even paler than when I first showed him the drive on the doorstep.

'Who else knows you have this?' he asks.

'Just us and Daisy Beauchamp, as far as I know. We came up here the moment she handed it over.'

'Have you checked what's on the device?'

My chest tightens as I picture the windows opening on the screen and the thousands of files that appeared. 'I had a brief look, but it isn't easy viewing.'

He stands and crosses the room in three strides, holding out his hand. 'I want to see what's on it.'

The only way to fight an infection is to produce antibodies, and maybe that's what Rawani sees himself as. I don't argue, handing the drive over, before repeating my warning that it isn't easy viewing.

He turns the device over in his hands, contemplating the weight of his next actions, before turning and heading out of the room. He summons Jack to follow him, leaving just Rachel and me in the room, with the dog watching us.

Chapter Forty-One

NOW

Chiswick, London

Jack and Rawani have yet to emerge from the room beyond the closed door, and I can't help feeling out of place in this beautiful and well-organised living room. Rachel has been checking her phone for the last twenty minutes, and I too can't be certain whether we've now served our purpose here. After all, what's required next is real police work – investigation and detection, rather than the amateur deduction that I've specialised in for the last few years. I've dug up histories and I've followed clues to the best of my ability, but I'm not able to bring these victims the justice they deserve.

I've never felt more redundant my entire life.

My sister is alone and in a prison cell, and there's nothing I can do to help her. Regardless of whether she was telling the truth when she said she hadn't killed Tomlinson, she is in the frame for his murder, and if the CPS do agree to press charges along with any charges she might face for the abduction of Daisy, it will be a matter for a jury to determine her guilt, and I do fear for her long-term future. Daisy said she'd sacrificed herself to get the evidence to me, but surely she wouldn't have reached out in Market Harborough if she didn't at least hope I could keep her out of prison.

And then there's Mum, who battled for years to find Anna, but I didn't manage to reunite them in time, and she died not knowing that her first daughter was still alive. I didn't manage to tell her that it wasn't her fault that Anna went missing that day; that she couldn't have known an organisation of paedophiles and traffickers would stumble upon her. But then I think about her dying words to me: *for years I've wondered whether I made the right choice.*

Did she really go her entire life thinking that she was somehow culpable for Anna's disappearance? Did she believe that on some level she'd chosen to protect me over Anna? Or was she just confused as her body fought to keep breathing? I feel like I may never know the truth, and if Anna has repressed that time like Zara Edwards did, then maybe the truth about that day is already lost.

I'm not expecting my phone to ring, but it's a welcome distraction from the troubling thoughts in my head. The number isn't withheld, but isn't one saved in the new SIM card.

'Hello, Emma Hunter speaking,' I say, answering the call, but moving over to the patio doors so that Rachel doesn't have to listen to the conversation.

'Hi, Emma, it's Marina Oakley, can you hear me okay? Signal is terrible here.'

'Yes, hi, I can hear you.'

'G-good,' comes the stuttered reply, followed by broken words that are indecipherable.

'Um, Detective Oakley, I missed that because you broke up, can you repeat what you said?'

There are more vocal sounds that leave me checking my own phone's signal, which is only at two bars, so I fiddle with the key in the lock, and when the door opens, I step outside. An extra bar registers, but the call ends. I attempt to phone DI Oakley back, but the number goes straight to voicemail, and I don't leave a message.

'Everything okay?' I hear Rachel say from behind me, and I offer her a smile and reassuring nod.

'It was DI Oakley,' I reply, waving the phone, 'but we got disconnected.'

She holds her phone out. 'Do you want to try mine?'

I shake my head. 'Thanks, but I think the problem's at her end. Are you okay?'

Her eyes widen and she smiles warmly, but her eyes are artificially large and I'd say she's trying to look happier than she is.

'Yeah, yeah, things are fine.'

'But…?' I add, drawing out the vowel.

'It's nothing… It's fine.'

I tighten my lips, and cross my arms.

'Okay, it's Daniella,' she yields. 'She's just landed at Heathrow, and she's asking whether I'm free to meet her for afternoon tea. I've told her I'm not, but I'm just wondering how much longer you think the other two will be before they let us know what's going on?'

I don't blame her for wanting to bail, and in fairness if I had a beautiful fiancée offering to distract me from the maelstrom we find ourselves in, I'm not sure I could ignore the offer.

'You can go if you want,' I tell her, but she's quick to shake her head.

'That's not what I'm saying. I'm not looking to ditch you, especially when you could be close to breaking what could be the story of the last decade! I just want to be able to let Daniella know whether she might see us today, or whether she should make other plans.'

I'm about to ask her how long is a piece of string when the phone in my hand starts ringing again. I shrug as I answer Oakley's call.

'Hello, Emma? Is that better?'

'Yes, I can hear you now.'

'Oh good, I've come outside now, but it's threatening to rain, so I might have to break off if the heavens open.' The sound of a lighter being flicked is followed by a small sigh of satisfaction as she exhales from the freshly lit cigarette. 'I wanted to give you an update on your sister, assuming her solicitor hasn't already been in touch?'

'I'm not sure she'd have my new number,' I reply honestly, though I'm not entirely sure how Oakley has this number, unless Rachel gave it to her when she called yesterday.

'Ah good, so my call isn't wasted.' She exhales again. 'Have you been allowed to speak to Anna at all?'

'No, but again, I don't think she'd have my number anyway. Have you been in touch with her or the arresting officer? Do you know whether they're planning on charging her with Daisy's abduction, because they need to know that—'

'I have no news about any of that, I'm afraid,' she interjects.

'I can make a call and see if the SIO will let me update you, but he has no reason to agree.'

'Thank you, I'd appreciate it.'

'Okay, I'll try my best. And you? Are you okay?'

I don't know where to begin with answering that question honestly, and I'm not sure it isn't rhetorical anyway, so I simply tell her I'm fine.

'The reason I was calling,' she says, 'is to let you know we no longer believe Anna had anything to do with Anthony Tomlinson's murder. I'm not usually in the habit of reaching out to suspects' long-lost siblings, but this isn't a traditional situation we find ourselves in, now, is it?'

My throat is suddenly dry. 'No, I don't suppose it is,' I try to say, but the words are like tar on my tongue, and I'm not entirely sure what I say.

'The Crime Scene Investigation team identified hidden security cameras all over the inside of Mr Tomlinson's property, and although we were aware that power had been cut to the six visible cameras outside of the house – two at the front and four at the rear – an hour before the gunshots were heard, it appears they weren't connected to the cameras inside. The type of devices and their locations would suggest that Mr Tomlinson was more than a little paranoid about his future, and with good reason based on the footage that was recovered.'

My knees are like jelly, and although I fall back against the closed patio door, I'm not convinced I won't simply slide down it to the damp concrete paving slab beneath my feet.

'This conversation is strictly off the record for now, Emma, is that clear?'

My neck feels so hot that I might be close to passing out, but I agree without question.

'Good. The footage shows two heavyset individuals in designer suits pushing Mr Tomlinson about, and threatening him. Unfortunately, the footage isn't high-res, and there's no sound, so it isn't clear exactly what their conversation is about, but there's a lot of shaking of heads, finger waving, and I would assume shouting. One of them pulls a gun, and fires point-blank at Tomlinson, before wiping the weapon clean and leaving it on top of the body. This is only minutes before your sister is seen entering the property from an upstairs window, and she is then seen heading down the stairs where she discovers the body, shortly before flashing lights can be seen though one of the front windows. Although your sister has yet to make a formal statement about what happened that day, if her version of events mirrors what's seen in the footage, then I have no reason to consider her a suspect in my investigation. We are already trying to identify the two men in question, but the footage isn't good enough for facial recognition. We're reaching out to colleagues in organised crime to see if they recognise them.'

My heart is racing, and it feels as though a blowtorch is being held against my neck and face, but this almost feels like light at the end of the tunnel.

'You're saying you're not going to charge Anna with murder?'

'Not at this time, no. I still need to interview her again, and that will be my next step. Hopefully she will be more cooperative this time.'

'She didn't force Daisy to go with her. Daisy was a willing participant,' I say urgently. 'You have to tell that to the investigating team. Get them to check Daisy's internet history, focusing on chatroom conversations. Daisy told me she was the one to reach out to Anna about bringing down her great-uncle.'

'Listen, Emma, I can't get involved in any of that. The best thing I can suggest is for you to contact Anna's solicitor and tell her anything you believe might be relevant, and tell her to encourage Anna to come clean about what's been going on. The truth is always the best place to start.'

I know she's right, but I worry that Anna has been fighting for so long that she won't welcome any kind of advice, even when it's in her best interests.

I thank Oakley for the update, and promise I will do all I can to get hold of Saira Mistry and relay the message. Pushing myself away from the door, I follow the stone path to the edge of the grass, sucking in lungfuls of breath as I try to regain my composure and concentrate on what else I can do to help Anna.

Rachel reappears at the patio door, her face as pale as snow. 'They want to speak to you,' is all she manages before Jack's face appears like an apparition behind her shoulder. The deathly pallor tells me the infection has him, and I so want to tell him how sorry I am for ever involving him in this mess, but how grateful I am that he has been there every step of the way.

Heading in through the patio doors, I follow him across the living room, and to the small office door. The room is dimly lit, and at first it takes a moment for my eyes to adjust. The blind at the far side of the room is drawn, but I can see there is a large map on the wall into which Rawani is sticking coloured drawing pins.

'You weren't kidding when you said how much information was on here,' Jack says, straining to keep the sadness from his voice. 'There must be five or six times as many videos as were found on Turgood's drive. It's… it's sick.'

My bottom lip trembles as our eyes meet, and I nod. 'Did you watch them all?'

He shakes his head, and the dim light reflects in his watering yes. 'Couldn't…'

I know what he means, I couldn't bear to watch more than a few seconds of the files I opened, and I'm not sure what level of courage would be required to catalogue this discovery. I pity the poor souls who will ultimately be assigned such a horrendous task. Their futures will be permanently dimmed by such activity.

'The DCS says we need to involve specialist teams within Anti-Corruption to ensure proper oversight of what is to come,' Jack says quietly. 'I don't know whether you looked at any of the names in the spreadsheet, but this spread far wider than I think we ever considered. We're talking decades of abuse and corruption at the highest levels, and heads are going to roll. This is bigger than Operation Yewtree, and you saw the media coverage that garnered. This may indeed become the biggest multi-agency investigation ever coordinated in the UK.'

I nod as if I understand any of the repercussions of what Jack is saying, but I don't think I'll truly understand just what this means until it's all over.

'We'll need a statement from you confirming how this drive came into your possession,' Rawani offers, glancing from the screen to the map, and jabbing another pin into it. 'We'll also need to know who else was involved in obtaining it, and what steps you followed to bring it to our attention.'

'Sure,' I reply, suddenly overcome with fatigue. 'Whatever it takes.'

Jack places a protective arm around me, and kisses the top of my head. 'You did it, Emma.'

I huddle into his warmth. 'No, this was all Anna's work. We need to get her out of that cell, and into protective custody. She's been locked up for too long.'

Chapter Forty-Two

NOW

Weymouth, Dorset

Rachel offered to drive me home, but I told her we all need a night off before the real work starts, and the gentle rock of the train carriage brought on a dark and turbulent sleep that I'm relieved to wake from as the train guard announces our arrival in Weymouth. Jack promised to call with an update once his and Rawani's meeting with the Anti-Corruption division is complete, but it wouldn't surprise me if he's forced to sign a non-disclosure agreement and can't provide an update. If their assumptions about the scale are right, then they'll want to keep a lid on matters.

I want to call Anna and tell her she's made the difference, but in her current circumstances, she's not available to hear such great news. I've left messages with Anna's solicitor, Saira, but she has yet to return any of my calls. Something tells me Anna is going to need her now more than ever. But I do worry that her life will be at risk of reprisal when the truth does get out, and I'm also terrified that she might just as easily drift back into the ether, and out of my life. We didn't exactly hit it off or slip into a familiar pattern when we met at Jane Austen's house. What if we're never able to find that sibling bond after everything that's happened? What if she has no desire to reconnect with me?

There's an older couple sitting across the table from me. Her silver hair is tied in a tight bun, and her head has been buried in a book of crossword puzzles since we left Reading. He, on the other hand, with hair almost as white as snow, has been fast asleep, his head resting on her shoulder and his mouth wide enough to catch flies. She presses a hand to his arm and gently wakes him, telling him they've arrived at their destination. He looks to be in a blind panic as he opens his eyes, as if he has no idea where he is, but then she brushes his cheek and closes his mouth with the tips of her fingers.

'Glasses,' he says, loudly enough to turn the heads of those seated in close proximity.

'Around your neck, my sweet,' she says, rolling up her book and tucking it and her pencil into her handbag.

His hands fumble around his shirt until his fingertips brush the cord, and he quickly slides them back up and onto his face, stifling a yawn in the process.

'What would I do without you?' he asks, leaning over and kissing her cheek.

'Well you'd probably end up in Timbuktu with no idea how to get home,' she teases, 'but the real question is what would I do without you? Come along, we don't want to be late for the bus.'

He pushes up the armrest and slides off the chair, straightening and rubbing the base of his back, before offering her his hand and helping her from her seat. The love between them radiates, and I can't help envying that level of intimacy, something that has sorely been lacking in my life for far too long. But with Jack's likely heavy involvement with the investigation, how long will I have to wait until we can consider crossing that bridge? And then taking into account the distance between our homes and lives, it just isn't going to happen. I care deeply for Jack, and I wish him nothing but joy and success in the future, but maybe friendship is the most we can expect of one another.

I follow the couple as they slowly make their way down the carriage and wait for the door to slide open. She allows him to step out first, and then he holds her arm as she clambers down onto the platform. She catches me watching them, and although I quickly turn my head, I already have her attention.

'Oh Finn, look who it is,' she says to her husband. 'You're Emma Hunter, aren't you?'

My cheeks flush as I step onto the platform, offering a nod and a slight shrug. 'Hi, yes, I am.'

'Oh, what a treat! We've had a lovely day sightseeing in London, and then we get to meet a local hero. It's truly an honour to meet you, Emma.'

The temperature in my face cranks up another notch. 'That's very kind of you to say, but I'm no hero.'

'Oh, I'm sorry, I didn't mean to embarrass you, dear. I'm a big fan of your books.'

'Thank you, it's always nice to meet a fan. Are you two local then?'

'Oh, yes. Finn's mind isn't what it once was, so we try and get out whenever we can to make the most of the time we have left. I imagine you must have a line of suitors waiting to escort you home.'

'Have you two been married a long time then?' I ask as we make our way to the station's exit.

'Thirty-five years next month. When you meet the man who makes you smile every day, you grab hold of him and don't let go.'

Her husband Finn has wandered off along the platform and she wishes me well as she hurries after him and steers him back towards the exit. I think about my parents' marriage, and how they'd seemed unsinkable until the worst happened that Sunday afternoon. When they were then forced beneath the microscope, the cracks soon appeared and quickly widened, but does that mean they weren't suited? What would have happened if Anna hadn't been taken that day? Where would we be now? And would they both be alive now? I still have so many unanswered questions about that period in my life, and with Mum gone, I can't see how I'll ever find those answers.

The walk home from the station is brief, and I collect a fish and chip supper on the way as I'm too exhausted to think creatively about food. It smells so good, and I'm glad I chose to come home rather than staying at Rachel's. She needs a night of normality with Daniella, and I need to hear the call of the seagulls when I wake in the morning.

'Spare a chip for an officer of the law?' a familiar voice calls over my shoulder as Rick bounds over, dressed in jeans and an anorak rather than his more familiar high-vis vest and PCSO uniform.

I stop and offer the open bag to him as steam rises up and hovers around his face. He takes a chip and puffs out his cheeks as it burns the tip of his tongue.

'Thanks. Is there anything better than a fresh chip?'

I select one dripping in salt and vinegar and blow on it before putting it between my lips. 'Nothing,' I reply.

'Mind if I walk you home?' he asks.

I chuckle, as I could probably hurl the bag of chips and land it on my doorstep, but I nod as a bit of company might not be a bad thing. After all, Rick's made it perfectly clear that he's interested in more than just friendship, and I didn't really give him much of a chance because of my confusion over Jack. Maybe Rick's appearance here is fate's way of giving me a much-needed nudge in the right direction.

'I wanted to return something of yours,' he says when we reach the steps, removing my old phone from his inside jacket pocket and passing it over.

I hand him the chips in exchange for the device, but am a little disappointed to see the large crack across the screen.

'Yeah, sorry about that,' he tells me. 'It got damaged in the scuffle I had with the thief it helped me apprehend.'

I'd almost forgotten about the mugging.

'You caught him then?'

'Yeah, just a chancer, but thanks to your phone we were able to track his movements and catch him. The inspector I report to was very pleased, and there's going to be a story about it in tomorrow's *Echo*.'

'You'll have to autograph a copy of it for me,' I say proudly, unlocking the door and inviting him inside. 'How's your mum?'

He closes the door slowly, but remains in its shadow. 'She's fine, thanks. Keeps asking me when she can expect to read the next Emma Hunter instalment.'

'In about five weeks,' I say, reminding myself to give

Maddie a call in the morning and chat through the proposed outline for the next book. 'Hey, do you want me to split my dinner with you? I can probably rustle up a couple of slices of stale bread and butter to bulk it out.'

'Sure,' he says, remaining by the door.

I head out to the kitchen, flicking on the light and cursing when I can't find any ketchup in the cupboard. I don't remember running out, but in fairness I haven't been very good at keeping rations well stocked these past few months. Here and now, I make a vow to improve my lifestyle, including cutting down on the number of takeaways I buy when I can't be bothered to cook.

Splitting the fish and chips between two plates, I set the table, placing the larger of the portions where Rick will sit.

'Do you want a cup of tea?' I call out, moving to the door to see what's holding him up.

He's by the desk, but hurries over when he hears me. 'Yes, tea would be great.'

I put the kettle on, but am too hungry to wait for it, so we sit and tuck in.

'You look exhausted,' he says when we've finished eating.

'Thanks a lot!' I exclaim. 'Crikey, what charm school did you get excluded from?'

He laughs and collects my plate, carrying them both to the sink and beginning to fill it while I make the tea.

'Seriously though,' he says, as the bubbles rise to the surface, 'you should take a few days for yourself. I'm sure it's been a crazy week, what with discovering your sister is alive and well, and then haring off after her yesterday.'

Something stirs in my mind, but I shake it away as I splash milk into our mugs.

'What did you have in mind?' I ask. 'Are you offering to take me away on some all-expenses paid mini-break?'

'Ha! Not on my salary, but I'm sure I could wangle a couple of days off if you fancied some company.'

I really should get my head down and start writing, as there's so much to tell, but maybe a rest and a break are precisely what is needed.

'It must have been weird coming face to face with your sister after all these years,' he comments, as he places a soap-covered plate in the rack on the draining board. 'What did the two of you talk about?'

'It's funny, I'd pictured the moment for so long, but when it came I didn't know how to react. I can't even remember what my first words to her were.'

'Did she tell you where she's been hiding for all these years?'

I yawn, wondering the same thing myself. How could she have stayed under the radar for so long undetected? And how long would she have remained under had she not sent me those pictures of Faye McKenna and Cormack Fitzpatrick?

'I'd rather not talk about it,' I say, stifling another yawn, the prospect of bed and a good book to read drawing me in.

'And then she went and kidnapped that girl in Southampton! Did she explain why she did that?'

I frown at the question. 'Sorry, Rick, but do you mind if we talk about something else? Sorry, it's just it's all I've thought about for days, and I'd rather talk about something with a happier ending.'

'Sure, sure,' he says, placing the second of the plates in the rack. 'It's just such a fascinating tale: long-lost sister turning up out of the blue like that, and then abducting a child herself. I was just curious about what she'd hoped to achieve other than throwing a giant spotlight on herself.'

'Who knows why some people do the things they do?' I respond, carrying my mug through to the living room and sitting on the sofa.

Rick dries his hands on the towel on the radiator in the kitchen, before following me through.

'I heard Anna was finally caught breaking into the girl's uncle's house. The funny thing is, the police have yet to find what she stole.'

Alarm bells are ringing in my head. Rick seems far too well-informed about my actions over the last couple of days, which is odd when I haven't spoken to him since he raced away from the scene of the mugging to catch the thief.

'Yes, well, as I said, let's change the subject,' I say, smiling thinly at him.

Rick lowers his mug to the table and moves across to my front door, locking it in one motion. 'I'm afraid I can't do that, Emma. You see, they know what was taken, and all you have to do is tell me what you did with it.'

Chapter Forty-Three

NOW

Weymouth, Dorset

This must be some kind of joke are the only words playing through my mind, and yet the darkness that's come over his eyes, and the pained grimace on his face, tell me it's anything but.

'Rick?' I try to question, but the words stick in my throat. 'What's going on?'

He moves away from the door, and I've never seen him looking so pained and confused, like a man battling internally with a decision he has no choice but to make. He looks back at me before hurrying over.

'We don't have long.' There is heightened tension in his voice, and fresh urgency. 'They're sending people over. You need to tell me where the information is, Emma, before they get here. If you don't… Please just tell me how you got the files and where you've put them.'

The pieces of the puzzle are falling before my eyes like

giant snowflakes, settling in place on the ground. Beauchamp's surprise visit this morning to thank me for saving Daisy was exactly the ruse I suspected. He must have been trying to suss out whether I knew the others had broken through his firewalls. Even though I didn't actually know at the time of his visit, I can't have been sufficiently convincing. Daisy said there was no way he would know she'd got in, and maybe he doesn't know it was her specifically, but clearly he knows something was taken.

Rick sits down beside me, his hands fidgeting as he stares at them and tries to make sense of this place we now find ourselves in. He isn't the only one.

I think back to the first time we met. It was only a couple of months ago when he appeared on my doorstep to escort me to the police station in Portland; Jo-Jo Neville's parents had reported her missing when really they'd faked the whole thing to cash in on media exposure. He'd seemed sweet, and fairly full of himself, but I don't remember any kind of vibe that he wasn't on the level. I'm usually such a good judge of character, and now I'm feeling nauseous.

'You were the one who helped me track Cormack Fitzpatrick's grave in Hayling Island,' I say quietly. 'But all this time you've been working for them. How could you?'

He is quiet for a moment. One, two, three, four seconds pass, and then finally he looks up at me, his eyes narrowing as he speaks.

'It wasn't like that... in the beginning... Our meeting was by chance. I meant it when I said I'm a big fan of your work, and I meant it when I told you I care for you. I do, Emma. I really do.'

'Then why? How could you...?' The words trail off as I

hear doors being slammed outside, and clomping footsteps moving towards the door.

'It isn't what you think, Emma,' he says, glancing nervously at the door. 'I'm not one of them… Not like you're thinking. I got into some trouble, and they found out, and then they told me I was to keep tabs on you, to update them on your activities. I didn't know who *they* were at first, but then I started to realise, only, by then it was too late.'

There is a loud thump at the door, and I can see the concern in Rick's eyes as he turns back to face me again. 'It isn't too late, Emma. Just tell me where the data is. You must have downloaded it to some kind of drive, right? That's all they want. Tell me where it is and I can make all of this go away. Please?'

There's a second thump, and his concern now has my pulse racing. I shake my head as vehemently as my anxiety will allow.

Rick shakes his head in silent resignation, before standing and moving back to the front door. With a deep breath, he unlocks it and steps to one side. The two men who enter can barely fit through the door without turning sideways and ducking slightly. The moment I lay eyes on them, I hear DI Oakley's words in my head: *the footage shows two heavyset individuals in designer suits pushing Mr Tomlinson about and threatening him.*

The light in the hallway reflects off their shiny suits as they speak privately to Rick, who promptly closes and locks the door behind him.

This cannot be happening. I've always been so careful about who I welcome into my life since Anna disappeared.

And then another piece of the jigsaw slots into place.

'You were the one who uploaded the tracking software to my phone and laptop,' I say, but it isn't a question.

He breaks away from the two men who remain lurking near the door, but thus far their threat is worse than their bite.

'Yes, I did. Okay? You want honesty? Let's do honesty.' The words are tumbling so fast from his mouth, it's as if he's jacked up on something. 'Ask me anything you like, and I'll tell you the truth. Okay? I want you to trust me, Emma, but we don't have much time. Let me convince you that I'm here in your best interests, and then maybe… maybe there might just be a way out of all this for us.'

He falls onto the couch beside me and dares to take my hands in his. I try to snatch them away, but he grips them firmer.

'They know that a copy of Beauchamp's files was downloaded. Okay? They don't know how you or your sister did it, but they know you did it. So there's no point bullshitting and claiming otherwise. The only question is what you did with the download. Is it here? Please don't make us ransack the place looking for it.'

I look over to the goons by the door, but I can't tell from here whether they're carrying weapons. Even if they aren't, I don't doubt they could be just as effective with their hands as with a gun. There is no backdoor out of this flat, and they're blocking my only exit. My only chance is to keep Rick or them talking, and hope that by some miracle someone comes by that I can call out to, or that they move away from the door for long enough that I can make a bolt for it. If I could just get out I'm sure I could outrun both of them. But maybe not Rick. I'll need some means of incapacitating him if I'm to escape.

'How could you work for an organisation like that?' I ask

Rick, softening my voice. If he's looking for absolution, then maybe I can convince him it's available here.

'I told you, it isn't like that. These people… they're connected. It's all connected. Don't you see, Emma? I'm not working for *them* directly, but the people I owe money to, they're making me help them indirectly… I'm not even sure how it all works. I only know what I'm told to do down a phone line. It's only because I know the work you've been doing that I've even managed to connect the dots.' He glances nervously back at the duo before meeting my gaze, his eyes imploring me to give him what he wants. 'Please? Just tell me for both of our sakes.'

'Is it drugs? Is that what you got caught up in?'

His eyes are watering. I'm sure I'm getting through to him, but he's resisting. He lowers his face. 'Mum's care doesn't come cheap… On my salary there isn't a lot I can do to help them financially.' He sighs, but his shoulders relax a fraction, like some great weight is finally being lifted. 'So I did what I could to scrape together more by any means I could. But I ran up gambling debts, and then I had to borrow more from others to pay back what I owed to the first, and things just spiralled. They didn't give me any choice, and I didn't think I was doing anything that would jeopardise your investigation. It was like I was just giving them an advanced look at your next book.' He snorts slightly, maybe seeing how lame an excuse he's offering. But then his face snaps back up. 'These people, Emma… they don't react well to bad news. I don't know who these two guys are, but I do know they've been sent here to get those files by any means necessary. Please just tell me where it is. I'm desperate.'

I lean in closer to him, even though I'm sure he must be

able to hear my racing heart. 'If you really do care for me, Rick, you won't let them hurt me.'

He snatches his hands away, standing and turning his back to me. 'I don't have a choice, Emma. Why can't you see that? You either give them what they want, or… or neither of us lives to tell the tale.'

I keep trying to think what Rachel would do in this situation. She's the bravest and most forthright person I know, and she wouldn't give up without a fight. But then, she's also fairly pragmatic, and I can almost hear her telling me just to give them what they want. It's not like the drive is here. It's safe with Jack and Rawani. When they learn I don't have it, there's a chance – and I realise now just how slim a chance this is – that they'll leave and go on their way.

I stand, figuring that if I'm moving about, there's a chance the goons might follow, or at the very least, clear a path to the door.

'All right,' I say desperately, trying to keep the quiver from my voice, and channelling my inner Rachel. 'Yes, we did download a copy of Beauchamp's files. That's what Anna and I were doing in his study when the alarm sounded. We managed to smuggle the drive out of there and gave it to the police.'

I pause and study their three faces, waiting to see any look of resignation or acceptance, but they're giving me nothing.

'It's over,' I say firmly. 'The police know that Beauchamp is involved, they have the evidence and all the names of everyone connected, and now it's only a matter of time before the lot of you are arrested and locked up. So you can come here and threaten me, but you won't find the drive, because it isn't here. Ransack the whole sorry place: you won't find it.'

The apparition of Rachel to my left is punching the air and

cheering me on, but vanishes in an instant as the nearest of the thugs marches through her and I feel the pressure of his fat, warm fingers thrust against my throat. But he doesn't stop once he's made contact. Instead, he's thrusting me backwards until I slam into the wall, sending the table lamp crashing to the floor. I claw at his hand, but it's so big that my tiny fingers can barely grip it, let alone pull it off. His palm is crushing my larynx, and suddenly I can no longer breathe, and that's when the real panic cuts in.

'Rick...' I manage to gag, but he isn't even looking. His back is turned, maybe so that he doesn't have to watch as I'm throttled.

The goon's hand is so hot, and I can feel my life suddenly slipping through my fingers... and there's nothing I can do to stop it. And then I realise that none of these men is wearing gloves, and that sends a shudder the length of my spine. They're making no effort to cover their tracks, and the only people who do that are naïve first-timers or those who consider themselves above the law, and these aren't the former.

'R-Rick,' I try again, but there is no breath left in my lungs, and I can see black spots as my vision starts to blur.

The grip around my neck loosens a fraction, and a tiny, fresh wave of air sneaks through, as the man is distracted by crashing on the other side of the room. I can just about make out Rick and the other goon fighting. My laptop crashes to the floor, and then the two of them roll into the coat stand, sending that against the front door.

Another gust of air seeps through as the grip loosens a little more as he weighs up whether to help his partner or finish the job.

I kick out with my right leg and stub my toes against his

knee, but it has no effect other than to draw his attention back to me. A sickening grin spreads out across his fat face, and I have no doubt that he's enjoying this power over me.

I kick out again, this time aiming more centrally, but he blocks the attempts with his knee, and I slip down as my standing leg slides on the floor. Suddenly, his fat hand is the only thing keeping me up, and that puts even more pressure against my throat.

The black spots grow larger, and despite wanting my fingernails to scratch at his hand, my arms drop uselessly to my sides, and I have to accept that this is the moment it will all end.

The front door crashes open, and this time the gorilla does let go of my throat, and I plummet to the ground, unable to feel any pain when my bottom breaks my landing. I focus on the door as I will my body to find the energy to kick-start my lungs, but I can no longer tell if what I'm seeing is real, or whether the vision of Freddie Mitchell is another apparition, come to escort me to the afterlife.

I cough, and breathing returns in stuttering waves as I suck in new air. I can't yet move, but I silently champion Freddie as he squirts hot soup into the face of the gorilla who had, seconds earlier, been killing me. He squeals like a piglet as his hands shoot up to his eyes, and he flails around in the direction of Freddie, who simply steps to one side, before driving a heel into the goon's lower back, sending him tumbling into the sofa, where he flips over the top and crashes down onto my antique coffee table, smashing it into a thousand splinters.

Freddie hurries over and helps me to my feet. 'Come on, let's get you out of here,' he says.

But just as we're standing, he's suddenly yanked away

from me, and I crash back to the ground, but this time I'm able to use my hands to take some of the pressure off my bottom. The second thug has pulled Freddie into a bear hug from behind, and it looks like he's delivering the Heimlich manoeuver. He lifts Freddie's legs into the air, and I desperately want to help him, but as I stumble to my feet, I see Rick lunge at the two of them and smash the fallen table lamp over the aggressor's head, and suddenly Freddie is free.

'You two go!' Rick shouts over their moans and groans. 'Get her to safety, and I'll sort out these two.'

Freddie doesn't need telling twice, slipping the soup canteen from his back to the floor, and then thrusting my arm over his shoulder, helping me back up and leading me to the door. Rick is now kneeling on the back of the goon he hit with the lamp, and is securing his wrists behind his back with two cable ties.

'I'm sorry, Emma,' I hear him calling out as we bustle through the splintered doorway. 'I'll do what I can to fix things.'

Chapter Forty-Four

NOW

Dorchester, Dorset

It's been twenty minutes since Freddie and I arrived at Dorchester police station, and my heart rate is yet to slow. It was my idea to get a taxi here, even though I knew they wouldn't be open to the public this late at night. Having phoned 999 on the ride over to report Rick and the goons in my home, I told them I was making my way to the police station, and was assured we would be given refuge. What the telephone operator couldn't have known is we'd have to wait in the reception area for someone to come and deal with us.

I should feel safe. They wouldn't be stupid enough to come after me again behind the locked door of a police station, and yet, until I know who is and isn't on their books, I may never feel safe again.

'I used to hate places like this,' Freddie says beside me. 'Lots of bad memories.'

Poor Freddie. When I told the taxi driver to bring us here, I didn't even consider how he might feel to be back in a police station where his cries for help were once overlooked. He smiles reassuringly when I look up, and pats my hand gently.

I don't think I'll ever be able to repay Freddie for coming to my rescue like that. In the taxi, he explained that he'd been walking past my place on his way to the shelter, and only decided to call round when he saw the lights were on. He said he heard the commotion inside, and feared the worst, which is why he kicked in the front door. I don't want to think about what would have happened if he hadn't.

I haven't cried yet, not because I'm trying not to, but because I think my entire body is still in shock about tonight's revelation. I keep replaying my interactions with Rick over in my mind, trying to find the chinks in his façade that I missed. His excuse that he ran up gambling debts trying to support his mother rings true as I've met her and I'm aware she is suffering with MS, but it isn't an acceptable excuse for what he has done. How many more victims have suffered at *their* hands as a result of his interference? How much quicker might we have found Anna and the truth had he not been helping them stay one step ahead? Rick claims he isn't like them, but he has collaborated and in my book that means there's blood on his hands too.

I've yet to hear whether the squad car sent to my flat rounded up any of the three of them, but I'd imagine Rick probably set the other two free the moment Freddie and I were out the door. I will never forgive him for putting my life at risk, and I have every intention of reporting him as soon as someone comes out to speak to us.

I've tried phoning Jack to warn him, but his phone is switched off. I'm hoping that means he is still in discussion with the Anti-Corruption team, but until he calls me back, I won't know for sure. I've also phoned Rachel to warn her to be careful. She assures me that both she and Daniella are fine, but offered to drive back down here when I told her what had happened; I've told her they'll have to go through Freddie if they want to get to me.

It's funny how things have come full circle. Meeting and then interviewing Freddie was what sent me along this course, and I wouldn't want anyone else at my side right now. I have no doubt Freddie will do anything to keep me safe, and as I link my arm through his, he rests his head on top of mine.

'How're you holding up?' he whispers.

'I'll be better when I know Jack and Jagtar are safe.'

'If I'd known how much trouble you'd bring when we first met, I might have thought twice about speaking to you,' he says, trying to lighten the mood. 'And to think, you described yourself to me as just a nosy busybody with boring taste in books and music.'

I feign shocked hurt. 'I never said I was boring.'

'Oh, didn't you? I must be misremembering. Seriously though, can I do anything to make you feel better?'

'Your being here with me is comfort enough.'

A door buzzer sounds at the far side of the reception area and a petite woman in smart trousers and a dark blouse emerges through the door there. The close-cropped bleached locks and stern stare can only belong to one detective I know, and I grimace as she approaches.

'Well, look what the cat dragged in,' DI Zoe Cavendish crows as she takes a seat next to me. 'What brings you to our station this evening, Emma?'

'They called you?' I say, feeling as though fate is having a cruel joke at my expense.

'I am the on-duty senior detective this evening, and from what I've heard you called 999 to report a break-in and assault at your home. What have you been getting yourself mixed up in now?'

I feel Freddie tense, ready to leap to my defence, but I squeeze his arm. I lift my head and show her the bruising around my neck.

'This is what one of them did,' I say, and her animosity disappears in an instant, as she leans in for a closer look.

'We'll need to get that photographed. Have you been checked over medically? Are there any other wounds or injuries we need to be aware of?'

'No, this is it. Did you send a patrol car to my flat?'

'We'll come to that. Can you talk me through what happened, so I can make some notes and determine how we take this forward?'

I recap everything that happened from the moment I got off the train at Weymouth. Cavendish listens intently, scribbling notes in a small pad as she goes, only interrupting to clarify points I've said. For all the difficulty she's given me in the past, I can't say she's anything but professional and thorough with me now.

'So Rick Underwood is involved with this group as well?' she asks, her tone dripping with disappointment.

'I'm afraid so. At least, that's what he told me before one of the men he'd allowed into my flat attacked me. If you don't believe me, phone Jack; he'll validate everything I've told you about this group and what we've found.'

She lowers her pen and looks into my eyes. 'I do believe

you, Emma. Okay? But I also think we should get you looked over, just to be safe. We have a first aider in the station who can do a preliminary check, and if they have further concern about your health, we can request an ambulance, or take you to the hospital.'

'That really isn't necessary,' I deflect, reluctant to leave the safety of the police station.

She picks up her pen again and rattles it against her teeth. 'Three men were apprehended at your flat when the patrol car arrived. Rick Underwood had subdued two larger men and was escorted to the police station in Portland, where he's made a full statement, which more or less corroborates what you've just told me. He specifically asked that we check on your whereabouts and make sure that you're safe and well. He's given up a burner phone that was used to make contact with his handler, and I'll ensure the details are passed to Jack as soon as I can get hold of him.'

I'm not totally surprised to hear that Rick did remain behind, and I hate myself for it, but I do have sympathy for what his future now holds. How stupid is that? He used me and put my life in harm's way, and yet I'm pitying him. I suppose it's because I had considered the possibility of a future with him, and that thought sickens me now to my core.

'The other two have refused to answer any questions,' Cavendish continues, 'and will probably be interviewed in the morning when their solicitor arrives from London. For now, I'd say you're as safe as you can be. It isn't standard protocol to allow overnight stays here, but I can probably find a free cell if you want to get your head down for the night?"

After what happened last night, the last thing I want is to be anywhere near an enclosed cell, and I shake my head.

'Can you keep trying to get hold of Jack, or DCS Jagtar Rawani? I'm concerned about their safety too. If the group thought to come after me, then...'

I don't finish the sentence, as fresh fear explodes across my chest. Rick knew all about the break-in at Beauchamp's, and how the files were copied when the alarm sounded. He knew I was there, and that Anna was with me. If they were prepared to send him and the goons to my address, what else would they do in their desperation to get the data back?

'You need to contact the police station in Chichester,' I shout with urgency. 'My sister is in custody there, and I think her life might be in danger too.'

I can't believe I didn't consider Anna's safety before. My first thoughts were Jack, Rawani, and Rachel, but she's as big a pawn in this game too. What if I'm already too late?

Cavendish's face tautens with confusion. 'Your sister?'

'Too long to explain. Please just phone somebody there and check that Anna is okay.'

She's up and off her seat a moment later, heading to the front desk and switching on the computer there, searching for a number. I stand and begin to pace, my legs not allowing me to sit still.

Freddie watches on in silence, but I wish he'd offer me reassurance that everything is going to be okay, and that this anxiety peppering my mind is nothing but paranoia brought on by the shock of the attack.

Cavendish now has the phone to her ear, and is talking to whoever has answered.

This isn't right; none of it is. Anna is just as much a victim in all of this – more so than most – and she shouldn't be sitting in a police cell waiting for fate to roll the dice again. I'm not going to let her come to harm again.

Marching over to Cavendish, I cross my arms in muted defiance.

'It's okay, your sister is fine,' she relays. 'They've just tucked her in for the night. You can relax.'

'That's not good enough,' I fire back. 'Get DI Marina Oakley on the phone. I don't care what it takes or who needs to be kicked out of bed. I want my sister out of that cell this minute.'

Chapter Forty-Five

NOW

Dorchester, Dorset

Cavendish perches on the edge of one of the desks and reaches for the telephone. She's moved us up to this dimly lit open-plan office where it's more private and slightly warmer than the chill of the ground floor. I'm pacing because I'm too anxious to sit. I've stressed to her how important it is that Anna be moved to a place of safety, but the look on Cavendish's face offers little optimism.

They came for me in my home, I can't get hold of Jack and Rawani, and my mind is jumping to paranoid conclusions. What if it's already too late and they've made simultaneous moves against the pair of them too? Together, we're strong, but without them I'm a lone voice. Who's going to believe the tinpot theories of a writer without corroboration? The only reason *Monsters* managed to secure an investigation against Francis Turgood was because Freddie, Mike, and Steve came together to share their brutal stories. I was just the stagehand pointing the spotlight on their experiences. Freddie's claims had been ignored for years, until Mike and Steve backed him up.

I can't do this on my own. I need Jack. I need Rawani. I need my sister.

Oakley isn't answering her phone either. She told me Anna would be safe in Chichester, but now I can't get hold of her. Why is nobody contactable?

Cavendish nods at me as the line connects, and my pacing halts instantly so I can listen to the conversation. She switches it to speakerphone.

'Hi, this is Detective Inspector Zoe Cavendish from Dorset Constabulary, who am I speaking to, please?'

The line crackles with static.

'You've come through to PS Nikesh Choudhury. I'm the duty sergeant. What can I do for you?'

'Thank you, PS Choudhury. I am concerned about the wellbeing of one of your custody residents this evening. I – *we* – believe her life may be in danger.'

There's a pause on the line. 'Wait, where did you say you were calling from?' Choudhury asks, his words tinged with cynicism.

'I'm a DI with Dorset Constabulary, and am calling from Dorchester. I can give you my warrant card number if you want to verify it.'

'Right,' he says, elongating the vowel, 'and you're concerned about the safety of one of our occupants?'

I can only assume the slight chuckle in his tone is as a result of being the brunt of more than one practical joke in his time. I want to interrupt their conversation, to shout and yell that this isn't a joke and that someone might be making moves on Anna already, but Cavendish's eyes are warning me to keep quiet.

'Her name's Anna Hunter, and she was brought in earlier today on suspicion of burglary. I just need you to go and check on her, and confirm she's well.'

'Hold on,' he says, and there's the sound of typing nearby.

My feet have me pacing the well-worn carpet again. Freddie is sitting in a dark corner of the office, keeping out of the way, but I wish he'd grab me and tell me everything is going to be okay.

'You said Anna Hunter?' Choudhury's voice comes back on the line.

'Yes. H-U-N-T-E-R,' Cavendish confirms.

'There's no record of anyone in custody with that name.'

I freeze, and my body temperature lowers as dread crawls the length of my spine.

Cavendish's eyebrows arch as she glares at me. 'There must be some kind of mistake. Can you look again please?'

'Maybe Oakley listed her under the name Kylie Shakespeare,' I call out to her.

'PS Choudhury? Can you also check the name Kylie Shakespeare?' Cavendish relays.

'As in the playwright?'

I nod, and Cavendish is about to confirm, when the static disappears, and the line drops.

'W-what happened?' I stammer hurrying over.

Cavendish lifts the handset and stabs the receiver. 'I-I don't know,' she replies. 'The line is fine at this end.' She redials the number for Sussex Police HQ, but it fails to connect.

The icy dread reaches my toes.

Cavendish tries again, but there's no connection. 'It could be nothing,' she says unconvincingly.

My head snaps around to Freddie. 'What if…?'

He races to my side and throws his arms around my shoulders. 'Here, listen to me. Your sister will be just fine. They've probably just had a powercut or something. There's no reason to assume that something's happened. I mean, these people would have to be pretty stupid to make a move on someone inside a police station.'

'Or desperate,' I counter.

Cavendish hops from the desk and holds her mobile up to indicate she has a call, and heads away from the two of us as she answers it.

I grab the phone Rachel got for me and try Jack's number again, but it's still switched off, so I leave him yet another message, begging him to call me ASAP. Given how late it now is, I can't believe he's still with the anti-corruption unit, and it's unlike him to leave his phone off. I'm trying to ignore the voices in my head, but they're screaming so loud that I wish I was back on Weymouth seafront, running through the sand, and yelling at the world.

I picture Jack in that hospital bed after he was driven off the road. What if the same people have come back and finished the job? What if my meddling has stolen Mila's dad from her?

Cavendish returns, but her face is ashen. 'That was Gold Command,' she says quickly. 'Apparently, there's been an attack on the police station in Chichester. An explosion of some kind apparently. All on-duty commanders are being contacted and warned to stay vigilant, *in case* it's terror-related.'

My knees give way and I crash to the floor. No, not Anna. I've only just found her.

'Are we safe here?' Freddie asks Cavendish, coming to my aid and taking my hand, but allowing me to stay crumpled on the threadbare carpet.

'Ordinarily, I would have said yes, but given what you've told me tonight… I don't know. I think it's in everyone's best interests to get you to safety, Emma. Let me figure out where we can go, and then I'll be back.'

She disappears out of the room, but I can't speak as I look at Freddie. I know in my heart that this explosion isn't terror-related, and now I need to get myself to Chichester ASAP. We're hours away, but I need to see for myself.

I've never been this scared in all my life.

The Dorchester office has been a hive of activity since Cavendish received the call from Gold Command. She's moved Freddie and me to one of the soft interview suites downstairs until she can arrange transport for us. My phone has no signal down here, so I have no way of knowing *if* Jack, Rawani, or Oakley have returned any of my calls. I don't want to just sit tight and wait, but I also can't be certain there isn't a gang of armed conspirators waiting for me just beyond these walls.

I kicked the hornets' nest and angered them. I've put us all in danger.

I can't stop my mind replaying everything that's happened these last few months. We kept pushing and probing, trying to expose those in the ring of paedophiles and traffickers so they could face the justice they deserved, but maybe I did underestimate the lengths to which they would go to keep their identities hidden. They've attacked each of us as individuals, but still I continued. We're so close to unpicking the whole thing, and I've forced them to play their final card. Without Anna, we lose Daisy Beauchamp. Without Jack, we lose the NCA's investigation.

I don't know who's left I can trust. I'm taking a huge chance in hoping that Cavendish is on the level, but what if she's holding us here until someone arrives to finish us off? I trusted Oakley, but what if she was the one who told them where Anna was being held? I know my brain is leaping to irrational conclusions, but I had no inkling about Rick, and I'm not prepared to repeat the mistake.

But I swear now: as long as there is breath in my lungs, I will never stop fighting to expose every last one of them. I won't allow their victims to continue suffering in silence.

I stand and move to the door.

'W-where are you going?' Freddie asks.

'*We're* getting out of here, Freddie,' I reply, with more bravado than I'm feeling. 'We need to get off the grid and plan our next move. I know somewhere we can go where they'll never find us, but we need to move now. Are you game?'

He stands without hesitation. 'You lead, and I promise I'll do whatever I can to keep you safe.'

My eyes fill, but I don't have time for emotion, and so I give him a firm nod and reach for the handle.

But it slips from my grasp as someone from the other side depresses it, and the opening door slams into my foot. I start and scuttle back across the room, my mind already picturing a masked assassin coming for us, but just as I'm searching for anything I can use as a weapon, I see Jack's face in the gap, and

I can't stop myself rushing over to him and throwing my arms around him.

'Oh, thank God you're safe,' I hear him whisper, his breath warm against my ear.

I can't keep the tears at bay, and they blot between my cheek and his shoulder. 'I thought…' I begin to say, but I can't finish the sentence, as he moves forwards and shuffles me out of the doorway.

'We kept our phones off so they wouldn't be able to track us,' he adds, and peels me away to watch as Oakley enters the room, with Anna cuffed behind her.

My bubble of anxiety explodes, and I silently thank all the angels who have brought them to me safely. I break free of Jack and embrace Anna, the tears now flowing freely.

Anna keeps her shoulders tight, not yet ready to let emotion show. 'So, is this guy your boyfriend then or what?' she asks, nodding towards Jack.

Our cheeks flush, but neither of us speaks. I guess it's too late for formal introductions.

Oakley clears her throat. 'Jack called me and said he didn't think Anna would be safe in custody, and then convinced me that we should move her. Just as well we did, based on what I just heard on the news. But I don't think we can stay here either. We need to get you all to safety for a debrief and to plan next steps. Who've you been dealing with here?'

'DI Zoe Cavendish,' I just about manage to say.

'And you trust her?'

I look at Jack, and we both nod.

'Okay, I'll go and find her, and then we'll get moving. Something tells me there's a lot you need to fill me in on.'

'I know somewhere,' I say, glancing at Anna. 'Mum's best

friend Hayley still lives in Weymouth. She won't bat an eyelid, and will be over the moon to hear that Anna is back.'

Jack lifts his phone. 'I'll let Rawani know to come and meet us.'

Oakley leaves the room, and I try to convince myself that everything will be okay now that we're back together, but I still don't know what the next step looks like. If the people we've been chasing were prepared to go on the offensive, I dread to think what else they have in store. And for the first time, I'm doubting the strength of the evidence we have. Will it be enough to convince Oakley and Cavendish to pursue an investigation or charges against Beauchamp and his cohorts? All I know is that I need to get things straight in my head before they'll consider options. These next twenty-four hours are going to be critical.

Chapter Forty-Six

NOW

Chichester, West Sussex

30 hours later

It's cold enough out here that every breath emerges from our mouths in elongated clouds of white. I wouldn't have it any other way though. Jack's mouth is chattering away beside me, as excited as I've ever seen him, I think. Dressed in thick Kevlar, he's busy telling me how privileged I am to be so close to the action of this unfolding scene. Up ahead I can see DCS Jagtar Rawani deep in conversation with the head of the armed response unit and, like Chess Grandmasters, they are hovered over a board, carefully placing their pawns ahead of this enormous game, while the head of the unit relays their instructions courtesy of a headpiece and microphone. From where Jack and I observe, we can hear those messages being received, and then carried out with discreet rustling.

I glance at my watch and see it's nearly five in the morning.

The sun is starting to peek through the clouds behind the large house in the distance, but if anyone inside happened to glance out, they wouldn't see anything beyond the large screen that has been carefully erected around the estate to covertly hide the volume of activities underway beyond it. This morning's endeavours have been carefully planned for the greatest impact, and most of those this side of the enormous curtain have been awake every minute of the planning.

Today marks the first chapter of Operation Cicada, and with Rick's testimony hot off the press, Rawani's plan is to cut off the snake's head. Although he hasn't admitted as much, I can see from the excitement in his eyes that he's relieved his proposed retirement has been postponed. From our first meeting in his office all those months ago, I never would have thought that he would end up leading the charge. I wouldn't trust anyone else to handle the reins.

Rick has accepted responsibility for his small part in trying to derail my own investigation, and whilst he can't directly tie Beauchamp to the conspiracy, he has confirmed that the conspiracy exists, and has named a handful of others, which has helped identify the hierarchy. Like a house of cards, it will tumble. I hope one day I'll find it in me to forgive Rick's betrayal. Grudges are for those who don't want to find closure.

'Here they are,' I hear Cavendish's voice declare from behind me.

Turning, I just about make out her face moving towards us, with Oakley in close proximity. The pair have been roped into the task force at Jack's request, each representing their respective areas, and considered above reproach. Their credentials have been checked and double-checked against the list of names recovered from the hard drive provided by Daisy

Beauchamp, and against the names considered in Jack and the NCA's original investigation, as has the name of every officer involved in this morning's operation.

Oakley and Cavendish join Jack and me at the perimeter edge of the activity, and offer the cups of tea they have brought with them, which we gratefully accept.

'DCS Rawani wanted you to know things will be starting any minute,' Oakley says, 'and to make sure that you both have a good viewing spot of the house as they move in to arrest Mr Beauchamp.'

Jack nods and looks at me to make sure I've understood. I nod my agreement and follow as they lead us through the gathered crowd, and to the far side of the area.

'How is Anna?' Cavendish asks quietly as we pick up speed.

'I have no idea,' I respond carefully. 'I haven't heard from her since you two insisted she go into protective custody. I was actually hoping you might be able to give me more of an update.'

Cavendish exchanges a glance with Oakley before meeting my gaze. 'I'm sorry, but I hadn't realised that had happened already.'

'Don't look so glum,' Jack says next. 'She's there for her own protection, and it doesn't mean you'll never see her again. Once all the arrests have been made and those involved have had their day in court, there'll be no reason for your sister to remain off the grid.'

I nod, even though I don't agree with either of their conclusions. I understand the rules of protective custody, and that she won't be allowed to make contact with me, even if she wants to, and that's the part I'm most uncertain of: even if she could, would she want to?

We stop as we arrive at the far side of the screen, now beside a television screen, which is showing an undisturbed image of the front door of the property. There is a group of five men in black waiting in the wings of the door, and the one at the front holds out his hand, fingers splayed, and each slowly lowers, counting down, and when his fist is tight, they move forward as one, forcing an entrance to the property.

I can almost hear them shouting that they are armed police as they move through the door, and then the image on the screen flicks to the bodycam footage of the officer at the front as he holds his weapon aloft and moves up the stairs, calling out as he goes.

He stops at the first floor with another armed man, and they move from door to door, until a dressing-gown-clad and confused-looking Ian Beauchamp emerges from one of the doors and is quickly tackled to the ground, his wrists secured behind his back, and the paper warrant for his arrest pushed before his face. The screen flicks to a second bodycam which moves into the room from which Beauchamp emerged, and a woman is seen huddling beneath the duvet cover, presumably Mrs Beauchamp, though it is difficult to see in the darkness of the room.

The screen returns to the first bodycam, as Beauchamp is lifted to his feet and is being led down the stairs, and then the screen flicks back to the view of the front door as Beauchamp is pushed through. He blinks against the bright light shining in his face. He looks as pompous as when he walked into my flat three days ago, so certain of himself, as if this entire scene has been planned. I can't bear to watch it unfold and I step away.

'Where are you going?' Jack asks, hurrying after me.

'I'm sorry,' I reply, keeping my eyes low so he won't see them watering. 'You stay,' I encourage. 'I just need some air.'

'You want me to drive you back to Weymouth? Or the train station?'

I stop and pull him into my embrace. 'Thank you, but I'd prefer to walk. Besides, you're probably needed here.'

He allows me to go, but I can feel his eyes on me for a long time, until I finally have the courage to turn and see that I'm alone. And that's when I duck to the left and in through the trees. Once I'm off the main road, and certain I can no longer be seen from the main house, I follow the path through the trees, only stopping when I arrive at the new campervan that's parked at the top.

'Ah, good, it's you,' Anna says, stepping out of the shadows. 'I thought you'd never make it.'

I double-check that I haven't been followed before turning back and smiling at my sister. 'I said I would. Are you ready to go?'

She nods, and opens the passenger door.

Chapter Forty-Seven

NOW

Wareham, Dorset

Ken Bruce – apparently no relation to the Radio 2 DJ – told me on the phone that he is the private investigator my mum hired almost twenty years ago when it seemed like the police had given up hope of ever finding Anna. Unprepared to accept never seeing her daughter again, she would visit him every time I was at Dad's place in Swanage. I always did wonder what her special appointments were all about as her hair never looked any different when she collected me at the bus stop, and Dad never seemed any the wiser either.

Wareham is an historic market town, situated on the River Frome, and as we arrive I have a tingle of excitement, recognising the quay and some of the pubs along the main road. Watching Anna's face, I'm sure there are traces of recognition in her eyes too. It's funny, but when she suggested telling everyone that she'd gone into protective custody so she could slip under the radar, I thought I would never see her again, but she gave me a burner phone containing one number, and promised she would ring once she'd sorted out some new wheels.

I'm pretty sure this campervan is even older and more rickety than the last one, but it was bought with cash, and she says it's all she needs. I suppose after a lifetime on the run, it must be hard to put down roots. After I'd spoken to Ken, the investigator, I asked Anna if she would come with me. Even if she can't remember Mum, she deserves to hear how hard Mum tried to get her back.

We park at the Streche Road Car Park and make our way towards the fire station and away from the town centre, following the directions on my phone's app, until we arrive at a small bungalow on Worgret Road. It is the smallest property amongst much larger detached houses covered in solar panels. I double-check the address, but this is what he gave me. I was expecting some kind of rundown office like in those old gumshoe movies Mum would watch late at night when I was supposed to be asleep. This must be Ken's home, rather than his office.

Heading up the drive, Anna is wearing a baseball cap to cover her head, and a tracksuit that makes her look as though she's just left a gym. I'm in black jeans and a jacket, so as a pair we're a bit of a before and after photograph.

The man who comes to the door is out of breath, his large belly practically bursting out of his shirt and trousers. He's wearing a confused expression until I give him my name.

'Oh yes, of course, of course,' he mutters moving back into the house and beckoning us to follow.

Anna looks back along the road before stepping inside,

keeping the peak of the cap pulled down over her eyes. I close the door behind us and take in the narrow corridor through which we are now walking. There is barely room for Ken to fit along it, and I can see nails poking out of the walls where frames must have once hung, but no more. Ken heads through the door to his left, where a large bay window adorns the room in sunlight. There is a battered leather armchair facing the window, but as Ken drops into it, he uses his feet to swivel it around to face us.

The only other chairs in the room are the two hard-backed ones tucked under the table, so we each pull out a chair and sit. The room isn't big, and there's no sign of a television or radio. There is a chess board standing on a small table in one corner of the room, a couple of wooden units with drawers, and more hooks in the wall with missing frames. The paint on the walls looks old and faded, and in fact the carpet is threadbare in places; now that I'm looking at the windows, I can see that they're probably the original single panes that came with the property. The bungalow is in dire need of renovation, much like its owner.

'I was sorry to learn of your mother's passing,' Ken says to me, wiping his mouth with a handkerchief.

He's probably wondering who Anna is, though he hasn't asked. I'm tempted to introduce her, but I don't want to make him feel bad that he never managed to find her. He has a full head of hair, despite his age, which juts out at all manner of angles, like I'd expect to see if someone had just been electrocuted. Despite that, he has a kindly way about him, and in some way I'm reminded of my grandfather, my memories of whom are limited. Maybe that was what first attracted Mum to seek his help.

'You said on the phone she hired you about a year after my sister's disappearance?' I ask encouragingly.

'Aye, that's right. That was back when I rented a room in an office in the town centre. I was still newly qualified, and your mother was only my second ever client. I've never met a woman so heartbroken, and as soon as she told me her story, I made a promise to her that I'd never stop looking for her missing daughter. She said she couldn't afford much, but I told her just to pay what little she could whenever she could, and that I would give her updates as and when I had any to give. It was an unconventional arrangement, but that's how it was for a long time.

'At the start we'd meet once a month, but most of that time was spent with her sharing background information about your sister, and family life, to help me paint a picture of who I was looking for. As I said, she was only my second client, so I had plenty of time I could dedicate to the search in those early months, but as leads dried up and I became busier, unfortunately I wasn't able to give the case as much time as it deserved. Still, every now and again I'd come across a rumour or fragment of information and I'd let her know. I know also that she never stopped looking for evidence, that is until she moved into the nursing home. That was the last time I spoke to her, just before. She came here to this house, and she told me what the doctor had diagnosed, and she asked me to keep a few bits and pieces for her. That was why I called you, you see, now that she's gone; I thought you might want her things back.'

'Thank you, Mr Bruce. Yes, if you're happy to give them to me, I can make sure they're dealt with.'

He stands with a strain and crosses the room, disappearing through the door and promising he'll return in a few moments.

'Are you okay?' I ask Anna, who hasn't spoken a word since we parked the campervan.

She nods, but it is so hard to make out her face beneath the shadow of the peak. Maybe it wasn't fair for me to drag her along today. At least she's heard for herself how hard Mum kept looking.

I can hear Ken shuffling about in the room next door, but then he appears in the doorway carrying an old and fairly large cardboard box, with a crisp manufacturer's name prominently in the middle. He stumbles into the room, practically dropping the box onto the table, pausing to wipe the sweat from his forehead before shuffling back out.

'Do you need any help?' I call after him, but if he does answer, I don't hear it.

I can't see Anna now over the top of the box, and so I stand and check whether she wants to look inside, but she leans back in her chair and nods for me to do it. The box isn't taped up, but the worn panels have been woven shut, and easily come apart as I pull at one of the ends.

'It contains books,' I say, reaching in and extracting one of the notebooks. 'This one says 1995 on the spine.' I flick it open and rummage through the pages, gasping when I realise what I'm staring at. 'This… These are diaries.' I close the notebook and rest it on the table, before reaching for another. 'This one is from 1992,' I continue, 'and this one's from 1993. I never knew Mum kept a diary, did you?'

Anna has picked up the first notebook and is skimming the pages. 'I had no idea.'

I flick through the spines until I come across the year 2000 and pull it out. It feels heavier than the others, as if it contains a world of secrets, or maybe it's just that I know how significant a year it was for her. I don't want to open it, knowing that it must contain her deepest and darkest thoughts. I'm concerned that if I see that version of her, my memories will somehow become tainted.

Ken lugs a second crisp box onto the table, and Anna moves out of his way, allowing him to rest his hands on the table to catch his breath. 'There's one more box,' he pants, 'but it's smaller. I won't be a second.'

I return the 2000 diary to its box and open the new one. There are a handful of diaries in this one too, but also a dust-covered shoebox. Gripping my fingers around the edge of it, I take it out and place it on the table, lifting the lid. My heart brightens when I see a photograph of Mum, me, and Anna staring back up at me. I extract it and pass it to Anna, and I swear there is the briefest glimpse of a smile. She must also recognise the old house the three of us are standing in front of – a house that looked just the same when we were there a couple of days ago.

'I remember this,' I hear Anna say, but I can hear the strain in her voice.

I return my attention to the box, extracting a child-sized gold bracelet and a matchbox, which makes me gag when I open it.

'What is it?' Anna asks, and she bursts out laughing when she sees inside. 'My teeth? I can't believe she kept all my baby teeth!' She takes the gold bracelet from me and holds it up to the light. 'I was given this the day I made my First Holy Communion. I remember being told it was very precious and that I wasn't allowed to wear it at school in case it got broken or lost. I was to save it only for special occasions. But look at it now; it isn't even real gold.'

Ken huffs and wheezes as he carries another shoebox into the room, but I sense it is the strain of walking, rather than what's contained in the box, that is causing his breathlessness.

'Are you all right?' I check. 'Do you want me to get you a glass of water or something?'

'Thank you,' he replies. 'The kitchen is at the end of the hallway, and you should find a glass on the draining board.'

I follow his instructions, trying to ignore the pungent smell of rotting meat emanating from the dustbin. I return with the glass of water. Ken is back in his chair and smiles gratefully when I hand him the glass.

'Feel free to take as long as you need looking through those bits and pieces. I'm not entirely sure what's in there. She just asked me to look after it for her.'

I turn and see Anna has now opened the final box, but she's staring at the contents with a puzzled expression.

'What's wrong?' I ask as I move next to her so I too can look inside, but I gasp as I realise what I'm looking at. And then I hear my dad's voice: *I left something in the garage. It's a box of sorts, a green case but small. It contains something very important and I need you to get it for me.*

Chapter Forty-Eight

THEN

Portland, Dorset

The day before John Hunter's death

'John? What are you doing here?' Bronwyn asked, opening the door to her ex-husband, racking her brain for a forgotten meeting or appointment.

His shirt was soaked through, despite the relatively clement forecast, and his red cheeks puffed as he looked to the left and right and then met her questioning gaze.

'I'm sorry to just turn up unannounced like this, but I need to speak to you, Winnie.'

She pulled the door closer to her body. 'Oh no, John, whatever it is, I don't want to hear it. If you have anything you want to say, put it in a letter. I have to go and collect Emma from school soon, so I don't have time to hear about your latest error of judgement.'

'Please, Winnie,' he said pushing himself closer to the gap in the doorway.

She grimaced at the smell of stale beer on his breath, but didn't have the heart to close the door on him, promising herself no matter what he said to her, she wouldn't give him any money.

'You have five minutes,' she said, stepping back from the door holding her breath as he bustled in past her.

He strode to the sofas before turning and looking at her awkwardly, as if he didn't know if he was allowed to sit. Although he'd once lived in this house, it was no longer his. Most traces of him had been removed after the divorce.

'Sit,' she said, closing the door and crossing to the armchair and making a point of looking at her watch so she'd know when his time was up.

'No chance of a drink then?' he asked, as he dropped into the sofa, but her raised eyebrow told him all he needed to know.

Pulling out a cigarette, his fingers trembled as he pushed it between his lips and lit it. He knew she hated him smoking, but he needed something to settle his nerves. To his surprise, she didn't instantly evict him, just slid a saucer across the table for him to drop his ash into.

She looked at her watch for a second time, but for his benefit rather than her own. 'I do have to collect Emma shortly.'

He inhaled deeply, closing his eyes and tried to recall the speech he'd spent all morning rehearsing. 'Before I begin, I want you to know how sorry I am. For everything. If I could have my time again, I'd do everything differently, I swear. I never meant to be the cause of so much pain.'

Bronwyn rolled her eyes. How many times had she heard this speech before? Every time he'd *accidentally* bet the housekeeping money on a sure thing that had failed. Or when he'd missed an appointment at the marriage guidance counsellor's office because he'd *forgotten*. He was always so sorry, but if he truly meant the words, he wouldn't keep screwing up. The day he moved out had felt like lifting a stock from around her neck.

'Yes, well, none of us can change the past, can we, John? If it's money you're after, you're out of luck as it isn't pay day until the weekend. I don't even have enough to buy milk this week.'

His eyes flew open. 'You want money? I can spare you a few quid if it would help?' He rested the cigarette on the edge of the saucer, and reached into his pocket, rattling the change inside.

Bronwyn frowned at the stain the cigarette was leaving on her best china, but at least it wasn't burning a hole in the carpet or leaving a scorch mark on the freshly polished coffee table.

He dropped the change on the table and began to sort it into pounds, silvers, and coppers.

'That really isn't necessary, John,' she said, determined not to provide absolution by accepting a few dirty coins.

Hayley had already agreed to pick her up a few groceries when she went to Safeway later.

He continued to sort the coins, sliding all bar his bus fare over. 'There you go. I'm sorry it isn't more, but I don't want little Emma going hungry.'

Bronwyn ignored the gesture, as she didn't want to give him more time by getting into an argument with him.

He picked up his cigarette and took a long drag, blowing

the smoke away from her, though there was little point as that only served to spread the disgusting smell further. 'Where was I?' He paused, trying to recall how far into his speech he'd got, before realising he'd barely started. 'I need to tell you something, and I don't know how to find the words. Now that I'm here with you, they just don't want to flow. You know?'

She crossed her arms, taking another glance at the watch.

He looked her straight in the eye. 'The thing is, Winnie, I found her. Our Anna, that is. I know who took her.'

Bronwyn narrowed her eyes, her mind trying to predict what his endgame was. Why had he shown up today if not to ask her for money? He'd claimed to know where Anna was when he was at the hospital, before clarifying that he knew a person who'd claimed to know. One of the inmates in his care, or so he'd claimed. She'd taken it all – as she always did – with a much-needed pinch of salt.

He stubbed out the cigarette and immediately lit a second. Bronwyn coughed, but it didn't deter him.

'What do you want, John?' She sighed quietly under her breath.

'I had this plan… to get her back, like, you know. I thought if I could get enough money together, I could pay off my debt, and then they'd have to let her go, but they refused, and so then I threatened to go to the police and just come clean about everything—'

'What are you talking about, John? Coming clean about what?'

He looked at her, the tears already leaking out. 'I can't say, but there was some stuff… Stuff I did a long time ago, which I'm not proud of… But that's why they took her… as insurance, like… I didn't know that's what they'd do… but I don't want to make the same mistake again… That's why I'm telling you all this.'

He buried his head in his hands.

Bronwyn sat forward in her chair. 'All what, John? What are you saying? You're saying that the people who have Anna took her because of you?

She could hear him sobbing as he nodded frantically.

Bronwyn leapt forward, crashing to the carpet on her knees and crawling over to him.

'John, you need to tell me everything. I need to know where she is.'

He kept his eyes covered as he shook her heart. 'It's… no… use. They won't let her go. Not now.'

'I don't understand, John. Who is holding Anna? I need to know.'

He rubbed at his eyes with his hands, until she reached for a tissue from her bag and passed it to him.

'It doesn't matter anymore,' he said as the blotting didn't ease the flow of tears. 'We're never going to be able to get her back.'

'Rubbish!' Bronwyn shouted, slapping him hard across the cheek to snap him out of his self-pity. 'If she's still alive, then that's the best news I've ever heard. We'll phone the police and let them know, and then they'll go and get her.'

'No, Winnie, you don't understand,' he said, shaking his head again. 'They'll have moved her by now. It's what they do.'

'It's what who does, John? Who are these people? How do you know people who would abduct an innocent child?'

His eyes met hers, but he still couldn't find the strength to tell her everything. He'd written it down so he could get the confession straight before memorising the bitter words. But now that he was faced with the moment to clear his conscience, his brain wouldn't let him.

She stood and crossed the room, picking up the telephone and listening for a dialling tone.

'What are you doing?' he said, standing and blocking her way. 'Who are you phoning?'

'The police. If you won't tell me whatever it is you know, then maybe they'll have a better method of extracting—'

He snatched the phone from her hand and it killed the words on her tongue.

'You're not listening to me, Winnie. We can't phone the police. They'll find out, and then they'll come for little Emma.'

Bronwyn shivered as her blood ran cold. 'What did you just say?'

'They said if we go to the police they'll come for Emma as well.'

She slapped him again, this time with much more force, but he didn't move.

'What the hell have you done, John?'

'None of that matters. All you need to know is that I'm going to do whatever I can to fix all this. I have a plan. Okay?'

'No, it's not okay!' she erupted, but he grabbed at her arms and held them firm.

'I'm sorry, Winnie, but this is the way it has to be now. We don't have a choice.'

'The hell we haven't! Start talking, John, or I swear to God I will phone the police. What are you mixed up in? Why did people take our daughter, and who the hell is threatening Emma? We need to phone the police.'

He squeezed her arms tighter, as the stress worsened. She

wasn't listening to him, but he had no doubt they would fulfil their threat if he didn't get her on side.

'Damnit, Winnie, you're not listening to me,' he shouted. 'These people… they're serious fucking people! They have moles everywhere, and the moment they learn that we've contacted the police, we'll have signed Emma's death sentence.'

She tried to pull her arms free, but he continued to press tighter, leaving white marks on her arms. Pulling him closer, she drove her knee into his groin and he instantly released his grip, turning and hunching over to protect himself from a second attack.

Bronwyn hurried across the room, putting the sofa between them to buy her enough time in case he reached for her again.

He grabbed the edge of the sofa, using it to support his bulk as he composed himself and muttered, 'I'm sorry,' over and over.

'Don't be sorry, John, just bloody fix this. If it's your fault Anna was taken, then tell me why this had to happen.'

Stooped over, he met her gaze, but still the words wouldn't come. 'I'm sorry, Winnie. If I could go back and fix things I would. All I can do is make sure they don't come for Emma too. I have a plan, and I will make *them* listen if it's the last thing I do.'

She couldn't concentrate on any one question as her mind flooded with dozens at the same time. John continued sucking in deep breaths and finally straightened before returning the phone to its cradle. He looked at his ex-wife and knew instantly that she would phone the police the moment he left, unless he convinced her why moving on was their only choice. The best they could hope for was keeping hold of the daughter they still had. It was time to get everything off his chest, even though he could already foresee how much pain it would bring her.

'Sit down, Winnie, and I'll tell you everything. You deserve to know what happened. I won't let those bastards take Emma, no matter the cost. One way or another, it'll be sorted by tomorrow.'

Chapter Forty-Nine

NOW

Wareham, Dorset

'I know that case,' I say to Anna, moving closer and recognising the rust around the hinges on the lid. 'Dad made me fetch this for him back in the day. He said it contained something important, and I wasn't allowed to mention it to Mum.'

I turn and look at Ken, but something has either caught his attention outside the window or he's deliberately choosing not to look at me.

'What was in it?' Anna asks, lifting it out of the shoebox and slowly turning it over in her hands.

'I never looked,' I tell her, instantly fearing the contents but with no idea why.

'It's not very heavy,' Anna says, shaking the box. The same rattle I heard all those years ago echoes around the room.

'It's locked,' I tell her. 'Is there a key in the box?'

She lifts the shoebox and tips it upside down but nothing falls out. 'What do you think it is?'

I can picture Dad's face when he first told me about the box and how he took me for a special lunch after I'd retrieved it and brought it to him in Swanage. I also recall how we returned to the bedsit to find it had been burgled, and how someone had then thrown a brick through his window. Whatever it contained, it had brought heat to his door, and now I fear just what damage it will do here today.

'It's probably nothing,' I say to Anna, hoping it will be enough for her to put it away so we can move on. I don't know why, but I feel like opening the box will only bring more pain and heartache, and God knows we've had enough of that already.

But Anna is rattling the box again, and now her eyes are studying the lock. For the briefest second we're twenty-one years younger and in the yard and she's refusing to listen to me because I'm just her little sister and how could I possibly know more than her.

I reach out to take the case from her when she places it on its edge on the floor. I'm about to ask what she's doing when she drives her trainer hard onto the rusting hinge, and the case cracks open. She collects the mangled box and smiles proudly at me.

'Never found a lock I can't get into.'

Lifting the lid, her excitement drops to disappointment as she sees the cause of the rattling. Extracting the small VHS-C cassette. It seems so old fashioned now, but this is the sort of tape that would have been used in a handheld camcorder, back before everything went digital. I don't remember Mum and

Dad ever owning such a camcorder, but then it could have been before I was old enough to remember.

'A tape?' Anna questions, turning it over in her fingers, as if just staring at it might reveal the reason it has been so carefully hidden for all these years. The green case is now back in the shoebox, an unwanted trophy.

I look over to Ken again, who is still choosing to show us his back, but if this case has remained locked and hidden for all these years, there's no way he could know what's on it. Is there?

Anna puts the tape on the table, now more interested in the diaries and mementos from the second box. It's the right thing to do: ignore the tape. Yet I can't take my eyes off it. It's like I'm no longer in control of my own thought processes. Even though every sinew in my body is telling me to walk away and never watch the tape, I find myself reaching for it, and then carrying it over to Ken.

'I don't suppose you have anything we could watch this on, do you?'

His head dips slightly and he sighs audibly. 'I was afraid you were going to ask that.'

'Why?'

'Your mum liked to keep herself to herself, but I always got the impression that there was something about that tape… Like it was the key to something she couldn't live with. I always assumed it had something to do with your dad. She never did believe he committed suicide.'

The cassette suddenly feels unbearably heavy in my hand. 'What's on it?'

'I've never watched it.'

'That isn't what I asked, Mr Bruce.'

He doesn't elaborate. Instead, he crosses the room and disappears again into the room at the back.

'Could one of you give me a hand with this?' he calls a moment later, and Anna heads after him, returning a moment later carrying a hefty television-video combi unit, not dissimilar to one some of my friends had when we were growing up.

It looks ridiculously bulky compared to modern televisions, and as Anna lowers it to the table, I can see it's covered in a thick layer of grey dust. Ken waddles in a moment later carrying what looks like a VHS tape, but he slides a switch and a small window opens.

'Now,' he says, pausing to regain his breath. 'Are you sure you two want to watch this?'

'Why wouldn't we? I thought you didn't know what was on it?' Anna asks, stepping forward, and instantly looking far more menacing than I ever could.

It's another example of just how much we've grown apart, and yet our endgame is still the same. I do my best to make myself look as intimidating as Anna, and Ken picks up the small cassette and inserts it in the larger version before handing it to me. He fishes for the plug and then hands it to Anna.

'There's a socket in the wall beneath the table. Would you mind plugging it in?'

Anna takes the plug and crawls under, and a moment later a small red LED of warning appears on the front of the television.

'I've no idea where the remote is,' Ken says, 'but if you push the tape in it should turn itself on and play automatically. I'm going to need a drink.'

He heads out of the room without offering refreshment to either of us, but I follow his instructions and slot the cassette into the player. There is temporary black, grey, and white static, and a gentle humming, before the tape engages. I cover my mouth as I see our dad appear on the screen. He's sitting in what looks like one of the old wooden dining table chairs we had in Portland. And as I allow my eyes to blur him out, I'd swear he's in the kitchen of that same house.

My eyes fill instantly and my chest constricts as I hear his voice for the first time in almost twenty years.

'My name is John William Hunter, and I am making this recording of my own volition.' He pauses, and lifts a tumbler of what I would guess is scotch, and sips from it.

'I remember that voice,' Anna whispers beside me, and I instinctively put my arm around her, remembering it's been even longer for her.

Dad lowers the glass but he keeps his fingers wrapped tightly around it. 'I am neither proud of my actions, nor seeking forgiveness for what I have done. God will judge me soon enough.'

My hand shoots out and a finger stabs at the faded pause button which is just below where the tape was inserted.

'What are you doing?' Anna asks.

I open my mouth to respond but I'm not sure how best to word it. 'My instincts are rarely wrong about certain things,' I begin. 'And every one of them right now is telling me that Dad kept this tape hidden for a very good reason. I have no idea how it fell into Mum's possession, but she too kept it hidden. Maybe there's a reason they didn't want us to see it.'

Anna snorts and her eyes water. 'It's funny, you calling them Mum and Dad. That's not how I see them; not anymore. I know that man on the screen was a part of my life, and if you say he's my dad, I have no reason to doubt what you're saying, but I don't remember having a mum or a dad. My first memory is of a man I didn't know trapping me inside the back of his car. I remember being taken to a caravan on some farm somewhere, and my life being threatened. I remember men taking photographs of me, and calling me darling and sweetheart, and then I remember other men pushing their tongues into my mouth, and forcing my head down between their legs. What I don't know is why I had to endure all of that. The life I once had is long gone, but if this man on the screen wants his confession to be heard, then I say we should listen.'

My lips tremble, and I feel the warm splashes on my cheeks. The torture she has just described… I wouldn't wish it on my worst enemy, let alone my own sister. But what upsets me most is the thought that there is nothing I can say or do to ever come close to easing her pain.

I press the play button, honouring her wishes.

Chapter Fifty

NOW

Wareham, Dorset

'Many years ago,' Dad's voice sounds again, as I do my best to hide my own upset, 'before all of this, before I fell in love and was blessed with two wonderful daughters, I agreed to work for a man who promised me wealth beyond my wildest imagination. He told me he was a movie director, and he needed someone with a steady hand to work the camera for him. I was stupid – naïve maybe – but I idolised this man, and when he took me to his movie set, I closed my eyes to what was going on in front of the camera.' He takes another sip of the scotch. 'I knew it was wrong. I knew that although the actors weren't screaming or crying… ultimately they were children, and they shouldn't have been doing the things that were asked of them.

'Eventually, I came to my senses, and I packed it all in… moved away and started my life over, but I never forgot. I fell in love and got married, and it felt like I'd been given a second chance; a new shot at life. A better life. I took a job in the prison service so I could give something back, and help keep the public safe. I worked hard. I tried to make amends, and I swore I would do whatever I could to make others' lives better every day. To make my family proud of me.'

He drains the rest of the scotch from his glass, and even through the grain of the low-resolution video, I can see how deathly pale he looks.

'But I should have known that something like that would come back to get at me. You can't see what I've seen and hope to get your hands clean. Two years ago, a prisoner was transferred to Portland. A seedy good-for-nothing, always trying to get one over on others. He recognised me from that time, and he tried to blackmail me. I tried to pay him off. I gambled but lost more than I won, so then I borrowed more to give to him. And then it was like my prayers had been answered. He crossed the wrong convict and got shanked in one of the bathrooms. But only after he'd revealed his grubby little secret to his cellmate – someone who was not so easily bought off. He wanted more than I could pay, threatening to reveal the truth about me unless I did as he said. He said he wanted me to prove my loyalty, and that to do that I'd have to help some of his crew pull off a heist.'

He tops up his glass and drains more than half of it, his words now starting to slur. 'I refused to comply. Told him just to tell the prison governor or the police and leave me to take my chances. But he didn't like that, and then Anna went missing. At first I didn't connect the two incidents, until he then said he'd made a recommendation to an acquaintance and that the only way I'd get Anna back was to go ahead with the heist. I didn't believe him until a package mysteriously appeared in my locker at work. It was the top Anna had been wearing the day she disappeared. I was going to take it to the police, but it would be my word against his, and it wasn't like I knew where she was. I tried for so long to resist, but they kept ramping up the pressure, so I did the only thing I could… I went along with the robbery.

'I only had to drive the van away, so it never really felt like I was doing anything wrong. I was convinced someone would screw up and they'd get caught inside and at least I'd get away, but it all went like clockwork. They were in and out in minutes without any alarm being triggered, and I was back home in bed just after midnight. Winnie never had a clue what I'd done. If she knew any of my bullshit, she never would have looked at me twice.'

He shuffles forward in his seat, pulling out a packet of cigarettes and lighting one, the exhaled smoke making the footage even less clear.

'When I next saw him inside, I demanded to know where Anna was, but he started saying that there'd been some trouble with her. At a party somewhere, she'd caused a lot of embarrassment and she'd been moved, and he didn't know where to. I was furious, and I told him I would tell the police everything, and that's when he threatened Emma. Said if I so much as looked the wrong way, he'd have the same people come for Emma, and then I'd have both their deaths on my hands. If I can get close enough to him… threaten him somehow… or offer him enough money, then maybe I can get her back and keep them away from us for good. I still remember the faces of who I saw at that film studio, and I know how much they'll give to keep their pasts a secret.

'And that's why I'm now making this video. I don't care

what's going to become of me in the future, so long as I keep what's left of this family safe. There needs to be a record of how we ended up in this mess. It's all my fault, and I don't...'

He suddenly stands and heads to the kitchen door, opening it a crack, as if he can hear something on the other side, before hurrying back, and the screen cuts to the same black, grey, and white static. I leave it playing for a minute in case there's more footage, but Anna eventually tells me to switch it off.

I don't know what to say. I want to comfort Anna, but no words will be enough, and I want to shout and swear and scream that that wasn't my dad on the tape; it must have been some lookalike whose voice just happened to have the same rhythmic burr as my dad's. But it couldn't have been him. My dad was a sweet, and warm, and loving man. He wasn't perfect, and my memories of him have probably been rose-tinted following his tragic early death, but the man I knew and loved couldn't have been capable of such horrific actions.

And yet...

When I consider how the tragedy I've witnessed over these last few years, from Freddie Mitchell to Cassie Hilliard, Natalie Sullivan to Sally Curtis, Aurélie Lebrun to Jemima Hooper, Jo-Jo Neville to Zara Edwards, all were let down by parents or guardians or betrayed by those charged with caring for them... should I even be surprised by this revelation?

Anna turns and moves to the bay window, but even from here I can see she is wiping her eyes. I know there's nothing I can say or do, and I'm not even going to attempt to add context to the confession we just watched. My fingers entangle as I take a deep breath and invoke my inner Rachel. Appearing behind Anna I put my arms around her and hold her still. At first she shuffles and battles to break my grip, but I've lost her before and there is nothing in this world that's going to stop me holding onto her this time.

'I know you probably don't want my love and support, Anna, but whether you want to believe it or not, we *are* sisters, and I am going to fight every day to give you a better life than you've had.'

She balks and tries to break my hold again, but it is as firm as it can be.

'We will bring all of them to justice. I swear I won't stop fighting until every single name on that hard drive has been exposed. The world will know what they have done, but I'm not going anywhere. We only have each other. Please let me in. Nothing you can say or do will frighten me off.'

We both start as Ken clears his throat just inside the door. 'I'm so pleased to see you found each other. Your mum always used to say you wouldn't give up, Emma. I take it you watched the tape?'

I'm still holding onto Anna, and I feel compelled to show her just how much stronger I am than the little brat she may or may not remember.

'Did Mum know?' I say, the sob so close.

'Honestly I don't know. Shortly after your dad's passing, she asked me to look into the names of prisoners under your dad's care at the prison, with the possibility that one or two could have had something to do with Anna's abduction. It wasn't an easy job back then, and I gave it my best go, but there was nothing conclusive. She never let on why she asked me to do it, and when I told her I hadn't found anything, all she said was to keep looking. When she brought those boxes over, she asked me to pass them on to you, Emma, once she'd passed, in case there was anything useful in your quest. I never actually thought I'd survive her. She was an incredibly strong woman, your mum, and when I see your name mentioned on the news, Emma, I always think of her. You're far more like her than you realise. And as I said at the start, I truly am sorry for your loss.'

Anna's shoulders soften and I allow her to turn until we are facing each other. She pulls me into her embrace. 'Did you mean what you said? About exposing every one of those names?'

I pull myself away far enough that she can read my eyes. '*Every* word. I will never let you down, Anna. Whatever you need, however you want to proceed, I'm all in. I need you in my life more than anything else, and I think you'll be pleasantly surprised by my resourcefulness.'

Her despair is broken by just the hint of a smile. 'Are you freaking kidding me? I'm your number-one fan. I have no doubts about the lengths you'll go to for justice.'

It's my turn to smile slightly. 'I heard you were arrested with one of my books in your possession. How would you feel about helping me write the rest of this story? I think my readers want to hear your story from the very beginning. I've promised to send my agent, Maddie, an outline for my next book, and I think it should start with you, if you're happy to share your story?'

'Yeah, but can we get a drink somewhere? My stomach thinks my throat's been cut.'

Chapter Fifty-One

NOW

Windsor, Berkshire

Six months later

The gentle hum of the room feels so reassuring, although I don't know half the people in the lavish suite, but that doesn't matter; today isn't about me. From the outside I appear cool, calm, and collected. The carefully applied makeup is still shining, and my hair remains in the delicate shape the stylist wrestled it into shortly after the first glass of prosecco. Even the dress Rachel chose for me is doing a decent job of keeping my wobbly bits under control. I don't recognise the woman who keeps staring back at me from the mirrored hall we're seated in.

Inwardly, all is not so in check. I feel physically sickened by the prospect of the speech I'm required to deliver in the next five minutes. Rachel knows I detest public speaking, but when she asked if I'd be willing to make a small Maid of Honour toast, I couldn't turn her down. I know how much it will mean to her, so the compromise we reached was that I was allowed to write down what I want to say, so all I have to do is read it, while keeping my eyes firmly fixed to the page, rather than on everyone else who will be staring at me.

I reach for the glass of Chablis on the table and see that my fingers are trembling as I press the glass to my lips. Why is it so hot in here?

I look over to Freddie, who is sitting with Rachel's cousins, regaling them with anecdotes as they fall about laughing. He must feel my eyes on him because he looks up and tilts his glass in my direction. I hear his words on the phone this morning, 'Stand tall, thrust out your chest, and *own* the room.'

Easier said than done, if you ask me, but I can't help but admire his new zest for life. Since Beauchamp's arrest, Freddie has enrolled on an Open University psychology degree course. That anyone can suffer as he has and now want to help others suffering with similar trauma is a testament to his character. I want to make him as proud of me as I am of him.

A cool hand presses mine and I catch Rachel leaning in. 'Are you okay?'

She looks beautiful in her peach one-piece studded with pearls, topped off with a decadent tiara that I know for a fact had to be insured for today's ceremony and reception. But I've never seen her look so happy and comfortable in my life. Even the less than happy expressions her parents are wearing don't seem to be enough to spoil the day. They're not seated at the head table for that very reason, instead seated with Daniella's parents at the round table off to our left. Daniella's parents flew in from Italy a week ago, and have helped the two of them move into their new Marylebone apartment. Their English isn't great, but Rachel has started learning Italian so she can communicate better with them. Daniella's mum hasn't stopped smiling all day, and every time I see her dad, he's dabbing his eyes to catch the joyful tears.

I take another sip of my wine. 'I'm fine,' I whisper to Rachel, squeezing the tips of her fingers.

'You don't have to say too much,' she says, reading my mind as she always does. 'Just thank everyone for coming, say how beautiful the brides look, and then raise your glass. Easy.'

If only it were that easy. My chest prickles with heat, but the sooner I start, the sooner it will end. I know I wouldn't feel nearly as nervous if the chair beside me weren't noticeably empty. Rachel had addressed my plus one invite to Jack specifically – another attempt at matchmaking – and he did say he would be here, but he's missed the ceremony and wedding breakfast, and his phone is switched off, so I guess that tells me everything I need to know about the prospect of us pursuing anything romantic. It isn't a criticism – I have no doubt he's been called in to work at the last minute – but I do wish he were here to champion me on.

I suppose I only have myself to blame for him being such an integral part of Operation Cicada. What started with the arrest of Ian Beauchamp quickly snowballed, focusing initially on those police officers listed in the spreadsheet recovered from Beauchamp's files, but spreading to include former senior civil servants. Some names on the list will avoid prosecution because they've died, but enquiries are ongoing. They've targeted the biggest names first, but Jack has told me they won't stop until every named individual has been arrested and interviewed.

What I didn't expect after Anna and I reconnected in Wareham was how difficult she'd find it to adapt to regular life. I insisted she move in with me, and although I offered her my bed, as well as the sofa bed, she moved back into her campervan after two days. Tragically, I think she's been running for so long, she doesn't know how to slow down. So, rather than restraining her, we reached an impasse, and she went 'back to work', offering those running Operation Cicada her full cooperation. She's been granted temporary powers so that she can attend briefings and share the wealth of her knowledge, experience, and trauma. With Rawani's retirement postponed, and at his suggestion, Jack and Anna are focusing on finding the victims in the MP4 files, and providing the necessary support they undoubtedly need.

'Are you ready?' Rachel asks, touching my hand again.

I don't answer, instead unfolding the printed sheet I brought with me and skimming the opening lines so I know how to frame my tone. Picking up the dessert fork I didn't use, I tap it against the fresh flute of prosecco, and stand. The hum in the room quells, and all eyes turn to me. My toes are curling inside my Louboutins, but thankfully nobody can see them beneath the table cloth.

The words on the page blur slightly, as I try to focus on them. 'Um, thank you for your attention.' My mouth is so dry that my lips are sticking to my teeth. I don't want to screw this up. 'Um, for those of you who don't know me, my name is Emma Hunter, and I'm the Maid of Honour today.'

Someone wolf whistles from the audience, but I daren't

look up to see where it came from. I read on, but the lines before me sound so carefully worded that there's no longer a natural rhythm to them. This was such a bad idea. I should have told her that I'd mess up the speech, and she'd be better off asking her other bridesmaid to do it instead.

Now I realise seconds are slipping away, and I'm not speaking. Everyone is staring at me as I stutter and fail at yet another public speaking event. How did my mouth get so dry? Rachel is shuffling uncomfortably in my periphery, and I just wish I could wake from this nightmare.

I reach for the Chablis and drain the glass, swilling slightly to hydrate my gums, before swallowing.

I only glance up for the briefest of seconds, but there he is.

Standing at the back of the room, out of breath and desperately tucking his pressed shirt into his black trousers, holding up his hands in apology. He remains where he is, not wanting to interrupt my big moment, even though I wish he would make some kind of entrance to distract everyone's attention.

Rachel takes my hand and whispers, 'It's okay, you don't have to do this if you don't want to. Just raise your glass and toast us.'

I look down at her and can see the concern etched around her eyes. She deserves so much better.

I lower the page of notes and press my hand against her cheek, welcoming the cool relief on my palm. 'You are the most amazing friend I ever could have asked for,' I say, feeling my eyes filling, but no longer caring. 'Today you've transformed from my funny, ditzy, brave university housemate into an elegant swan. I see you sitting here with your beautiful bride, Daniella, and I feel honoured that I get to call you my friend.

Public displays of affection are not really my thing, as you know, but today I stand here prouder than I've ever felt, because you chose me to share in your most special of days. What most of your guests probably don't realise is just how big an influence you've been on my life. And I can, hand on heart, say I wouldn't be half the person I am today if I hadn't had you supporting me from the sidelines. So all I really want to say is thank you, Rachel, for being my personal cheerleader, and I hope you'll let me continue to ride on your coat tails as you set off on your new life with Daniella.'

I pause to allow Rachel to wipe her eyes, and turn to face the audience, though I concentrate my attention on Jack's face. 'Ladies and gentlemen, please raise your glasses and join me in a toast to the bride and bride.'

Chairs scrape in unison as all the guests stand and raise their glasses. This gives Jack the opportunity to circle the edge of the room and drop into the chair beside me. He leans across and quickly apologises to Rachel and Daniella for his tardiness.

A waiter comes over and fills Jack's flute with prosecco, topping up mine in the process. We sit quietly and listen as Daniella's dad delivers his speech in his native tongue, while Daniella translates for him, gushing at his warm and kind words, and then we hear Rachel's dad offer a brief toast to the pair of them, and then the Master of Ceremonies informs everyone that there will be a break in proceedings so that the room can be set up for the evening reception. Jack and I head to the bar, and find a table in a quiet corner.

'I'm sorry I didn't get here sooner,' he says once we're seated. 'Today's been a bit of a mental day, but I'm so pleased I got to see your speech. You almost had me sobbing buckets.'

'I'm just glad you've made it now. Where's Anna?'

He glances around as if looking for her, before returning my stare. 'She said she was going to change quickly and then she'd be out. I gave her the key to my room, so she's probably up there now.' He pauses and takes a sip of the lager he ordered at the bar. 'There's something I need to talk to you about.'

A shudder courses the length of my spine as I see fresh anxiety in his eyes. The last time he looked like this was when he was about to break the news that he'd found Anna's face on one of the videos in Arthur Turgood's collection. I don't need more heartache after this turbulent year.

'I don't know where to begin,' he says, now fixing his attention on his shoes.

'Just bowl out with it,' I reply quickly. 'Whatever it is, just say it like you're ripping off a plaster.'

He looks up and begins to speak, before thinking again, and looking back at his feet. 'Chrissie and her husband are moving to Bournemouth, because he's just got a new job that requires him to be closer to the sea. And they're obviously taking Mila with them.'

'Oh, Jack, I'm sorry,' I say, knowing it will be a two- to three-hour journey for him to see her from London.

He shrugs. 'It's fine. I understand why they need to move, and they did speak to me about it before making their decision. It's much better money for him, and Mila is super excited about being so close to the beach. So it's okay.'

I sense there's more bad news to come, and take a long sip of my prosecco.

'So, the reason I was late arriving today was because today was my last day working on Operation Cicada. As of Monday morning, my transfer will be complete, and I'll begin work at my new station.' He looks up and fixes me with a pained stare. 'I've left it all in great hands, and your sister is doing an incredible job of keeping everyone focused on what's at stake. She's so resilient, and reminds me a lot of you, but maybe a touch more fiery. She's even got Rawani planning on postponing his retirement for another year.'

He sits back and pulls down his tie a fraction to unfasten his top button. 'I'm leaving London, Emma, and I've just put a deposit down on a flat near Dorchester, so you'll be seeing a lot more of me – if you'll let me, that is.'

My mouth drops open. 'But you love London.'

He shakes his head, his lips turning down at the edges. 'Not anymore. When you spend enough time in the smog and swamp, you eventually reach a point where you'll never be able to get your hands clean. The atrocities I've seen there these past few months have really put things in perspective. I don't want to become just another faceless commuter unable to claw my way out of the detritus. I need a fresh start, and transferring to Dorset police gives me that opportunity.'

'How come this is the first I'm hearing about this?'

'I didn't want to let on until it was all sorted. I wasn't sure the transfer would be approved, but it helps having a fierce recommendation from one of the former detective inspectors.'

'Zoe Cavendish,' I mouth.

He nods, smiling awkwardly. 'With her now transferred to London, they've just promoted a sergeant in her team into her role, so there was a vacancy. She had a word with the recruitment panel, and I can't have screwed up the interview too much because they offered me the job.'

'But you haven't taken the sergeant's exam...' I start to say, but he is nodding his head again.

'I passed it last year, but then the opportunity came up with the NCA so I put applications on hold. Now feels like the right time to move.'

My shoulders finally relax. 'Congratulations.'

'Thank you,' he says, but there is still caution to his tone. 'The thing is, Emma... What I wanted to speak to you about... I was thinking... well, actually, I was hoping... that you might be open to the prospect of maybe you and me... seeing a lot more of one another.'

My entire body stiffens.

'You know that I like you, don't you,' he says rhetorically. 'But the thing you don't know is that you're the first person I think about when I wake up in the morning. I wonder, what will Emma be up to today? Should I call her? Or will she call me? Every time you're close, my brain reverts to its twelve-year-old state, and I don't know how to tell you how much you mean to me. I don't expect you to give me an answer now, because I've put you on the spot, but I'd like you to think about the possibility of letting me become your boyfriend at some point in the very near future.'

Poor Jack is deathly pale as he waits for me to speak, but I don't know how to answer him. It feels like a dream, and I'm terrified I'll be woken from it any second and none of this awkward but cute exchange will be real.

'Yes,' I eventually say.

He blinks several times. 'Yes?'

My eyes fill as I nod. 'Yes.'

He smiles like the cat who's got the cream. 'Can you hear

that?' he says a moment later. 'Sounds like the DJ is starting the music. Do you fancy having a boogie with me?'

He should know better than to ask me to dance in front of a room full of people, but for the second time today, I swallow my fear and doubt, and stand.

'I should warn you,' Jack says, standing so close I can smell his cologne, 'Mila says I'm the worst dancer because I've got two left feet. My counter argument is that I'm the best worst dad dancer, so in a way I'm good at something. I'll try not to embarrass you too much.'

Our eyes meet, and in a surge of awkward anticipation, I lean forward and place my lips on his. Only, with my eyes closed, I misjudge exactly where his mouth is, catch the tip of his nose with my top lip, and his moustache with my bottom one. My cheeks burn instantly.

Jack looks shocked at the awful attempt, and I'm convinced he's about to take back all the nice things he just said, but instead he apologises.

'I'm sorry… I wasn't ready. Can we try that again?'

My humiliation is hovering precariously above the precipice, so I just nod.

Jack wets his lips and places his warm hands on my even warmer cheeks, and tilts my head slightly as he pulls me towards him. And this time the kiss is everything I've dreamed it would be: soft, tender, and my heart feels ready to explode.

'Oi, you two, get a room!' Rachel calls out to our left.

I turn and smile at her, as she clings tightly to Daniella.

'Come on,' she urges, as she approaches, 'we've got to do our first official dance in a minute, and I want you pair up on the dance floor straight after, so your clumsiness will make the two of us look more graceful.'

She collects each of our hands and pulls us along into the hall, which has been quickly transformed into a neon-lit wall of sound. There are tables and chairs around the edge of the room where a few guests are sitting, waiting for their cue to hit the dancefloor.

Anna appears through a side door, and I actually gasp as I lay eyes on her dress. It's the first time I've seen her in an outfit that accentuates her femininity. She is beautiful, and I couldn't be prouder to beckon my sister to join us. She remains at the back of the room, reluctant to let her guard down. I cross through the tables and take her hand in mine.

'Just one dance,' I promise her. 'Please?'

For the briefest moment, it's like we're back in our parents' yard in Weymouth arguing over that stupid skateboard, but rather than retreat, she takes a deep breath and nods, following me back to where Jack is patiently waiting.

'Do you mind?' I ask him, but he shakes his head.

'I've waited long enough for this moment, I can hold out for a few minutes more,' he adds with a smile that warms my soul.

But he doesn't have to wait long as Freddie sashays up to us, clasps Jack's hand and tells him he can lead. Poor Jack doesn't know where to look first, but doesn't resist and my heart could explode with the love I have for these five people.

My family.

Because that's what they are, and there is nothing that will break us.

And that is where this story ends. There is strength in unity, in the family we choose as well as the one we inherit. I wouldn't be who I am without them, and that is why I will continue to fight for all of them.

And as for the monsters who still lurk in the shadows, physically and emotionally abusing those they should be caring for, know this: I'm coming for you, and this time my sister will be right alongside me.

We won't stop until you're caught.

THE END

Acknowledgments

And just like that our time with Emma Hunter draws to a close. I'm in tears as I write this, having just completed the copyedit of *Exposed*. Living inside Emma's head has been as much of an adventure for me writing her as it has been to the legion of loyal fans who have clamoured to devour each new entry in the series. She was my best friend during the pandemic in 2020, and I'm really going to miss her outlook on life, and how she always wants to put others first in her struggle to uncover the truth.

I hope the ending to the series was as satisfying for you as it was for me. From the first book I always planned that Emma would discover the truth about what happened to Anna, I just wasn't certain about some of the developments that would come along the way. And what do you think the future holds for Jack and Emma? Will they live happily ever after, or is there more pain to come their way? I'd love to hear your thoughts and opinions on what happens to Emma, Jack, Anna, Freddie, and Rachel in the years to come.

I am active on Facebook, Twitter, and Instagram, so please do stop by with any messages, observations, or questions. Hearing from readers of my books truly brightens my days and encourages me to keep writing, so don't be a stranger. I promise I *will* respond to every message and comment.

I'd like to thank my editor Bethan Morgan, and the brilliantly creative team at One More Chapter, for supporting me in the creation of this book and the other books in the series. I've never been prouder of a writing project than I am of this, and it wouldn't have been possible without all of you. Thanks to Lucy Bennett for her work in producing the series' covers; to Lydia Mason, whose copyediting was painless; and to Tony Russell, who kindly completed the proofread to pull out those all embarrassing spelling mistakes.

I'd like to thank my own parents and my parents-in-law for continuing to offer words of encouragement when I'm struggling to engage with my muse.

Thank you as ever to my best friend, Dr Parashar Ramanuj, who never shies away from the awkward medical questions I ask him. Thank you to Alex Shaw and Paul Grzegorzek – authors and dear friends – who are happy to listen to me moan and whinge about the pitfalls of the publishing industry, offering words of encouragement along the way.

I want to send my love and gratitude to my wife, Hannah, and my children, Emily and Ethan, who put up with me staring off into space when imagination takes over mid-conversation. You are the reason I continue to write, even when my confidence is shaken or I'm struggling to put words on the page.

And thanks must also go to YOU for buying and reading

Exposed. Please do post a review to wherever you purchased the book from so that other readers can be enticed to follow Emma's quest. It takes less than two minutes to share your opinion, and I ask you do me this small kindness.

One More Chapter is an award-winning global division of HarperCollins.

Sign up to our newsletter to get our latest eBook deals and stay up to date with our weekly Book Club!
Subscribe here.

Meet the team at
www.onemorechapter.com

Follow us!

 @OneMoreChapter_

 @OneMoreChapter

 @onemorechapterhc

Do you write unputdownable fiction?
We love to hear from new voices.
Find out how to submit your novel at
www.onemorechapter.com/submissions